A *Whisper* in *Time*

BOOK TWO IN THE WHISPER FALLS SERIES

ELIZABETH LANGSTON

SPENCER
HILL
PRESS

Spencer Hill Press

Contact: Spencer Hill Press, PO Box 247, Contoocook, NH 03229, USA

Please visit our website at www.spencerhillpress.com

First Edition: April 2014.
Elizabeth Langston
A Whisper In Time : a novel / by Elizabeth Langston – 1st ed.
p. cm.
Summary:
An 18th-century indentured servant teen girl immigrates to modern-day North Carolina and, along with her boyfriend, fights to establish her identity and protect her sister in the past.

The author acknowledges the copyrighted or trademarked status and trademark owners of the following wordmarks mentioned in this fiction:
Armani, Disney, iPad, Lexus, Mercedes, Netflix, Propel, Rolls Royce

Cover design by Lisa Amowitz
Interior layout by Marie Romero

ISBN 978-1-937053-81-9 (paperback)
ISBN 978-1-937053-80-2 (e-book)

Printed in the United States of America

To Bobbye and Chuck, my first model of selfless love

CHAPTER ONE

WHATEVER THE TERM

Although I had lived in this century for five weeks, I had still not grown accustomed to its vehicles. They moved too quickly and stopped too abruptly. Even now, as Mark drove me downtown, I pressed against the passenger seat, comforted by the belt strapping me in, and kept my eyes closed. It was best if I did not watch.

His truck lurched to a halt. The driver's seat creaked. When Mark's hand closed over mine, I turned to him.

"It's going to be all right," he said with a reassuring smile. I tried to smile back. "Will it?"

"Yes. I promise." The warmth of his hand slid away as the truck whined forward, its speed increasing at an alarming rate as it rushed toward a version of Raleigh I had never seen before.

I first visited the capital city in 1796, which had been only two months ago—or perhaps I should say two hundred and twenty years. The town in my memory held buildings of wood, huddled beneath tall oaks. Its air had been filled with the crack of hammers and the scent of fresh sawdust.

A different capital city stretched before me. Trees were dwarfed by large buildings of brick, glass, and stone. Wide streets of rough pavement divided the city into blocks. While my previous visit had been exciting, the Raleigh of today overwhelmed me.

There had been little opportunity to travel since my arrival in the twenty-first century. It had taken most of August to recover from my injuries. I'd stayed the initial three weeks at Mark's grandparents' lake house, soaking up the simplicity of the country as my body healed.

When Mark returned to high school near the end of August, I moved into his parents' home. Their neighborhood rested along the quiet fringes of the city and felt nothing like downtown.

Mark turned the truck onto a driveway and through a large door in the side of a tall brick barn.

"What is this?" I asked.

"It's called a parking garage."

His answer was not helpful. We drove up and up a winding road, as if climbing a concrete hill.

We were in a building that contained nothing but cars.

He pulled into a parking spot and shut off the vehicle. I could sense his scrutiny on my face.

"We're here, Susanna. The building we want is just down the street."

I gave a nod. Why had I come? Was I truly ready?

"Hey. Are you okay?"

"Yes," I said in a firm voice that belied the quivers in my belly.

He hurried to my door and held it open. I stepped out, smoothed the loose folds of my best gray skirt, and took the hand he offered me. As I walked beside him, my nose twitched at the smell of smoke and fuel.

We crossed a street and entered the tall building that housed the Register of Deeds. Mark preceded me through "security" and then strode toward two metal panels in the opposite wall. When he pressed a button beside them, the panels hissed open, revealing an empty closet.

He stepped in. I did not.

"Get in, Susanna, before it leaves."

I stared at the small space he stood in, not trusting its ominous clanking. "What is the purpose of that closet?"

His forehead creased. "It's called an elevator. It'll lift us to a different floor, so that we don't have to walk up the stairs."

Two men pushed past me and waited beside Mark.

He gestured for me to come. "You don't need to be worried. It's the fastest way to travel in a building like this."

"I prefer to travel slowly."

One of the men cleared his throat. Mark stepped out. The panels hissed shut.

"All right," he said, his expression patient, "we'll take the stairs."

We climbed to the third floor and stopped before a gray-bearded gentleman, sitting at a desk with a sign that read *Check In*. I waited until he looked up.

"Hello, sir. I am here to speak with Mrs. Heather Cox."

"Name?"

"Susanna Marsh."

He inclined his head. "Go down that hall. I'll let her know you're coming."

The hallway had bright lights, plain walls, and a shiny floor. A woman appeared in the doorway at the hall's end. I studied her as she beckoned to us. Mrs. Cox was tall and thin, with skin of dark brown and the most elegant hands I had ever seen.

"Please sit." She gestured toward two chairs in the midst of many stacked boxes. "Don't mind the mess. We're going through renovations."

I had never seen a black person or a woman in such a position of authority. Though the concepts were new to me, Mark claimed that it was common; Negroes had been free for over one hundred fifty years, and women had experienced increasing freedoms for not quite as long. After a too-long pause, I said, "Thank you."

She gave a business-like nod and then donned a pair of glasses. "The circumstances of your case are difficult. I've never met anyone with such a complete lack of evidence of their birthplace or family. Do you know of an older relative or a doctor who was present at your birth? Their affidavit would be helpful."

I frowned at the unfamiliar word. "An affidavit?"

"A written story of his memories," Mark said under his breath.

I met her gaze calmly, glad that deception was not needed yet. "My father and mother were the only witnesses to my birth, and they are both dead."

"Any older siblings?"

"My brothers Caleb and Joshua."

"Would they be old enough to remember anything?"

"Caleb is ten years older than I. Joshua, eight."

Mark broke in. "Susanna has no idea where her brothers are or whether they're even alive."

My lips tightened. He had promised to let me answer the questions until I stumbled, which I had not.

The woman laid her hands on the keyboard of her computer. "What is your father's name and birthdate?"

"Josiah Marsh. I do not know his birthdate, but he was twenty-eight when I was born."

"Your mother's first name and maiden name?"

"Anne Barron. She was a year younger than my father."

A long minute passed as Mrs. Cox concentrated at the screen, her hand clicking frequently on the mouse-device. "I can't find either parent in the system."

I said nothing. Had she found a trace of my parents, she wouldn't have believed they were mine.

"Your parents were also in this cult?"

The lie stuck in my throat. I looked to Mark for help.

"They were," he said. "We call it 'the village.'"

Her gaze flicked over him and then back to me. In a kindly voice, she asked, "Can you contact anyone from the village to see if they might have school records or a family Bible?"

"I cannot." I shifted on my chair, ill at ease whenever my thoughts strayed to my former life. "My master and his family are long gone."

"Your master?" She blinked. "What does that mean?"

Mark leaned forward until his elbows bumped the edge of her desk. "Susanna's stepfather gave her to another family. She was pretty much forced into slavery by the age of ten."

A shudder passed through my body at the images his words evoked. Was slavery the right way to describe the way I had lived? It didn't seem right somehow to compare my lot to what slaves endured, but my servitude had been wretched—whatever the term we used now.

The woman pursed her lips in sympathy. "Ms. Marsh, I believe that you were born in our state, but I'm not sure what we can do without acceptable documentation."

While her words held a glimmer of hope, her dark eyes did not. "If you believe me, why is that not good enough?"

"My opinion doesn't trump the law. As far as North Carolina is concerned, Susanna Marsh simply doesn't exist."

CHAPTER TWO

SCREWED-UP PRIORITIES

Beside me, Susanna gave no outward sign of emotion except for her hands clenching in her lap.

"You know I exist. You can see me."

"I'm sorry," the woman said. "I don't mean to discourage you, but you have a long battle ahead."

Time for me to break in. "Take me through this, Ms. Cox. What exactly do we need to get her a birth certificate?"

"If you have no secondary evidence from the family, like a baptismal certificate or affidavit...?" She shook her head, as if baffled. "It would help to have a Social Security card or a government-issued photo ID."

I'd already looked up the details on both and dismissed them, which was why we were here at the Register of Deeds office and not at the Federal Building or the DMV. But maybe Ms. Cox knew something I didn't. "How do we get a photo ID?"

"The most straightforward way? With a Social Security card and a birth certificate."

"Right." I knew what was next but I asked it anyway. "What does Susanna need to get a Social Security number?"

"A photo ID and birth certificate."

"So, I need a birth certificate to get an ID or a Social Security Card, and I need at least one of them to get the birth certificate."

"It sounds circular, I know."

"It sounds impossible."

The woman sighed. "Unless you can produce secondary evidence of citizenship, it's very difficult, short of a court order. Your best bet is to retain an attorney."

Susanna popped out of her chair. "Thank you. We have taken enough of your time." She noiselessly left the room.

Okay.

I blinked at the empty spot where, mere seconds ago, Susanna had sat. Better reach her before she got lost. "Thanks for your time, Ms. Cox," I tossed over my shoulder as I bolted from the room. I caught up with Susanna in the lobby. She stood outside the grim stairwell, motionless and quiet.

I held the door for her. "Are you upset?"

The words, "I am," echoed back to me as she hurried down the steps, one hand skimming the grimy banister.

We didn't speak as we headed outside and waited for traffic to clear at the crosswalk. People streamed past us, their gazes sliding over Susanna. It annoyed me to see them make snap judgments based solely on her clothes, although, honestly, what she wore totally sucked. Today she'd put on her "best outfit." The green, long-sleeved shirt was buttoned from her neck to her hips. The gray skirt was all kinds of ugly, from its elastic waist to the frayed hem brushing her ankles. Susanna looked like she belonged to a fundamentalist sect.

When the light changed, she glanced at me for guidance. I nodded and she took off, her dark braid swishing at her waist.

We rode home silently. She stared out the side window, completely closed off, until we pulled onto my street.

"Is your school holding classes today?"

Not a topic I wanted to discuss with her. "I'm skipping."

"What does skipping mean?"

"I've decided not to go."

The passenger seat squeaked as she turned to me. "Why did you make this decision?"

How could I say *"You're more important than a stupid day of school"* without launching into a discussion about priorities? For Susanna, who had to end her education before she was ten, school was a privilege that she envied. "I wanted to be with you."

"Will there be consequences?"

"I'm not sure."

The garage doors were up at my house, and both of my parents' cars were parked in their stalls. That was a very bad sign. No way should both of them be home at noon.

I didn't say anything to Susanna. It was better for everyone if she didn't witness the "consequences" that were about to be blasted my way.

We entered the house through the laundry room. I waited as Susanna ran up the back stairs and paused on the landing outside the apartment over the garage. Once she'd disappeared inside, I continued into the kitchen.

My parents stood next to each other, an army of two. Mom bumped her head against Dad's arm, as if prompting him.

"Mark?" His voice had that pained, *"What the hell were you thinking?"* sound to it.

The school had contacted them, of course. It was part of what my parents liked about sending me to Neuse Academy. Private schools had good communication with the people paying the bills. So even though it wasn't a surprise that my parents knew, I still hadn't planned how to play this. "Yes, sir?"

"Have you noticed that it's Wednesday?"

"Yes."

"Which is a day you would typically spend at school?"

It was rare for my dad to be this sarcastic. "Yes."

"Would you mind telling us where you were on *this* Wednesday?"

"At the Wake County Register of Deeds."

That should've sounded impressive, but it didn't have the desired impact on my folks.

Mom frowned. "Did you go with Susanna?"

I nodded. They could say anything they wanted to me, but they'd better not get started on her. "Appointments are only available during the day. We asked about loopholes for getting her a birth certificate."

The edge left my father's face.

It didn't leave my mom's. "Mark, there *are* no loopholes."

"That's basically what the lady told us."

"Susanna needs an attorney who specializes in immigration law."

"She's not an immigrant." I heard a faint creak on the back stairs. Susanna was there, listening. Was she visible to my parents?

"You're splitting hairs," Mom said.

"She can't afford an attorney."

"We'll cover the fees."

"She doesn't want that." We'd already been over this.

"They could deport her."

Did my mom have to bring that up with Susanna nearby, drinking in every word? "Where would they deport her to? No other country would take her in."

"I don't know, but it's something we have to consider."

Susanna's tread came steadily down the stairs. She drew abreast of me. "I was born in Wake County, Mrs. Lewis. America must recognize my claims."

Mom's face softened. "They're the government, dear. They don't have to recognize anything."

After spending fifteen minutes with Ms. Cox, a woman who had been both sympathetic and gloomy, I found myself reluctantly agreeing with Mom. "The government doesn't care, Susanna. You have to show proof. Maybe we should hire a lawyer."

"No, thank you. I would like to proceed on the path we are following until it fails me."

What Susanna didn't realize was that it already had. This was the only official path available to us, and it was a dead end. Time for us to find an unofficial route.

Dad's gaze narrowed on me. "So the trip downtown was a bust, *and* you missed school."

"Sure did." Damn. That came out snarkier than I intended, but too late now.

Susanna stiffened. Why? Was she concerned about their reaction or mine?

"Mark," Dad said, his voice tight. "You knew the school would text us."

No need to respond. They were leading up to the big scene. All I had to do was wait for it.

"You'll have an unexcused absence, and it's only the third week of the school year."

"Not if you write me a note."

He exchanged a glance with my mom and then shook his head. "We're not doing that."

They were just making me sweat. "Why not?"

"You made the decision. You live with the consequences."

"Susanna needed me."

"One of us could've taken her."

"She's my responsibility."

"You could've asked our permission to skip school."

"You would've told me *no*."

"Good guess. It's what we're telling you now."

My teachers in physics and English would understand, but not in American government. This was a disaster. "Do you understand what you're doing? I can't make up whatever I miss today."

"Sorry about that, son."

I was too pissed to be careful with my mouth. "Great. Just great. Perfect way to reward me for helping out a friend. Talk about having screwed-up priorities." I checked the clock. Two and a half hours left in the school day. Spinning around, I grabbed my backpack and stormed out through the laundry room.

"Mark," Mom called after me. "Are you going to school?"

"Where else would I be going?" It would be a bad idea for me to speak another word right now. I stalked out to my truck.

"Mark."

I looked over my shoulder. Susanna hovered in the entrance to the garage. "What?"

"Thank you."

Those two soft words flowed through my veins like a cool rain, diffusing my anger. Susanna could put more nuance into a simple phrase than most people could put into whole paragraphs.

"You're welcome." I smiled, hopped in the truck, and floored it.

My lifetime habit of waking before the sun had stayed with me. On Thursday morning, I rose, dressed, and skipped downstairs. The remnants of a loaf of bread I had baked the previous weekend sat in the breadbox. I cut and buttered thick slices and arranged them on a shallow pan for toasting in the oven.

Mark's father arrived next in the kitchen, dropped his luggage near the door, and then approached the counter to check the coffee pot. "You're up early, Susanna."

"Yes, sir." I smiled hesitantly, always shy in his presence. "Mr. Lewis, would you care for toast and scrambled eggs?"

"I would like that, as long as you join me." He smiled back, his teeth even and white. "And please call me Bruce."

I bobbed my head, glad for the opportunity to serve him. I'd learned to use their pretty pans and the appliances that cooked without fire. In only a few moments, I had filled two plates and handed one to him. "Here you are, sir."

"Thank you." He poured me a cup of coffee and placed it before my chair, a small but lovely gesture.

Mrs. Lewis strolled in, wearing yellow scrubs with pink flowers, and stopped before the coffee pot. "What's going on?"

"Susanna fixed me breakfast," her husband answered, as he slathered jam on his toast.

"Oh?" She carried a mug to the table and sat.

I nodded. "Toast is warming in the oven. Would you like an egg?"

"Okaaaaaay," she said, drawing the word out slowly as she gave Bruce a puzzled stare. "My health-freak husband hasn't eaten a breakfast like that in years."

I watched her carefully, unsure how to take her comment. The words were pleasant enough, but the tone was not.

He said, "It's nice for a change."

I smiled at his praise. Now that I felt well again, I could rise early each morning and cook. Moving to the stove, I reached for a bowl and a whisk.

"Fried, Susanna. Runny yolk."

I had seen Mark's grandmother prepare this dish before. It didn't look appetizing.

After I slid the half-cooked egg onto a plate, I set it in front of her and then returned to my seat. She ate silently, her gaze going from me to her husband. He had his attention trained on his phone.

She stood and collected the plates. When I rose to help her, she waved me back into my chair. "Thanks, dear," she said from the sink. "This was a nice surprise, but don't feel as if you need to do it again."

"It's no trouble, Mrs. Lewis." For five weeks, Mark's family had done nothing but give to me. Shelter, food, medical care, kindness. I wanted a chance to give to them. "I enjoy cooking."

"There's no need. We like cereal."

Those horrid bits of dried wheat that tasted like straw? I must have misunderstood. "Do you prefer oatmeal? I can—"

"It's okay," she interrupted. "Sleep in. We don't need you to fix our breakfast."

I closed my mouth. Finally, I *got it*—as Mark often said. She didn't like my cooking but was too polite to say so. I looked out the window, ashamed of the sudden hot moisture in my eyes, and willed my features to remain calm.

"Sherri, we're good." Bruce's voice was tight.

Her coffee mug smacked against the counter top. Arms crossed, she leaned back and scowled at him.

Tension hummed in the air, and it was because of me. I sprang to my feet and edged around the table. "Excuse me."

"Susanna?"

I paused. "Yes, sir?"

Feet thundered down the hall, drowning out Bruce's response.

Mark exploded into the room, full of energy. "Hey."

"Good morning." I tried to slip past him.

"Wait."

When he tugged gently on my braid, concern etched on his brow, I gave him a light smile.

"What's up, babe?"

Bruce spoke. "Your mother is being overly solicitous of my diet."

Mark's eyes narrowed on my face. "What did she say to you?"

Mrs. Lewis made an impatient sound. "Susanna's version of breakfast is full of fat and cholesterol. I'm merely pointing out that your father likes for us to eat healthy food."

"I made a mistake. It is nothing." I hurried up the stairs, but not before I heard Mark speak to his mother in a most disrespectful tone.

"Why can't you be nice to her?"

"Nice? There's no need to go overboard. You two treat her like she's about to shatter at any moment."

"We're trying to cut her some slack, Mom. Why can't you?"

"Your dad isn't doing her any favors by eating food he doesn't want…"

I closed the door softly, crossed to the bay window overlooking the back yard, and curled onto the window seat. Perhaps it was too soon to expect that I would be at ease in this world, but I'd expected to be useful at something.

Why had Mark's father neglected to share his preferences? Did he pity me? And why had Mark shown anger when his mother spoke the truth? It was bewildering.

The phone rang beside me. "Hello?"

"Susanna?" It was Mark's grandfather. "Norah is planning to do some shopping in Raleigh after lunch. Would you like us to drop by and pick you up?"

"Yes, please. Will you shop for groceries?" It was my favorite kind of shopping.

"We are, and we're stopping by the library. How about that?"

Mrs. Lewis had brought me numerous volumes from some library, but I'd not been inside one myself. It would be quite exciting to see so many books. "I should love to go with you there. Thank you, Charlie."

"Good. Can you hold a moment?" Without waiting for my response, he dropped the phone on a table. I winced.

A moment later, Mark's grandmother picked up the phone. "Hi," Norah said, in her cheerful way, "it's been a while since we visited. Why don't you pack a bag and spend the night with us?"

Pleasure filled me, swift and sweet. Mark's grandparents and their house beside the lake were like a much-needed haven. Nestled in a heavy forest, it would surround me with privacy and nature. "I should like that very much."

Chapter Four

Message Received

The teachers in my morning classes hadn't been as understanding as I'd hoped. All missed assignments for English and physics would be due tomorrow, with a whole letter-grade penalty. Good thing I hadn't skipped American government yesterday. Mr. Fullerton—the most feared man at the high school—would've been brutal.

I slipped into my seat in his classroom as the last period bell rang.

"Close call," the girl sitting next to me whispered.

I shot her a quick smile. Gabrielle Stone was the only thing about American government that could remotely be called fun. She was the most stared-at student in our school, and not just because she'd started here her senior year. Gabrielle was a celebrity—an international movie star, living in Raleigh while she finished high school like an ordinary teen.

Not that Neuse Academy—the area's most expensive private school—had all that many *ordinary* teens.

Gabrielle had been given a lot of freedoms the rest of us hadn't, like right now, when she had her tablet out to "take notes." I was probably the most aware of this privilege since, in addition to sitting beside her in government, I was also her lab partner in physics.

After school let out, I headed for the bike rack. As I was clipping on my helmet, Gabrielle strolled up, along with two of our physics classmates. An older guy, wearing aviator shades and an earpiece, followed a few paces behind them. He stopped when they stopped.

I looked from him to Gabrielle.

She smiled. "That's Garrett. He's my bodyguard."

Interesting. I'd never seen him inside the school, which was oddly comforting. We must be pretty secure if she didn't need him during the day.

She inclined her head toward the pair with her. "Do you know Jesse and Benita?"

"Hey, Jesse." Of course I knew him. He would likely be the valedictorian this year.

Benita shook my hand with a strong grip and a big smile. We'd never been introduced before, but I definitely knew who she was. It was hard not to notice her. She walked around our preppy campus in hippie clothes, hauling a cello case, her hands covered by gloves with cut-off fingertips.

Jesse locked his arm around her waist. "Benita's a sophomore."

Message received. They were an actual couple. I didn't bother to tell him I was already taken too. "A sophomore who takes physics?"

"I like science." She smiled down at her boyfriend, who was a head shorter. "And I wanted to take a class with Jesse."

Gabrielle laid a hand on my arm. "We're heading to Olde Tyme Grill to study. Want to come? We could share our notes from what you missed in class yesterday."

"Sorry. Not today."

"How about next week?"

"Maybe." I wasn't sure if I ever would, but there was no point in blowing them off completely.

"Good. We'll tell you after we decide for sure when we're going." Her gaze flicked to the parking lot and back again. "Do you ride your bike every day?"

"As long as the weather's good."

"So you live close by?"

"Yeah. Only six miles. Near Umstead Park."

She laughed. "*Only* six miles?" A black Mercedes SUV pulled to the curb and idled. "Here's my driver. If you ever want to join us, we can give you a ride."

"Thanks." Not going to happen anytime soon. Between needing to be with Susanna, mowing lawns for my lawn service, and wanting to squeeze in a training ride before sundown, I didn't have much time to hang out.

CHAPTER FIVE

SPEAKING SHARPLY

Norah drove to a large shopping center called Cameron Village. Charlie told me not to worry that it only had stores. "It also has the best library in the county," he said.

When we walked through the entrance to the library, I knew that he must be right. It was like a two-story mansion full of couches and books. Thousands of books. I was speechless with wonder.

Charlie patted me on the shoulder. "I'll be browsing in the mystery section. Where will you go?"

Swallowing hard, I whispered, "History."

He chuckled. "When will you ever tire of reading about history?"

"When I have caught up," I said without thinking.

"What?"

I hurried to give him a reasonable explanation. "There will be history on my high school equivalency examination. I must study what I have missed."

He cocked his head. "Didn't you take history classes in that commune?"

"Girls did not receive the same education as boys." That, at least, was quite true.

"Did you ever hear news from the outside?"

"Very little." Perhaps I should leave before he pressed the issue. I could make up no suitable response besides the truth, and he would not believe that. "I shall see you later."

I followed the signs to the history books, pausing with delight as I found shelf after shelf of true stories from the past.

It was the summer of 1796 when I escaped. Worthville, my hometown, had yet to be destroyed by a tornado. My sister was living and working in young Raleigh—a city of mud streets and a state government in its infancy. I wanted to know what life had been like for Phoebe after I left her behind.

A title caught my eye. *Architecture in the Nineteenth-Century Carolinas.* I drew the volume from the shelf, rested it on a table, and flipped through its pages with reverence. Many photographs, in shades of white and brown, awaited me. Photo after photo of historical buildings.

One of the pages held several views of a large house in Raleigh. The property had a side garden and two smaller buildings on its rear lawn. Neither the trees nor the grounds looked familiar, but I recognized the main house. My heart pounded faster.

I'd been here before.

The book called it the Avery-Eton House, but I knew it by only one name. Senator Nathaniel Eton, a much-revered member of North Carolina's first legislature, had built this house for his family. Mrs. Eton had offered my sister a position as a housemaid.

Charlie stopped beside me, a thick book in his hand. "Found something you like?"

"Indeed, I have." I handed the volume to him. "Do you know where this house is located?"

He read the caption. "Yeah. It's a couple of blocks away from the Governor's Mansion."

"Might we drive by it some time?"

"Sure." He glanced at his watch. "We could swing by today. Are you ready to go?"

I nodded eagerly and followed him to the place for borrowing the books. He added mine to the top of his stack and handed a small plastic card to the lady at the counter. As she reached for our books, she smiled at me. "Would you like your own library card?"

"Indeed?" My head buzzed with the possibilities. "How might I acquire one?"

"All you need is proof that you live in the county and a photo ID."

Disappointment stabbed me. "I do not have identification." I turned to flee, tired of the reminders that I did not belong in my own country yet.

Outside the library's front doors, a bench sat in the shade. I sank onto it to watch and wait.

The shopping center was quite busy. Cars pulled in and out. Women in tight garments and leather boots walked past, their hands gripping tiny children and phones. It was not long before Norah exited the grocery store at the corner, cloth sacks in each hand.

"Hello." She plopped onto the bench beside me. "Did you enjoy your visit?"

"Yes, ma'am."

"Where's my husband? Checking out books?"

"Yes, ma'am." I felt my cheeks warm.

"Susanna, forgive me if this is too bold, but I bought you something." She reached into one of the sacks and drew out a scrap of cloth. She unfolded it to reveal a shirt with sleeves of a peculiar length.

I brushed my fingers over the fabric. It was wondrously soft and in a pretty shade of crimson.

She laid it in my lap. "Red would be gorgeous with your coloring."

"Norah," I said with great reluctance, "you've given me too much already. I cannot accept another gift."

"It's not a gift. I'll make you work it off."

Interest curled in my belly. "We shall barter?"

"Yes. Based on what I paid for it, I think three hours of chores are fair."

"Three hours?" It didn't seem like much. Was I an object of pity to her too?

"Three hours of my *least* favorite chores, like weeding the garden and shoveling ashes from the fireplace."

I smiled. They were not favorites of mine either. It delighted me to receive them. "It's a deal."

She patted my knee. "Here comes Charlie."

"All right, ladies," he boomed, "I'm ready to go."

He strode to their vehicle. As he was helping his wife into the driver's seat, he said, "We need to run downtown by the Governor's Mansion for Susanna. I'll give you exact directions when we're closer."

I crawled into the back seat and buckled up. It took hardly any time to reach the government area and then the Avery-Eton House.

"Here we are." He whistled. "Holy moly. Somebody has done some major renovations on this place."

The house gleamed with burnished brick and new paint. It was nestled in a manicured garden, bordered by a low white fence, and framed by large oaks. The Etons' home was as elegant as I remembered. Age had merely made it more lovely.

Norah pulled to the curb. "If you want to go in, it looks open."

I did want to go in, but not without Mark. "I shall wait."

Charlie pointed at a large banner hanging in the yard. "They're about to have their grand opening celebration. Try to get down here Saturday."

Norah and Charlie retired at nine. Too restless to sleep, I rocked on the deck in the warm air, listening to the night creatures come alive to their work.

The phone rang with Mark's signal.

"Hello," I said, happy that he'd called.

"Hey." A neutral word said in a neutral tone. "How was your day?"

"Most enjoyable. I have a new book from the library." He made no response, his silence heavy. I wouldn't permit him to spoil my lovely day. "Are you working on homework?"

"Just finished. Why are you at the lake house?"

"Your grandparents invited me." I understood the usefulness of a phone, but not seeing his face made it more difficult to gauge his mood. "They drove me to the Eton house. It still stands, and I should like to see it more closely. Will you take me?"

"When?"

"Perhaps Saturday?"

"Yeah, I can do that." He cleared his throat. "Did Mom chase you away?"

"She would not do such a thing."

He mumbled an expletive. "Susanna, don't let her get to you."

"It is your mother's household. I must honor her wishes." At least, I would try to honor them. I didn't always understand what she wanted, and she seemed reluctant to tell me.

"I didn't like coming home without you here. I miss you, Susanna."

His words left me feeling warm and deliciously light-headed. "I miss you too. Will you pick me up tomorrow? I could make supper for you." Already my mind sorted through the options. It was grand to plan a menu without worrying about its colors. Mrs. Lewis insisted that we fill our plates with food of green, red, and yellow. I much preferred white: fried chicken, cornbread, mashed potatoes. And butter.

"I love it when you cook. Susanna?"

"Yes?"

"I love you."

My cheeks heated. "Indeed." I could say those words too, but he said them much more often and much more readily. Was it a unique part of Mark or was it common to the young men of his century? I desperately wanted to believe that Mark's words were especially meant for me, but perhaps it was the way of this world, like exposed skin. Or speaking sharply to one's elders. "I shall see you tomorrow."

"You will."

CHAPTER SIX

OPPOSITE OF SYMPATHETIC

Benita stopped at the bike rack as I was putting on my safety gear. "Jesse and I are going with Gabrielle to the football game tonight. Want to come?"

My gut reaction was *hell yeah*. I loved football, it was my senior year, and our team had a seriously good chance at the league championship.

But I also wanted to be with Susanna. I would offer to take her with me, except crowds still freaked her out. She would have a horrible time in a dark, noisy stadium watching a sport she didn't understand. Which was why I'd missed every game they'd played this season.

So there it was. The same battle I'd been fighting for three weeks in a row.

"Mark?"

"Thanks, Benita. Not sure if I can make it."

"Okay. Let us know if you change your mind, or just show up. We'll save you a seat."

Benita was way friendlier than I'd expected from seeing her around campus. It was nice that she hadn't let my vagueness deter her. "Maybe I'll see you there."

"Cool." She tossed me a smile as she loped away.

I called Susanna the minute I got home. "Hey."

"Hello. How was your day?"

"Great." I could hear the smile in her voice. She'd had a good day too. "When will supper be ready?"

She hesitated. "Why do you ask?"

Okay, I was just going to tell her, and I was *not* going to feel guilty—'cause she'd chosen to spend last night away from me. "Some kids from school asked me to hang out with them tonight, but it would mean I'd have to drive to the lake house now, eat, and get us back here by six-thirty." It would take forty-five minutes on three majorly clogged highways across two counties to reach my grandparents' house, but I would do it if she wanted me to.

"I think that is too much effort." Her voice lost its smile. "You should go with your friends."

"Okay." It was hard to tell with Susanna whether she was really upset or mildly disappointed. "Why don't you come with me?"

There was a long pause. "Where will you hang out?"

The way she repeated "hang out" almost made me laugh. She enunciated each consonant so clearly that it gave the expression a foreign sound. "We're going to a football game."

It was spooky how completely Susanna could fill silence with emotion, and this time, it wasn't positive emotion. "Perhaps I should remain at the lake house for another night."

Of course she would. Why had I even tried? I'd known the answer before I asked the question. "Sure. Whatever."

"Why does this make you angry?"

I bit off a sigh. "I'm not."

"You are. I do not know what to say, except that I am not ready."

"Yeah." She acted like a refugee, except she'd crossed centuries instead of continents. Everything was different for her. I was trying to understand, but it was getting old fast. "How can I help?"

"I need your patience."

"You have it." She really did, but forgive me for wanting my girlfriend on my arm. She was hot and amazing, and I wanted to show her off. "Any ideas when you'll be ready?"

"No, but you shall be the first to know."

Wow. Smackdown. "Fine. Just don't mind me enjoying life without you while I wait."

There was a stunned silence at the other end of the phone.

She wasn't any more stunned than I. "Susanna, I'm sorry. I don't know why I said that."

"It would sadden me if you gave up your friends for my sake. That isn't what I want," she said, a faint quiver in her tone. "Do as you wish. I trust you."

"You can trust me. I'm totally yours." This was where I should be noble and skip the game, but did I want to get into that habit? I shouldn't have to sacrifice hanging out with friends during my final year of high school while she adapted. Hiding away with her was taking its toll. "Maybe we could arrive late, after things have settled down."

"Mark, please go. Without me."

Okay, we'd said enough. "I'll call you when I get home."

"When will that be?"

"Ten o'clock. Maybe a little later."

"I shall have the phone in the bedroom. Mark, have you forgotten about tomorrow?"

Damn. She couldn't enjoy the twenty-first century with me, but I had to relive the eighteenth century with her? "I won't forget. I'll pick you up after my training ride. Nine o'clock max."

After we hung up, I frowned at the clock. It was too early to leave for the game. I had an idea about what to do with the extra time. I ran up to my room and booted up the laptop. At the meeting with Heather Cox two days ago, she'd thrown out a phrase I hadn't noticed in all of my early investigations into delayed birth certificates.

Short of a court order...

That implied judges. I needed to research what that meant.

It didn't take long to discover that judges could order the Department of Vital Records to create birth records, but that route required a couple of things we didn't have—decent evidence and a sympathetic judge.

Slumping back on my bed, I wondered how I might get them anyway. We had zero documents, but that didn't have to be a hindrance. Since the government wouldn't believe valid evidence if we produced it, I didn't have any qualms about producing fake evidence that they could believe. Susanna was the weak link there. She might balk, which meant it would have to stay a secret for a while.

The bigger issue was finding a sympathetic judge. I knew exactly one judge, and she was the complete opposite of sympathetic. Her son, a classmate who'd paid big for bullying me in middle school, went to Neuse Academy. Judge Nelson—and any judge who knew her—would be out of the question.

Neither of these problems, though, would stop me from pursuing the court order option. There had to be a way to make it work, and I was going to find it.

Tonight, Neuse Academy was playing Wake Day School. I expected us to win easily.

I rode over, locked my mountain bike, and strolled in. The game had already started and, since we were the visiting team, Neuse students had been relegated to the cheap seats. Fortunately, that made it easier to spot Gabrielle, Jesse, and Benita. The fact that Benita wore lime-green fingerless gloves didn't hurt either. The bodyguard was behind them, shades on, lips straight. Nobody sat anywhere near him.

A few rows down from them were Alexis McChord, Carlton May, and the rest of our old crowd. Last year, before Alexis broke up with me, I would've been sitting right in the middle. It was strange to admit it, but I didn't regret losing any of them—except Carlton.

My gaze slid back to Gabrielle. She hadn't been at Neuse for long, but she'd already started hanging out with three of the school's biggest misfits. Jesse was a scholarship kid and so smart that he'd been a loner for most of his time here. Benita had always seemed more interested in her cello than people. And me? Well, nobody considered my friendship worth risking Alexis's wrath.

I wasn't sure why Gabrielle had included me, but I was glad she had.

As I sat down beside her, she gave me a shoulder hug and immediately became engrossed in the play on the field. Yeah, just the way football ought to be enjoyed.

After the game, I hung back a few minutes with Jesse and Benita as the bodyguard murmured instructions to Gabrielle. Once he gave her the nod, we walked to the parking lot, where the SUV sat humming at the curb. Benita and Jesse crawled in first.

Gabrielle touched my arm. "Want to meet us at Goodberry's for ice cream?"

"It'll take me about fifteen minutes to get there."

"You rode your bike?" At my nod, she said, "The SUV can handle it. Throw it in and ride with us."

A quick glance at my watch showed that I still had an hour before I needed to call Susanna. "Okay."

We took our ice cream to Gabrielle's house, which actually belonged to her aunt. There was a movie theater in the basement, with a dozen amazingly comfortable seats, the best sound system I'd ever heard, and a concession stand (except we didn't have to pay). We finished our ice cream while watching outtakes from Gabrielle's latest movie release. It was almost midnight before her driver took us home. We dropped off Benita, then Jesse.

Honestly, Jesse's home shocked me. It was located in a row of townhouses at the center of a mildly scary neighborhood.

As we headed toward my house, Gabrielle said, "Where he lives is just another thing for Benita's parents to hate about him."

"What are the other reasons?"

"They think they have plenty. Benita is a nationally known cello prodigy, and Jesse's black, short, and poor." Gabrielle bit her lip. "Really poor. Neuse Academy puts extra money in his scholarship to cover his clothes so that he doesn't embarrass himself."

"How do you know this stuff?"

"Everything in my life is carefully choreographed." She gave a tiny shrug. "My aunt had all of you investigated."

Damn. "By who? The school?"

"The school couldn't tell us much. Privacy concerns. They cooperated as far as ethics permitted." She smiled. "They did, however, suggest you for my lab partner."

This information was vaguely creepy. Why was she telling me? I could've spent the entire semester being oblivious, and it would've been fine.

At some level, though, I could understand her caution. Even at a school filled with the children of the rich and locally famous, Gabrielle would stand out. "Okay," I said, staring at the back of the seats in front of us—just like she was. "Why did I get the job?"

"I asked for a person who was good at something outside of school. The person had to have a photo release on file, and —"

"Why a photo release?"

"When Gabrielle Stone takes AP Physics at a 'normal' high school, it's guaranteed that she and her lab partner will be photographed." She blew out a resigned sigh. "And most importantly, if my lab partner was a guy, he had to be unlikely to hit on me. I'm taken."

I was too, but I wasn't the kind of guy who would've hit on her anyway.

The driver pulled to a stop at the curb in front of my house. I released the seatbelt and turned to face her. "Did our personalities matter?"

She smiled but didn't meet my gaze. "Naturally, but I had to figure that part out by myself."

"Not entirely. We have to decide too."

She frowned at me. "Decide what?"

"If *we* want to hang out with *you*." I slid out of the car and went around to the back for my bike.

She leaned out the window. "Why wouldn't you?"

"Not everybody wants to have their friendships choreographed." I set my bike on the driveway. "Thanks. This was fun."

The window rolled up, but not before I'd seen Gabrielle's eyes narrow in surprise.

As the SUV slipped away into the night, I entered the side door of the garage. There were no lights on at my house. I tiptoed up the back stairs, heading to my room.

As I passed the landing beside the studio apartment, it hit me. I'd forgotten to call Susanna.

My brain became aware of a muffled sound. Someone jogged past my bedroom, their feet thudding on the carpet.

My eyes snapped open. The room wasn't the pitch dark of early morning. A thin line of sunlight edged the bottom of the door.

I checked the clock. Crap. Had I really slept until nine? I rolled to my stomach and buried my head in the pillow. This screwed up my whole day.

Feet thudded down the hall again, this time slowing as they neared my room.

"I'm up," I called.

The door opened with a sucking sound. "Are you sick, Mark?"

"No." I shifted my head to see my mother better. "I overslept."

"Oh." She frowned. "You were out late last night."

"Yeah. I went to the game with some friends from school."

"Did Susanna go?"

"She stayed at the lake house." I sat up in bed and rubbed my face. "I'm heading out there now. We have a date."

"Doing what?"

"Visiting some historical site downtown."

"Oh." She nodded. "Will she be here tonight?"

"I think so."

"Good. I'm going to do stir fry, but I'll get chicken for her."

"You don't have to treat her special, Mom."

"I do too. She's our guest."

I drove to the lake house without calling. I figured it would be better to see in person how Susanna reacted to my screw-ups.

When I parked in the driveway, my grandfather was sitting on the deck, drinking coffee and reading a paperback. He didn't look up as I approached.

"Granddad?"

He grunted.

"Something wrong?"

"I don't know, Mark. Is there?" He sounded pissed.

"Where's Susanna?"

"Maybe you should've called last night to find out."

This wasn't his business. "I got back from the game too late to call. Is she here?"

"Well, of course she is. Where else would she be?" He gave me a hard stare and then returned to his book.

When I entered the house, I found my grandmother in the kitchen, putting dishes away.

"Hey."

She scowled at me and then called out, "Susanna, he's here."

"I'll be down in a moment."

I looked up at the soft tread of her feet on the staircase and stared. Something was different about her.

It wasn't until she started walking toward me that I got it. She wore a form-fitting shirt, daring for Susanna. It was red, with a V-neck and no buttons. She was showing some skin and curves, plus it was the first time I could remember seeing her in a nice color. "You look great."

"Thank you." Her hands brushed at her exposed collarbone. "It will take time to grow accustomed to being without a scarf."

"I'm glad you gave it a try." I stood there admiring her, incredibly happy that she'd given something new a shot.

"Mark," Gran said. "Don't you need to leave?"

I nodded toward the door. "Oh, right. Let's go."

We walked out to the truck holding hands. I helped her in and then ran to my side.

She didn't say anything until I was on the highway.

"Why didn't you call?"

She didn't avoid the problem. I could appreciate that. "I didn't get in until midnight."

"I was awake."

That surprised me. Staying up late was obviously something she'd adapted to quickly. "If it happens again, I'll call."

"Do you anticipate that you'll stay out until midnight often?"

I couldn't tell if she were angry or not. "I don't know, Susanna. Maybe."

"Very well." She turned her head to look out the side window.

"Are you upset?"

"No."

How could she sound this neutral when I knew she couldn't be? "I wasn't alone."

"I didn't imagine you were. You said you would be with friends."

She didn't ask anything about them. Why not?

As I exited the highway, I glanced toward her. All I could see was her hair braided neatly down her back. "Would you like to meet them sometime?"

"Indeed, I would." Her head whipped around. "Are you sure you want them to meet me?"

CHAPTER SEVEN

BLOTS OF INK

Mark's fist banged the steering wheel. "Dammit, Susanna. What kind of question is that?"

This conversation made me weary. I'd been eager to hear from him. As the hours ticked by and the phone remained silent, I had put my book aside and watched the night sky through the window in my room. I didn't resent his evening away from me. I wasn't upset that he had friends.

But he hadn't called as he promised, and he hadn't apologized. Instead, he made me raise the subject. Why was this true? If this were merely an innocent mistake, why was it hard to discuss?

I gestured at the traffic light, which had changed to the color of green. "We can go now."

He muttered something unintelligible as the truck lurched forward. We were soon racing toward the downtown of Raleigh, with its man-made mountains of concrete and steel. I closed my eyes against the sight and rested my head against the seat back.

Moments later, we pulled to a stop near the Etons' house. It had been grand in my century, yet it seemed far less so when compared to modern homes.

Mark helped me from the truck but didn't release me at once. Instead, he kept his hands at my waist, his face grave.

"I'm sorry. I should've called."

I nodded. He should have. "It is past us now."

"No, it's not." He pressed his lips to my temple and then sighed, his breath tickling my hair. "I had a good time, but I should've called you."

"You have apologized. It is enough."

"I don't know if it is. We have to find things we can enjoy together."

I gestured toward the Etons' house. "Today is a start."

We crossed the street and stood on the sidewalk. I had never been inside the house. Two centuries ago, I would've been invited in only as a servant. Today, I would enter by choice. A sweet excitement gripped me.

There was a large crowd on the front lawn. I hesitated on the sidewalk and pressed closer to Mark's side.

"Come on." He gave my hand a reassuring squeeze. "I'm here."

We continued onto the property. Many of the people were dressed in late-eighteenth-century garb. They had done their research well.

"We came on the perfect day," Mark said. "It's like their grand opening or something. The sign in front says they started renovations a couple of years ago and took a lot of time to make sure everything was as correct as possible. See those people in costumes? They're called re-enactors. Most of them have studied how things worked in your century, and then they give demonstrations at events like this."

"I'm impressed at their accuracy." If I allowed myself, I could relax and pretend I was at a celebration of old.

We stopped in the midst of the activity. Children played games in one corner of the yard. An awning covered a table with lemonade and small ginger cookies. A lady, wearing the clothing of a shopkeeper's wife, sat under a tree, stitching a sampler. A well-dressed housemaid showed a cluster of visitors how to dip candles.

I laughed.

"What?" Mark asked, looking around.

"Truly, the Etons would've been unlikely to make their own candles." I gently detached my hand and started to turn away when I spotted a tent spilling over with young girls. Looking more closely, I could see baskets and racks of clothing. The sight drew me with an irresistible pull.

There were white aprons and caps trimmed with lace, tie-on pockets with heavy embroidery, and neck scarves of every imaginable color. Yet I bypassed them all to approach the shimmering folds of the ball gowns. I longed to touch them.

An older woman slipped a dress of gold silk from a hanger. "Would you like to try this on?"

"Indeed, yes." Had that light, breathy sound come from my mouth?

She beamed as she helped me into the sleeves. "There now. Here's a hat." She dropped a frilly confection of lace and gold ribbons atop my head. "You look adorable, hon. You're never too old to enjoy dressing up."

I stared at my reflection in the mirror. Never had I seen a garment so beautiful. It was the kind of gown I'd dreamed of as a little girl—the kind I'd imagined only appeared in great cities, for no event so grand had ever happened in the village of Worthville.

"Mark?" I looked over my shoulder. He stood a few feet behind me, holding up his phone. The camera flashed.

The look on his face charmed me. "Thank you, ma'am," I said to the woman as I reluctantly removed the garment.

"No problem. I completely understand. It's why I volunteer here."

When we emerged from the tent, Mark asked, "Where next?"

"I should like to go inside."

We drifted toward the small, square porch at the front of the house. I paused a moment, standing on a sidewalk that had long ago been part of a dirt lane, and shivered at the onslaught of memories. Mark's stillness suggested that he remembered too.

If I blocked out the trees and the smell of new paint, the magnificence of this place flowed over me as it had when I was here in July, except it had been July of 1796. The house had just been built, its bricks freshly mortared and its boards freshly nailed.

"Ready to go in?" he asked.

I nodded and then preceded him up the steps.

Ladies in period costumes stood at the entrance to each room. Mats covered the hardwood floors, with velvet ropes blocking the base of the grand staircase.

I entered the housekeeper's office. It was smaller than most of the closets at Mark's house, but it would have been considered quite extravagant for a housekeeper in 1800. I stood in its center, absorbing the sparse furnishings and rippled glass in the windows.

Had my sister spent any time in this space? I focused with all of my senses.

"Miss, may I help you?"

Mark spoke from behind me. "My girlfriend loves this period of history."

"Do you?" The lady's voice squeaked eagerly. "Do you have any questions?"

I turned to face her, full of questions for which I already had an inkling of the answers. "How many staff did the families keep?"

"Both the Averys and the Etons had many servants. Ten or more. At the very back of this property, you can see the foundation of an old dormitory for the slaves, and some of the hired staff had rooms on the property, like the housekeeper, butler, and cook."

"In the main house?"

"Mostly. The butler lived in the basement. The housekeeper had a small bedchamber through there," she said, pointing to a narrow doorway in the corner of the office. "The Etons had maids who slept over the kitchen."

"Truly?"

"Oh, yes. We're certain of that. We recently found a journal by a housemaid wedged into the attic wall. It's quite a find. Most maids would've been able to read some, but it was rare for someone in the working class to write so well." The lady's voice lowered as if confiding a secret. "The Eton family would've lived here at the time. Abigail Eton taught the girl herself…"

The woman's voice faded into the background, unable to compete against the hum of excitement singing in my veins.

A maid who could write?

I interrupted. "Where is this journal now?"

"Oh." The lady blinked at me through big round lenses. "It's exhibited in the dormitory above the kitchen."

I darted from the room, hurried through the length of the main house and out the back, rushing straight for the kitchen dependency. Two surprised ladies in costumes watched me run past and up the narrow stairs to the top floor. The maids' space was at the front of the building. It had unadorned walls and a tiny window. Two small bed frames slumped sadly against each other, topped with straw mattresses over ropes.

My eyes passed over the beds and moved on. This might have been the first true mistake I had seen in the reconstruction of this house. Bed frames were a luxury unlikely to have been provided to an indentured housemaid. My sister would've slept on the floor on a mattress that was not so thick as the ones shown here.

The journal rested on a stand in the farthest corner of the room, protected in a sealed case. I approached it with fear, wanting desperately to be right about its author.

Mrs. Eton began our studies this month.

Pleasure and pain whispered through my limbs. It was indeed my sister's handwriting—childish and poorly formed, yet recognizable to me.

"That journal is the greatest treasure of the Avery-Eton House Foundation," an unfamiliar voice murmured behind me. "A young maid wrote the entries in the last decade of the eighteenth century. She used the journal to practice her writing lessons. Her name was Phoebe."

The sound of her name ached through me. Phoebe Marsh. My beloved sister. "What do you know about her?" My voice was gruff.

"Only what her journal says and what we found on her indenture, which we found in the State Archives. Phoebe was likely fourteen when she arrived."

"Twelve," I said as I turned to face the lady. She was tall, thin, and dressed like a housekeeper in a cotton roundgown printed with stripes of green, gold, and brown.

"They did not hire someone so young." The woman shook her head, a patient curve to her lips. "A family of the Etons' wealth and position would've had their pick…"

I said nothing. The Etons had indeed hired someone so young. It wouldn't have been Mrs. Eton's natural inclination. Yet once she became convinced of the brutal treatment my sister would encounter elsewhere, Mrs. Eton had made an exception for Phoebe.

"…Mrs. Eton had forward-thinking ideas. It was unusual to teach a servant how to write."

"The girl knew how to write before she arrived."

The woman's smile deepened into something a bit smug. "That is an interesting guess. Some of the historians agree with you. Will you tell me why you think so?"

It would've been better to keep my knowledge quiet, but I couldn't allow them to think poorly of Phoebe or my parents. "The girl states that she began lessons that month, yet this journal demonstrates that she can write her thoughts as they flow, rather than copy a sentence crafted for her. Phoebe didn't learn to form the letters of the alphabet in a matter of weeks. The girl uses the journal to perfect her handwriting—not to learn how to hold a quill."

The lady wrinkled her nose as she stared intently through the glass.

"Was this the only journal you found?" I asked.

"I'm afraid so."

Disappointment tickled at the edge of my smile, but I wouldn't permit it to dim. "May I see the other pages?"

"I can't let you touch the journal, but we have all of the pages scanned. You can buy a DVD of the images in the gift shop."

Mark trailed me out the door and down the stairs, waiting to speak until we were alone in the bright sunshine. "Do you want me to stop in the gift shop?"

"Please." I studied his eyes. They reflected concern. "Are you worried about something?"

"I want you to be prepared." He cupped my shoulders lightly. "What if you learn that her life was miserable?"

I did not wish to believe it. But even if it were true, even if the Etons had been harsh with Phoebe, her years in their employ had rescued her from an indenture to my master, and there could've been no fate worse than that. "I wish to know how her life went. I do not fool myself to believe it would have been easy."

Mark's mother was in the kitchen when we returned home. Since Bruce was away on a trip, the table had been set for three. I declined her offer of lunch, anxious to be alone with Phoebe's journal.

Mark brought their old laptop to the apartment, set up the DVD, explained what I needed to do, and then left. After preparing a cup of tea in the kitchenette, I settled onto the couch and opened the collection of files. There was a preface from the foundation that ran the Avery-Eton House, explaining that the journal had been discovered this summer. I clicked on the first journal page and then looked away again in a bout of nerves. What if Mark were right? What if Phoebe had been miserable in her position as housemaid?

I sipped my tea, took a deep breath, and looked at the file again. I had to know. Why waste another moment?

Mrs. Eton began our studies this month. Patty is learning to read while I focus on my handwriting. Mrs. Eton says it is deplorable. She gave me this little book in which to practice.

Mrs. Parham reminds me without ceasing of my good fortune to have such a fine mistress. I need no such reminders.

I enjoy writing the letters with loops the best. My lines are never straight.

I smiled at her words, as if I could hear Phoebe's bright voice saying them aloud.

In an apparent effort to conserve paper, each day's entry had been written in tiny, cramped sections of the page. Phoebe had drawn a thin line to end an entry, and often left behind blots of ink. These imperfections had not dissuaded my sister from her goal.

July 28th, 1796
Raleigh, North Carolina

Mrs. Eton says that it is only right to begin each day's lesson with the date, for the months of the year are excellent words to write beautifully, and the ability to create elegant numerals has great merit.

Mrs. Eton says that clever girls are always able to think of lovely sentences to practice. I must not be clever, for I cannot think of a single lovely sentence.

How I wish Susie were here.

Perhaps I shall write to her. Indeed, yes. If I cannot be a clever girl with my journal, I shall be a good sister.

Dearest Susie,

I miss you greatly. Please visit me often. I have much to tell you...

I looked away from the laptop and shuddered. I would never see Phoebe again. How had she learned this fact? Had she hoped forever, or had she given up after months of silence?

If there were many more such statements from my sister, I wouldn't be able to read on.

...I shall begin my news with a description of the family.

Senator Eton is seen only at mealtimes, for his government duties are heavy and his hours long.

Two Eton children have married. Mr. John lives nearby and practices law. Mrs. Mary Johnson is the mistress of a plantation near New Bern. I do not believe she or her child has ever visited here, a fact which Mrs. Parham views as a personal slight.

Mr. William and Miss Judith are still in residence, although it will not be much longer before Mr. William leaves for college.

He winked at me once as I left the family parlor with dishes. Mrs. Parham would have thrashed me had she seen.

I must not forget Mrs. Whitcomb. She is Mrs. Eton's sister and stays in Raleigh for much of the summer. Mrs. Parham says that it is a pity Mrs. Whitcomb never had children, but I cannot see that it has harmed her. She is very beautiful and much admired.

Yours most affectionately,

Phoebe

August 2nd, 1796

Dearest Susie,

In today's letter, I shall tell you all about the household staff.

Patty works in the kitchen. She does not live in the house. Her family home is but a mile away. She walks to and fro each day.

There are five servants who live here. Mrs. Parham—have I mentioned the housekeeper?—has her own small suite in the main house, as does Mr. Fisk, the butler.

Mrs. Parham is a distant cousin to Senator Eton. I do not think she would be here otherwise, for she is disapproving of the household and, indeed, everything else she comments on.

Miss Trilby is a lady's maid to Mrs. Eton and sleeps in a smallish chamber on the floor with the family.

I sleep alone in the maids' dormitory above the kitchen. I suppose that more help will be added over time, but for now, I retire eagerly each night to my own small room.

Cook has a private bedchamber across the hall from me, and very possessive he is of the space. He will not permit me to clean it, for *which I am truly thankful. He has a smell about him that is most objectionable.*

Lessons are ending for the day. I shall write again soon.

Yours most affectionately,

Phoebe

I was relieved by what I'd read so far. Her first days had been acceptable, markedly superior to mine. My education had ended on the day I arrived at the Pratts' house. I slept in a coffin-sized wedge of space under the eaves of the attic and served a family of eight as their sole house staff. By the end of my first month, I had stopped counting the number of times I'd been thrashed for displeasing Mr. Pratt.

August 3rd, 1796

I have received a letter from Mama with news of infinite sadness. My beloved sister was swept away in a swollen river. We have lost our Susanna in the same manner as my father. We shall not have the comfort of the grave.

Mrs. Eton has permitted me an afternoon to grieve. There is a lovely willow at the back of their garden. I shall curl beneath it and remember.

Tears blur my eyes and threaten to stain the paper. I shall write no more this day.

My heart is broken. How can Susie be gone?

Chapter Eight

Together and In Sync

There was a sharp rap on my bedroom door Saturday afternoon. I looked up to find Dad leaning against the threshold, computer case in one hand, suitcase in the other. Fatigue etched deep lines into his face. "How's it going, son?"

"Great." I snapped my laptop shut and gave him my full attention. "Hard trip?"

"Just glad the travel is behind me for a while." He inclined his head. "Been thinking any more about colleges?"

"Yeah."

"I'd like for you to consider early decision at Virginia Tech."

There was plenty about his alma mater that interested me, not the least of which were the mountain biking possibilities. If we'd had this conversation in May, I would've had a different answer. But I had Susanna in the picture now and, as much as it surprised me that he'd forgotten that detail, I wasn't about to remind him. "I don't think I'll be ready to make a binding decision by November first."

Dad nodded. "Do you want to go back for another look?"

"I thought we might sign up for the Hungry Mother Cross-Country race. It's not all that far from Blacksburg." I'd never been to Hungry Mother State Park in Virginia, but I'd heard that their mountain-bike race was fun. It was close enough to Virginia Tech that some members of their cycling sports club might be there. Could be an opportunity to make some contacts.

Of course, it would also be fine with me for it to be just something I was doing with my dad. We hadn't gone on a trip—just the two of us—in a while, and with high school graduation only a few months away, the chance to do stuff like this was about to disappear. An easy race would be a good thing for him since he didn't have time to work up to anything remotely hard. And good for me too. With my focus on Susanna and school, racing had slipped in my priorities.

I'd already put it on the family calendar, but only as tentative. With my father, plans got canceled whenever a "high-revenue client" beckoned.

"Yeah. Let's do it," he said.

"Really?"

"I'll block it out on my calendar at work."

"Great."

After he left, I glanced at the clock. With my lawn service slowing down for the year, I only had a couple of lawns left to do this weekend. I had time to get them out of the way and then squeeze in some variety to my training.

Once the yards were finished, I loaded my bike in the truck and drove to a park in Garner. After a good, hard ride, I drove home, showered, and changed.

Then I went to check on Susanna. It was time for dinner, and still she remained alone. I went down the back stairs and hesitated on the landing outside the apartment. Her door was shut. There were no sounds.

As much as she liked her privacy, I didn't want to wait any longer to be with her. I gave a light tap on the door.

"Come in," she said in a husky voice.

I opened the door. The room was dim. It took my eyes a moment to adjust. She sat in a corner of the couch with the laptop on the table beside her and the lamp off.

"Are you reading Phoebe's journal?"

"Not at the moment. I was earlier."

Something didn't feel right. "What does Phoebe say?"

"She writes about her first weeks in the Eton household. Daily chores and such." Susanna's voice softened. "It wouldn't charm anyone but me."

There had to be more to this story. "Are you okay?"

"I am fine."

"You don't sound like it."

She held out her hand.

I didn't need another invitation. Walking more slowly than I wanted, I crossed the room and sat carefully beside her.

Her lips curved slightly. "You smell of soap and cologne."

"I went on a training ride earlier." I wanted to help her with whatever bothered her, but I couldn't if she didn't ask. "What can I do?"

"Kiss me."

I hesitated. If she were like other girls, I would think *hell yeah* and launch a make-out session, but Susanna still seemed breakable. Where she came from, people might not even kiss until after they married. So, even though she'd been in my world for over a month, I'd been careful to keep the physical stuff controlled within the *proper boundaries* that she expected.

Maybe I was thinking through this too hard. One gentle kiss and then I'd worry about where to go next. I leaned closer and pressed my lips to hers. Damn, she tasted good. I wanted to haul her up against me and explore the lean strength of her body with my hands, but it was too soon. She wasn't ready.

I really hated that phrase.

Her hand came to rest on my chest even as she drew back slowly. But instead of pulling away entirely, her head dropped to my shoulder.

"Susanna, I don't know what to do for you."

"Your instincts are serving you well."

My instincts wanted more of me touching more of her. I eased her onto my lap and took over her spot in the corner.

We stayed wrapped in each other's arms, listening to the hum of the A/C and the muffled calls of people passing on the greenway.

Linking her fingers through mine, she said, "Did you enjoy last night with your friends?"

I didn't want to talk about that right now. Not when we were together and in sync. But she'd asked and it would be a bigger deal to refuse than to answer the minimum. "The game wasn't very exciting, but we won by a lot, which makes it fun. Afterward, I went out with my friends to get ice cream."

"What are their names?"

"Jesse, Benita, and Gabrielle."

"Have you known them long?"

"I've known Jesse since our freshman year, but not well." Jesse was into chemistry and calculus. I'd always liked the "people" sciences more, like psychology and anatomy. We hadn't had many classes together. "Benita is Jesse's girlfriend. I only met her a few days ago. And this is Gabrielle's first semester at Neuse Academy."

"Is Gabrielle special?"

I stiffened. "What kind of question is that?"

"Your voice was different for her than the other two." She shifted until our gazes met.

"For one thing, Jesse and Benita are a couple. For another, Gabrielle is a celebrity."

"What is a celebrity?"

"A famous person. She's a movie star."

"On the TV?"

I smiled. It was a technology we'd introduced early to Susanna. "Gabrielle's films go to movie theaters first."

"Is she talented?"

"Gabrielle is, but a movie star doesn't have to be talented to be a celebrity."

"That sounds like politicians. They can be evil or honorable, but we know about them just the same."

"Exactly."

Her head dropped back to my shoulder. I could feel the tension bunching up inside her.

"Mark, why is this topic difficult for us to discuss?"

I swallowed a curse word. If I ignored her question, would it go away?

Nah, probably not. I had to admit the truth, because she'd be able to tell if I didn't. "I had a lot of fun, and you weren't there."

"Do you think I begrudge your evening away?"

"Of course not. It's just…" I didn't want to say anymore. Why did she keep asking? "I was out last night with two gorgeous girls, and neither of them was you."

She looked up at me, wide-eyed. "Should I be jealous?"

"No." The whole thing made me feel guilty, and I didn't know why.

"Do you love me?"

The question gnawed at my gut. Why had she asked that? To reassure herself or to remind me? "Forever."

"We would share a peculiar sort of love if it could not survive conversations with other young ladies." Her lips pressed to my cheek, close to my ear. "Do as you want with your friends," she whispered, "as long as you return to me."

"God, Susanna. How can you be so perfect?" I sought her mouth with mine and kissed her thoroughly, proper boundaries be damned.

It took a while to finish the make-out session, although probably *make-out* was too strong a term. It had been mostly PG-rated. Not that I minded. Susanna's struggle to let go was kind of hot, especially since I knew I'd be on the receiving end when she finally figured it out.

Eventually we both realized we needed food. "Burgers, fries, and chocolate shakes?" I suggested.

"Indeed." Her eyes gleamed.

I'd be willing to bet that, if Susanna made a Top Ten List of Best Things About the Twenty-First Century, a cheeseburger meal deal might be number one.

After we got our fast food fix, I searched through Netflix until I found an old movie of Gabrielle's. It was a period film, set in New England during World War II.

Susanna settled next to me with a bowl of popcorn and watched a few minutes. "This is your friend? She is much younger than I imagined."

"She's been in movies since she was a baby. This film was made at least six years ago."

"Indeed."

We didn't talk for another ninety minutes. That was one of the things I'd learned about Susanna. She wanted to absorb things totally.

Not until the credits rolled did she speak. "I enjoyed that story."

"Yeah." I rose and pulled her up beside me. "Want to go out for a walk?"

She nodded and then snuggled into my arms. "Mark, she thinks I'm dead."

I didn't have to ask who she meant. "Why does Phoebe think that?"

"The villagers assumed that Rocky Creek swept me away."

I wished Susanna had mentioned this earlier. No wonder she'd been down all evening.

I thought back to the day I'd helped Susanna escape. Images slipped through my brain like slides in a presentation. Susanna, weakened and bloody from abuse, thrashing through Whisper Falls into the safety of this century. Me, lying on a rain-slickened rock, trying to avoid being pummeled by her master. The men of Worthville, high above us on the bluff, watching silently, a gray blur of dogs at their feet.

Had my leap into the future looked like a death wish? From the villagers' angle, maybe so. But not to Susanna's master. He'd been close enough to see that the water wasn't dangerously swift or deep. "Not everyone thinks we were swept away. Jethro Pratt tried to jump through the falls because he could hear us talking. He does *not* believe that you're dead."

CHAPTER NINE

THE RIGHTEOUS SIDE

Mark and I strolled along the streets of his neighborhood, avoiding the other walkers with their dogs on treacherous leashes. It was a serene and lovely way to end the night.

"I don't get it, Susanna. Why did Pratt let everyone believe we died?"

I was happy to talk about things of no importance, but I didn't wish to speak of Jethro Pratt—the man who had made the past eight years of my life a misery beyond compare. "Perhaps he didn't know," I said, allowing my repugnance for this topic to color my voice.

"Don't think that's it."

I lifted my chin. "Must we discuss this?"

"Yes."

"Then discuss it alone. I have no comments to add."

"I'm on your side, Susanna. I just think it's weird—"

"Hush." I yanked my hand free from his and hurried in the direction of the Lewis house. Mark kept up easily.

I would distract him. "Have you spoken with your sister of late?"

"No." He caught my hand again. "It's been a while since I called her."

"She phoned your grandfather several times while I was at the lake house."

He stopped altogether, jerking me to a halt. "How often is several?"

"Perhaps four." His reaction was most puzzling. "Is this peculiar?"

"Maybe." He stared up through the trees, as if seeking a message from the heavens.

I looked too and sighed with pleasure. Pines waved their black bristles against the blue-gray of the evening sky. I had to take pleasure where I could, for the stars didn't appear with any brilliance in this century.

"Did she talk to Gran?"

"Not that I noticed." I sorted through my memory. "If I answered the phone, she and I would talk briefly, and then she would ask to chat with Charlie."

"Shit."

I stared at Mark through narrowed eyes at his choice of words, but he hardly paid me notice. Glancing at his watch, he said, "Let's get back. I need to track her down." He took off at a tremendous pace.

"Is there something wrong?"

"Probably." He made a low growl in his throat. "She has to be avoiding Gran, and that's not good. Fletcher is being an ass."

Such strong language for someone whose name I'd never heard. "Who is Fletcher?"

"The parasite who lives with my sister."

Parasite? That was a harsh claim. "Is your sister married?"

"No."

"Why have you not spoken of this to me before?"

"I don't know." We had reached the low fence that identified the perimeter of his yard. "Maybe because I can't stand the guy and wish he would disappear."

I understood such feelings, for I felt the same, but concerning Mr. Pratt.

When we entered the house, he lunged for the phone that lay by itself on the table top. Seconds later, he was talking—or rather, not talking. The conversation involved sharp sounds from his sister through the phone and much nodding of the head from him.

I had been forgotten.

Should I be annoyed at this fact or should I be relieved? I was unsure.

Perhaps both, for it allowed me to indulge more time with my sister's journal while still permitting me the righteous side in a later sparring match with Mark.

It was nine in the evening. I had hours left to read what came next.

August 5th, 1796

Mrs. Eton believes that Psalm 23 will bring me comfort. I wrote it yesterday on a slate, and today I shall write it with quill and paper.

Mrs. Eton found my first attempt to be competent while lacking inspiration. She is confident my second attempt will improve and encourages me to permit the loveliness of my embroidery to command my writing. I shall try harder this time.

Yea, though I walk through the valley...

A month followed in which Phoebe only wrote from the Psalms and complained of the brutally hot weather.

I had to admit that A/C was a lovely invention.

One page in the journal was so heavily stained that, truly, there could be no point in investing time in deciphering it.

The next pages contained a dull listing of her chores. How surprising that I should find anything she had to say as dull. But indeed, I did. I had no wish to recall the beating of rugs or the sweeping of floors.

Odd to think of all the ways I had already accepted this century and its conveniences. With machines replacing people at performing chores, people had time to do other things. There were different chores to complete, movies to watch, fast-moving vehicles to sit in. Were those other things better? I was still unsure.

September 2nd, 1796

We have settled into a routine for our lessons. Each Tuesday and Friday afternoon, Mrs. Eton instructs us in the classroom on the top floor of the main house. She uses a primer to teach Patty how to read. I worry that Patty will never succeed.

Mrs. Eton says that my letters show improvement. However, she insists that elegant handwriting must always include flourishes. I do not care a bit for flourishes. Adding them is impossible without blots on the page and ink stains on the fingers.

This entry proved that Phoebe was wise to be wary of flourishes because blots and smudges blighted the page. Row after row of letters followed.

The next date in the journal caught my eye. September 9th. Yesterday in my century.

September 9th, 1796

I should quite like to be Patty's friend, but she still will have no part of me.

Mrs. Eton has assigned The Lord's Prayer to me. I shall do my best to please her.

My sweet Phoebe was such an innocent. Of course Patty resented her. Phoebe had been given the job that Patty had originally had and doubtless wanted back. A housemaid had far more prestige than a scullery maid. Cleaning chamber pots, scrubbing pans and dishes in hot soapy water—could there be a worse position anywhere in a household?

Patty certainly had known that Phoebe's duties were less miserable. House chores had more variety and less smell. Not to mention that the gossip would be better among the housemaids. I could only hope that, with time, Patty had grown to love my sister the way Phoebe deserved.

September 19th, 1796

The Eton family left this week for a visit to their properties in New Bern. Mrs. Parham is to carry on our lessons, but I do not think she will. She complains that our mistress takes her responsibilities to us too seriously.

Patty does not like to read. She stumbles and stammers. Mrs. Parham asks her to read the same verse each day. I think Patty speaks it from memory so that she can scurry back to the kitchen.

Mrs. Parham gives me no assignment. She says to write a brief passage and date it. She says to do my best work, so that Mrs. Eton will not be angered when she returns.

September 26th, 1796

I am to polish the silver in the dining room today. If my mistress were here, I should not have to do this task. She cautioned me when I first came to save the sensitivity of my fingers for stitching.

Mrs. Parham, however, does not believe in coddling the staff and mutters egregiously about our mistress behind her back. How I will find the time to finish Mrs. Eton's instructions about the linens? I am to mend all sheets in the cupboard and strengthen their hems. There are a dozen plain new napkins without adornment which I am to embroider with sprigs of lavender, which is Mrs. Eton's favorite flower.

October 3rd, 1796
I have peeked at Mrs. Parham's ledger. She writes in a large hand and squints as she forms each letter. I am greatly relieved. I do not believe she can read small print. I shall keep my quill well-sharpened and make tiny letters, as tiny as my stitches. The housekeeper will not be able to decipher what I write. My journal will be as secret as if it were hidden.

October 7th, 1796
I broke a porcelain vase yesterday. Mrs. Parham beat my palms with a rod until they bled. I can scarce close them. Indeed, I lose my grip on the quill.

The entries ended at that point.

I closed the computer and snapped off the lamp. Wiggling under the covers, I rolled to my side on this comfortable mattress and became one with the dark.

It was late. The Lewises had been asleep for a long time. We would all rise early in the morning to attend the worship service. It was time for me to rest.

I plumped a pillow.

The journal gave me a measure of comfort. Phoebe had the ordinary life of a housemaid in the home of a family who didn't treat her badly. They had kept their commitment to increase her education. She had a safe place to sleep and no complaints about the food. It had been a wise decision to take her there.

Yet my sister had thought I was dead, a lie that grieved me. I'd mourned the loss of Phoebe since the day I left my old world behind. Only now could I see that grief reaching her. I knew it would be fierce and bewildering—a misery that had no cure.

Perhaps it was best this way. Was it not better to think me dead than to wonder why I lived and yet never contacted her again?

I had indeed passed away—to here instead of heaven.

CHAPTER TEN

SPARE X CHROMOSOME

Our physics class met in the lab on Monday, but the experiment was straightforward and we finished early. While Gabrielle cleaned up our station, I stared out the window. Rain had fallen all day. Flash flood warnings had ended, but the Piedmont portion of North Carolina was a mud pit. A slippery *wet clay* pit, if I wanted to be specific.

No way would it be safe to train in this mess, even if the nearby trails had been open. I'd have to ride on my stationary bike, which was fine. Endurance was important.

Gabrielle poked me in the back with a sturdy fingernail. "Jesse, Benita, and I are heading over to the Olde Tyme Grill after school to study. Want to join us?"

I did, actually. I had my truck today—so if I stayed only a few minutes, I could still be with Susanna close to normal time. "Sure. See you there."

I arrived first at the grill and grabbed a booth in the back corner. A steady stream of kids I didn't recognize wandered in, filling the booths and tables. I hadn't realized this was such a popular place, although there was another private academy and a public high school within easy distance of here.

All this popularity made Olde Tyme Grill a strange choice for us. Gabrielle would stick out like a beacon. Why hadn't they picked somewhere more secluded?

The three of them walked in together. Gabrielle went to the order line with Garrett right behind her in his regular uniform of khakis, polo shirt, and shades. His clothes might have looked casual, but he didn't.

Jesse and Benita headed over to my booth, flopped onto the bench across from me, smiled "hi," and then turned to each other.

I would've cracked up laughing if I stared that hard at a girl, but he seemed serious about studying every pore on her face.

It didn't take long for Gabrielle to show up with four smoothies and a huge basket of fries. She set them in the middle of the table and then slid in next to me.

The bodyguard took over the table nearest us. She didn't offer him anything or even acknowledge his presence.

Jesse picked up a fry that looked nearly as big as a breadstick. "Thanks for the food, Gabi."

She grimaced at the nickname. "No problem."

Benita twined both of her arms around her boyfriend. "Jesse thinks we'll have a pop quiz tomorrow."

He grunted. "I *know* we will."

I gave him a skeptical look. "How can you?"

"Research," he said as he frowned at another fry. "I interviewed some seniors from last year. Ms. Milford gives her first pop quiz the week after Labor Day. Based on the way she was emphasizing points today, I'm guessing we'll have one tomorrow."

Benita nuzzled his scruffy cheek. "You're amazing."

"You are too." This time, the solemn stare changed into an embarrassingly noisy kiss.

I watched them in surprise and then looked around to see if the grill's owner was around. He'd kick us out if he noticed.

There was a sucking sound as they separated. "We need ketchup. Excuse us just a second," Benita said as she slid from their side of the booth. Jesse slid after her, their hands joined. They headed toward the food counter.

Gabrielle smiled at me. "What's wrong?"

"I don't get what she sees in him."

"She doesn't *see* him. She's a musician. The sense she trusts most is hearing. The last thing she uses to judge people is her eyes."

I shrugged. Whatever. Still didn't get it.

"Describe Jesse."

It felt awkward to describe another guy, but Gabrielle had this laser-beam stare that I couldn't deny. "He's short. Probably works out with weights a lot. Shouldn't try to grow a beard yet."

"Describe Jesse without mentioning how he looks."

I hated it when girls got this way. Was it something bred into their spare X chromosome? "He's smart. Nice."

"And fun."

"Okay."

"That is what Benita *sees*." Gabrielle cocked her head to the side, as if studying me for the first time. "What sense do you trust most?"

That was easy. "Touch." As soon as I said it, I felt my face grow hot. I hadn't meant as in skin-on-skin— although I trusted that too. What I'd meant was the feel of the road through the bike. I trusted it way more than the way the road looked.

"Why do you—"

"Gabi?" Jesse interrupted. He dropped onto the other bench, one hand clutching a bottle of ketchup, the other clutching Benita's arm. "I've been reading *Teen Trash*."

Gabrielle answered without looking away from me. "That's a mistake."

Benita dropped her head on Jesse's shoulder and smiled. "It says you're secretly dating Korry Sim."

"Then I guess it's not a secret anymore."

Benita's head popped up, her mouth dropping open into a big O.

I looked at Gabrielle. "You're dating Korry Sim?"

She nodded and sipped her smoothie.

That was hard to take in. Korry Sim was in huge demand as an actor. He had a black belt and was willing to do his own stunts. He had to be older than her, four years or more, which seemed like a lot to me, but maybe it wasn't with actors. "Where'd you meet Korry?"

"On the set of *Flight Risk.*"

Wow. There was major buzz on that film. "I didn't know you were in that."

Benita let go of Jesse's bicep and leaned on the table. "*Teen Trash* says it's rumored that Korry picked you specifically to play Princess Aziza."

Gabrielle wrinkled her nose. "Why do you read that magazine?"

Benita laughed. "So I can keep up with gossip."

"I wish you'd stop. You can ask me anything." She took another swig of her smoothie. "They're right for once. Korry asked the producers to cast me as Princess Aziza. I wrapped my scenes over the summer."

"I know something they don't?" Benita slumped in her seat, eyes focused heavenward in abject joy. Jesse looked irritated at losing his spot at the center of her universe.

I was too interested in this news to pay attention to them. "How did you swing that?"

"Korry loved my performance in my last film and told the producers I'd be perfect opposite him. So they scheduled my scenes around my senior year."

Gabrielle and Korry Sim? I hadn't known this a minute ago, but now that I did it changed how I viewed her. A lot of the time, she did a good job of acting like a regular teen, but it was hard to hold that thought knowing that she was dating one of the best-known guys on the planet. "Where is *Flight Risk* being filmed?"

"Botswana."

Damn. "What's Botswana like?"

She gave the first real smile on this topic. "It's gorgeous. The land is varied and the animals…" Her voice trailed away on a sigh. "It's my favorite country in Africa."

Okay. Gabrielle had been to enough countries in Africa to have a favorite.

"Um, guys," Jesse said, "can we get back to physics? I want to pass the pop quiz."

"In a minute," Benita said, clamping her hand over his mouth. "How long has it been since you've seen Korry?"

"Four weeks."

Benita winced. "How long before you see him again?"

"Thanksgiving, probably."

"I wouldn't like that at all." Benita moved her hand from Jesse's mouth to kiss him, then stared into his eyes. "I want you around where I can get my hands on you."

If they thought four months was bad, what about two centuries? Until Susanna moved here, that's what I'd lived with. "Long-distance relationships suck."

The other three stared at me.

"Are you in a long-distance relationship?" Benita asked.

"Not anymore." Wait. That was misleading. "Actually—"

Jesse waved me to silence. "Better change the topic. Alexis McChord is heading this way."

Damn. "Is she alone?"

"No."

I crammed fries in my mouth just to have something to do.

Benita raised her eyebrows at Gabrielle. "Alexis is the girl who dumped Mark at prom."

I nearly snorted ketchup into my sinuses. Why make it sound like Alexis was the story here? She wasn't. It hadn't taken me long to get over her at all. We'd spent our entire relationship in one extended battle over how much I neglected her for my training schedule. On the rare occasions I'd thought about her since, it was more along the lines of *what the hell was I thinking.*

No, my problem wasn't how she dumped me. It was who she was with now. Carlton May had been my best friend until the day he started dating my ex. Now, we were...nothing. It was weird.

"Hi," Alexis said. Carlton halted behind her. His gaze met mine briefly before slipping to Gabrielle.

None of us responded. I snagged another fry.

Alexis tried again. "What's going on?"

Benita eyed her coolly. "Physics study group. Projectile motion."

Alexis stared hard at me. "I haven't spoken to you since school started, Mark. Do you ever see the colonial girl?"

I dropped my head to my chest. I should've known she'd try to stir things up. "Her name is Susanna," I bit out, "and I see her every day."

A ripple went through my study group, which Alexis must've felt, because she got even more persistent. "Where does she go to school?"

"Nowhere."

"She's already graduated?"

"Susanna had to drop out." My expression dared Alexis to keep going.

"What's she doing, then?"

I stared at her with cold fury. "I think she planned to bake bread today."

"That's an interesting hobby."

"She's the most interesting girl I know."

Alexis flushed. "Nice." She spun around and stalked to the exit. Carlton trailed after her.

"Who is Susanna?" Benita the Brave asked.

"My girlfriend."

There was a surprised silence.

"I can't believe that Alexis McChord's ex is dating again and nobody knew it." Benita slumped back in her bench. "Is there some reason you've never mentioned your girlfriend? Not even Friday night?"

I shrugged. I'd been to one football game and this study group with the three of them. I didn't share private stuff that easily.

"Okay, then," Benita continued. "How about explaining why Alexis calls her a colonial girl?"

"Because Alexis can't resist making bitchy comments."

"No argument here, but it seems like a fairly specific statement."

I wasn't going to let Alexis dictate how or when I explained Susanna to anybody, and now was not the time. So as rude as this might seem, I had to get out of here. "See you guys." I slung my backpack over my shoulder and gestured at Gabrielle to let me out. There would be no studying for me this afternoon. "Thanks for including me."

"Wait a minute, Mark." Gabrielle's brow was scrunched up. "I'd like to meet her. Why don't you bring her to the next game?"

"That's not likely to happen in this century," I muttered as I took off.

When I reached my truck, I heard the slap of running feet behind me. Gabrielle appeared beside my truck. Her bodyguard hovered nearby.

"You know how to make an exit," she said.

"Okay." I wrenched open the door to my truck and flung my backpack on the passenger side.

"So, are we your friends?"

"Yeah. Sure."

"Then don't we deserve a better answer than that?"

If this conversation was about to turn into one of those stupid-ass, touchy-feely things, I would dent my front quarter panel. "Maybe, but I don't have a better answer to give."

Her chin jutted out. "When you talked about long-distance relationships sucking, were you talking about Susanna?"

"Yes."

"But you see her every day?"

I hesitated. "She moved here in July."

"Where does she live now?"

"Close by." It was time to stop answering, and yet I couldn't seem to quit.

"Why haven't I heard about her before?"

"Why haven't I heard about Korry?"

"That's different. I have to protect him."

"It's not different. I'm protecting Susanna too."

Gabrielle's face settled into a smooth oval—as if she were posing for one of those "Madonna and Child" paintings at the museum. Beautiful and sad. "Are you ashamed of us, Mark?"

"No." I shook my head. "No, and I'm not ashamed of her either."

Damn. Why had I answered a question that she hadn't asked? I hopped onto the driver's seat of the truck, buckled up, and threw the truck into reverse.

Gabrielle watched me drive away, straight and still.

I was sorry that I'd acted like such a dick back there, but the alternative would've been worse. I couldn't describe Susanna in words that captured who she really was. She had this charm—this presence—that had to be experienced to be understood.

I would have to think of a way to introduce them, but in a time and place good for her. And once my friends had met Susanna, explanations wouldn't be necessary.

Chapter Eleven

A Level of Debt

Mrs. Lewis located a group of people online who were skilled at finding employment for immigrants. I called them and discovered that they were willing to assist me. I had an appointment at New World Family Services scheduled for Monday at two PM.

I could barely tolerate the slow passage of this day, but at last we arrived at the facility in the back of a church—a very large church, as if multiple homes had been combined around a central, beautifully landscaped courtyard.

A smiling young man greeted us as we walked in the door. "Miriam is waiting for you, Miss Marsh."

I nodded and headed in the direction he indicated.

"Susanna, do you want me to go in there with you?"

"No, thank you, Mrs. Lewis." I felt bold and confident about how the interview would progress. New World Family Services was accustomed to those who knew nothing about this America. I would fare well here.

"Are you sure?"

"Yes."

"I think it would be best if I came with you."

I was her guest. I would not refuse her again. "Certainly."

We entered a smallish room that had the feel of a library, with numerous bookshelves lining two of the walls. The woman who awaited us grinned tiredly when she looked up. She was older in person than her youthful voice had conveyed over the phone. After welcoming us, she gestured to a large volume of colorful papers and said, "You mentioned in our call that you're interested in employment opportunities."

I smiled. "Indeed. I am eager to find work."

She paused, as if expecting more and then glanced at Mark's mother.

"It may be a while before Susanna has an ID or a Social," Mrs. Lewis said.

The lady jotted down a note. "How much education do you have, Susanna?"

Mrs. Lewis answered before I could open my mouth. "She had to drop out of school at an early age, so she has no diploma. She's interested in a GED, but it's a long way off."

"You're fluent in English, Susanna. That's a good start." Miriam slid a brochure across the table to me. "Here's some info on how North Carolina handles the GED. If you want to get into Wake County's GED prep program, you'll need to take the placement exam first." At my nod of gratitude, she smiled and then flipped through the big black book that lay before her. It had three large metal rings along its spine and many sheets of paper. "As far as jobs are concerned, there are only a few possibilities, since we're limited in what you can do."

Truly? Perhaps she didn't realize how strong and capable I was. "Why are we limited?"

Mrs. Lewis patted me on the arm. "Most employers require a Social Security card."

I stared at her in dismayed surprise, willing my face to remain calm. It might be months before I had one of those cards. How had I not known this? Had the Lewises mentioned it and I'd been too perplexed to understand? "What are we limited to?"

"Primarily people who pay cash," Miriam said as she ran her finger down the sheet. "What do you think about babysitting? It's appropriate for someone your age."

I frowned, not confident about the term. "Sitting with babies?"

"Yes, although you could take care of children of all ages, from infants until age ten."

It wouldn't be my preference, but I was open to trying anything. "I have experience with minding children."

"Good. Do you know first aid and CPR?"

It seemed that I would recognize the terms if I knew how to do them. "I am not familiar with either."

She sighed. "That's not always a requirement. Can you provide your own transportation?"

"I can walk."

"That restricts your availability a lot—"

Mrs. Lewis interrupted. "We'll be happy to drive her, but babysitting isn't the answer. Susanna isn't used to the way kids are around here."

I swallowed words of denial. Mrs. Lewis was undoubtedly correct.

"Okay," Miriam said. "Delivering newspapers?"

Mrs. Lewis shook her head. "Susanna can't drive."

Miriam's smile became strained. "Food service?"

"The preparation of food?" I asked. "I can cook."

"You would start out washing dishes, cleaning tables, or sweeping floors."

I nodded. I could easily handle a job with such tasks.

"No," Mrs. Lewis said, "She's only just recovered her health after a serious infection. We shouldn't let her do anything that might expose her to contagious diseases until she's finished a round of vaccinations."

Miriam sucked in a deep breath. "Susanna, you're lucky to have a family so considerate of your welfare."

It might seem fortunate in her mind. In mine, it felt as if I were falling deeply into a level of debt that I could never repay. It took balance from my relationship with Mark's parents—and Mark.

Miriam slid heavy notepaper across the table. It had brightly colored lines and circles scattered about in irregular patterns. "This is a map of the bus system. If you learned to use it, you could gain a real measure of independence, and fare cards are quite cost-effective."

"None of the routes come anywhere near our house," Mrs. Lewis said.

I was aware that the pair of them spoke English, and that they were discussing vehicles, streets, places, and money. But it held no meaning for me. I didn't know what they discussed, nor why it had importance. The limited possibilities had been broached, only to have Mark's mother decline them. I had come filled with hope for finding a job, and I would leave stripped of even that.

Perhaps it would be best to think of something else. Something pleasant. Phoebe's journals. Fishing at the lake.

"Susanna?"

I looked up from the painted woodgrain of the tabletop to find Mark's mother eying me suspiciously. "Yes, ma'am?"

"Did you hear what Miriam said?"

"Pardon me. No." I refocused on the other woman's face. "Could you repeat?"

"We have an attorney who is willing to consult with you for a nominal charge. It might help you find a way to get your identity established."

"Why would he do that?"

"The attorney is female, and she is happy to provide this service through us."

I didn't know how much "nominal" was, but if it were more than zero, I didn't have it. Yet it seemed unwise to refuse completely. "I shall ponder this offer."

The other two women exchanged glances. Miriam cocked her head like a curious bird. "Certainly. It's your case. We can involve the lawyer later if you like."

They stood. I did too, greatly relieved that this interview had reached its end.

Chapter Twelve

Talking Around the Truth

The sky had cleared like magic while I was at the grill. It had been dark and threatening an hour ago. Now there were blue skies, thin clouds, and a milder temperature.

When I got home, both of my parents' cars were in the garage. I entered the house and hesitated in the doorway to the kitchen. Even though I couldn't see them, I could hear their voices clearly through a window overlooking the deck.

I probably would've continued onto my destination—the refrigerator—except one word stopped me.

"...*Susanna*..."

I froze, eavesdropping without shame. Okay, without *much* shame.

My father was speaking. "We told her she was welcome to stay here as long as she needed."

"She is," Mom said, "but I didn't expect it would be indefinite."

"It's barely been a month."

"Is there an end in sight?"

Ice tinkled in a glass. A deck chair squeaked.

"You're over-thinking this, Sherri. Susanna won't be here forever, and she's trying hard to be unobtrusive."

"I know." Mom sounded tired. "It's not her. She's a sweet girl, and I feel sorry about what a horrible life she's had, but I want my house back. It's never just us anymore."

"Your parents will take her any time you ask."

"I know." A noisy sigh. "Having her constantly underfoot isn't the only thing that bothers me. I'm worried about my son."

I leaned closer as if that would help me hear better, which was stupid since I could hear perfectly fine already.

"What about *our* son?"

"He's too serious about her."

Dad heaved a loud sigh. "Sherri, please."

"This is his senior year. He needs to enjoy everything it has to offer."

"He's having fun."

"I'm not sure that he is. He's too focused on her, and she's too traumatized to function. You have to admit—he sticks around the house way more than he used to."

I'd heard enough. I spun around to go out there and tackle them.

Susanna stood on the bottom step of the back stairs.

Damn. "How much of that did you hear?"

"I left the apartment when you came inside."

I crossed to her, but when I reached to pull her into my arms, she held up a hand to stop me.

"There is no need to comfort me, Mark. I admire honesty."

The back door opened, and my father stepped into the laundry room. He halted, his gaze widening on Susanna. My mom bumped into him and muttered a swear word.

Dad's voice was pained. "How long have you two been standing there?"

"Long enough," I said.

Mom peeked over his shoulder.

Susanna looked at them neutrally. "If you wish me to find another place to live, I shall."

"Not necessary," Dad said.

My mom shook her head, cheeks flushed.

They had not done a good enough job reassuring Susanna. "You're not leaving."

"Perhaps it would be best."

"It wouldn't be best for you. It wouldn't be best for me."

My mom leaned her butt against the washing machine and stared at the wall straight ahead of her, not saying anything.

"Susanna," Dad said into the awkward silence, "you have a home with us for as long as you need. That hasn't changed." He laid a hand gently on her shoulder. "Sherri and I have some issues we ought to discuss with Mark. May we excuse ourselves?"

"Of course." She ran lightly up the stairs.

"I'm sorry she overhead that," my mom said.

I was too. "Don't apologize to me. Apologize to her."

Dad pushed past me. "Let's finish this in the family room."

For the next fifteen minutes, they dragged through the same conversation again, only it took longer this time. Talking around the truth required a lot of words.

I waited until Mom paused for a breath and said, "Let me ask you this. Are you sorry I rescued her?"

They shook their heads.

"Do you regret that I brought her here?"

"No," they said together.

"So what's the real problem?"

Mom shook her head. "The amount of time it'll take to straighten things out."

"It's worse for Susanna."

Mom and Dad exchanged a glance, complete with eyebrows lifting and lips twitching. Dad looked back at me. "You're right."

Mom nodded.

"Anything else?"

"You," she said, hitching forward on the couch, propping herself up on my dad's legs. "This should be the most carefree year of your life. You're missing out."

"I miss out anyway because I train hard."

"Good try, but we all know that you'd hang out more with friends if she weren't here."

"Maybe not, Mom. Girlfriends are always a time drain. You only ever see me because my girlfriend lives *here*."

My dad patted her hand. "He's right about that."

She frowned at him and then me. "Can you promise that you'll try to be normal?"

I jumped to my feet and resisted the urge to roll my eyes. "It's strange to be holding this conversation right now. I went to a game with my friends Friday night, and I hung out with them today after school. I don't need to promise you anything. Susanna is not holding me back."

My mom gave Dad the *punting-it-back-to-you* look. He shrugged and didn't say anything.

I took that as a positive sign. "Are we good then?"

Dad smiled at Mom as he nodded. "Yeah, we're good."

"Fine," she said.

So it was settled. Now if we could just get past the fact that Susanna had overheard.

Susanna made supper for the two of us in her kitchenette, but she sat across from me, silent and withdrawn. After a couple of attempts to get her to talk, I gave up.

She collected the dishes as soon as I finished and set them in the sink.

I rose and followed her, rubbing my hands over her shoulders. "You cooked, babe. Let me wash."

"No." Her voice was husky and soft. "Work comforts me."

I took a step away. When she got like this—all shut down and closed off—I had no clue what to do.

She turned and looked at me. "Do you have homework tonight?"

"Yeah."

"Perhaps you should start it now."

"You want me to leave?" It was hard to say whether I was more hurt or relieved.

She stood on tiptoe and kissed my cheek. "I think it would be best."

"Okay." The faucet turned on as I shut the door behind me.

I spent most of the evening either completing homework or studying for the pop quiz that Jesse was sure we would have in physics.

Even though it was almost bedtime, I had a personal project that needed some attention. Creating a past for Susanna. I had to make up documents real enough that a judge would consider them for a court order and yet government agencies wouldn't scrutinize them too carefully.

Which documents would those be? I went online and checked the list.

Hospital records or midwife records were the most trusted. Not going to fake those. They could likely be verified over the internet, even by an overworked government official.

A signed and notarized affidavit from one of her relatives? Yeah, not going to happen.

Family Bible? It would be easy to buy an old Bible with empty "Births" pages. Maybe even too easy. It was the kind of evidence with the highest skepticism factor, but I wouldn't write it off yet.

A baptismal certificate seemed like it shouldn't be too hard—but even the Social Security Administration listed it as a possibility, which meant it must be harder to fake than I expected.

High school transcript? Maybe, especially if I could make up the school too. Private schools went out of business all the time.

My eyes skipped over one of the documents and then returned. I stared hard. Took a deep breath.

An original marriage certificate.

Damn.

CHAPTER THIRTEEN

SHARP RELIEF

I could hardly settle my thoughts during the night, but exhaustion must have finally claimed me, for the whine of the garage door startled me awake. As the powerful growl of Bruce's vehicle faded away, I glanced at the clock. Six-thirty.

Clogs slapped across the kitchen floor and into the laundry room. The door slammed. The garage door whined up again, followed by the light hum of Mrs. Lewis's hybrid car. She didn't put the garage door down. It was nearly seven. She would be late.

Mr. and Mrs. Lewis had kept to their daily rituals. I knew what that meant. The unpleasant scene had not affected them the way it had me.

Mark was the easiest Lewis to recognize unseen because his morning routine involved the most noise. His bike whistled into the garage and then clanged against the garage wall, signifying the end of his training ride. Footsteps stamped in from the garage and through the laundry room. Ten minutes later, with his shower doubtless completed, he tramped into the kitchen. It had become our custom to eat breakfast together before he left for his school. Today I wouldn't join him.

Cabinets banged. A chair screeched across stone. He walked into the laundry room, hesitated, hurried up the stairs, hesitated again, and tapped lightly on my door.

I held my breath, not wanting to speak with him. What if a night's sleep had changed his feelings about my presence in his parents' house?

He had defended me yesterday, but would he defend me forever?

No, I could not speak to him when I was facing yet another day with nothing to do. I stayed silent so that he would leave.

The bike rattled again. The garage door shrieked back into place. I ran to the window and watched as, helmet on, he rolled down the drive and disappeared around the bend in the lane.

With an odd sense of defiance, I reached for yesterday's clothes. For my entire life, I'd had two sets of clothing—one for Sunday and one for the rest of the week. There had been one bath per month. I'd worn the same shift for weeks on end.

Mark's world had changed all that. Bathing every day, sometimes twice. Fresh clothes every day, sometimes twice.

The blouse I slipped on was stale but not truly bad. I stepped into a rumpled skirt and ignored socks and shoes. I didn't look my best, but there would be no one here to scold me with words or scowls.

I ought to find something useful to do. Perhaps it would be best to study English grammar for my GED, but a stack of library books beckoned. I picked up a volume on history and turned to the early years of the nineteenth century, to learn of the times my sister had lived through without me.

After an hour of immersion in the political turmoil of the young United States, I set the book down. Two months ago, had someone offered me a day to do nothing but read, I might have fainted from sheer joy. The reality was far different. The printed word was not as happy a companion as I might have believed. I enjoyed people more.

I left the apartment and wandered down the back stairs into the kitchen and then to the family room. This space made me yearn for Mark, so I hurried through it to the front foyer, careful to step around Toby, who had kindly accompanied me. I paused in the living room, a place the family hardly ever visited. There were lovely paintings on the wall and a fireplace—rarely used. Shelves held books, small sculptures, and gilt-framed photographs of smiling children.

I stopped to browse the books that no one ever read. There were six volumes by Jane Austen. I had only read *Persuasion*. A delightful story. Perhaps I should read the others. Miss Austen had much to say, more than she could say in a single book.

Like Phoebe?

I pondered this thought. Might Phoebe have written more?

Indeed, yes, if I knew my sister. The first journal had ended abruptly, and Phoebe had much to say. There would surely have been others if she could afford the cost.

Might other journals have also been preserved?

Would the internet know?

I raced back to my apartment. It was good that Mark had shown me how to search the web on the laptop. I brought it up, but there my hands hesitated. What did I ask for? I had only tried in the past to find food recipes. He always seemed to know exactly what to ask for, but he was in school. I would go mad awaiting his return at past three.

Perhaps the easiest thing to try would be my sister's name.

Phoebe Marsh proved to be more popular than I would've anticipated—and in many countries. I added *journal* and *North Carolina*.

The list of links altered dramatically, but all seemed to reference Phoebes in the twenty-first century.

I tried *servant*, *Raleigh*, and *18th century* next.

A promising website appeared. I selected *North Carolina State Archives - Artifacts from the Colonial and Early Federal Periods*.

There was a brief paragraph of introduction.

"Little is known about the daily lives of the working class from this period. Few could write more than their names and, for those who did, time was too short and paper and ink too dear to encourage their writing. Most of what remains are letters of correspondence. They have proven to be a treasure trove of information. Much of the current understanding of the lives of the working class has been gained from this small collection of documents."

I smiled. The greatest treasure trove they could ever know sat right here—reading their words—yet they would never find me.

I scanned the list of materials and found what I sought on the third link.

Primary sources from house servants: 1795 - 1830

Phoebe's indenture lasted from 1796 until 1802. Could she have any documents among these?

The reference claimed that these diaries and journals were stored in a special warehouse but they were available for public viewing. Most had yet to be transcribed.

It didn't matter to me that the materials were not transcribed. If any of those journals had been written by my sister, I could read them as well as any printed book.

I wanted to investigate further, but I didn't have the skills and Mark wouldn't be home for hours.

I prepared and ate my dinner, washed the dishes, and put them away.

There was nothing left to do in this place.

Life had been simpler for me in the first few weeks after I moved to the twenty-first century. I had been ill. It had taken time for my ankles to heal and my infection to cure. I had slept, eaten, and slept more. I'd been told what to do and when to do it.

Mark had barely begun to teach me about my new world when he had to return to school. When would there be time to teach me again? How many more such days would I have?

Perhaps a stroll about the lawn would lift my spirits. I hurried down the back stairs and out the rear door of the laundry room, hopped across the over-warm lumber of the deck, and sighed with pleasure at the cool prickle of grass under my feet.

Rose bushes adorned the foundation of the house, their bright pinks bringing a smile to my face. I left the shadow of the house to walk along the edge of the property, to the waist-high fence dividing their yard from the greenway. A large corner of the lawn had made way for Mrs. Lewis's garden. It was evident that she'd taken great care with its design.

There was a pool at its center with a small fountain. Nearby, in the shade of a dogwood, squatted a white iron bench. It looked like a piece of Phoebe's embroidery, with curling vines and graceful leaves. I sat on the bench and reflected on this world I had joined.

Behind me, the greenway wound through tall pines and spreading oaks. It ought to be a place of beauty yet, to my mind, it could not be—not with its acrid surface and heavy traffic. With so many people seeking refuge, the greenway would fail to bring true peace.

A pair of women ran past in their shorts. It no longer jolted me to see exposed skin, but neither did I envy them. I might be willing to wear a shirt that revealed my collarbone, but I had no wish to bare my limbs.

Not that I should. There were too many scars tracking across my legs. Dozens of them crossed like a wide weave, thin and straight. The recent ones had plumped up pink and puckered. The older ones had faded to a lightening of my skin tone, perhaps more like shadows than scars inflicted by beatings from a switch. I considered them now with an odd detachment, even though I had received each and every one of the beatings without flinching or crying out.

I slipped down onto the grass, lifted the long skirt to my knees and exposed my legs and feet to the warmth of the sun.

The screams of a baby roused me from a light sleep. I checked the position of the sun. Mark would be home soon. I had best go inside, bathe, and change into fresh clothes.

The knob of the back door refused to turn. I frowned in concentration. Had I locked myself out?

I tried again. It was indeed locked, and I had no key.

There were numerous doors to this house. Perhaps one of them was open.

It took very few moments to discover that every door was locked.

I tried the garage last. It had a keypad that could raise the garage door, if only I could remember the correct numbers.

Mark said that the numbers changed each month and reflected a special occasion. What was the holiday for September? Had it not occurred this Sunday?

9-1-1. Yes, that had to be it. I pressed the three buttons. Nothing happened.

I tried again. There was no difference. Perhaps I should abandon the keypad.

There might be a window left open.

I walked to the midpoint of the driveway and assessed the distance from the ground to the apartment. I had left a dormer window undone to allow in fresh air, but the pitch of the roof and the lack of trees would make climbing to that window most difficult.

A vehicle rolled behind me on the lane and stopped. A car door shut slowly with a deep *ker-thunk*. I glanced over my shoulder. A man in a dark uniform approached.

He must be a member of law enforcement. An unfortunate circumstance.

"Hello," I said, clasping my hands before me. "Are you a police officer?"

"I am," he said, his voice clipped. "Who are you?"

"Susanna. How may I help you?"

"I was about to ask you the same thing."

Were there not crimes to manage in this city? My problem seemed entirely too mundane to concern the police. "I cannot get into the house."

"Why not?"

"It's locked, and the keypad doesn't work."

"Ah. Do you know the combination?"

"Apparently not, else I should be inside now."

His gaze narrowed. "Is this your house?"

"No, indeed. It belongs to the Lewis family, but I do sleep here."

"Where do you sleep?"

"In the space over the garage."

"Miss, I'll need to see some ID."

"I do not have any."

"Is your ID in the space over the garage too?"

Had he not heard me? "I have no identification card. The government will not give me one." I shook my head. America was far too concerned with identification.

"Miss, why don't you come with me?" He caught my elbow and tried to tug me down the driveway.

"Pardon me, sir," I said, pulling my arm from his grasp. "It isn't proper for you to touch me so."

He reached for me again. "Okay, that's enough—"

"Hey," a voice shouted.

"Merciful heavens," I said. "There is Mark. Perhaps he can explain matters to you."

Mark braked to a stop behind me. "What's going on here?"

"Who are you?" the police officer asked.

"Mark Lewis. I live here." He nodded toward me. "So does Susanna."

"She lives here?"

"Mark, truly, that is too strong a statement. Your parents—"

"Shut up, Susanna." He frowned at the officer. "Is there a problem?"

"We received an alert. I'm here to check on it."

I was glad that Mark had come. He seemed far better prepared to address the police officer's questions than I. Yet I didn't think the lack of courtesy was warranted. "I'm locked out," I explained to Mark.

"Did you try the keypad?"

I nodded. "I couldn't get it to work."

Mark closed his eyes, released a tight breath, and opened them again. "I apologize, Officer. This is just a big mistake. Susanna is new to the city and doesn't understand how things work. But she does live at this house, and I have the key code. We're good." With that, he took out his phone, tapped out four numbers on its surface, and the garage door opened.

Mark asked me to hold onto his bike as he and the officer made their way back down the driveway. Out came the wondrous identification card that consumed this century.

A few moments passed and the vehicle sped away. Mark walked back to me, took his bike, and proceeded to put it away. He remained silent throughout.

I walked past him, into the house, and up to the apartment. Ten minutes passed before I heard his tread on the stairs. There was a light rap on the door before he entered.

"What happened this afternoon?"

"I sat in your mother's garden. I didn't realize the door had locked behind me."

"Don't you know the code?"

"A rather foolish question, is it not? Had I known it, none of the remainder would've happened." I did nothing to hide my frown. This first encounter with a law enforcement officer had been an unpleasant experience. Mark's impatience was not helpful. "I thought it might be your Patriot Day but it—"

"Did you try 9-1-1?" At my nod, he groaned. "That's for emergencies."

"I am certain you mentioned it at one point."

"Yeah, as in *never use that code* unless you have an emergency." He shook his head. "Granddad's birthday is September twenty-sixth. That's the code." He crossed the room and slumped onto the couch beside me. "Why did you go outside at all?"

"I had some hopeful news. It needed space to breathe."

He exhaled noisily and then shifted to meet my gaze. "Tell me your hopeful news."

"There may be more journals written by Phoebe."

"How did you find that out?"

"I searched on the internet." I turned on the couch to face him. "There is a warehouse at the State Archives with documents that haven't been transcribed. They have a section for house servants in the years that Phoebe served the Etons."

"It's a stretch to go from that information to *my sister has more journals out there.*"

"I know this to be true. Phoebe didn't write one journal. She would've loved recording her thoughts. I must go to the Archives. Tomorrow, if possible. How far is it to the warehouse?"

"First, we have to figure out where the warehouse is." He shook his head. "If it's in the Archives building, it'd be insane to walk there, Susanna. I'll have to drive you."

He pushed off the couch, drew out his phone, and made a call, walking to the rear window to stare out. The sunlight etched his profile in sharp relief. How beautiful he was.

How fortunate I was.

He slipped the phone in his pocket and then rejoined me on the couch. "Many of the documents are located in a large storage facility in the basement of the Archives, but you have to have an appointment to get in. They'll let us down there tomorrow at four. We'll have at least an hour."

I tensed. "Will you arrive home that early?"

"I'll take the truck to school. If Phoebe has journals down there, we'll know tomorrow."

Chapter Fourteen

Ways to Exploit

It took me a long time to fall asleep, because I couldn't stop thinking about Susanna's run-in with the law. The *what-ifs* were horrible.

What if I hadn't arrived when I did? As I'd ridden down the lane, he had his hand on her arm and she was on the verge of freaking out. Would she have struck him? That could've been all kinds of bad.

If I'd stopped for a smoothie or come down the greenway instead of taking the main roads, Susanna might've been on her way downtown to the Police Department without me seeing. Would she have known what to do? Would she have talked too much? They'd never come across anyone like Susanna, and she'd never come across anyone like them.

What if she'd landed in jail with the real crazies?

What if I couldn't find her, and we couldn't figure out where she'd gone?

It made me sick to think about it. It made me want to lock her up in the house and throw away the key until she made it all the way to normal. If that ever happened.

I took the truck to school the next day for two reasons. I had to hurry home to pick up Susanna, and my guidance counselor wanted to talk to me about college. Not that I was looking forward to it. There were a lot of things I liked about my final fall semester. Answering questions about my college search wasn't one of them.

I paused in the open doorway of his office. "Mr. Rainey?"

He looked at me with a smile. "Come in, Mark. Close the door and take a seat."

A smiling Mr. Rainey made me nervous. It could mean either bad news or something squishy. Dropping onto a seat, I waited for him to start.

"So, when we talked last semester, you were looking at Virginia Tech and Brevard College."

I'd finished my junior year with my serious college list narrowed down to two. Both in the mountains. Both with great mountain biking teams. One was a huge, out-of-state public college; the other, a small, in-state private college. "Yes, sir, with App State as my safety school."

"You won't need one." He glanced at his computer. "Your SATs are excellent. Your AP exams are..."

"All fours and fives."

He gave a sharp nod. "Your unweighted GPA will be the weakest part of your application." He stared at me over the top of his glasses. "What's up with that, Mark?"

I shrugged. "Priorities." The difference between a B and an A at Neuse Academy wasn't worth the training time I would sacrifice.

"Hmm." He frowned at his computer screen again, his mouse clicking rapidly. "You've taken a lot of science..."

"*Life* sciences." I'd only taken physics and chemistry under duress.

His lips twitched. "*Life* sciences, which colleges love to see. Any ideas about a major yet?"

I wasn't sure what I wanted to do, but being outdoors had to be part of it. "Something to do with the environment, maybe."

"Fine. You have time to get more specific." He plucked at his lip. "Are you thinking about early decision to Virginia Tech? You're a shoo-in, especially being a legacy."

"Probably not. I haven't decided if it's where I want to go." Even though it would please my dad, two hundred miles seemed a whole lot farther away right now than it had last spring. "I'd like to consider something smaller. I might look around here again."

Mr. Rainey's gaze narrowed on me. "Really? I thought mountains were a requirement."

They had been, but Susanna changed everything. And mentioning my girlfriend to a guidance counselor would start a lecture I didn't want to hear. "I may have written local schools off too quickly."

"If enrollment size is important to you, the only one I'd recommend is Duke."

"I don't have the GPA."

"You might be surprised." Fingers tapped briefly, then he smiled. "If you're serious about looking in the Triangle area, Duke is a strong option. Drop by and give them a visit. If you text me, I'll mark you excused that day. "

Mr. Rainey wasn't prone to exaggeration. Shifting to the edge of my chair, I got ready to leave. "Thanks, maybe I will."

"Before you go…" His face scrunched. "Newman College is another school that might interest you if you're feeling undecided. Four thousand students. In the mountains. Heavy into life sciences. It'll have several majors which might interest you."

"Never heard of it."

Mr. Rainey's lips curved. "That's why you have guidance counselors."

Okay. "Where is Newman College?"

"The southwest corner of Virginia. Near the town of Damascus. It has a beautiful campus."

"Thanks, but—"

"They started a mountain-biking program last year and are looking to recruit some strong racers for the team."

He had my attention now, just in time for the bell to ring. I stood, hesitating. "Do you know anything about the coach they've hired?"

"I'll look into it for you. Any chance you could drop by at the beginning of last period?"

"I have American government."

"With Mr. Fullerton?"

"Yeah."

Mr. Rainey sighed. "Another day, then."

I smiled as I left the room. Nobody wanted to take on Mr. Fullerton.

Gabrielle walked into the physics classroom, but instead of stopping at her assigned seat on the front row she continued down the aisle until she reached the desk behind me.

"Jackson?" she said in her soft, clear voice.

"Huh?" Jackson Mott coughed. "Yeah. You need something, Gabrielle?"

"Would you please trade seats with me? I'd like to sit behind my lab partner."

I glanced over my shoulder to see what would happen. Jackson scrambled out of his seat. Very interesting that he'd given in so easily. It would also be very interesting to see if our physics teacher let the change stand.

I looked back at her as she settled in. "We have assigned seats."

"This will work out."

"Really?"

She nodded with confidence.

I faced forward. Ms. Milford was watching us. She'd observed the switch and said nothing. I looked back at Brielle. "I'm impressed."

"There are a lot of things about being a celebrity that suck. I might as well exploit the ones that don't."

I laughed. "Just don't try to exploit me. Like, did you get your half of the lab report done?"

"Here it is." She held up her part. Several thin specimens were tacked carefully to a board.

"I forwarded my half to Ms. Milford last night."

"And copied me." She leaned forward and lowered her voice. "We're trying the study group again today, since we didn't get much done Monday. Want to join us?"

"Can't. I promised Susanna I'd hang out with her." No way would I let her down.

"Maybe next time." Her phone hummed. When she read the caller ID, her face clouded. "Excuse me. I have to take this." She put it up to her ear. "Wait a sec. I need to find somewhere private to talk."

She strolled up the aisle, whispered to the teacher, and left the room.

Seemed to me there were a lot of not-sucky ways to exploit being a celebrity.

Susanna waited for me on the front porch of the house. I didn't need to shut off the truck. She ran to the passenger side and climbed in.

"Mark, we must hurry. The Archives close at five-thirty."

I kind of knew that, since I was the one who had told her. "We have plenty of time." I backed out and headed downtown.

It turned out that I was wrong. Traffic was horrible. There were orange barrels everywhere.

Susanna set her hand near mine. It meant she wanted to have her hand held, but she wouldn't come right out and do it herself. *Most improper.*

When I linked my fingers through hers, she gripped them tightly.

"I cannot wait to find my sister's journals."

It made me smile to hear the excitement in her voice. It had been too long.

"What makes you sure they'll be there?"

"Because I want it to be true."

Even with my favorite shortcuts, it took forever to arrive in the general vicinity of the Archives, and parking was even harder. The main lot was full. I circled the building three times before giving up and had to settle for a parking space between the Governor's Mansion and the Avery-Eton House. It would be a bit of a hike.

She didn't wait for me to open the truck door. By the time I reached the sidewalk, she stood there, nearly hopping from impatience.

"It's three fifty-five. Will we have time?"

I nodded confidently. "Come on. Let's go."

We ran down the sidewalk, but between Susanna's long skirt and traffic lights that hated us, it was after four when we entered the lobby.

"Hey," I said to the security guard. "We have an appointment in the warehouse."

"Sign the register, and I'll need to check your IDs."

Holy shit. How could I have forgotten something so important? I'd been here often in the weeks preceding Susanna's escape, scouring through ancient contracts and wills. I'd been through the security here enough to know that the Archives staff carded visitors every chance they got.

"I don't have one," she said, her eyes wide with panic.

The guard shrugged. "We can't admit you without ID. You'll have to come back another day."

"But I can't—"

I pulled her away from the desk and over to a bench in the corner. "We need to think this through."

"What is there to think about? I don't have identification. What am I to do?" The excitement died in her eyes, like someone had snuffed out a light.

I wanted to kick something. Why hadn't I thought about this? I knew we had to have ID. It was such a common thing that I hadn't thought about it at all. "I'll go down there and see what I can find."

"You don't know her handwriting."

"Maybe she wrote her name on the cover."

"What if she did not? What if there are hundreds of journals?"

"There won't be hundreds." I pulled out my phone. "I have a camera. I'll take photos of the pages and show them to you."

She took a deep breath and averted her face to stare out the window. "It will take a long time."

"We'll come back as often as we need to find Phoebe's journals." I didn't wait for her to respond. I showed my ID at the guard and slammed down the stairs.

The girl with pigtails, the one who'd helped me do research earlier in the summer, waited behind the desk. "You?"

"Yeah. Me."

"What do you want this time?"

"I'm looking for diaries, letters, journals, anything from the last years of the eighteenth century."

"Is there a specific range?"

"1796-1802."

She nodded and disappeared behind a row of metal cabinets. When she returned, she carried a tray of beat-up, crumbling, musty books and papers. "Here are the artifacts we have from the 1790s through 1810."

There were about a dozen or more items to choose from. "Can I open them?"

"No, I'll do it for you." She snapped on a pair of gloves and picked up the best book of the bunch. "This one was written by a printer's apprentice."

"Can you tell whether it was written by a guy or a girl?"

"A printer's apprentice would be a guy."

"I only want to look at stuff by girls."

"Okay." She set it down and picked up a tattered pile of pages, barely held together by something that looked like string. "This one was written by a housemaid, and there is a second journal that we're confident she wrote as well."

Anticipation feathered down my spine. The helper carefully drew back the top page. Inside, row after row of text had been jammed onto every square millimeter of paper. There were loops and lines in faded ink. Impossible for me to read.

I felt a prickle of hope. "I have a friend waiting in the lobby to see this, but she doesn't have ID. Can I take some photos with my phone?"

"Sure, but don't use the flash."

"Do we have enough time?"

She nodded. "I lock the doors at five-thirty."

Ten minutes later, I emerged from the basement with shots of handwriting from both journals by the housemaid and a few samples from letters by a tavern keeper and a dry goods merchant.

Susanna sat on the end of the bench, hands clasped tightly in her lap, nothing moving on her face but her eyes. They tracked me across the floor, never wavering.

"Do you have news?" she asked, her tone husky, her face stiff with the effort to keep hope at bay.

"I think so." I dropped onto the bench beside her and held up the photo gallery on my phone, trying not to shake. I wanted this to be right for her sake. *Please let the writing be Phoebe's.*

As she stared at the image, she choked back a sob. "It's hers."

I swiped. "How about this one?"

She nodded, biting her lip.

I jumped to my feet, grabbed her into a hug, and spun her around, right there in the middle of the lobby. She laughed and clung to me, arms locked tightly about my neck.

When the spontaneous celebration ended seconds later, I set her back on her feet. "I'll go back down there and see what I can do about getting access for you."

"Oh, indeed." Her eyes clouded. "What will happen if I cannot visit that special room?"

"Don't worry. If I have to snap every page, I will." I dropped a light kiss on her forehead and raced back downstairs.

It was quarter after five when I made it back to the special area. That was calling it close. "My girlfriend is interested in the books by the housemaid. Do I have enough time to photograph every page?"

The girl shook her head. "No need to. All pages have been recorded as digital images. For twenty bucks, I can burn you a DVD."

"Deal."

"Cool." She scowled at me a moment and then nodded her head, as if reaching a decision. "It'll be hard for your girlfriend to read the text. These documents are in worse condition than most of the collection, and the way they wrote in the eighteenth century is different from the way we do."

"Susanna is good at transcription."

"You sure?"

"Yeah."

The girl's eyes widened. "Ask her to capture the transcriptions. We'd love to have the help."

Susanna bounced on the passenger seat all the way home. Her hand kept straying to the DVD, as if she could feel her sister's presence on its surface.

We didn't even discuss what to do when we reached my house—just ran up the stairs to her apartment and placed the DVD in the old laptop's drive. I pulled up the first page of the first diary from the Archives.

Susanna shook with excitement. "Here, let me," she said, pushing my hand aside.

"Sure."

She paged through the images, her lips moving as she read the scrawled text. I could hardly make out anything.

"Can you read this stuff?"

"Of course." Her voice had that hollow ring that meant she was only half-listening.

It didn't take long for the silence—and being ignored— to get old. "Do you want me to stay?"

"It isn't necessary."

That stung. Not sure why, except that she wouldn't have gotten this far without my help.

Yeah, I did know why. I didn't like being dismissed.

CHAPTER FIFTEEN

CHAOTIC ASSORTMENT

Most of my sister's first journal—the one we purchased at the Eton House gift shop—had had little of an exciting nature. My sister had delighted in recording the most boring details of her life. Naturally, it would be better to have a boring life instead of a miserable one.

Yet I had hopes that the next two journals would be more interesting.

Mark had passed along the request from the young lady at the Archives. I was confident about transcribing Phoebe's words and would be glad to provide this small service. Although it might not be their expectation, the Archives staff would receive a report prepared in my most careful and modern handwriting, since I had no desire to use a keyboard for anything other than the unavoidable requirements of searching on the internet.

I gathered paper and pen, preparing to do my best. With great anticipation, I opened my sister's second journal and prepared to transcribe the first entry, which began six days after the housekeeper beat Phoebe's hands for breaking a vase.

October 12th, 1796
The family returned to Raleigh yesterday, arriving in the late afternoon in a flurry of horses, wagons, and carriages.

Mrs. Eton voiced great displeasure at the progress Patty and I made with our lessons during her absence. She came to stand over my little table and asked to see my hands.

It ached to open them.

Mrs. Eton said, in the most mild of tones, that she would bandage my wounds and that I was not to permit them to become wet for two days. Then she turned to Mrs. Parham and smiled—a most peculiar smile, I must say—and asked her for a word in the parlor.

I was coming down the servant's staircase when Mrs. Parham left the mistress' parlor. She walked quickly past me, head bowed, but I did note cheeks flushed an unbecoming shade of red.

October 13th, 1796

Mrs. Parham has left the household. I cannot be sad. She was not kind to me or Patty. Nor did she hide her irritation with Mrs. Eton's gentle treatment of the staff.

I wonder how long it will take to find someone. Mrs. Eton is most particular.

October 20th, 1796

Our mistress talks to many candidates in search of a replacement. Her standards are quite high and many leave abruptly.

The next few entries showed Phoebe's interest in the new objects of art that the Etons had brought with them from their plantation near New Bern. She described them in fascinated detail. Lacing through her narratives was a chaotic assortment of chores as she poured out the calamities of a household without a housekeeper.

Her awe at her mistress continued unabated.

November 3rd, 1796

Mrs. Eton is wondrously skilled in the healing arts.

Patty became afflicted with a most peculiar pain in her back. Cook swore that Patty required a hot poultice but our mistress would have none of that. She assured Patty that the pain began in her belly. Mrs. Eton prepared a noxious tea from her own secret recipe and made Patty drink the whole of it. Cook was most displeased. He claimed to be incensed at the number of visitors tramping through his kitchen, but I believe he has a more prideful reason. Cook does not like to be told he is wrong. Indeed, I should think the mistress is the one woman alive who is permitted to hint at such a thing.

The episode ended well, for Patty was quite strong the next day.

The next few entries documented the search for a housekeeper. After meeting with many candidates, Mrs. Eton had finally found someone who promised to meet her exacting standards. Mrs. Jasper, "tall of body and strong of limb," arrived with great energy and skill. A widow without children, she made her mark quickly.

December 1st, 1796

My mistress told us today that it would be her last in the classroom. "I shall come no more to teach you," she said, "for Mrs. Jasper has graciously agreed to take over your education."

I shall miss Mrs. Eton fiercely, but I do admit to relief. It is unseemly to be the recipient of so much attention from the mistress of the household.

The next four pages were either torn or crumbled. I read as much as I could but soon grew frustrated by sentences and paragraphs only partially decipherable.

It was truly unfortunate, for the damaged pages covered what, for me, would've been the most interesting time of the year. The effort to support a large household in the dead of winter would make for entertaining reading. I should very much like to know how many food stores they had put up or if they continued to serve meat. In Mark's world, the effort to eat had become so very easy. Fresh food, in bewildering quantities and varieties, was no more than a short car ride from the house—any time of day or year.

Numerous months were lost on the damaged pages, for I reached the spring of 1798 before the journal became readable again.

April 9th, 1798
There will be a ball at the State House in May, with dancing, music, and a feast. My master and mistress will attend.

Mrs. Eton has commissioned a new gown. She especially loves whitework and asked the seamstress to leave the hem unadorned. My mistress told Mrs. Jasper that there is none so clever with thread as I and asked for me to embroider whitework on her hem and sleeves. She is especially partial to ivy and sprigs of lavender.

I am pleased and honored that she remembers my talent although, truly, I have kept my skills alive by adorning their linens these past two years.

May 2nd, 1798

A new lady's maid arrived today. Her name is Millie Pritchard and she hails from Fayetteville. She brought much baggage with her.

Miss Pritchard does not speak to us. She walks about the house with her chin tilted just so. I heard her whisper to Mrs. Jasper that good servants should blend with the wallpaper. Mrs. Jasper laughed. I do love our housekeeper's laughter. It is impossible not to join in.

Patty does not like Miss Pritchard at all, but then Patty doesn't like many people. She has relented about me and confessed that she no longer resents that I have the position she wanted.

I find two years to be an excessive length of time to hold a grudge, nor can I find it in me to feel compunction about the merit of her complaint. Much as I should have liked to be friends with Patty all along, I should have disliked being a kitchen maid more.

June 20th, 1798

Mr. William left today for a journey north to Boston, where he resumes the study of medicine.

Mr. Eton has never reconciled himself to Mr. William's wish to be a physician. The Senator wanted his younger son to follow him into law and, perhaps, politics. Mrs. Eton is delighted. The healing arts have always been her special concern, and she is deeply gratified to have a son who wishes to pursue them as well.

We were allowed to watch his departure from the windows of the upper floor. He is a most handsome man.

Handsome? A curious reaction swirled in my belly at the word. It was not unreasonable for Phoebe to notice such a thing about a member of the family. It was, however, peculiar to have felt strongly enough about it to include it in her journal.

I came to the last page of the second journal and considered shutting off the computer, as my eyes were strained and my fingers sore.

"Hey."

I glanced toward the apartment door. Mark was here. Excellent.

"Wait a moment." I shot him a quick smile and then dropped my gaze back to the computer, to close the files I'd been reading and seek the button that would turn this device off. I'd been apart from Mark for too long.

CHAPTER SIXTEEN

HEALTHY RELATIONSHIP SKILLS

From the moment we reached home, Susanna was absorbed by her journals. That was cool. It meant I had nothing to distract me from homework, and I had plenty of that to consume my evening. Mr. Fullerton never let a school night pass without expecting us to think about the history of American democracy.

And, of course, I had physics. Gabrielle had emailed me the stuff that she and Jesse/Benita put together. She tried to make it sound like they'd had a lot of fun, but I didn't care. I'd wanted to spend time with Susanna.

Except look how well that had gone.

Maybe I should focus on Susanna's ID. Tonight, I would look into Social Security cards.

We couldn't be the first people to ever try to fake one before. Could it be as easy as simply asking the question?

I tried: *how to fake ssn card.*

Oh, yeah. Lots of hits. Ask.com had the best answer.

Get a real Social Security card.

Get a real typewriter.

Type the new name over the old one.

Put the card in the pocket of a pair of jeans.

Wash. Dry. Done.

And what would we have? A realistically beat-up Social Security card.

My card was in Dad's office. Gran had an old-fashioned typewriter. We were golden.

I was in a seriously good mood, and I wanted to share it with Susanna, even though I couldn't tell her why. I headed to her apartment. The door was ajar and I nudged it open.

She didn't even hear me enter the room.

"Hey."

She flashed a quick look at me and then returned her gaze to the computer. "Wait a moment."

Right.

How long was I going to be on hold this time?

When I took the Consumer Living class last year, we'd spent a lot of time talking about healthy relationship skills. They made us watch these videos that emphasized how much girls liked to be asked questions. It made them think the guys were interested. I could try that. "Have you learned much?"

"Indeed." She smiled at the computer, brushed her hand against the keyboard, and closed the lid.

"Want to tell me what Phoebe said?"

"Not yet." She straightened a pile of loose papers sitting next to the computer.

Was I getting the brush-off again? "Come on, Susanna. Take a break for the night. Those journals will be here tomorrow."

She looked at me, her brow wrinkling. "Why are you using that tone?"

"I didn't expect that getting those documents for you meant I wouldn't see you tonight."

"We are seeing each other now."

"Not really." We wouldn't be in the same room if *I* hadn't made the effort.

"What a charming invitation this has become." Her chin lifted. "You are quite correct about the documents. I can read more in the morning. It isn't as if I have anything else to fill my days."

Her words felt like a slap. I turned and left, thumping my way to the second floor. Once I reached my room, I stood in the center, fuming, looking for something to do that didn't involve punching a hole in the wall. It wouldn't be homework, since that was done. My mom had cleaned in here today, so I didn't have anything to clean, even if I'd been motivated, which I wasn't. There was a pile of folded laundry that Mom left at the foot of the bed. It would take me ten seconds to put away. And then what?

"Mark?"

I whipped around. Susanna watched me from my bedroom door. "Yeah?"

"I do not wish for our evening to end this way."

Opening my arms wide, I said, "Come on in and we'll talk."

Her cheeks reddened. "You know I cannot enter your bedchamber."

It was one of my parents' rules—rules that Susanna would never break. There could be no sleepovers in her room and no visits of any kind in mine. "Talk from there. I'll hear you."

"Why are you angry?"

"I'm feeling a little stupid right now. I thought *I* was something you could use to fill your days."

She clasped her hands at her waist. "I spoke too harshly. That comment isn't a reflection on you."

"Yes, it is."

"Indeed, it is not. You are not here during school hours when I have no chores. I cannot bear to be idle."

"Damn. Like I've never heard you complain about that before." I scooped up the pile of clothes and stuffed part of them in my dresser.

"Mark." She hung on the threshold. "Do not speak to me this way."

"Sorry, but I don't want to have this out with you right now." I crossed to my closet and stared in, hardly remembering why I was there until I realized I still clutched bike jerseys.

"Do you want to have it out at all?"

Why did girls like fighting? Maybe because they were better at it than guys since it involved words. "Sure, Susanna. Why not? Go ahead and let me have it. You're dying to say something."

The silence stretched.

I glanced over my shoulder. She was gone.

CHAPTER SEVENTEEN

AN UNDETERMINED DAY

I'd been too angry with Mark to rest easily during the night.

It would've been most pleasant to have the house to myself. Mark and his father were gone on Thursdays, but not Mrs. Lewis. It was hard to miss her presence. She filled her day off by cleaning the first floor. The house rang with the noise of her cleaning machines.

It did seem best to remain in the apartment, a situation that suited me perfectly well since I was eager to read more of Phoebe's thoughts.

The next journal skipped forward nearly a year, for its first entry started in March of 1799.

I learned of the tedious preparations for the Eton household's spring cleaning. It was less complicated for my sister than it had been for me—but then, the Etons had many more servants than had the Pratts. My spring cleaning efforts had rarely gone smoothly or unpunished. Perhaps I should feel a sense of gladness that one of the Marsh sisters had escaped weekly thrashings.

I carefully turned the next page and was surprised to find a long entry, perhaps the longest she'd written. Another three months had elapsed. I put the pen down on the sheet of transcriptions and prepared to read the entry through once completely before transcribing it.

June 14th, 1799

It was a rare treat to be invited into the housekeeper's office. Mrs. Jasper honored me thusly after breakfast on Tuesday of this week. While she wrote numbers into her account books, I had the task of mending a fine damask tablecloth, illuminated by the good light spilling in the window.

A knock disturbed our peace. Mr. Fisk rose from the small desk he kept in the corner of the room and crossed to the front door, greeting the early-morning visitor with a dignified welcome.

The light voice of a young girl responded and asked if Mrs. Eton were in. When Fisk requested the caller's name, she replied that it was Miss Dorcas Pratt of Worthville.

I looked up, shocked and pleased. What business did my childhood friend have here?

While Mr. Fisk led Dorcas to the formal parlor, Mrs. Jasper inquired if I knew Miss Pratt. I assured her that I did.

Rising to my feet, I pressed my face to the window overlooking the lane, straining to see outside. A lovely carriage stood on the street before the house. Two horses stamped their hooves, held in check by a gloved pair of hands. Their owner remained hidden by the roof of the carriage.

Little time elapsed before Mr. Fisk returned to the office and said that Mrs. Eton required my presence.

I glanced anxiously toward the housekeeper. At her nod, I ran to the mistress' parlor and rushed in.

Mrs. Eton stood beside the fireplace, her face grave. I bobbed my head respectfully, my eyes searching the room for the visitor from Worthville.

Dorcas hurried toward me. We clasped hands and shared a moment of delight in seeing each other after so long an absence. In retrospect, I am ashamed to admit that I forgot my proper demeanor before my mistress.

How lovely Dorcas has grown. She wore a stylish gown of printed cotton, trimmed with ribbons of scarlet. Life must be good in the Pratt household.

My beloved Dorcas. How good it was to hear news of her. There was nothing I regretted more about abandoning my old life than losing Phoebe and Dorcas.

In the three years since I moved to the Etons' home, I have only been to Worthville once. A terrible dysentery had swept through the village. Many had succumbed. I returned to attend the funeral of three of the Pratt children. Dorcas had been too distraught on that occasion to speak.

She is twelve now and displays the promise of beauty and poise.

A sudden sting of tears ached behind my eyes, and I had to look away. It had happened. I'd known it would. Mark had already discovered that my three youngest babies had not lived until the 1800 census. But I had put it from my mind, and now here was certain knowledge of their passing.

John, Delilah, and Dinah. They had not been born of my body, but I had loved them just the same.

I rose and paced about the room, pausing to peer from the rear bay window over the glory of the back lawn. Once the initial shock lessened, I returned to my chair and searched for Phoebe's description of her meeting with Dorcas.

"I am afraid I bring sad news."

This solemn statement struck fear in my heart. I listened anxiously as Dorcas informed me of my mother's death, saying that Mama had passed away on Sunday. Since my brother Caleb and his family had moved there recently, he was at her side.

The pain of this announcement was great, indeed. Yet knowing that Mama had not been alone at her death provided great comfort.

Dorcas continued, quietly relaying the arrangements. Caleb and Frances were tending to details. Since Mr. Pratt had business in Raleigh, he had offered to collect me, if the Etons could spare my time.

Unease prickled my skin at the mention of Dorcas's father. My sister had warned me about him. As much as I wished to be with my family at this time, I did not relish the thought of an hour or more in his company. I allowed my wariness to take over. It held the grief at bay.

Mrs. Eton drew our attention with a soft sound of sympathy and urged me to attend the funeral, which was to be held the next day. "Phoebe, you may go. We shall do without you until Friday."

Truly, I can hardly remember what happened next. The events rushed by quickly, a jumble of moments toppling onto one another. I shall write of them another day.

"Susanna?"

I looked up from my study of the computer screen to find Mrs. Lewis standing in the door. I could not remember leaving it open this morning. Had she come in without knocking? I didn't like to think she'd entered my private haven uninvited, but naturally I would say nothing. I was here on her sufferance. "Yes, ma'am?"

She released a heavy sigh. "You might as well call me Sherri."

Perhaps not as gracious as I would've liked, but it did ease my mind. "Thank you."

"What have you been doing up here all morning? You've been quiet."

I sat back in my chair, surprised at the passage of time and melancholy at the news of Mama's death. The grief must remain contained and unspoken. "I'm transcribing an old document for the State Archives."

She peered over my shoulder. "You can read that?"

"Yes, ma'am."

"Are they paying you?"

Of course not pressed against my lips, but I held it in. This was the most comfortable discussion we'd had since I moved in. I should not like to spoil it now. "I have volunteered. It is a pleasure."

She picked up one of my sheets and gasped. "Is this your handwriting? It's lovely."

"Thank you."

She pulled out a chair and sat down. "I hadn't thought much about what you do all day."

I remained silent. She knew that I would work in this house—*wanted* to work for her—if only she would permit it.

"Have you thought any more about the type of job you might be good at?"

Sherri had ruled out all opportunities that involved cooking or going near people who might have illnesses. Perhaps she should be the one to suggest possibilities to me. "I can think of nothing else I can do."

"Let me give it some thought." She stood. "I'm about to go to the grocery store. Is there anything you need?"

I should dearly love to leave this house for an errand, but she hadn't asked. I shook my head.

"All right." She drifted out the door without closing it and thumped down the steps.

I closed my eyes and waited for the sounds of her vehicle purring up the lane. Only then did I ponder my sister's entry, love and regret tugging at my heart.

My mother and I had never understood each other. She liked to be around people, especially children. Perhaps if she'd been born in Mark's time, she would've made an excellent babysitter. Nothing made her happier than to cuddle and rock babies.

I had very much been my father's daughter, a person more interested in learning and observation. Nature had fascinated us both. He and I had loved to discover how things worked or to argue how to make things better.

Now my mother was gone. Naturally, if I considered my current life, she'd been gone for many years. I'd accepted this with my mind, but it had flowed no further.

I wanted to be with my sister and brothers and share in their grief, as we had when my father had drowned. Would Whisper Falls let me return to my home?

What was I thinking? These were the thoughts of a girl gone mad. The waterfall might let me cross, but on what day? The one immediately following my escape? An undetermined day twenty years hence?

No, indeed, Whisper Falls had always transported me and Mark to the same date we left. If the waterfall permitted my passage today, it would also be September fifteenth on the other side. But what of the year? Would it deliver me to the year I requested? I thought, and hoped, that was true.

And what if I were to arrive at the right time for the funeral? Nothing changed that fact that I was a runaway. A common criminal. The mourners would be honor-bound to throw me in jail.

Much as I might long to be with my family in our grief, my mother's funeral was a risk I could never take.

Chapter Eighteen

National News

I drove to Neuse Academy Thursday morning, fighting the distraction of Susanna's new obsession and another problem, too. My sister.

Marissa wasn't ready to admit it yet, but she needed to dump the arrogant prick who was living with her. While Fletcher was off partying with his MBA classmates, she was working her ass off to support them both. I wanted her to cut her losses and come home, but she claimed (whenever she wasn't crying her guts out over him) that he was always so sweetly sincere with his apologies.

Yeah, well, he continued to do whatever it was he had to apologize for. Didn't sound very sincere to me.

Why couldn't the women in my life all be happy at the same time?

School was a relief. I threw myself into paying attention. The harder I focused, the less time I had to worry about personal stuff.

After the final bell rang, I took a detour by Mr. Rainey's office, and then made my way to the senior lot. It was nearly empty by the time I reached my truck, but I wasn't the only one there. Gabrielle leaned against the bumper with her ever-present bodyguard a few feet away. She straightened as I arrived.

"Hey," I said, puzzled to see her here without Jesse and Benita in tow. "Congratulations on making Homecoming Court."

"Thanks. They only elected me because it'll bring a lot of publicity…"

No use in denying it. She was right.

"…which leads me to a huge favor I want to ask. As a friend." She flashed me one of her killer smiles. "Korry can't be here, of course. He's busy."

"Okay."

"I need an escort, and it can't be my boyfriend. So…will you be my escort on the Homecoming Court?"

Had not seen that coming. I unlocked the truck door and tossed my backpack onto the passenger seat. It gave me a moment to wonder what I would say. "That's quite an honor."

She wrinkled her nose. "Is that how you begin a *no*?"

"I'm not saying *no*, it's just…there's Susanna. I'm not sure how she'd feel about it."

"You can still sit with her for part of the game."

"Susanna won't be coming to the game."

"Why not?" Her voice was light and curious.

A chill rippled through me. I didn't want to talk about Susanna, and I was surprised that Gabrielle was pressing the issue. "Susanna doesn't like sports or crowds."

"If she's not coming anyway, would she mind if you escorted me?"

"I don't know." Gabrielle really wanted me to do this. It was unexpected and flattering.

"We won't be on an official date. You'll be free after the halftime show." Her voice intensified. "Korry thinks that this is the perfect solution. If he can't be here, he wants me to find someone who is also taken. That way, he won't have to worry about my escort getting the wrong idea."

It sounded logical enough. Why did I feel guilty for even considering it? "I'm not sure—"

"Don't answer now, Mark. Give it some thought. Ask your girlfriend." She smiled again. "I'll wait."

When I got home from school, I checked out the apartment, but the door was closed. So I headed instead to my room, put on my gear, and went biking in Umstead Park. Normally, this would be the kind of training I could do in my sleep, but there had been a light afternoon rain. The trails were slippery and fun.

Dinner was still an hour away when I finished the ride and my shower. I needed to study.

I wanted Susanna.

Maybe I could have both. Like a date—but not. I got stuff ready in the family room and went looking for her. The door to her apartment stood wide open now. When I reached the landing and looked in, I found her sitting at her kitchenette table, laptop closed and eyes closed, with Toby napping against her feet.

"Hey. Are you okay?"

When her eyes opened, she met my gaze calmly. "I am."

Something was wrong. It wasn't her expression. She always looked that calm, and her voice sounded unemotional, which was typical too.

I wasn't going to ask. If she wanted me to know, she'd tell me. "I'm studying in the family room. Want to join me?"

"I should love to."

She had the most gorgeous smile ever made. I wished I could figure out how to make it appear more often.

She picked up a thick paperback book from a bookshelf and preceded me down the stairs.

"I have your favorite tea ready."

She stared into the family room, her lips rounded into a surprised *oh*. "What a lovely thing to do." She turned to me, stood on her tiptoes, and then hesitated, blushing.

"Come on, Susanna," I said, leaning down. "My parents aren't around. Kiss me already."

She did. Not as enthusiastically as I would've liked, but we could work on it. Her instincts were improving.

We settled on the couch, Susanna curled up in the corner. I lay with my head in her lap.

There was a thick book in her hand, but she didn't open it. Just kept staring into space.

Her not-doing-anything was distracting. "What did you bring down?"

"A study guide for the GED." Susanna spoke in a sleepy tone, like she wasn't entirely there. "Your mother asked me to call her by her Christian name today."

That was a shock, but a good one. "She's getting used to you."

"Do you truly think so?"

"Yeah." Their wariness around each other had been uncomfortable, but maybe it was thawing out.

"She does not think I am capable of a job."

"That's not it." I shook my head. "It's just hard given your lack of ID. Plus she's hoping that studying for your GED becomes your main job."

"Studying is not a job. It's a pleasure."

"In this century, it's a job."

"Indeed." She drew the word out slowly, thoughtfully. Then, with a quick shake of her head, she flipped through the book, stopped a third of the way in, and read.

I settled back against Susanna, opened a textbook on my iPad, and did my best to focus on the Articles of Confederation and the Continental Congress.

Both had happened in the 1780s, which brought up an odd thought. I tried to brush it away, but it persisted.

"You were alive while they were trying to write the U.S. Constitution."

"I was." Her voice was warm and focused. "My father was most displeased with the Articles of Confederation. Had his life not ended abruptly, I'm sure I would've learned more. Neither my stepfather nor my master would tell me about the Constitution, although I do know that North Carolina would not ratify it."

"We did eventually."

"Truly?" Her gaze dropped to mine. "We follow our own path." Her smile faded.

Who was she talking about? North Carolina or herself?

"Susanna, did something happen today? Something with Phoebe's diary?"

"My mother died."

I sat up again, this time tossing the iPad onto the coffee table, done with everything except listening to Susanna. "When? How?"

"When Phoebe was fifteen. I do not think they saw each other often. There is certainly no mention of visits in the journals." She sighed softly. "I would never have seen my mother again, but the finality aches the same."

We slouched side by side on the couch for a while, leaning into each other, holding hands, having abandoned the pretense of studying long ago. It was quiet. There was no need for words. She grieved for her mother, and I waited.

"I do not wish to sit in somber silence for the rest of the evening," she said, her head against my shoulder. "Please tell me about your day."

I tensed. Not a topic I wanted to cover. "It was busy. I have a lot of tests next week."

She straightened, her warmth leaving me. "I believe there is something troubling you too. Something you're hesitant to mention to me. Do not let my sad news stop you."

Damn that sixth sense of hers—that frickin' ability to see past what I was hiding. I wasn't ready for this conversation, and I was going to screw it up. But she would dig until it came out. "I want to go to a special football game we have. It's called Homecoming."

"An interesting name. Do people come from all around to attend, as if they are coming home?"

"Exactly." So far so good. I rolled my head until I could meet her gaze. "Will you go with me to the Homecoming game? There's a dance afterward."

"How many people will attend the game?"

"Thousands."

"And the dance?"

"Hundreds."

"Mark, I don't—"

"A special ceremony happens in the middle of the game." There was a sick feeling in my gut that told me she was about to refuse to attend, and I didn't want her to. I wanted her to come with me and give me an excuse to show her off, to be a couple in front of everyone. "The students at Neuse pick girls to represent each class. Then the girls put on these big fancy ball gowns and parade around in front of everyone at halftime."

"Why?"

"It's a type of celebration."

"You celebrate football by dressing girls in ball gowns?"

"Yeah. We call them homecoming princesses. They walk out into the middle of the football field, carrying flowers and waving." I hadn't realized how lame it sounded.

"Then what happens?"

"The crowd screams."

She laughed. "It sounds foolish."

I shouldn't have let her goad me into talking about this. "Homecoming is a tradition."

"Traditions are not always good."

"They're not always bad either."

She unlinked our fingers and clasped her hands in her lap. "There must be more to the story than this. It is too trifling of a thing to upset you so."

"The princesses pick guys to escort them."

"Their boyfriends?"

"Usually, but not always. If they don't have a boyfriend around, they can ask a guy friend." This wasn't going well, and it was about to get worse. "A princess on the homecoming court asked me to escort her."

"What was your answer?"

"I haven't given one yet."

She rose smoothly from the couch and walked a few paces away, arms crossed. "You didn't say *no*."

"I wanted to talk to you first."

"Why?"

"You're my girlfriend. You might object."

"A wise inclination." She spun around to face me. "Your attitude gives me pause."

"Oh, come on, Susanna." I hated when she went all superior. "She has a boyfriend, but he can't be here. It's not like Gabrielle and I would be out on a date."

"Gabrielle, the movie star?"

"Yeah." I slid off the couch and stalked across the room to where Susanna stood. "Her boyfriend is in Africa right now. He's fine with the idea."

Susanna stared straight at my chest. "You want to do this thing?"

"Yeah."

"Why?"

"It's flattering. I might even make the national news."

Her arms dropped. "Then say yes." She turned towards the door.

What had just happened here? Had she really given me permission? "Are you saying you don't mind?"

She hesitated in the doorway. "I do mind. You should say *yes* anyway."

CHAPTER NINETEEN

THE TWITCH OF A SKIRT

Mark's request unsettled me in a way I could not understand, and it wasn't because I feared there was more to the event than he described. It was his reaction, as if he had cause to be guilty. That he expected me to be angry.

My eyes popped open and sought the clock. Four AM.

I had tried long enough to sleep. In the quiet before dawn, with the house and its inhabitants still, I had my own little world that wouldn't be disturbed. After dressing in fresh clothes, I wiggled into a position of comfort on the couch and indulged more in my sister's story.

June 15th, 1799

The funeral was both somber and sacred, a fitting goodbye to our mother. All three of her remaining children sat on the front row. Joshua had come from Hillsborough on his own. His wife had stayed behind to care for an ill child. Caleb, Frances, their tiny daughter, and their twin sons were there with us.

We had a respectable turnout from the townsfolk. There was the Foster family. Mr. Pratt came with his young wife, their baby son...

My head jerked back as if slapped. His first wife, my mistress, would've delivered her youngest child in the spring of 1797.

Even had she died in childbirth, he must have married and bred again in less than two years. How could I have forgotten? Mark's research had determined that the second wife was the indentured servant after me—a girl even younger than I.

Mr. Pratt came with his young wife, their baby son, Deborah, Dorcas, and their littlest sister Drusilla. Naturally, the Worth family attended—Mr. and Mrs. Worth, Solomon and his wife, and Jacob.

I did not want Mr. Worth to lead the congregation. I could never forgive him for demanding shackles be placed on my sister. Fortunately, Caleb had arranged things well, for his preacher from Ward's Crossroads officiated.

Afterwards, the Worths offered to return me to Raleigh since they had business there the next day. I agreed because it afforded me a chance to visit with Jacob, and it meant I would not be required to accept another favor from Mr. Pratt.

Jacob and I rode in the rear of the wagon while his mother and father rode in the front. Her snores were loud enough to be heard over the rattling of the wheels. Mr. Worth, who had become hard of hearing, could not have heard us had we been shouting.

Jacob has grown into a fine young man, strong of body and handsome in both look and manner, not at all imperious and disapproving like his brother and father. I found Jacob's love of laughter most appealing.

I had to agree with Phoebe. Jacob had always been the most admirable member of the Worth family. I'd never seen him without a ready smile—except, perhaps, with Deborah. But then, her relentless pursuit of him years ago would have irritated even the kindest soul.

Jacob announced his plans to go to the College of William and Mary in the mournful tones of a man facing prison. When I inquired why he sounded so distressed, he replied that his father wanted him to study to be an attorney while Jacob preferred to pursue the life of a farmer.

Perhaps if anyone else had said such a thing, I would have been surprised, but it sounded like the most natural desire in the world coming from Jacob Worth.

We spent a pleasant ride discussing his plans. He would never be permitted to farm Mr. Worth's land. Solomon Worth had a prior claim as the elder son. Yet Jacob showed little concern. He had no interest in raising tobacco.

"I should like to try my hand at orchards," he told me. Jacob remembered his one visit to the mountains as glorious, and longed to return and claim a bit of rich land for growing trees of apples and cherries.

I told him it sounded quite beautiful, a comment as polite as it was honest, for I did like the sound of mountains even though I knew they were something I was unlikely to ever see.

Mark loved the mountains dearly enough to want to attend college there. I had seen photographs, and they did look beautiful, but my mind could not conceive of their size.

Truly, the mountains of North Carolina and Virginia were something I didn't wish to ponder.

As the journal continued, another year passed in my sister's life—a year of embroidering linens, scarves, and sleeves. A year where her housemaid chores lightened with the arrival of another housemaid.

April 24th, 1800
Mr. William has journeyed home. He arrived on horseback from New Bern, after a voyage aboard a fast clipper ship. Senator and

Mrs. Eton are wreathed in smiles to see him. A great family feast was arranged for this Sunday past after they returned from church. Mrs. Cornelia Whitcomb, Mr. John Eton, the Eton daughters, and the grandchildren filled the house with noise and laughter.

This morning, as I brought Mrs. Eton her tea, I discovered Mr. William had arisen early to join his mother for breakfast. As I served his meal, he asked when I would be leaving their household.

Mrs. Eton's response surprised even me. "I believe that today is Phoebe's sixteenth birthday. We are but a year away from the time I plan to end her indenture." She went on to say that she intended to assist me in finding a position outside their household—perhaps even with Mrs. Simpson.

I swallowed a gasp at this statement. To work in Mrs. Simpson's establishment would be a greater honor than I could have imagined. I would work on beautiful ball gowns. Perhaps, if I were truly fortunate, Mrs. Simpson would permit me to try my hand at elegant headpieces.

With the tea poured and the dishes laid, I hurried from the room, my mind already dancing through daydreams of my future.

I paused to reflect on an interesting bit of information that had appeared in this entry. Mrs. Eton would release Phoebe on her seventeenth birthday, not the eighteenth as the contract had been written. That was very kind. I wondered how long Phoebe had known.

July 15th, 1800
Senator Eton hails from Charleston, a city whose citizens hold themselves in higher esteem than they deserve. His sister, who still lives there, has sent her stepdaughter, Miss Margaret Dunwoodie, to stay with the Etons for the summer.

I do understand why Mrs. Dunwoodie sent her to us. It cannot be pleasant to live with Miss Margaret yearlong. I anticipate that, as the weather grows hotter, we shall suffer ever more greatly from the sharp sting of her tongue.

September 25th, 1800

Miss Margaret's birthday ball is nearly upon us. She has planned each detail and then set them all aside for a new list. Our housekeeper is ever patient and tries to please her, but truly, there is no pleasing that one.

Her lady's maid claims that her ball gown is the loveliest ever sewn. Snow-white from its neckline to hem, embroidered with whitework fleur-de-lis, enjoying a train. I cannot believe this claim, though. Mrs. Eton is never outshone.

Our newest calamity is the weather. Miss Margaret had hoped to set up the refreshments in the garden, but Mrs. Eton has dissuaded her. We have had several uncommonly hard rains of late, and the ground is quite soft.

Miss Margaret, thankfully, has agreed with the wisdom of this suggestion.

September 30th, 1800

My hand trembles to hold the quill, but I am anxious to record my thoughts while they are still fresh.

Mid-evening, I was pulled from my duties serving food at the ball and ordered back to the kitchen.

Mrs. Jasper awaited me, her usual unflappable nature nowhere in evidence. With a sharp command, she beckoned me to follow her, explaining that Mrs. Eton had particularly requested my skills with the needle. I changed my apron and hurried to keep up.

Mrs. Jasper spoke in short, piqued bursts about an unfortunate situation that had occurred only moments before. Miss Margaret's clumsy dance partner had stepped on her gown and ripped it most dreadfully.

The housekeeper led me to the family parlor on the ground floor of the main house. Miss Margaret stood near the mantle, the fire illuminating the skirt of her gown, her legs thin smudges of shadow beneath it. The gown had torn near its train, through the heavy embroidery of the hem, a rough tear that rose to mid-leg.

She frowned at our entrance, hissing that it was time for her birthday dance and for us to be quick about our business. Mr. William was to be her partner.

I rushed to her side, knelt, and assessed the damage, my heart sinking at the sight. It would be impossible to hide the repair. When I murmured an estimate of ten minutes of stitching, Mrs. Jasper reminded me that excellent work was more important than the clock.

Miss Margaret had decided, no doubt, that I failed her expectations and stepped out of reach. I hesitated, unsure what to do.

"What progress has been made?" Mrs. Eton asked as she floated into the room, dressed like an angel in gossamer white. Her gown had been trimmed with golden lace, each swag held in place by rosettes of gold ribbon. It was a glorious garment.

Neither the housekeeper nor I needed to reply. It was evident from the stiff manner in which Miss Margaret held herself apart that no progress would be made without the intervention of Mrs. Eton. She gestured at Mrs. Jasper and bade her bring white thread, a delicate needle, and pins.

"Aunt Abigail, why do you let a housemaid touch my gown?"

My mistress chided her niece, reproof clear in her tone. "Phoebe has the most clever fingers in Raleigh. Your gown could be in no better hands."

Such a remarkable statement from Mrs. Eton. I shall cherish it always.

My mistress perched carefully on the sofa and asked if the repair would be noticeable. When I nodded, the young lady made an undignified squawk.

Mrs. Jasper returned shortly and handed over the requested items. Her gaze flicked to our guest, her expression strained.

Mrs. Eton talked lightly with her niece. The young lady's sulky tone faded away as the topics turned to the success of the ball and Miss Margaret's glad surprise at the sophistication of the people of Raleigh.

It took me more time than I'd predicted, no doubt in part because Miss Margaret was incapable of remaining still.

I had completed the work and was making my final knot when she jerked at the folds of her skirt.

It was a disastrously timed movement. The needle leapt from my control and plunged into my right thumb. I fell back, cupping my injured hand, lips pressed to hold in my cry of pain. I focused my gaze straight ahead and noted with horror that my blood stained the hem of the dress.

"Oh, you stupid, stupid girl."

The young lady's shrieks only added to my shame.

"Aunt Abigail, how can you let her take advantage of your kindness? The time you spent pretending to be a maid during the war has made you overindulgent—"

With a sharp word, Mrs. Eton silenced her niece even as she crossed to my side. She took my hand in hers and studied my thumb carefully. Her face reflected her concern.

The parlor door creaked open to reveal Miss Judith and Mr. William. At the sight of her stepcousins, our guest became all elegant posture and liquid smiles.

Mrs. Eton wordlessly offered my hand to her son. He considered it a moment with a critical eye. After frowning toward his mother, he murmured that he hoped it would not cause me distress. Mrs. Eton shook her head and vowed to watch the injury for me.

I nodded, awed by her generosity on my behalf.

Briskly, she asked me if anything could be done to hide the blood stain on the dress. I assured my mistress that, indeed, with a bit of white ribbon, I could add the same type of rosette that adorned her gown.

For the first time all evening, Miss Margaret expressed delight.

And so the incident ended, with light praise from my mistress and a smile from her son.

I did not care for Miss Margaret's airs, but I could not suppress a sigh of pride at my handiwork on her gown.

Phoebe had written in a larger script, no doubt attributed to her injury, and it took up a page and one-half of the journal. By contrast, the following pages held short entries.

October 3rd, 1800

Three days have passed and still my thumb aches. It is swollen and hot. Even Mrs. Eton's ointments and soothing teas have not helped.

I fear that something is wrong.

The pain makes my hand tremble. I shall perform no more delicate work until this affliction has passed.

October 6th, 1800

The prick from the night of the ball will not let me go.

Tonight, as I was leaving the dining room with a tray of soiled dishes, my mistress beckoned to me from the parlor doorway.

I obeyed but stayed out of view of the family.

"I sense great pain, Phoebe. Are you using my remedies?" At my nod, she took my hand. "Despite our efforts, an infection has taken hold. We must do something before it is too late."

She asked advice from Mr. William, and he suggested bleeding the finger. Mrs. Eton will hear none of it. Instead, she has given Mrs. Jasper another stronger remedy to aid me.

I do not know what to do. I can barely hold the quill.

On the next page, I was shocked by what I saw. Huge letters, punctuated by large blots, each letter formed more like carvings than writing.

The meaning of the words was far more ominous.

October 9th, 1800

My thumb has swollen to the size of a fat sausage. It oozes dreadfully. The quill slips so that I cannot hold on much longer.

Mrs. Eton has given me fearsome news. The infection has spread disastrously. Even now, it pushes me along the path toward death. The remedy is to sever my thumb.

I must decide now. Tonight.

It is a simple enough decision. I shall, of course, trade my finger for my life, although it appalls me to form the words of assent.

Mrs. Eton has asked Mr. William to perform the amputation. I am glad it will be he, for I have known and admired him all of these years. He will do his best to save as much of my hand as possible, of this I have no doubt.

Oh, dear Lord, I am frightened. My hands are my voice—the only way I can sing.

What will become of me?

I snapped the lid down on the laptop and hopped to my feet. Tears burned at the back of my eyes, but I wouldn't let them fall.

Yet, my sister's own question spun through my mind. What became of Phoebe?

There were a few images left on the DVD for that final journal, but I knew great reluctance to read them. Phoebe's once-bright future had dimmed at the twitch of a skirt.

I left the apartment and tiptoed down the steps. On swift feet, I crossed the green velvet of the back lawn and tread on the prickly pine straw at the greenway's edge until I reached the muddy trail. Careful in the faint gray light of dawn, I picked my way through the trees, ignoring the thump of my heart as I approached Rocky Creek.

It was my first visit since the day of my escape. The early hour made it difficult to see clearly. I had to experience this place instead with my other senses. The earthy scent of free-flowing water, musty rock, and decaying leaves. The heavy coolness of the forest. The muffled murmurs of the night creatures.

As I had throughout my youth, whenever I needed solace, I returned to the falls.

Chapter Twenty

Colored by the Emotions

I'd been a complete dick to Susanna last night, and I wanted to make things right with her before I left for school. I cut my early-morning training ride short to give us a few extra minutes together at breakfast. After showering and changing, I hurried to the kitchen, but there was no sign of her. Biting back disappointment, I went carefully upstairs to the apartment, not wanting to awaken her if she slept.

Her door was ajar, only Susanna wasn't inside. It was neat as always, yet it had an abandoned feel.

I crossed to the back window. She wasn't sitting in Mom's garden.

She must be seriously upset if she wasn't in the apartment or the back yard. I called the lake house.

"What?" my grandfather barked into the phone.

"Is Susanna out there?"

"What time is it where you are, Mark?"

"Seven thirty."

"It's seven thirty here too—which is damned early, if you understand what I'm saying."

"Did I wake you up?"

"No."

I really didn't need this. "Okay, then. Is Susanna there?"

Granddad heaved a sigh. "Did she leave you a note?"

"No."

"Does she normally leave a note when she comes out here?"

"Yes."

"Then there's your answer. She didn't magically turn inconsiderate today."

"Thanks, Granddad."

"Happy to help."

So...not at my grandparents' and not in the house.

Where could she be?

Whisper Falls.

The thought gripped me with its truth, and I really hoped I was wrong. She hadn't been there since her escape. She'd told me she didn't want to see the waterfall ever again. It would be too painful to remember.

But had the pain faded? Had whatever new pain that had shown up in those journals driven her back there? Or was this about me?

I'd better go check. It wouldn't take long.

The sun was low in the sky. Dry leaves rattled as I walked past. I stepped off the greenway onto the hard-packed dirt trail that forked into the woods, down the incline, and along the banks of Rocky Creek. The waterfall poured in a steady hiss.

She sat on a fallen log, back off the path in the shadow of the trees, motionless as a statue, almost blending into the background in her black tunic over a gray skirt. Curled leaves swirled over her bare feet and tumbled away on a gust of wind. A wayward lock of hair brushed across her face, but she didn't even reach up to tuck it behind her ear. If I hadn't been looking for her, I might not have noticed her there.

I'd been standing on this same spot when I'd first seen her. She'd been standing in the mouth of the cave behind the falls, stunning in a way that took my breath away still. Her reason for coming today worried me, but it also reminded me that a part of Susanna belonged in these woods.

"Hey," I said as I sat beside her.

"Hello."

I loved her voice. It was low, husky, and colored by the emotions she fought to keep hidden. After four months of listening to her, I knew enough to recognize sadness.

"Why are you here?"

"I miss my home."

The soft response jolted me. It held yearning. It excluded me. "This is your home."

"Is it?"

"Yes!" I scoured her face, hoping for some sign that she hadn't meant that. "You aren't thinking about going back, are you?"

"I cannot. In that world, I'm either dead or a fugitive."

Good. I was glad she remembered that. "Then why did you come here today?"

"It was time." Her face creased in confusion. "I didn't like the way I lived before. The endless chores, the bad smells..."

"The beatings."

"...the injustice. I knew I would like to be free of it. I do not miss the misery." She looked at me, her eyes searching my face. "I am a burden to your family. Can you understand what that means to me? I have never been useless in my life."

"You're not a burden."

She shook her head. "I have read nearly to the end of Phoebe's journals. There is an accident—a bad one. My sister needs me, and I am not there to help her."

"If you were there, you would be dead now."

"Stop, Mark." She sprang to her feet and stared down at me, shaking with intensity. "Thank you for rescuing me.

As often as you remind me, I shall say thank you. I may be useless, but I am also grateful."

I stood too. "Don't say that—"

She shook her head and looked away from me. "There is little in the life I live now to be proud of. How long will you be satisfied with a girl like me?"

CHAPTER TWENTY-ONE

UNDUE ATTENTION

I had shared my greatest fear with him but had not had the strength to linger and watch his reaction. I ran back to the house, hurried to the apartment, and closed the door with a definite *click*. I needed to be alone.

For the first time since I'd arrived, this space felt like a cage. A large, comfortable, dull cage. And, unlike with my indenture, I had no idea when I would be free.

My gaze fumbled about the room until it landed on the table. My sister's journals. I ran to the chair and opened the laptop with determination.

The stack of papers I shoved to the edge, uncaring that they fell off in a messy stack. I had abandoned the effort to transcribe my sister's life. No doubt others would. Someone else would make it possible to learn about the past from Phoebe's words.

How would she react if she knew that her private observations and painful secrets had become fodder for aloof historians?

I wouldn't be the one to make it happen. It was a betrayal.

The last images in the journal were filled with blots and wavy lines. Letters were large and ill-formed. There was page after page of practice. Phoebe must have been trying to write with her left hand.

She proceeded with diligence. Each entry showed a measure of progress. Letters grew smaller. Lines straightened. Loops became consistent.

Then I reached the final page of her journals. It held three brief entries.

November 30th, 1800

With my position forever gone from Mrs. Simpson's dress shop, I shall pursue a position where clumsy hands can be borne.

December 8th, 1800

My mistress has offered to let me stay as a housemaid for as long as necessary.

It is a charitable gesture. I should dearly love to refuse, but what other choice do I have?

Mrs. Eton had been kind and well-intentioned, but I hoped that my sister had not accepted. To spend an entire life as a housemaid would be hard and lonely. My sister should marry and have children.

January 14th, 1801

Silas has asked me to marry him. He leaves in the spring to work on a horse farm near Hillsborough. I would be near Joshua and his family. It is an offer worth considering.

I stared at the screen for so long that the words seemed to wave and blur before my eyes. How dearly the loss of her thumb had cost her.

Despair washed over me. I longed to find my sister and advise her on what to do. Surely there were other possibilities. A desperation marriage to Silas, the stable lad, or a lifelong position as housemaid could not be all. Her remarkable beauty and generous heart were deserving of much more.

To think on my sister's plight a moment longer was intolerable. Until Mark returned from school, I would fill my hours with familiar activities. I baked bread in the big kitchen and scrubbed its already-spotless floor. I began a new Jane Austen novel and watched TV about the science of flight.

By mid-afternoon, I was too weary to think any longer. I climbed into my bed, lay in the middle of its mattress, huddled under a light quilt, and slept.

The roar of a lawnmower awakened me.

I remained where I was, for the warmth and comfort of my spot held me captive. Mark must be home and doing his chores. He would want to be with me later, just as I wanted to be with him. But would I be good company? Would the awkwardness of our last meeting cast a pall?

A tear leaked from my eye and dripped to the sheet. How had I come to this place in my life? I lived under the same roof as the man I loved, yet not as his wife. It was a situation completely opposite from everything I was raised to believe was proper. My heart could not let go of the expectation for marriage, even as my mind accepted that such a commitment from Mark was years away, if he ever made that decision. He had things to do. Important things. He had choices to make that could not include me.

Even though I had a strong body, willing hands, and many good skills, I had no choices.

I needed a birth certificate.

I needed a job.

I needed to save my sister.

With a swiftness that sent the blood thrumming through my veins, my mind flooded with purpose. I had no control over the first two needs, but I might over the third.

I could warn my sister about what was to come. To stitch with care. To wear thimbles. To anticipate twitching skirts.

No, I must slow down and think this through. I had changed Phoebe's future once before. To prevent her ruination by Jethro Pratt, I had moved her to the Etons' house. Was damage to her hand a consequence of my interference, the price history demanded for saving her from one awful fate? How would her life have progressed had she been Mr. Pratt's wife? Mark hadn't checked on anything after his 1800 will.

Perhaps this was a consequence, but I didn't regret the choice, even now. Life with a crippled hand or marriage to a stable boy was better than living as Mrs. Pratt. If this change had created ripples in time, surely they had been small and absorbed by history.

I had led her onto the path she traveled now. Would it be so very bad to nudge her again—when another person's carelessness threatened the tiny measure of contentment Phoebe had achieved?

Yes, I would consider whether I should go and what I would need to prepare.

Besides, wouldn't it be lovely to see her again and hold her in my arms! The sweet hum of excitement trembled in my limbs. There was such pleasure in imagining the Raleigh of old, a world that made complete sense, a world where I did not strain to understand every sentence uttered.

A visit was illogical and dangerous. Many things could go wrong, but could I anticipate them?

The most fearsome risk was being captured. A grave risk, indeed. Yet, with care and planning, I could remain hidden from the wrong eyes. Could I not?

Worthville and its residents would be easy enough to avoid. I should simply not go there. No one would recognize me in Raleigh—except Phoebe and, perhaps, Mrs. Eton. They wouldn't turn me in.

I could travel under the cover of the trees on the journey over and back. No one would see me. Indeed, the only time I would be vulnerable was the minute-long walk from the edge of the forest until the flow of the falls.

Unless, of course, there was no sparkle to the water. What would I do if I could not pass back through?

No, truly, I wasn't concerned about the volume of water this time of year. The falls were strong in our century, and Phoebe had mentioned an overabundance of rain in hers. The only reason I could not pass back through would be the whim of Whisper Falls, and it was my friend. I could trust it to make the right decision there.

Could I make this work?

I leapt from the bed, on fire with resolve, and hurried to my table, eager to see Phoebe's last entries and reacquaint myself with the details of her injury. The ball had taken place on September thirtieth. That was but two weeks away in Mark's century. Was there sufficient time to plan?

As much as I should like for Whisper Falls to return me to the date of my choosing, I could not count on such an idea. It had always moved us on the precise date in both centuries. I had either to finish the plan in a few days or risk waiting another year, and that I could not bear to do.

What would the journey require?

I would need clothes, of course, and sturdy shoes.

No doubt Phoebe could feed me.

It would take three hours to walk from the waterfall to Raleigh and then three hours back. There would be no reason to arrive at the Etons' house before supper. Phoebe would be too busy to talk during the day anyway. I would have to stay the night.

This necessity sobered me. Bruce and Sherri had been good to me, and they would be greatly distressed by my decision.

Even more, my absence would terrify Mark. If he discerned my plan before I left, he would do everything in his power to stop me. He wouldn't succeed, and it would cause a rift between us.

Indeed, could this trip cause a permanent rift in our relationship?

No, I wouldn't think these thoughts. He would be angry, perhaps for a long time, but he loved me. He would grow to understand.

Still, it would be best to hide my intentions, and if I left during the day when no one was about, it would delay their concerns until it was too late.

The simplicity of my plan calmed me.

The clothing must be investigated to ensure that I wouldn't draw undue attention. The bodice and petticoat I had worn when I moved here wouldn't be appropriate. They had been cast-offs that Mrs. Pratt had given to me as work garments. The women in the upper and merchant classes of Raleigh had worn frocks that were nothing like my old clothes. Fortunately, Mark had taught me the skills I needed to discover information on the internet. After logging in, I searched for "gowns" and "1800."

Hundreds of links appeared, many calling themselves "The Federal Period." The links revealed paintings of gauzy dresses, pale or white, with wide ribbons emphasizing a high waist. Mrs. Eton had worn such a gown at our last meeting.

There was no need for me to dress as one of the upper classes. Phoebe wouldn't believe it, and I couldn't pretend well, though I should still like to dress as a lady who had prospered. My mistress had embraced roundgowns, which appeared to remain popular into the early nineteenth century. I approved of the modesty and practicality of these garments. Unlike what I'd worn as a servant, a roundgown had its bodice attached to its skirt. I could take the simple cotton nightgown given me by Norah, a yellow "granny gown," as she put it, printed with clusters of cornflowers, and make a fine imitation of a roundgown.

I no longer had stays, nor would I acquire any. The twenty-first century was to be commended for the undergarments worn by its women.

The nightgown hung in my closet, just as I remembered. It would make an acceptable costume for a woman of the merchant class. With a white cap and apron, I would blend in with the crowd.

If I decided to go, the only true difficulty would be to convince Whisper Falls to grant me passage to the year 1800.

CHAPTER TWENTY-TWO

BAD TIMING

Susanna had acted strangely all last night. Really distracted and excited. There had been no mention of the scene yesterday morning at the waterfall. We ate fast food, watched a movie, and walked around the neighborhood. She talked and laughed and even flirted.

We drove out to the lake house Saturday morning to spend the day with my grandparents. From the very first time she'd ever ridden in any type of car, she'd huddled on the seat, refusing to watch the world rush by. Today, she sat beside me, relaxed and smiling.

What was up with her? It was weird, but I liked it.

I turned onto the narrow paved road that wound through the community my grandparents lived in, although "community" was too strong a word. Each house was lakefront, with its own dock and heavily wooded five-plus acres of land.

We parked on the driveway and got out. My grandfather stood on the deck, fishing poles in hand. He barely nodded at me before smiling at Susanna. "Want to help me catch lunch?"

I could practically hear her smile widen.

"Indeed, I would."

"Are you going to let me catch the most this time?"

"Victory is only sweet if it's earned."

Their laughter faded as they wandered down the trail. It made me a little jealous. I hated to fish, so it wasn't that. It was the way the two of them disappeared around the bend, strolling along with the silence that comes from an intense friendship. How had Susanna managed that? Granddad barely tolerated most people.

I walked in the screen door, only to be stopped immediately by a small hand smack in the middle of my chest.

"I need you to go out to the shed and bring in the stepladder," Gran said, "and hurry."

"Why?"

"We have to get this done before your grandfather gets back."

I didn't bother to ask what "this" was. She would tell me when I returned. But it sure didn't seem fair that Susanna was off having fun with Granddad while I did his unwanted chores for Gran.

I found the stepladder, which was a cobwebby mess, cleaned it off, and carried it inside the house. "All right, Gran. What's next?"

Her eyes narrowed to slits—in a creepy, squinty glare that reminded me of my mother. "Don't use that tone of voice with me, young man."

Mom used that phrase too. She'd be horrified if I told her she was turning into Gran.

I nodded in my best imitation of humility. "Yes, ma'am. How may I help you?"

"Much better. Lightbulbs."

"Lightbulbs?"

"Yes. I want to use those high-emitting thingies they rave about at the hardware store, but your grandfather refuses to put them in. We'll take care of it while he's gone."

"Now wait, Gran." I backed up a step. "The last thing I need is Granddad mad at me."

She shot me another squinty-eyed glare. "Would you rather have *me* mad at you?"

"Point taken." I picked up the stepladder. "Where do I start?"

"Next to the mantle."

It took forty-five minutes to finish the kitchen, great room, and master bedroom before Gran called a halt for the weekend. "Susanna usually catches a lot," Gran said. "I'd better have the frying pan ready." She waved me toward the bathroom. "Put the ladder away and get cleaned up. They could be here any moment now."

Susanna came in a few minutes later, carrying some decent-looking crappie. Granddad trailed her, stopping a few steps into the great room. His head swiveled in my direction.

"Lightbulbs," he muttered.

"What about them?" I asked with all of the innocence my guilty ass could muster.

"You picked your grandmother over me."

"I did."

"Smart boy." He shuffled past me to the bathroom. "I still haven't forgotten about the leaf vacuuming you promised."

"Yeah, Granddad. I haven't either."

We were eating fish and fried potatoes half an hour later when Gran stood suddenly, her chair scraping loudly against the floor.

I hoped that meant it was time for pie, but her words let me know I was wrong. She tapped her husband's palm with an index finger. "You have a puncture."

He rolled his hand palm down and kept eating.

"Where did you get that? I'm serious, Charlie."

He shrugged. "At the dock."

"On a fish hook," Susanna said.

Gran stalked into the kitchen, pulled a first-aid kit from the cabinet, and returned.

"You're overreacting, Norah. I've stabbed myself before, and I'll stab myself again."

"Better safe than sorry." She pulled out antiseptic wipes, ointment, and a bandage with smiley faces on it.

Susanna gripped the edges of the table until her knuckles turned white. "What are you doing?"

"Making sure my husband doesn't get a nasty infection."

"May I watch?"

"Certainly."

Susanna's behavior surprised me. She ran around the table and knelt on the floor, watching everything my grandmother did.

"I do believe I like all of the attention," Granddad said.

Gran snorted. "Yeah, don't be getting any ideas, old man."

"Norah," Susanna said, rocking back on her heels, "Is this the same medicine you used on my ankles when I first arrived?"

"Uh-huh. Bacitracin. It's an antibiotic ointment."

"I also took pills."

Gran nodded. "Your infection was too advanced for a topical antibiotic to do the trick. You needed oral antibiotics as well." She smoothed the bandage across my grandfather's palm and scooped up the trash. "There you go. Now, who wants cherry pie?"

Susanna was quiet on the ride home, and the whole eyes-open thing was still going on.

"Hey, babe."

She looked at me and smiled. "I had a lovely afternoon."

"Are you okay?"

"Indeed. There is nothing wrong. In fact, quite the opposite."

"You like fishing that much?"

"I like visiting your grandparents that much." She turned to watch out the side window.

When we reached home, I found a note from my parents. They'd left for an evening out with friends.

"Hey, Susanna," I shouted up the stairs. "There's enough time left to get in a good training ride. I think I'll head out."

She appeared on the landing outside the apartment. "Certainly, Mark. I shall have a meal awaiting you when you return."

As I rolled down the driveway, I looked back over my shoulder. She watched from the bay window at the front of the house.

I frowned at the sky as I headed onto the main trail into Umstead. Black clouds boiled in the distance. Maybe not such a long training ride after all.

The first clap of thunder sent me home, which pissed me off because I had a lot of pent-up energy after a day climbing up and down the stepladder, and I really needed to work it off.

As I jogged up the stairs to the second floor, I pulled my jersey over my head, and then tossed it onto the bathroom floor in passing. After grabbing a towel from the linen closet, I was just reaching for the shower faucets when I heard a noise coming from my room.

That was weird. It had to be Susanna, and that meant she was breaking one of my parents' major rules: *Susanna may not go into Mark's bedroom for any reason.*

It was a stupid rule and, for most kids I knew, completely unenforceable unless we were total idiots. Yet my parents had made it, and Susanna and I had stuck to it—*because of her.* What had happened to make her break it now?

I crossed the hall and stood in the doorway. Susanna was rifling through the top drawer of my dresser.

"What the hell are you doing?"

Her head jerked up, her face and neck flaming red. "What is this?" She held up a condom.

She wasn't going to distract me from the main point, which was why she'd invaded my bedroom—my privacy—and risked whatever happened if my folks caught her. "I'll answer after you tell me why you're in here."

"Is it one of those items gentlemen use to prevent pregnancy?"

Shit. "Yes, it is. How do you know about that?"

"Norah has magazines." She held it up with one hand as she slammed the drawer shut with the other. "Why do you have these?"

Double shit. "Obviously, to prevent pregnancy."

Her face appeared sickly pale in the dim light of the room. "Have you ever…?"

"Had sex?"

She nodded.

I would rather have put my fist through the wall than have *that* conversation right now. "I have."

She swayed on her feet. "With whom?"

"I'm not getting into this with you—"

"Were you with Alexis?"

I pressed my lips together. Alexis McChord was the only girl I'd ever really dated. Why was Susanna putting herself through this?

"Perhaps you should have a shirt on while we talk."

I crossed my arms over my bare chest and leaned against the threshold. "Maybe you should tell me why you're in my room."

She placed the condom on the end of my bed and walked to the door. I braced my hand on the opposite side of the doorframe, blocking her path.

"What were you looking for, Susanna? It had to be huge to break a rule."

She stared straight ahead. "I do not wish to say. Now please let me pass."

"There's nothing in that drawer except briefs and socks."

"And those items."

It was all I could do to keep from grinding my teeth. "They're called condoms."

"You have never asked me," she whispered.

"Asked you what?"

"To go to bed with you." She ducked under my arm and disappeared down the hall.

The storm passed and left behind a clean, earthy scent. The sun had already faded, leaving a silver-white glow on the western horizon, which showed the tall pines in the clear black and white of an Ansel Adams photo.

I wanted to go to her, to finish the conversation that I hated we'd started. To coax her into telling me why she'd invaded my room.

But I wasn't sure what to say. What to ask. How to answer.

I walked into the kitchen, the tiles cool against my bare feet, and looked around. A movement on the deck caught my eye. Susanna was out there, standing beside the brick fireplace. She'd changed clothes.

I joined her. "Hey."

She spun around, her hair fanning loosely around her shoulders. I got a whiff of rose shampoo.

"Hello, Mark."

"Drying your hair out here?"

She nodded.

"I love you, Susanna."

"I love you."

Marissa always talked about how love felt like melting and tingling. It didn't for me. I felt strong. Tough. Caveman and fierce. When I reached for Susanna, she launched herself, her arms winding tightly about my neck.

Holy shit, she smelled amazing. Felt amazing. "Susanna?"

"Yes?"

I ran a hand down her spine until it reached the small of her back. I pressed her hard against me. "Do you know what that is?"

She shivered. "Yes."

"I want you. Okay?" I kissed her hair, her temple. "I haven't asked because it's not right for you yet. Which means it's not right for *us*."

She nodded against my neck.

"Look at me."

She leaned back until I could see the glittering pools of her eyes. "Yes?"

"You have to be the one who asks."

"Why?"

"I have to know that it's what you want. If you ask, I'll be sure."

Her gaze dropped to my chin. She looked calm, but her breathing quickened. "What if it takes a long time?"

"Then we wait."

Her gaze snapped back up to mine, only this time her look made *me* breathe faster. "I doubt I shall ever be that brave."

"You will be with me."

Her lips parted. I took that as an invitation to kiss them.

I loved the feel of her mouth under mine. I loved the way she tried to give back. It wasn't enough, but it wouldn't be much longer before it was too much. I wrapped her in my arms and swayed to music that only we could hear.

Without even coming up for air, I slow-danced with her on the deck. Susanna was an eager student.

This was a gorgeous moment. That other question would have to wait for another day.

My folks and Susanna headed to church Sunday morning, while I went out for a training ride. I got back before they did, so I worked on my room. It hadn't been aired out since last week. Even I could detect the funky smell. Clothes and sheets went into the washing machine. Then a quick vacuum. When I turned the vacuum off, I saw my dad standing in the hall outside my room. Good. I got bonus points for being caught in the act of cleaning my room. I couldn't have planned it better.

"Didn't mean to disturb you," Dad said.

"No problem. Is there something you needed?"

"Your mom says you might want to take a look at Newman College."

"You know about Newman?"

"Yeah, it has a good reputation. Do you want to take a look at it the same weekend as the Hungry Mother race? It's a bit farther than Virginia Tech, but we could visit while we're in the area."

"Sure. That'd be great."

He scratched the stubble on his chin. "Where have you booked a room?"

"Nowhere." I'd completely forgotten. It was my responsibility to make reservations for a place to stay, and I hadn't done a thing yet.

His face tightened. "I thought we agreed…"

"We did, but I haven't."

"If it coincides with an open-house weekend for Virginia Tech, everything decent within miles might be booked by now."

"Then we'll stay further out." Not sure what was worse— my attitude, or just admitting I'd forgotten.

"No skin off my back, Mark. If you've screwed this up, I'll be happy to blame you."

"Thank you." I hated when my father went all rational on me. It made me feel like a child.

"Have you at least registered us for the race?"

"No."

"So you've done nothing more than think about that weekend?"

I nodded.

"All right. Let me know when you're serious about college, and we'll talk again."

Serious about college?

What did he mean? I *was* serious. There was a whole lot going on right now for me to think about. This conversation was just bad timing. "Wait, Dad."

He gave a shrug and kept walking.

CHAPTER TWENTY-THREE

A SLY THIEF

The decision was made. I would return to the past. Yet I would do more than merely warn my sister against the dangers facing her. I would leave behind a cure.

Mark had not asked me again why I'd been in his bedroom last evening. I was glad, for I would've refused to answer, and Mark was wise enough to know that something was not as it should be.

I had one orange bottle in my bathroom with three pills remaining, which was the reason I was on a mission to find more. Although Mark's dresser had held no pills, there might be more elsewhere in the house.

But first, I needed to know what would be needed. I had taken so many pills during my illness that I'd lost count. How many would Phoebe need to overwhelm her infection?

I crept down the stairs and opened the door to the garage. Mark's bike was gone. That was good news. I could talk to his mother without fear.

I found her in the living room. "Sherri?"

"Hmmm?" She didn't look up from a puzzle that spread across an entire coffee table.

"What is the difference between oral and topical antibiotics?"

She pressed a tiny piece into place, gave a small whoop of triumph, and looked up. "Why do you ask? Are you hurt?"

I was prepared. "Norah put ointment on Charlie's hand yesterday when he punctured himself, but I had to take pills this summer."

She nodded and then picked up another piece. "If you get the ointment on fast enough, you might not need oral medication. With puncture wounds, it makes sense to be cautious. They can get scary fast." She smiled. "I'll take a look at his hand next time I'm out there, just to be on the safe side."

"How many pills are enough?"

She frowned but didn't look up. "Depends on the problem and the drug, but two weeks is typical."

"Thank you."

As I started to turn away, she asked, "Is medicine something you might be interested in?"

I hesitated. "As a job?"

"Yeah." She looked up. "I know you didn't have any exposure to health care in your cult, but there are a wide variety of specialties to pursue. It's more than nurses and doctors."

Facing her fully, I considered the idea—not only about medicine specifically, but the entire concept that I could pick a profession because *I* wanted it. My stepfather had determined when I was ten that I would be a kitchen servant. There had never been time to dream of something different. "I shall consider your suggestion."

"Would you like to try a first-aid class? You might enjoy it, and I'd be happy to drive you in the evenings. It would probably only last two or three days."

I swallowed against the huskiness in my throat, overwhelmed at the kindness of the offer. "I should like that."

"Great. Do you want me to find a class for you?"

"Yes, please."

She gave a quick nod, then returned her attention to her puzzle.

With slow steps, I returned to my apartment, pondering the conversation with Sherri. I wanted to accept her offer, not only because *she* had made it, but also because it sounded intriguing. Would my trip to the past ruin this too?

No, I could not let myself be dissuaded. My sister needed medicine, and I must get it.

Sherri had answered in time instead of pills. How many pills would I need for two weeks? I would have to check on the internet.

My next chore was to convince the waterfall. It had proven helpful in the past, but might it be unwilling to let me take this risk?

I would just have to be persuasive.

Mark had returned and disappeared into the bathroom. I had thirty minutes or more before he would come to look for me. I would go now and make my plea.

The day was glorious, hinting that autumn must be hovering nearby. Sunshine feathered through the trees in thin bands of light. The scent of pine mingled with wood smoke. People jogged along the path without speaking, as if they too understood that words could only detract from the beauty of the morning.

When I reached Rocky Creek, I remained on its bank and tried to gauge the mood of the falls. There was no feeling about the place today. It was ordinary. The water didn't sparkle. The air didn't listen.

Disappointment coiled in my gut, but I forced it to be still. I wouldn't be dissuaded. The falls *would* let me through. They had to.

Standing on Mark's favorite rock, I stretched my arms until my fingers breached the flow.

"Would you take me back if I asked?"

The waterfall whispered steadily.

"I must rescue my sister. She needs me, and I can't get there without you. Please."

The water slid—cool, wet, and utterly normal—around my fingers.

"The date will soon be upon us. If you could take me back to this date in the year 1800, I would be grateful. Will you help?"

A branch snapped behind me.

"Hello? Are you alright?"

I spun around. A tall woman of indeterminate age stood on the rutted trail. She had dark skin, short black hair, and an unfamiliar, yet lovely, accent.

"I'm fine, thank you."

Her gaze searched the shadows around the waterfall and its cave before returning to me. "If you're sure?"

I nodded.

She continued along the trail, her arms pumping and her steps strong.

I swung back to the falls. "I shall return tomorrow, and I shall be careful next time to speak without an audience. It is my sincere hope that you'll do your part as well." I walked away and glanced over my shoulder for one last look.

The water sparkled, twinkling like stars, before returning to its clear flow.

Had that been a warning, or a *yes*?

I awakened Monday morning with a new sense of confidence. If I were to see my sister this week, I had to be prepared.

How long would the trip on the other side of the falls take? As I mentally mapped the route from the waterfall to the house where Phoebe lived, I thought through every detail. How would I remain undetected in the area around Worthville and along the Raleigh Road and still move swiftly? How much food should I take? If I carried a sack, how much weight could I tolerate for the hours I would walk? How much medicine could I take without raising suspicions in both centuries?

The last question had an easy answer. Suspicions didn't matter. I would take as much as I could find.

It was a horrible breach of trust to even contemplate what I was about to do. Mark's family had been only generous toward me, but my sister's future was at stake. I could make no other choice.

Once all three had left for the morning, I sprang into action. I searched Mark's bathroom and bedchamber again. Then the guest bathroom. In all of those places, I found a single pill.

The action I'd been dreading needed to be taken. I had to enter his parents' suite.

I stood at its entrance and gazed about me in wonder. A black four-poster bed, wider than I was tall, waited regally in the room's center. Encircling the bed and against the walls were a black chest, an armoire, and a table with a large TV. Opposite the bed waited a small fireplace and two wing chairs within easy reach of a fire's heat.

Sherri had decorated the room with linens in dark green and dull gold. It was truly the most beautiful space I had ever seen, like a small home in its own right.

I gave myself a shake to remember my purpose. I lurked here as a sly thief. Admiration was profane.

Bypassing the furniture of the bedchamber, I made straight for the bathroom, as if searching there was somehow less despicable than searching in the room where my hosts slept. I found a cache of small orange bottles in a shoebox at the top of the towel closet. Most had one or two pills left.

I placed the shoebox on the counter and carefully copied the name of each drug. Then back the box went on the top shelf.

It took me over an hour on the internet, but I discovered information for the different pills. The purposes of these drugs, at times, made me uncomfortable. I would do my best to put them from my mind.

Five of the bottles held antibiotics. I returned to the master bathroom and retrieved my treasure of white, red, and yellow pills.

The guilt over my activities left me feeling oddly powerful. Why should this be so? Should I not be cowed by shame rather than excited and bold?

It was time to press the waterfall more urgently.

CHAPTER TWENTY-FOUR

AFTERNOON SHADOW

I coasted into the garage after school and then left my bike leaning against the wall. There would have to be a harder ride before it got too late. My training recently had been subpar.

Above me, I heard the sounds of water running. Susanna must be taking a shower. I'd check on her after getting started on my work.

My life felt a little crazy and out of control. I'd been too distracted with Susanna and schoolwork. And decisions. There were too many decisions to make. What to major in. Whether to go after any scholarships. Apply now or in January.

Was there some kind of conspiracy of silence out there about the final year of high school? Everyone was always saying how wonderful it was. *The best time of your life.*

Wrong. It royally sucked.

With Dad going with me to check out Newman, Mom might want to come, which meant I had to plan for her too. Launching their last kid from the nest was a team sport. By letting me make the arrangements, they were showing their trust in my maturity. Crap. I'd rather not be trusted.

I hadn't found much available for lodging when I checked this weekend, so I'd dropped by Mr. Rainey's office this morning—hoping he might have insider information.

He'd told me about a special website. That was my first project this afternoon, even before training and homework. I logged into the internet and went to the Blue Ridge section of the VisitVirginia site. Every Mom-quality hotel room between Blacksburg and the park was booked solid for that weekend.

Of course they were.

I tried mom-and-pop type places. A few vacancies popped up, but they looked funky.

I tried the "Vacation Rentals" section.

Someone had converted an old country church into a rental property. The photos of the inside looked cool. The sanctuary became a great room, complete with a fireplace and kitchenette. The balcony had a loft bedroom, and the narthex held the bathroom.

One of the photos showed a glass case displaying old church things. A hymnal. A baptismal certificate. A Bible opened to the Marriages page.

As I flipped through the images of the outside of the rental-church, I wondered how much business the place got. Probably not much. It had no access to the internet or TV, and then there was a serious weirdness factor of hanging out in a church.

I was about to leave the website when a thought tickled at my brain. Something about the glass case…

Returning to the image of the glass case, I hit the magnifier a couple of times, focusing on the Bible with its marriage ceremonies.

Damn, I still hadn't checked about original marriage certificates. What would it take to get one? If that opened up the possibility for Susanna to get a legal identity, would I take it?

I loved her. Completely. But marriage?

Where Susanna was raised, life meant husband and kids as a teen. For me, marriage was in the same relative category as death. I knew it was coming, but *way* in the future.

A marriage certificate would have to be a last resort. We weren't there yet.

I turned my attention to the baptismal certificate instead. Someone had written in the child's name, place and date of birth, and names of parents. A pastor and lay leader had signed and dated it.

As long as the church was still active, it would be difficult to fake. But what if the church had closed? There would be no one to call.

If I had an old Bible and a defunct church, I might be able to produce some decent evidence. I brought up a rare books website and searched for *Bible*. I had to refine the search a bit, but eventually I found one. Circa 1930. Forty bucks.

Sold.

Maybe Susanna was about to get a fake family.

High-voltage energy coursed through my veins. I had to keep this quiet until it worked out, but it was going to. I was psyched. A quick check of the time showed that I could fit in a short training ride before dinner, homework, and Susanna.

I'd finished putting on my gear and was about to leave my room when the laptop chimed an incoming video call. Charging to the bed, I checked the ID. Gabrielle?

"Hey, what's up?" I asked as I adjusted the screen.

She scowled. "Are you about to train?"

I nodded. "We'll finish the lab report at eight, right?"

"I was hoping to do it now."

"Sorry. What's wrong with eight?"

"Korry just texted me." She smiled shyly. "He's going to call me around seven. I don't know if we'll be done by eight."

"Anytime after that is fine." Okay, I hated to ask but I would anyway. "I thought he was in Africa. Isn't it kind of late over there?"

"It'll be midnight his time." Her smile faltered. "They've wrapped up in Botswana. He's shooting in England now."

"You hadn't mentioned that. When did he get there?"

"Friday." She shrugged. "He's been busy."

He'd moved to England and told her through a text two days after he arrived? Korry Sim might be a great actor, but he could be a real jerk to his girlfriend. "He's a lot closer to you now. Could he fly over for Homecoming?"

Her eyes narrowed as she considered the idea. "Maybe," she said, nodding slowly. "Would you mind?"

"No." Okay, that wasn't entirely true. I'd been leaning toward saying yes. Being her escort had sounded like it would be fun—especially when I considered that, six years ago, I'd been the fat kid that the cool kids kicked around. But having Korry Sim on our homecoming court would be awesome in every way possible. "Hey, enjoy your talk, and catch up with me when you can."

"Thanks for understanding." The screen faded.

This was weird. I had inside information on one of the most recognizable couples in America. I knew *her* well enough to form an opinion, and I felt sorry for them.

After shutting down my laptop, I stowed it away and then headed straight for the garage. As I was passing through the laundry room, the door to the apartment opened. Susanna came bounding down the stairs, stopping on the bottom step.

"Hey," I said, my hand on the garage door.

She gave me a slow, sexy smile. "Come to me."

Wow. Even as my brain was reeling, my legs were obeying the command. I reached out for her, my arms automatically closing around her hips, our eyes at the same level for once.

Her hands cupped my jaw, one grazing lightly over the afternoon shadow of my beard while the other slid toward the back of my head, her fingers threading through my hair.

"What are you doing, Susanna?"

"You told me to be brave with you," she said, pulling me closer until her lips touched mine. "I am trying."

My brain stopped working. All that was left was her mouth "trying." And succeeding.

I pulled away first. "Holy shit."

She laughed. "Truly? Is cursing the only encouragement I am to get?"

"That was hot, and you know it."

"Hot?" She inclined her head, puzzled. "Did you not tell me once that hot means pretty?"

My turn to smile. "I told you it had another meaning too."

"Will you tell me, or must I tempt it from you?"

Damn. I needed to say it before she totally screwed up my training plans. Fortunately, she had a better vocabulary than most college professors. "Hot also means seductive."

"Indeed."

When she reached for me again, I backed away. "You stay there. I need to train." The next hour could be painful.

"You are a man of admirable willpower."

"Shut up," I said with a grin as I slipped out the door.

Chapter Twenty-Five

Unfettered Nature

My trip to Old Raleigh would keep me out overnight. There was no way this could be helped. Because I didn't wish to worry my hosts, I had to provide a note of explanation. I would leave it for Bruce. He was sensible and less inclined to judge me.

Mark would receive no note. I regretted this necessity and dreaded the inevitable argument when next we met, but there was no helping it either. If he returned from school before the waterfall allowed me to pass, he might try to talk me out of my plans or go with me. Neither was acceptable.

Tuesday, after everyone had left, it was time to assemble the supplies. I squeezed a tube of Bacitracin into a fat glass jar, then added a cork stopper. Into a tiny cloth bag, I added the pills. Seventeen in all. Three different kinds, but each and every one an oral antibiotic. At two per day, this treatment would only last for nine days. It was the best I could do, and I hoped it would be enough. I pulled the drawstring and tied it snugly.

After packing these items into a canvas sack, I added a few more. For hunger, I included an apple, a package of beef jerky, and two granola bars. For emergencies, there was a cloth bandage, a pair of socks and a rain poncho. And, of course, toilet paper.

Missing was the costume. I cleared my mind and donned my clothing. Full slip, silky and trimmed with lace. The granny gown. A wide blue ribbon at my waist. Thick trouser socks. Black sneakers.

With sure fingers, I wound my hair, secured it to the top of my head, and pinned on a cap I'd fashioned from a square of cloth. The transformation was complete.

A quick look in the mirror reflected a girl I barely recognized. It stunned me how completely I had changed in only seven weeks. With the costume came memories, unpleasant in their intensity. I fought back the sense that I was still a servant girl, bound to an unseen master in every way except physical.

I snatched off the cap and forced it into the canvas bag. There would be time enough to pin it on once I reached Old Raleigh.

Now for the letter. Sherri had a delicate mahogany secretary in her husband's office. It held beautiful notecards of creamy vellum with gilded edges. A special set of pens rested in a carved wooden box. I hurried there, wrote the note quickly, addressed it to Bruce, and laid it on his desk.

It was noon when I emerged from the rear of the house, engaged the alarm, and crossed quickly to the greenway. I ran for the rutted trail and picked my way carefully to the banks of Rocky Creek. There was no one about.

"I am ready, Whisper Falls. Take me back, please."

There was no sparkle—no indication that the falls would accommodate my wish.

I crept as close as I dared and held out my hand. The water was wet. I laughed. Of course it was. Water was supposed to be wet, was it not?

"Are you toying with me?"

The rhythmic thud of running shoes slapping pavement of the greenway filtered through the thick forest. The sound grew louder and then faded around a bend in the greenway.

I crossed to an old hollow log and sat, clutching the canvas sack to my lap. I could wait and watch.

One hour passed. Then another. No sparkle or shimmer. Mark would be home soon. I must hurry, retrieve the note, and hide my supplies. I could wait here no longer.

I stood stiffly and stalked to the closest boulder. "I shall come tomorrow and the day after that. As long as it takes."

The water ignored me.

After hurrying home, I let myself into the house and retrieved the note from Bruce's desk. Then I ran to the apartment and hid the canvas sack in the cabinet below the window seat. Soon, the granny gown hung in the closet, and my normal clothes were back on.

A bike rattled in the lane and up the driveway. Mark was home. Moments later, the door slammed. Feet thundered up the stairs to my apartment and then two light raps.

I faced the door nervously, as if my guilt reeked from every pore. "Come in."

"Hey, babe," he said as he flung his backpack on the floor by the door and strode across the room. A few feet from me, though, he stopped. "Why do you have your hair like that?"

Merciful heavens. I had forgotten. "I thought perhaps..." My words faltered as I reached for the hair piled on my head.

"Don't. Let me do it."

I nodded wordlessly and turned my back to him. One by one, he drew out the pins. A lock fell, then another. With the third pin, the mass tumbled down.

His arms slipped around my waist and drew me back against him. "That was hot."

I relaxed into him as his lips pressed to my cheek. "Indeed, and how was your day?"

He groaned against my neck.

"I have two major projects due later this week and two big tests next Wednesday. I'm drowning in homework."

"May I join you in the family room? We could study together."

"Sure." He dropped a light kiss on my lips and took a step toward the door. "See you down there in ten."

I held my breath until his steps merged into the noise of the house and then released it on a sigh. I'd made too many mistakes. I must increase my vigilance. There could be no room for error once I set foot in the past.

Eight days went by, and still the falls wouldn't let me through. Three days remained until the night of the ball in 1800.

I would not give up. My sister needed me. Surely the waterfall would relent, though it had to be today. Tomorrow was Thursday, Sherri's day off. What if she were to engage me in an activity and I could not slip away? Worry ached in my belly.

I hurried to the falls after my noon meal and waited on Mark's favorite rock. "Please." My voice wavered with a mixture of dread and hope.

The water glimmered. I plunged my hand into the flow. It wound around my fingers like ribbons, silken but *not wet.*

Hugging the canvas sack tightly to my chest, I stepped through the waterfall and into the past.

I stood on the narrow ledge of rock between Whisper Falls and the tiny, moss-strewn cave behind it, opening my senses. The world of my birth was as I remembered. The sounds were crisper. The smells fresher.

The creatures in the forest murmured without fear, undisturbed by the presence of humans. I hurried downstream along the pebble-strewn bank before cutting into the woods, then set a course that paralleled the creek, far enough into the trees to avoid detection. When I emerged on the Raleigh Road, there was no one in sight, just as I had expected. I turned toward the capital city.

The road was rutted, the inclines steep at points. How I wished I could ride a bike. The distance in time would be shorter, and the hills not so high. I needed to cease such thoughts, for they made the hours of walking that lay ahead less tolerable. I would be alone with unfettered nature.

Was this not a much-missed part of this century? There was no whining of motors, no planes overhead. How could Mark's world permit the racket of clashing metal to drown the lovely sounds of the forest? I decided I must relax my mind and allow sweet solitude to ease me onward.

I arrived at the ridge overlooking the capital in late afternoon and paused to drink in the sight. A wave of homesickness rolled over me.

There were new buildings everywhere. New streets encroached into the surrounding woods. Yet it moved and changed at a familiar pace. I understood this world.

With a resolved shake of my head, I plunged down the other side of the ridge. In the ensuing years—four on the nineteenth-century side of the falls—the road had been much-improved. Gone were the weeds that hid snakes, and the rocks that lamed horses. It shortened my time into the heart of the city.

The pounding of hammers had been replaced by the shouts of merchants and the screams of those unwary enough to step into the path of a wagon.

I still had not worked out how I would gain access to my sister, but perhaps an idea would come to me when I got there.

The Eton house looked deserted. There was a bit of movement in the kitchen but none visible on the ground floor of the house. I walked along the street until I could stop in the shade of an oak. While I stood there, clutching the short wooden fence and debating what my next move should be, a young woman in a dark roundgown and white apron exited the kitchen building. Her gaze swept the garden, focusing curiously on me.

Her hand crept to her mouth. "Susie?"

"Indeed, yes, Phoebe," I said in a voice brimming with joy. "It is I."

Chapter Twenty-Six

Random Events

The final bell rang, signaling the end of school and this frickin' American government test.

Mr. Fullerton asked insane questions. The only thing that saved me was Susanna. Her father, as the village tutor, had been on top of the politics of that time—which meant Susanna had been, too.

When I walked out of class, Gabrielle stood in the center of the hallway, talking with Jesse and Benita. They waved me over.

Three weeks ago, I'd been dreading this year, worried that I'd be a loner during the school day. Somehow I had just merged into this circle of four friends. It felt nice.

Benita nudged me with her elbow. "We're celebrating how well the teachers colluded to give us a Wednesday marathon of tests. Want to come with us?"

I resisted the urge to check my watch. "Sure. Where?"

"Olde Tyme Grill?"

"Yeah. Great."

Gabrielle smiled. "Did you bike today?"

I shook my head. "I drove."

Fifteen minutes later, we were seated in our booth, drinking smoothies and eating fries. Jesse wanted to compare notes on exam questions, but we outvoted him three-to-one.

"Fine. You win." He elbowed Benita. "Want to tell them about your audition at the School of the Arts?"

"Sure. It went great."

Was it modesty or boredom that kept her from saying more? I was actually interested. "Is that where you want to go to college?"

"I don't know yet. I guess it depends on whether I get into their high school program."

"You'll get in," Jesse said.

Ignoring him, she propped her chin on one of her gloved hands. "Where do you plan to go?"

"Don't know yet. I'm mostly looking at schools in the mountains."

"Jesse wants to go to Berkeley."

He shook his head. "Where I want to go—and where I will end up—might not be the same thing."

She rolled her eyes. Obviously something she'd heard too often. "Let's talk about Gabrielle."

Beside me, Gabrielle laughed. "What do you want to know?"

"Are you going to college?"

"Eventually. It'll have to wait, though. I have a couple of films lined up after graduation."

Benita nodded in sage agreement, as if all of her friends took gap years to star in movies. "How does it feel to be on the homecoming court?"

"Busy."

"Do you have a dress?"

"I will." Gabrielle shrugged. "My agent is flying in a few to pick from."

"Oooh." Benita's eyes widened. "Is Korry coming?"

Gabrielle exchanged a glance with me. "Korry can't get away from the movie set."

How long had she been holding onto that piece of information?

"Then who's going to escort you?"

"I asked Mark."

Her statement shut up Benita and Jesse, and it pissed me off. I turned sideways on the bench and pressed my back to the wall, putting maximum space between me and Gabrielle. I'd stopped thinking about it, expecting Korry to show up. Why did she wait until I had an audience? I didn't like being put on the defensive. From the way her gaze skittered away from mine, she had gotten the message.

The silence lingered an entire minute, quite a record for the four of us.

Jesse was the first to break it. "What did you say, Mark?"

"I haven't answered yet."

"Why not? I would've said yes before she finished the question."

Benita punched him in the arm. "You're taking *me* to the homecoming game."

"I know," he said, "but if Gabi asked me to be her escort, you would just have to spend some time alone in the stands."

I grabbed a fry and chewed slowly, glad the couple had pulled the attention back to themselves. The rest of the dining area was beginning to fill with Neuse classmates. All were looking about as mentally worn-out as we were.

"So what's the holdup?"

Okay. Center of attention again. Not happy about that. They would want to know what I thought, and I hadn't made a final decision before the request got put on hold. I liked the irony of ending up on the homecoming court, I had Susanna's go-ahead, and yet it still didn't feel quite right. "I'm working through the angles."

Gabrielle settled against the booth and crossed her arms. "He has a girlfriend."

Had she really just deflected this to Susanna? Not exactly the way to get my agreement.

"Oh, right. I'd forgotten about her," Jesse said. "Does she know that Gabi asked you?"

"She does, and she's okay with it." Why did I let that slip out? By defending Susanna, had I backed myself into a corner?

"So it's all good." Jesse scooped up his complete share of fries and dumped them on a napkin.

"Then you'll do it," Gabrielle said with satisfaction.

That wasn't what I'd said, but it was what I wanted to do. And Susanna *had* said it was okay. Grudgingly. So why did I feel played?

"What's your girlfriend's name again?" Benita asked.

"Susanna Marsh."

"What's she like?"

Gabrielle's words floated back to me. *Describe without mentioning looks.* "She's quiet. Smart. Loyal. Pure." Plus both slang meanings of hot, except I wouldn't use that word with them. It was private. Just for the two of us.

"Where is she right now?" Benita asked.

"Home."

"Where's home?"

Shit. Where was my brain today? Had the tests turned it into mush? "My parents have a studio apartment over the garage. Susanna is living there for now."

Jesse gave Benita a wide-eyed look. "Wish you had parents like him."

He might not think that if he'd heard the rules my parents laid down.

"What does she look like?" Jesse asked.

Oh, yeah, guys had their priorities straight. I pulled out my phone, opened the gallery, and hunted for the photos from the Eton House. I'd taken the first shot secretly. We'd just arrived, and she'd been absorbing it all. The booths. The docents in costume. The little kids giggling over the games. She'd smiled in total wonder, hands clasped against her waist, in love with the place and the day.

I handed it to Jesse.

He sucked in a quick breath. "I see why you've been hiding her. I'd hide her too. Damn."

We fist-bumped.

Benita looked over his shoulder, frowning. "Okay. She looks...nice. But I don't understand..."

Jesse and I said in unison, "The hair."

"What about it?"

Jesse and I laughed. He said, "Oh, yeah."

Benita took the phone and swiped to the next shot. "What's she wearing?" She showed us the image, the one inside the dress-up booth.

Gabrielle studied the photo closely. "Federal-period costume."

I nodded, impressed at Gabrielle's knowledge. "We were at the Avery-Eton House, near the Governor's Mansion."

"She likes that kind of stuff? Is that why Alexis called her the colonial girl?" Benita smiled. "I hope so. I think that's seriously cool. When do we get to meet her?"

"Not in this century," Gabrielle said.

I cut a sideways glance at her. "What is up with you?"

"Nothing. Sorry." She closed her eyes. "Long-distance relationships suck."

"Yeah. Sounds like it. Maybe you should discuss that with *him*." I retrieved my phone. "I'd better be going."

Gabrielle got out of the way. I slid from the booth, grabbed my backpack, and started across the dining room. I'd barely made it halfway when I felt a light touch on my shoulder.

It was Gabrielle. "I apologize. It wasn't right to take that out on you."

"Agreed." I stared down at her, wondering if there was more, not cutting her any slack at the moment. Normal teens didn't get automatic forgiveness for crap like that.

"Korry can't come, but he's already okayed you, and my publicist is pressuring me to announce my escort. And…" She bit her lip and looked around the room. People were staring. "You're the perfect solution. I didn't know what I would do if you said *no*."

"Well, you got your *yes*." I backed up a couple of steps and turned to go.

"You'll need to rent a tuxedo," Gabrielle called to me.

The sound in the dining room dimmed significantly. Message sent and received.

I didn't understand what had gotten into Gabrielle. "No, I won't. I own one."

The noise around me rose again. Now everybody knew that Mark Lewis would be escorting Gabrielle Stone on the homecoming court.

Once I got home, I raced up the back stairs and found Susanna's door closed. I tapped lightly, but there was no response.

Maybe she was taking a nap. I'd try again later.

Bike ride. Shower. Change.

By the time I made it to the kitchen, Mom had dinner on the table. I detoured to the back stairs to get Susanna.

"She's not there," Mom said.

I looked over my shoulder. "Where is she?"

"I don't know. I haven't seen or heard her since I got home."

"Is she at the lake house?"

"She didn't leave a note."

Weird. I walked to the window overlooking the back yard and peered out. No sign of her in the garden.

"I wouldn't worry, dear. She's probably walking on the greenway and lost track of time."

"Maybe."

"Are you talking about Susanna?" Dad asked from behind me.

I whipped around, uneasy at the odd inflection in my father's voice. "Yeah, Dad. We can't find her."

"Then I guess you need to see this." He held up some of Mom's fancy stationery. "She left this on my desk."

"Why for you?"

"I'm not sure."

Dread jolted through me. There could be no good reasons for Susanna to write a letter to my father. "Let me see that."

I charged across the room and snatched it from his hands. The note was brief, written in her precise, elegant handwriting.

Dear Bruce,

When you read this, you may have noted my absence. I have left for an errand that will likely keep me away overnight. Do not worry. I shall return tomorrow.

Please say nothing to Mark until he asks. He will be unduly concerned, and I should not like to distract him from his studies.

Sincerely,

Susanna

After reading it a second time, I tossed it on the table, stalked to the window, and glared at the setting sun. This was bad. Really bad. I clenched my fists in front of me, so my folks couldn't see.

The card rustled behind me as my mom picked it up. "Do you know where she's gone?"

"Not for sure." One idea kept tickling at the periphery of my brain, but surely Susanna wouldn't be that stupid.

I had to think. She hadn't gone to the lake house or she would've said so. Who else did she know? How had she gotten there? Bus?

No, the destination was likely within walking distance. I frowned over my shoulder. "Dad, has she said anything to you recently? Anything that seemed strange?"

He shook his head, his eyes narrowed on me with suspicion.

I needed to take a deep breath. Until I had this figured out, I couldn't act too "unduly concerned." It took all of the acting skills I possessed to hide from them how bad this was. "Mom?"

"Hmmm?" She looked up from the notepaper. "Susanna has gorgeous handwriting."

"Mom. Focus."

"Watch it, son," my dad growled.

Another deep breath. "Has Susanna said anything to you? Like, maybe about her sister?"

Mom wrinkled her nose at me. "I thought her sister had escaped."

"She has, and I don't have any more information than that."

"Okay, dear. Nothing about the sister."

"Has she said anything recently that seemed weird?"

"Nooooo," Mom said, drawing the syllable out.

I turned to face her fully, jamming my fists into my pockets to hide their tension. "Have you thought of something?"

"She asked me about the difference between oral antibiotics and topical. We ended up talking about first-aid classes."

It felt like someone had put a metal clamp around my chest and squeezed hard. Random events clicked into place, like colored glass in a kaleidoscope falling into a pattern.

Granddad's wound.

The top drawer of my dresser.

Her eighteenth-century hairstyle.

I gave my mom as relaxed a smile as I could manage. "That can't be it. Maybe I'll go up to her apartment and look around for hints."

Tearing up the stairs two at a time, I burst through the door. It looked perfectly neat. Perfectly kept. Perfectly empty.

The laptop sat in its orderly spot on the table.

I popped it open and brought up a browser, hunting through the recent history of links she'd visited.

Women's fashions from 1800.

Treatment of puncture wounds.

Prescription drugs.

I checked the list of drugs she'd researched. Many were antibiotics, although some were…unexpected, indicating health problems that I didn't know anything about. Problems that old people had—like maybe my mom and dad.

Had Susanna gone in my parents' room looking for drugs?

Damn. They didn't have a rule about that because no one would've ever imagined Susanna would do such a thing. Including me.

Okay, I'd have to deal with those thoughts later. For now, I had to forget how angry I was and refocus on why she did this.

She'd spent a lot of time with her sister's journals recently. Had something happened to Phoebe—something related to her health?

I brought up the file containing Phoebe's last journal, went to the end, and worked backwards, skimming the words as best I could. I didn't have to go far when the word *amputation* jumped out at me.

Phoebe's thumb had been amputated.

Was that something Susanna would feel compelled to prevent?

Of course it was.

Emotions exploded inside me, a volatile mixture of anger and fear. Susanna had returned to the past.

CHAPTER TWENTY-SEVEN

FOREVER FROM VIEW

"Where have you been, Susie?" Phoebe raced across the lawn and into my arms, the wooden slats of the fence our only form of separation. "I have missed you."

"And I have missed you. Oh, my dear sister." I hugged her tightly to me, but she no longer had the frame of a little girl. She'd grown taller than me by two inches, and her body had curved into the form of a young woman.

I dropped back a step. "Let me see. You are lovely."

She smiled and bobbed a half-curtsy. "I do thank you, ma'am." She reached across the fence again and caught my hands. "I cannot stay. I am needed in the house. How long will you be here? We thought you were swept away. Where have you been? Please say we can be together for a time. I have many questions."

"I shall not leave until the morning. May I stay here?"

A scowl settled on her face. "I share a room with Letty. She is our newest chambermaid." The scowl cleared. "Of course, Letty will not tell. You may sleep in my room. Come here after dark."

"I shall."

A horse and carriage clopped to a halt in the street. Phoebe gave a quick glance and gasped. "I must go and so must you." She squeezed my hands briefly. "I shall see you soon. You will not forget?"

"I shall not." I stepped deeper into the shadows as she darted across the gardens and down some steps into the basement of the house.

Where would I go until nightfall? Where could I stay hidden from view? A lone woman, regardless of attire, was bound to attract notice if she wandered about without purpose.

There were no churches yet in Raleigh, and I hadn't thought to bring anything to barter with, so I could not slip into a shop or a tavern.

Merciful heavens, I had not made a perfect plan.

I watched as a fine-looking young man alighted from the carriage and then turned to offer a hand to his three companions. This was, no doubt, Mr. William Eton. The first woman I recognized as Mrs. Abigail Eton, elegant and cool in her pale gown, even from a distance. Next came a young lady, likely Miss Judith Eton, for she was a younger version of the mistress of the household—both in countenance and dress.

Last he helped a girl of tremendous beauty, delicate in stature. Her ink-black curls were cut stylishly short. Her dress flounced with row after row of lace. Doubtless I was seeing a glimpse of Miss Margaret Dunwoodie, the young lady who would've ended my sister's dreams had I not shown up this day.

Quickly, before they could spot me, I trailed along the lane in the opposite direction and followed the boundaries of the Eton property. When I reached their neighbor to the east, I paused. The Etons had planted a high, sturdy hedge, as had their neighbors, leaving a small gap.

The sight made me smile. A feud, a past unpleasantness, or perhaps merely a desire to be left alone echoed in that narrow space. It would serve my purpose well. I plunged between the hedges to lie on the grass in the cedar-scented shade.

The growl of my stomach awakened me from a light doze. As I nibbled on a granola bar, I peered at the sky. The sun perched on the horizon, although there was sufficient daylight to see. Supper could not be more than two hours away. Phoebe's duties would end once the meal had been served.

I crept back to the Etons' side yard and hid beneath the branches of a willow. The servants scurried about. Mr. Eton arrived and handed his horse over to a waiting slave.

I tracked that young boy as he led the horse down the block, disappearing behind a row of buildings, doubtless the stables. It was hard to reconcile my thoughts on the enslavement of people. I too had been bound out against my will. My enslavement had promised an end date, although I had not known at the time that my release would only have come with death. Mark's world had taught me how desperately wrong this system was. Yet where was my rage for that young boy? Or the girl I had been?

In my new century, the very concept of one human being owning another had been long abandoned in America. Nor were women viewed as lesser than men. Clever ideas and hard work had been added as measures of worth.

Yet, even with this enlightened thinking, I had learned through my quest to prove my birthplace that there were still plenty of ways to keep people in their places.

Motionless, my back against the willow's trunk, I watched as the Eton household settled into its evening routine.

An hour passed before a cap-covered head emerged from the basement of the main house and tiptoed into the garden.

"Susie?"

I stood, remaining behind my curtain of willow branches a moment longer. "I am here."

She skipped to my spot, linked her hand with mine, and held a hushing finger to her lips. We crept around the perimeter of the property, slipping from shadow to shadow until we'd circled all the way around to the kitchen building.

"Phoebe?"

She shook her head to silence me.

"Truly, is such stealth necessary?"

She leaned closer and pressed her lips to my ear. "My delight at your arrival is so excessive that I suspect all who see us together will have to know that you are not a mere cousin or friend. Let us not tempt fate."

I shuddered at the wisdom of her statement. My sister had matured more than my heart had anticipated.

She tiptoed up a pair of steps to the ground floor of the kitchen, looked about, and then waved me in. I rushed straight past her to the upper floor, hesitating on the top landing.

She waved me into the chamber to the right and closed the door behind her. "Letty will retire soon. Shall we share our private stories before she arrives?"

It took no more than a second to reclaim our hold on each other. I wanted to weep and laugh and dance out my joy. I would not think on the brevity of this visit, for that would surely change its feeling. No, indeed, I should think only of her and now.

"Do you wish to store your sack while we talk?"

The sack? How could I have forgotten the entire reason I had risked this visit? "There is medicine in this sack that I have brought to you."

"Medicine?" She waved airily.

I grasped her by the shoulders. "It is the reason I have come. I traveled a great distance to bring it to you. Please accept its grave importance."

"Indeed, Susie." She blinked in surprise. "Tell me what you wish me to know."

I set the sack on a scarred table and drew out the ointment jar and the drawstring bag of pills. "Did you ever hear what happened to me after I brought you to Raleigh?"

"Jacob Worth told me the entire tale after Mama's funeral." She shook her head. "He was most disgusted by his father's role in your suffering."

"Then you know Mr. Pratt shackled my ankles."

She nodded, her lips trembling.

"The pain was fierce and the infection deadly."

"But it did not kill you."

"No, it did not. Mark took me to a place with powerful medicine."

"Mr. Lewis?"

I nodded. "Without this medicine, I would surely have died from poisons in my blood. As it was, I nearly lost my feet."

"They would have been severed?"

"They might have been." I leaned forward, hoping that she would remember my urgency. "Phoebe, I put myself in danger to bring this to you."

"Why should I need it? I shall not be shackled."

"Perhaps not. Yet you often handle sharp things, like knives and scissors."

Her brow creased. "And needles."

I shuddered with relief. Would she not recall better what she had concluded on her own? "Indeed. Needles too. If you cut or puncture a limb, try this ointment. Perhaps it will hold the infection at bay. If not, you must swallow these pills. One at night and one in the morning until you run out of them. Promise me?"

She smiled. "I shall not forget, but do not worry. I am most careful with sharp things, and Mrs. Eton is most wise in the ways of healing."

"It is better to prevent a wound than to heal it after it is there." Mrs. Eton could never be as wise as the science in Mark's world. "Do you have a place to hide these remedies?"

She nodded. Reaching beneath the corner of her pallet, she drew out a simple wooden box. Inside, I could see a small stack of letters, tied together with a thin blue ribbon. She placed the jar and bag inside and then closed the lid.

"Who sends you letters? You've never—" I bit off the rest of what I was about to say. She had never mentioned them in her journals.

"They are from Jacob Worth. He writes me of the adventures he has in Williamsburg." She smiled. "He attends college there."

"Do you write him back?"

"Naturally. It would be inconsiderate not to return a letter now and then."

I didn't know how I felt about this news. "Is Jacob Worth your beau?"

"No, indeed. We are very, very good friends. I think that such pleasantries are possible between a man and a woman. Do you not?"

"I do." I didn't know how I felt about the view of my sister as a *woman* either.

She gestured toward a washstand against the wall. It held a candlestick with a stub of a candle. "Let us go over there where I can see you better."

We sat beneath the washstand, cross-legged with knees touching, and held hands.

She sighed sadly. "You will go again in the morning."

"Yes."

"Tell me where you live now, that I might visit when I am free from my indenture."

"I live far away in a strange land. You can never visit."

She shook her head firmly. "It can not be very far away if you can visit me. Perhaps, if it is wonderful, I should want to live there too."

Could I consider bringing her forward? Would she be able to survive in Mark's world?

I gave my head a quick shake, to clear my thinking. No, she could not endure it. The only reason I had moved was the push that the fear of death gave me. I survived because I had no other choice.

Neither could I be sure that Whisper Falls would permit her passage. It would be devastating to make such a decision, reach the waterfall, and have it end there. "Phoebe, I should dearly love to have you visit me, but the journey is arduous and the customs are peculiar. I do not think it is wise to make such a plan."

"Very well. We shall see." She smiled primly. "Do you live with Mr. Lewis?"

"I live in the same home."

"Have you married?"

"I am devoted to Mark, and he is devoted to me. One day, we shall marry, but the time is not right."

Her eyes narrowed in outrage. "You are nearly twenty-two, Susie. It is long past time to have a husband and children. If Mr. Lewis loves you, why does he allow you to languish so?"

I'd forgotten the difference in time. What had been only two months for me had been four years for her. I shook her hands lightly, as if reassuring a child. "We do not have an improper relationship, Phoebe. I cook in his parents' home, and I clean. I have my own room above the…stables." It was only a slight deception, yet it still ached in my throat.

Her face clouded. "Why does a servant talk of marriage to a member of the family?"

This conversation had become treacherous. How much of the modern world had I absorbed in the months I had lived there? "In Mark's city, there is more familiarity between the classes. It is not frowned upon."

"Truly? His parents would consent to an alliance between you?"

I tried to imagine the reaction from Sherri and Bruce if we were to announce our marriage. I nearly choked on a bubble of laughter. "They do not consent at present. They wish for us to wait until Mark has finished his studies."

"And then it will be allowed?"

I nodded. "Indeed, no one—not even his neighbors—would bear us ill will."

"A most unusual place, sister." She bit her lip, thoughts racing behind her expressive eyes. "I must think on this idea."

"Let us not talk of me." I smiled with encouragement. "Tell me of your life."

"I have but a few months left on my indenture. Mrs. Eton will release me on my seventeenth birthday."

A fact I already knew—yet I displayed the most profound surprise. "So early? How generous! What will you do after?"

"I hope to work for a seamstress and work on beautiful gowns." She rose to gaze out the window. I stood too and followed the direction she looked. There was the Eton house, ablaze with candlelight. "Earlier today, when the carriage rolled up and I departed, that was my mistress returning with two of her children." Her voice grew wistful. "They were accompanied by Miss Margaret—she is Mr. Eton's sister's stepdaughter. She is to have a lovely new frock for her birthday ball. I have glimpsed the gown. It is…"

"Snow white from neckline to hem, embroidered with whitework fleur-de-lis, enjoying a train."

"Indeed, that is precisely how I would describe it. Have you seen this gown?"

I yielded to a naughty urge. "Where I live, that style is too common to be distinctive."

"You have moved to a wondrous place, sister. It is no surprise you do not wish to return here." She linked her arm through mine and stared out into the peace of the night.

We slept on a pallet meant for one. Across the room, Letty stirred fretfully. I suspected my presence was to blame. Letty had been confused by Phoebe's quick, vague explanation.

The other girl arose before dawn and began her day. Phoebe, as the senior housemaid, could claim an extra thirty minutes of sleep. She did not rest this day. We rose, donned our gowns, and stood before the tiny oval mirror that made a pitiful adornment on the wall above the washstand.

"Here, let me dress your hair," I said, taking the comb from her. I pulled her locks into a golden plait before pinning it neatly at the back of her head.

Silently, she did me the same favor. When the work was done, Phoebe moaned a sob, and quickly cut it off.

"Please do not cry," I said.

"We shall soon say our final goodbyes." She made her statement with certainty.

There was no use in denying what we both knew to be true. "You will never be far from my heart."

"Can you write me?"

I shook my head, unable to speak the response that would cause her such hopeless grief.

"I hate what Mr. Pratt's actions have done to us. Without him, we could be together. We could be a family still."

"Do not say hate. Mr. Pratt deserves no emotion from us except contempt."

"He must have done horrible things to you, sister, to make what has come afterward worth the pain." She covered her mouth with her hand and whispered, "I did not know, Susie. I am sorry."

"Keeping you safe from him is worth the sacrifice. I regret nothing."

She nodded, dabbed her face with her apron, and then smiled, wobbly but sweet. "Oh, sister, my chores await me. I shall stop in the kitchen, put together a packet of breakfast for you, and leave it in the garden." She grasped the doorknob and turned it with a squeak. "You will find your meal on a bench near the rose bushes, midway between this building and the lane. Give me ten minutes and then go."

"I love you, Phoebe," I said, my voice cracking. "Do not forget."

"Never." Her smile widened. "I love you, dearest Susanna." And she was gone.

I didn't stay as directed. Instead, I crept from the kitchen building, retraced our route around the perimeter, and hid beneath the shelter of the willow. My sister burst from the kitchen moments later, ran first to the bench, and then down the brick steps leading to the basement, her white cap bobbing forever from view.

CHAPTER TWENTY-EIGHT

POTENTIAL ACCESS

Last night had been maddening. My parents had insisted on seeing the "place where Susanna lived." Again. I'd taken them once before—and there was just as much nothing now, only it was darker at night.

We walked through the woods of Umstead Park with flashlights, before emerging into the meadow that held the crumbling foundations of the meetinghouse and store. I waited as they looked for clues that might lead us to where the village had gone. We found nothing useful other than a bit of litter that, of course, I knew hadn't been left by the Pratts.

When we returned home, I was grilled for an hour, sitting at the kitchen table while they pounded me with questions. Mostly, I said "I don't know," which was true in this case. I didn't know where Susanna was, although I could guess. I didn't know when she would be back, and I didn't know whether she was in imminent danger.

My mom had left abruptly, eyes shiny with tears. Were they tears of frustration? Tears of fear?

Yeah, I totally got that.

When I awakened this morning, I didn't bother to follow my normal routine at all. No training. No preparing for school. It would be useless to go today. I wouldn't be able to function until Susanna returned.

Both parents were out of the house by eight. Before I jogged down to the falls, I sent an email to Mr. Rainey that I was on a college visit. If I were lucky, he wouldn't press too hard about which one or, even worse, ask my folks. I didn't want to have another conversation with my parents about skipping school.

I reached Rocky Creek without thinking about what my plan was. I didn't know where Susanna was. Probably with her sister, but where was Phoebe? Still with the Etons? That was most likely.

Much as I didn't want to, I also needed to consider the possibility that she'd failed at whatever mission she was on. She could be injured somewhere. Or...

Nope, not going to think about this. I'd play it by ear. Standing on my launching rock, I studied the flow. It was clear. Normal.

"Are you going to let me through?" I let the water pour over my fingers. It was wet, dammit. I hadn't planned out what I would've done on the other side, but it pissed me off that it hadn't let me through.

"She came through here yesterday," I said, drawing my hand back. "I know she did."

Nothing. Nada.

Okay, I wouldn't get mad. It was just a waterfall with an attitude. "Why won't you let me through?"

Even more nothing.

All right, if it wasn't going to let me through right now, I would wait. Until it changed its mind. Or until she came back.

I ran home and got ready for a stake-out. Food, drink, stadium blanket. I grabbed the iPad and put a note—just in case—on my dresser. The last thing I did was program the home security system to text me if anyone entered the house, and then I hiked back to the falls and positioned myself, hidden among the trees, to see as much of the cave and bluff as possible.

The first half hour passed slowly. I watched with vigilance, which was stupid on a logical level. If she were in old Raleigh, it would be mid-morning or later before she could safely, realistically walk back. That assumed she was coming back today.

Stop. She was.

That's when the emotions hit, rolling over me like a tsunami. The first wave brought anger—fierce, white-hot anger pulsing through my veins. How dare she? How dare she scare me and my parents this way? There had better be a damn good reason—and even then, it wouldn't be okay.

The second wave of emotion was even worse. Raw, agonizing betrayal. She'd planned this, executed this, and deliberately kept it away from me. Could I ever trust her again? This was a huge lie, a huge slap in the face. It made me deeply…sad.

And that sense of sadness was the final, lingering emotion. This action changed our relationship, and not for the better. I wanted the old relationship back. I wanted the pure Susanna. The Susanna I trusted. And she was gone.

I turned my attention to the iPad. Might as well use the time that I was sitting here doing nothing. I checked my Bible order. It was on the way.

Next I visited the VisitVirginia site and booked subpar lodging, hoping that my mom decided to stay home.

It had been a while since I'd checked historical records for Worthville. I searched on it, except this time I added the names of people I remembered.

Phoebe's name popped up nowhere, but the last name Marsh did. Susanna's brother Caleb had made a Last Will and Testament and it was available online. He'd lived to be pretty old and left his farm to a son. They must have survived the tornado that hit the area in 1805.

I'd have to remember to pass that along to Susanna after she returned. Well, not right after, because I was mad at her and I was going to take all the time I needed to get that out of my system.

Who else should I try? Pratt?

Nope. Didn't want to think about him.

Maybe I should put some attention on this century and Susanna's identity. I started a search on court orders and found a bunch of information, so much that it would take some effort to narrow it down.

I had plenty of time today.

An hour later, I had some interesting things to consider.

I'd finally checked out the marriage certificate thing for North Carolina—and South Carolina, Tennessee, and even Nevada. We had to have a photo ID and probably a Social Security card at every one of those places.

At the moment, I was so pissed at Susanna that my reaction to this reprieve wasn't worth analyzing.

Moving on.

There are a lot of judges in Wake County. They all seemed to belong to the same clubs with photos popping up in the society pages. Which meant they might be friends with Judge Nelson. Not good.

But the best fact was unexpected and potentially very helpful. Judges had law students filling in as interns. I'd have to see how hard it was to find one who liked to talk.

Cramping muscles reminded me of my whereabouts. After shutting off the tablet, I stood, stretched, and did some pacing along the trail. The waterfall droned on, but it still didn't sparkle.

My stomach rumbled. It was weird how much energy it took to sit still and search the internet for nuggets of information.

I checked my watch. A little after eleven. I was hungry— and the later it got, the more likely Susanna was to show up.

I'd just finished cleaning up my snack when I noticed a glint in the falls. A sparkle or two. Not much. There was definitely something going on. I went over to the falls and slipped my hand in the flow. It wasn't wet. It also stopped my hand at the wrist.

What did that mean? Was this reassurance that things were okay? Or was it hedging its bets, giving me potential access in case things were about to go wrong?

I heard voices coming from the other side. No, make that one voice. In a swirl of pale blue fabric, a girl appeared, leaping onto the boulder at the cave's mouth, golden curls flowing down her back like a shimmering cape.

She wore better clothes than Susanna ever had. She was model-beautiful and happy as she leapt from rock to rock on bare feet. There was something familiar about her. I stared hard, waiting for the glimmer of memory to surface.

And then recognition came. She was Dorcas Pratt, several years older than when I'd last seen her two months ago.

Placing my hand in the flow, slowly so that I didn't startle her if she noticed, I tried to see how far I could cross. But the waterfall stopped me at my wrist again. I withdrew my hand, backed away, and sat down on the flat rock to wait and watch.

Dorcas tiptoed into the cave, sat on the low rock that served as a great bench, and kicked her legs before her, humming a soft tune.

I stared, rigid with fear. If there was one Pratt nearby, there might be two.

CHAPTER TWENTY-NINE

A SECOND BLOW

Morning was a good time to walk. The day was bright, the temperature mild.

Many traveled the Raleigh road this day. I remained among the trees, safe from prying eyes. The thick soles of my modern shoes made the walk easy.

It was mid-morning as I passed the turnoff to the farm where I was born and had lived until I was ten. My footsteps slowed, nerves fluttering. My brother's care for the property was evident. Fences had been mended. The lane had been cleared.

The sight of it made me pant with homesickness. What would my reception be if I visited?

Without reflecting on my decision, I turned onto the lane and reached the yard moments later. There was a stillness to the farm, as if it awaited something.

Caleb's wife appeared in the door, a basket in hand. The edge of her cap shaded her eyes. Otherwise, I suspect she would've seen me instantly.

She left the porch and made a turn toward the vegetable garden. With a whip of her head, she glanced my way and halted. Her smile held polite curiosity. "Hello?"

"Hello, Frances." My voice was gruff.

Recognition dawned in her widening eyes. Dropping the basket, she grabbed for the porch railing. "Susanna."

I nodded. "I did not drown."

Her free hand clamped to her forehead, and she shook her head, speechless.

A little girl came running to the door with cries of "Mama, Mama."

"Go, Mary," my sister-in-law choked out, and then immediately reversed herself. "No. Find Papa. He is in the barn."

My gaze hungrily followed the tiny girl—my niece Mary—across the short distance to the barn. She reminded me of Phoebe, dainty, lovely, graceful with innocence. Mary disappeared into the cavernous structure, strong and newly-built, more evidence of industry.

"How old is she?" I asked.

"Three." Caleb's wife wrapped her arms across her chest, as if protecting herself against a deep chill. "Why did you let us think you were dead?"

"I am free of the Pratts, Frances. I cannot go back there. I risk much to be here now."

"You are not free. For the rest of your life, you will always watch over your shoulder." She hung her head. "Why did you run away with release close at hand?"

"Do you know Jethro Pratt?"

She shuddered. "I do."

"He took pleasure in my pain, Frances." I reached out to her and she strained away. "He shackled my ankles and observed them sicken and bleed. If I had not left, I would have died."

"You cannot know that—"

"Hullo." There was a shout from the barn. My brother crossed the yard, holding his young daughter in his arms. Two boys stood in the entrance to the barn, watchful and silent.

"Do we have a visitor?" Caleb asked with a smile as his gaze fell on me. His good humor vanished, replaced by blazing eyes and twisted lips. He swung the girl down and barked, "Go inside. Now."

She blinked, lower lip trembling, and ran to do his bidding.

He stalked closer until he drew even with his wife. My brother registered no surprise at seeing me, although his fury was fearsome, the heat of it blistering across the space between us. "Where have you been for the last four years?"

"I live very far away."

"Where?"

"I cannot say."

"Can not—or *will* not?"

"In this case, they are the same."

Caleb sneered. "Has the boy married you?"

"He has not."

"Whore."

A vile word—*whore*. I staggered a step backwards from its impact. It had been hard to hear from Mr. Pratt—but to hear it from my brother?

Despair weakened my resolve. I watched Caleb silently, even as all the joy of visiting with my sister, of seeing my niece and nephews, drained away from me, leaving me debased.

Would contempt always be my lot in this world? If I were ever to return, if somehow my name were cleared, would I still always be *the whore who lived in sin with Mr. Lewis*? For Caleb to believe this of me scarred my heart as surely as my master's switches had scarred my limbs.

His wife placed a hand on his shoulder. "Caleb."

He shook her off and took a step closer to me. I stood my ground, not taking my gaze from him.

"What are you doing here, Susanna?"

"I have come to ask for the Bible."

He gaped, surprised at last. "Why?"

"I cannot marry Mr. Lewis without it."

"Do not mock me with your falsehoods. There is nothing to block a sacred union with him except unholy will." He snorted. "You dishonor our family. I shall not defile the Scriptures with your foul hands."

I studied him, this man who had teased me good-naturedly when we were children. Taught me how to fish and ride a horse. Tugged my braids and swung me around until I had laughed myself breathless. I did not recognize the man who frowned at me as if I were dung to be kicked aside—all because he believed something that was not true.

He lifted an arm and pointed toward the lane. "You are not welcome here. Leave and never return."

I gasped, shocked at the ferocious finality of what he was saying. "No. You cannot mean that."

"Get off my property before I tie you up and turn you over to the magistrate."

His demand fell like a second blow. "You would not do that."

"I would."

Frances clasped her hands together, as if in prayer, her gaze locked on her husband's face, but she said not a word.

"Caleb, please, do not send me away like this," I said, desperation making me beg. "Please let me have the Bible. I am lost without it."

"Stay a moment longer and you will be in jail before nightfall."

I ran, blinded by tears, feet pounding and stumbling. I didn't notice my surroundings until I'd reached Rocky Creek. Only then did reason reassert itself. I was close to the falls. Now was not the moment to lose my vigilance. For a few moments longer, I must not think on the sorrows of this day.

To avoid travelers on the well-worn trail, I paralleled the creek bank in the shelter of the trees. Progress was slow but detection unlikely.

The forest ended at a meadow of tall grasses edging the Pratt property. I paused, listening and watching for the presence of people.

Safety awaited me a hundred feet up the creek bed and through the falls. I darted onto the bank and into the shadow of the granite bluff, picking my way carefully across slippery boulders.

"Hello?" a girl's voice called.

Shock froze my limbs. Before me, in the cave behind the falls, the girl stood, bare feet peeking out below a pale gown with a muddy hem, with golden curls flowing freely to her waist.

"Susanna?"

"Dorcas!"

Her smile was warm and cheerful.

We approached and then halted, a few inches apart, grinning foolishly. There could be no surprise happier than my beloved Dorcas.

"You are not dead." She giggled. "I am overjoyed."

I breathed in the delight of her. "And you are most improperly groomed." I caught her in my arms and rested my chin atop her golden head.

It took long minutes to slake my thirst for the feel of her. When at last I stepped away, it was to study her carefully. "Let me see you."

She laughed and twirled slowly.

"Yes," I said. "You have grown into a fine young lady."

"And you look just the same."

"Thank you." I reached for her again. "This is an unexpected treat."

"I know." She sighed dramatically.

I laughed. "Why are you not surprised to find me here?"

Her smile vanished. "Papa does not believe you were swept away. He still comes here to look for you."

"My sweet Dorcas." I kept my smile in place, not willing for her to see how much this news shook me. But he wasn't here now. I wouldn't waste my precious moment with her on fear. It was a day for hugs. I relished the feel of her, the girl I had raised from a baby and loved as my own. "You are a rare beauty. I am so happy that we have met again. What brings you to this place on this day?"

"You spoke of a refuge once, when you were in jail. You did not say directly where it was." She gave me a pitying look. "You might as well have told me, for when I found this place, I knew instantly that you had loved it before me. It is my refuge too."

"A refuge from what?"

"Papa's wife. She was our servant after you." Her face grew thoughtful. "Papa ignored her when she first arrived, but she never ignored him. Especially after Mama died. Joan hoped to take her place, I think, and she succeeded." Dorcas beamed at me, eyes twinkling. "She wants me to call her 'Mother,' but I prefer 'ma'am.' It annoys her most dreadfully. It is a good thing she does not know that, in my refuge, she is merely Joan."

"I am glad you love this place of respite, as I do."

"Do you love it still? I never see you here."

I blinked at my own foolishness. Had I said too much? "I…"

"Do not worry. We can none of us determine how you vanished so completely from the other bank of Rocky Creek. Jedidiah once spoke of it as magic, for he could hear you speak but could not see where you were. But Papa quickly hushed him. Joan is most anxious that we do nothing to alarm the townsfolk, lest they think us mad. Therefore, we keep our ideas and questions to ourselves."

"Indeed. It is the best course of action." I wouldn't tell more and she wouldn't ask. It was an advisable way to enjoy our friendship. "Does the new Mrs. Pratt treat you well?"

"Oh, yes. She must. She is the same age as Deborah and not much older than I am. Papa could not tolerate for the three of us to have any unpleasantness." She bobbed her head. "He is most proud of my beauty and speaks of me with the same pride he uses with his favorite horses. No, indeed, Joan does not dare upset me. I should not get away from the house as often as I do if she had her way." Dorcas lowered her voice, as if to share a secret. "Joan enjoys our position in the town, although she does overlook an important truth. She married Papa a short while before my baby brother was born. I am sure the entire village has noticed."

I smothered a laugh. "But we shall not speak of such things."

"No. It is enough to think of them." She brightened. "How do you fare in your new home?"

"Quite well, thank you."

"And Mr. Lewis?"

"He is well, too." I smiled as I hurried to return the conversation to her. "Tell me about the rest of your family."

"Deborah has abandoned all thought of Jacob Worth. She is trying to catch the eye of one of Mr. Foster's sons instead." She frowned. "Papa has sold the mill to Solomon Worth."

"Indeed?"

"Oh, yes. Papa could not make the mill prosper. It was dreadful for a time." She gestured behind her. "Shall we sit in the cave and continue our chat? I have so much more to say."

"I cannot."

She nodded, smile still bright. "You will return. I shall write you letters."

Her confidence was charming and misguided. "I cannot give you an address, little one."

"I do not mind. I shall write them, and perhaps one day you will find them."

"Dorcas, I shall not—"

"I know what you plan to say, Susanna, but do not. They said you had drowned, but you are here. I have waited in this cave, hoping to see you, and you have come. I believe that, if I write letters, you will one day answer them, and we *shall* meet again."

"Do you think so?" Her words dredged a yearning from deep inside me. For two months, I had kept my need for Phoebe and Dorcas locked away. It made the risk of the visit worth the reward of their smiles. "Perhaps I shall receive those letters, if you leave them in the cave—"

"Dorcas," a harsh voice shouted. "Where are you?"

We looked up.

On the bluff high above us, a man appeared, leading a magnificent bay horse. It was Dorcas's father. My former master. As his gaze locked on mine, he seemed to expand, his cloak flapping around him like a bird of prey. "Susanna, stay."

At the sound of his command, my limbs became sluggish with dread and the remembered sense that doom would soon follow. It was as if the habit of obeying his voice had not relinquished its hold on my body.

In an instant, Mr. Pratt had dropped the reins and stormed toward the bluff's edge. "You will not escape me this time."

Dorcas stepped between me and the granite wall. "Susanna, run."

Her words urged me into action. I stumbled backwards and landed against the rock wall, my gaze never leaving Mr. Pratt's. He scrambled down the granite cliff, his laugh of imminent victory jolting through me with an electric shock that broke the spell over me.

I had to go. Now. With a mighty leap, I passed through the waterfall and two centuries. Once on the safety of Mark's rock, I spun around to view the world I'd left behind.

Mr. Pratt had just made it down the cliff and charged past Dorcas, knocking her aside. Her scream of agony mingled with his grunt of effort as he lunged for the falls. Once again, the falls sent him backward, flinging him against the mouth of the cave.

"Merciful heavens—Dorcas!" Every instinct urged me to return to her.

Before I could decide what to do, an arm clamped about my waist. I gasped and tried to twist away.

"No, you don't," Mark said, staring down at me with fierce eyes.

"Dorcas," I said, pushing at his arms. They didn't budge.

A sob echoed from the other side. I peered through the falls to see Dorcas lying on her side, clutching her ankle, her face contorted with pain. Mr. Pratt lurched closer to her.

"Let me go," I said, straining away from Mark, but it was too late. Whisper Falls had lost its sparkle, restoring itself to normal water.

"*No,*" I shrieked. What had happened to Dorcas? Would I ever know?

She had saved me again, and a veil had fallen across time before I could know the consequences.

My body ached from emotions it could hardly absorb. The joy of being with Phoebe and the despair of saying goodbye. The pleasure at meeting a new niece and the horror of my brother's rejection. The delight of Dorcas's sweet nature and the fear for the results of her courage. And, underpinning it all, anger that Mark and Whisper Falls had worked against me.

CHAPTER THIRTY

FAVORITE CURE

Relief ripped through me as Susanna jumped through the falls.

When I'd seen Jethro Pratt appear at the top of the bluff, it had nearly driven me crazy. I wanted to get to her, and the waterfall wouldn't let me. I'd had to stand there, fighting the urge to yell, silently begging her to run.

Once she reached on our side of the falls, I didn't even think. I grabbed her and hung on. Now that she was safe, not even wild relief would affect my hold.

"What happened to Dorcas?" she asked. "Tell me quickly."

I'd heard screams like that at sporting competitions, and they usually resulted in doctors running onto the field and stretchers taking the injured athlete to the hospital. "I don't know for sure, but it's not good."

"Is she hurt badly?"

"Yeah, I think so." I loosened my hold on Susanna's waist as waves of reaction rippled over me. "Pratt almost had you."

She peeled my hands away. "Please. Not now."

The three words were like a match to a bonfire. "Excuse me?"

She inhaled deeply. "I am not prepared to discuss this trip with you."

"Too bad, 'cause I plan to discuss it a lot." My arms ached to yank her back into them, to feel her solid and alive and safe. Instead, I ran my fingers through my hair to give my hands something to do. Anger was beginning to smother my relief. "Are you insane?"

"Indeed not," she said, her voice clipped and icy. "I was quite clear in what I wished to do, and I successfully completed that task." She circled around me and started up the path.

It took me four strides to catch up. "There's no way you can outrun me."

"I am not trying to outrun you. I am merely attempting to elude your voice."

Talk about pressing all my hot buttons. I'd never become so mad so fast at anyone in my entire life. "Where are you going?"

"To learn how history changed."

I grabbed her arm. "Stop. You're not going anywhere until you tell me what happened the last two days."

"I went home."

A thousand questions crowded into my brain. Where exactly had she gone? Was Phoebe's problem so awful that Susanna had been willing to risk capture? And why did she call the past her home? *Here* was home now.

But I'd wait to ask questions until I was less pissed off and might actually remember the answers. All I wanted to do at the moment was chew her ass out. "That was incredibly stupid."

"I am weary. Might this argument wait until later?"

"No. It'll take a long time to finish. No reason to postpone getting started."

She jerked her arm from my grasp and continued down the greenway. "I shall not speak with you when you are acting this way."

"Acting what way, Susanna? Like I'm justifiably horrified that you put your life in danger? That I'm freaked out by how much effort you put into hiding your plans? That you went all sexy on me to divert my attention?" My voice almost cracked over that last one. How long was it going to take me to get over *that*? "What about the way you've kept secrets from me?"

She stalked along, head high, ignoring me.

I kept up easily. "Do you remember the last time you screwed with history? That didn't turn out so well until I rescued you."

"Thank you for the reminder that, without you, I lack competence."

"Holy shit. That isn't what I meant and you know it." Some of the pedestrians stared at us as they walked past. Guess I'd better bring my voice back under control. "What makes you think that tampering with the past will work this time?"

"I had to try. My sister needed me."

"You can't race back there every time she has a little problem."

"This problem affects the entire course of her future."

"So will other problems. Life is full of decisions that have serious impacts. Just because Phoebe has someone living in the future to watch out for her doesn't mean she gets a free pass on bad stuff happening. She has to learn how to handle things." We'd reached the back gate to my yard. "You can't jump through Whisper Falls every time you feel the urge to mess with history. You're safe, but Dorcas is hurt and Jethro Pratt knows you're alive. What if there're long-term consequences? Why can't you admit that what you did was stupid?"

Susanna stared into space, jaw flexed. "I shall be most grateful when you have run out of words, for I have run out of interest in hearing them." She banged open the gate and strode purposefully across the lawn.

"Stop and look at me."

She spun around. "What else can you want?"

"Did you at least find Phoebe?"

"Yes." Her face softened. "She is well and happy."

"What were you trying to solve?"

"She will get a puncture wound in her thumb. They were going to amputate as a result."

"That's bad. I get it. But bad enough for you to risk arrest? Jail time? Being controlled by Pratt again?"

"She would've been unable to work. She would've lost a great talent—one that she loved. She would've been forced to accept marriage to someone who viewed her as a burden."

Okay, her sister's life would've been awful after that, but Phoebe wasn't exactly a wimp either. "She would've figured it out."

"She does not have to anymore."

Did Susanna feel any remorse at all? "Because you gave her antibiotics that you stole from my parents."

"I did," she said, averting her face. "I regret the necessity."

"It's against the law to give drugs written for one person to someone else."

"This crime will be hard to prosecute."

"Dammit, Susanna. It's not only against the law. If they're administered incorrectly, they can actually harm her." Her gaze narrowed on me, assessing the truth of what I said. That just upset me more. "It looks like you may have given your sister different types of pills. Not cool. Antibiotics aren't interchangeable. You could make her sicker."

Her chin lifted. "You're saying that to frighten me."

"I hope it does, because I'm not making this up."

She turned her back on me. "Must I listen to this now?"

"You scared me shitless, Susanna."

"I apologize, Mark. I'm sorry that I frightened you, your parents, perhaps even the cat. May I go?"

Hands on hips, I closed my eyes and gritted my teeth against a stream of expletives.

The security system beeped.

She went inside? Really? I looked up in time to see the door swing shut.

By the time I caught up with her again, she was in the apartment, yanking pins from her hair.

She looked at me over her shoulder. "I would prefer my privacy."

"No."

"Should you not be in school?" She pulled out the last of the pins. Her braid swung free.

"I would've been worthless not knowing if you were okay."

Her shoulders slumped. When she spoke, the words ached with something soft and sad. "I had to take the risk, Mark. I could not enjoy this life while knowing Phoebe lived in misery."

I crossed the room, ready to do...I didn't even know what. I wanted to yell and argue and shake her and kiss her and never let her go. I hauled her into my arms, clinging to her like she was a lifeline. "Don't ever do that again."

"I didn't mean to frighten you." She nuzzled against me, her arms locking about my waist. "I shall not do that to you again."

"Waiting was like a living hell." What if she had never come back? I pressed kisses all over her face, every square inch of skin, eager for the taste and feel of her. When our lips touched, it was like an explosion of hunger. We had to break the kiss to breathe.

"I'm sorry that you suffered." She sighed, her breath warm against my neck. "I have suffered too. Today I said goodbye forever to my sister. I lay beside her all night and barely slept, knowing what the morning would bring."

"You said goodbye to her the day she was indentured."

"I said goodbye with a heart full of hope that I might see her again someday. I do not have that hope any longer."

It hurt to hear the pain and yearning in her voice. The twenty-first century was so much better than the nineteenth, but damn, she'd given up her family. Yet as awful as that must be, she couldn't have stayed there, or Pratt would've killed her. Which was why she should never go anywhere near him again.

"Okay, Susanna," I said, pressing a kiss to her brow. "Done." The whole scene had left me drained. I disagreed with her decision. She'd risked too much, and it hadn't been a bad enough problem. Nothing either of us said to the other was going to change our opinions. "Let's take care of you now. When was the last time you ate?"

"At dawn."

"Do you want to take a shower?"

"Are you telling me that I need to?" Her lips twitched. "Yes, I wish to be clean."

I untangled our arms and turned toward the door. "I'll fix you something to eat. Come down when you're ready."

It took all of ten minutes to cut up an apple and zap some soup in the microwave. I had the table set for two when she arrived.

She ate in her efficient way, as if she expected to be ordered away from the food at any moment. Only when she'd set her spoon down and folded her hands in her lap did she look at me. "I went to see my brother and his wife."

"You what?" I understood the thing about Phoebe, but there was more? Totally confused. "Which brother are we talking about?"

"Caleb. He inherited the farm at my mother's passing."

She had her calm face on, but her voice was toneless in a scary way. "How'd it go?"

"It was most uncomfortable." She rose.

"Why did you do that?" I got up too.

"I wanted to see him and his children. I asked for the family Bible."

"Did he give it to you?" I hadn't seen her carrying anything that big.

"He did not." She left the kitchen and wandered into the family room.

Weird. Susanna paced around, her hand drifting restlessly over furniture. Stopping at a bookshelf, she scowled at some books and then crossed to the farthest corner and plopped down on a low, padded bench.

It was dark over there. In her neck-to-ankle brown outfit, she nearly blended into the background. I flicked on the lights.

"No, Mark. Please."

The lights went out again. I stared at her rigid body across the room, arms on knees, head bowed. I finally got it. She hadn't just been rescuing Phoebe. She'd been trying to rescue herself—from my world and its crazy-ass rules.

Didn't she realize that we couldn't use their Bible here? Nobody would believe it. Maybe I should tell her about my plan to create her identity and set her mind at ease. "It's okay he didn't give you the Bible. We'll work something out."

When she shook her head, her braid slid off her back and across her shoulder until it hung between her knees. She left it there, either not noticing or not caring.

"What are you leaving out, Susanna?"

"I'm forbidden to return to my brother's home." She hunched there, still as a statue.

I crossed the room and sat beside her. "Hey, babe. It's okay. You're never going back anyway."

"Perhaps not," she said, her voice rasping. "Yet it does pain me to learn of his contempt."

"Why does he feel that way?"

Her head dropped even lower, denying me an answer.

I got along fine with Marissa, and from what Susanna had said previously I had never detected hostility to her brothers. They hadn't intervened in how the Pratts treated her, but distance and society probably contributed more to that attitude than lack of sibling emotion.

What had happened to cause her brother to bar her from the place where she was born? "Is he mad that you ran away from Pratt?"

"My brother loathes Mr. Pratt. It enraged Caleb when our stepfather bound me to that family." She pushed up until she could press herself against the wall, ramrod straight. "I suspect that he has felt a small measure of shame from my decision, but it is certainly eased by the pleasure of seeing the Pratts humiliated."

So if it wasn't the fact that she ran away, what else could it be? He didn't know anything about her life now.

Damn. There was one thing Caleb knew. "He's pissed because you're living with me."

She didn't answer, but I knew I was right. Of course, I was. Everyone from her past would condemn the choice they thought she'd made. If they only knew. "I'm sick of this conversation too." I stood and held out my hand. "Come on. Let's sit on the couch and hold hands and stop talking."

"An excellent idea," she said, slipping her hand into mine.

"Mark."

There was an annoying voice trying to interrupt my dream, and an annoying hand shaking my shoulder hard.

"Mark," Mom said in a loud whisper.

I didn't want to wake up. After a night of no sleep, a nap now was highly desirable.

"How is Susanna?"

Since ignoring my mom wasn't working, I opened my eyes and looked around. I was still in the family room, slumped on one end of the couch with a sleeping Susanna stretched out beside me, her feet in my lap.

I rolled my head until Mom's face came into view, where she knelt at the couch's end. "She's fine," I whispered back.

"Where was she last night?"

I swallowed words of impatience. After all, my parents had been worried too. "She went to search for her sister."

"Did she find her?"

The less my mom knew about this situation, the better off everyone would be. "Susanna spent the night with Phoebe."

"I thought the girl was in a safe place."

"She is. Susanna needed reassurance." I wiggled some on the couch cushion. My butt felt a little numb. "She took Bacitracin with her. The people Phoebe lives with are not into modern medicine." The stolen antibiotics would have to remain a secret that I hoped my mom never uncovered.

"Was Susanna ever in danger?"

"Not really." I had to defuse this. I wanted my parents to get past Susanna's absence fast. "She got to speak briefly with her favorite young friend. That went well too."

"You made it sound like a bigger deal last night than you are now."

"I guess I overreacted." Damn. How did I get those words out with a straight face? "I forget sometimes how strong she is."

"True." Mom patted my hand and stood. "I'll make dinner."

I watched my mother walk away to prepare her favorite cure for any problem. If we were lucky, the cure would include mashed potatoes.

"I was not in danger, Mark. I am fine."

I looked toward the other end of the couch. Susanna watched me solemnly. "Something bad almost happened."

"But it did not."

"The next time, you might get caught."

"I shall not go back."

"You might."

She shook her head emphatically. "I shall commit more deeply to adjusting to your world. I should like to start by learning how to ride a bike."

"Really?" I frowned. Where had that idea come from? "I thought you were afraid of them."

"I prefer the word *wary*."

"So what's changed?"

"I need to get over myself."

I smiled. "You've been listening to me talk to my sister."

"Indeed, since those conversations generally occur with me sitting next to you."

My smile faded as my brain raced through the possible reasons for her sudden interest. The first one that came to mind might piss her off if I asked it, but I had to anyway. "Are you trying to cut how long it takes to get from the waterfall to Old Raleigh?"

"I shall not go back. My request is about this world. I want independence."

"Okay." That was a good reason. I should be happy about it, shouldn't I? Why then did it make me uneasy?

"There is another reason." She sat up and reached for my hand with a shy smile. "You spend a lot of time on your bike. When I learn how to bike, I could go with you."

I kissed the back of her hand. "I'm all over that."

CHAPTER THIRTY-ONE

UNNECESSARY CAUTION

Mark's parents barely alluded to my overnight absence during supper, other than to say they were glad to see me safely home. I didn't expect Mark to share the details of my experience, but the intensity of the silence surprised me.

Mark left in the truck after supper, to seek out friends who could tell him what he'd missed this day.

Bruce retired, as always, to his study to "catch up."

Sherri and I carried plates to the sink.

"Let me do the dishes," I said.

"No, dear, I'll take care of it. You've had a hard day." She opened the dishwasher and added the plates. "Before you go, though, I have a couple of things I'd like to know."

"Certainly." I waited by the island.

She finished loading the dishwasher, closed the door, and then leaned against the counter. "How long had you been planning this trip?"

"Two weeks."

Her brow creased. She dropped her gaze to her feet, as if the tips of her shoes held answers she needed. "Why did you work so hard to hide what you were doing?"

"Mark would've fought my decision. I chose to delay this disagreement until my return."

"Maybe we could have all gone with you."

"I didn't want you with me."

"Wow, Susanna."

I kept my gaze steady. "I will not satisfy your curiosity further. Please drop this."

"It's more than curiosity." Her face flushed. "Why won't you tell us where these people are? They should be brought to justice."

"You have looked for them before. You have pressed me on this issue many times. Yet I have never cooperated." Tension rose within me. I took a deep breath to calm myself. "There were only two truly bad men, and their authority was diminished when I left. The others in the village are good, ordinary people. I shall do nothing to disrupt or confuse their peace."

She pushed away from the counter and stepped closer to me, genuine distress in her demeanor. "They must not live all that far away if you got there and back this quickly."

"Please, Sherri. This subject must remain forever closed."

"Why do you resist our help?"

"Because I do not require any." How could I make her understand? We had been warming to each other of late, and I was sorry my absence had altered that. But I wouldn't apologize for my choice. "My sister leads a life of contentment. The bad men cannot hurt her. You must trust me on the matter."

"Did you see the man you used to call master?"

I drank in another breath before responding, for the thought of him was never without discomfort. "I did indeed see Mr. Pratt. It was unpleasant, but as you can see, I am here and unharmed. He has no power over me."

"Fine." She grabbed a pot from the stove, walked to the sink, and flipped on the faucet.

Taking her actions as dismissal, I returned to the apartment, alone with Toby and the journals, finally ready to discover how history had changed.

If Phoebe had taken my advice, had the treatment worked? Could Mark be correct that the mix of pills might have made her more ill?

I sat in my chair, hands folded, eyes closed. I did not make things worse. I was certain of this. I had no need to sit here nervously.

Enough. It was time. I opened the laptop and went to the folder marked "Archives." There were three journals present. Not two.

An ember of joy burned in my belly. Phoebe had written an additional journal because she could use her hand. Because she had more to say.

I opened the second journal and went directly to the end—to see how the story had altered—and browsed through the pages until the week of the birthday ball.

September 29th, 1800

I received the most glorious surprise yesterday. As I walked from the house to the kitchen, I caught a glimpse of a person, standing on the lane. It was Susanna.

The sight of my sister froze my limbs and my thoughts, even my breath.

She wore a most unappealing gown and shoes more ugly than a laborer's boots. Her body and face had rounded from too much good food. Yet it was my sister. I would have known her anywhere.

Was she saying that I had grown fat? It was true that the supply of food here was endless, even decadent. I could eat my fill, but had I become noticeably rounded?

Perhaps I should ask Mark, although he would be unlikely to agree if he were wise.

I had been told Susanna was dead. Yet she had not been swept away. She stood before me, strong and well.

The night was not long enough. I know I dozed at times, but I could not sleep deeply for fear that she might slip away.

The morning came too quickly, but for a time it felt as if we were little girls again. We braided each other's hair and talked quietly and then went our separate ways.

Phoebe didn't mention the medicine. Had she forgotten already?

I went to the next page, eyes hot with the need to know more.

September 30th, 1800
My hand trembles to hold the quill, but I am anxious to record my thoughts while they are still fresh.

Mid-evening, I was pulled from my duties serving food at the ball and ordered back to the kitchen...

This entry, from the night of the ball, was identical. I couldn't tell that a single word had changed.

October 1st, 1800
Two days have passed and still my finger aches. It is swollen and hot.

Mrs. Eton is worried. She has plied me with a potent tea. It tastes so foul that surely it will work.

My sister brought me medicine but it is too soon. I should take it only for a fearsome injury like she described. The hole in my thumb is no longer visible.

I shall wait a little longer.

Still, the pain makes my hand shake. I can perform no delicate work until this affliction has passed.

I ignored the flutters of anxiety over her unnecessary caution. There was a new journal. Something *had* changed.

October 9th, 1800

It has been a week since I last wrote and yet much has happened. Indeed, a week ago I wondered if I would ever write again.

I have my dear sister to thank.

For many days after the ball, the pain from the needle prick would not let my finger go. I dabbed on a bit of the ointment each night and hoped it would be enough.

Late one evening, as I left the dining room with a tray of soiled dishes, my mistress beckoned to me from the doorway of the family parlor. I obeyed but with reluctance.

She asked to study my thumb, expressing great concern over my discomfort and that their efforts to heal my thumb had yet to succeed.

She called to her son, who joined us in the hall. "A nasty infection has taken hold of Phoebe's thumb. We must do something before it is too late."

Mr. William took my hand in his, casually at first. Then his attention sharpened. He laid a probing finger on the joints of my thumb. I could not contain my hiss. He commented that the pain must be severe.

I agreed in a voice so hoarse that I hardly recognized it.

He closed the parlor door behind him, shielding the three of us from curious eyes. When his mother asked him what he had learned in college about such afflictions, he nearly smiled as he said "blood-letting."

She snorted in contempt. I would not receive that treatment.

Drawing me closer to a candle, she pressed her fingers gently yet firmly to my wrist and asked her son if he had ever performed an amputation.

I gasped in horror and tried to pull my hand away.

Mr. William nodded and then took over the scrutiny of my hand, turning it this way and that. With a sigh, he agreed with her assessment.

Mrs. Eton declared her intention to "consult my book."

We all knew what that meant. Mrs. Eton's mother had been a noted healer. Her recipes and wisdom had been written into a secret book—a volume that was the envy of doctors and healers throughout the Carolinas.

She summoned the housekeeper, who had been standing in the shadows nearby. "Mrs. Jasper, ask Cook to boil a measure of vinegar with rosemary and lavender. Dip a bandage in the brew and wrap Phoebe's finger while it is still as hot as she can stand. William and I shall assess her again in the morning, when the light is better." She slipped cool fingers under my chin and observed me solemnly. "We shall do our best to save your hand, but you must be brave."

Mrs. Jasper walked to the kitchen to consult with Cook while I hurried up the stairs to my bedchamber.

No longer questioning the seriousness of this injury, I fetched one of the pills. It had an acrid taste, but I swallowed it down.

As Susanna instructed, I took another pill first thing in the morning and coated my finger with her ointment.

223

When I reported for chores to Mrs. Jasper, she ordered me back to Cook's office in the kitchen building.

Mrs. Eton and Mr. William arrived shortly thereafter, unsmiling and quiet. She carried a basket with jars and bandages. He carried a locked wooden box. The sight of it made my heart lurch.

With exquisite gentleness, he scrutinized my thumb and palm, and then gently turned my hand over. The furrows in his brow deepened as he repeated his study. Silently, he released my hand and took a step back.

My mistress began to unpack her basket, but then she hesitated. With a bewildered frown, she too examined my hand and then asked what I had done. I shook my head, not understanding the intent of her question.

She touched her cool fingers to my forehead and announced that the infection had lightened in such a dramatic way as she had never beheld. She demanded to know if I had tried a special remedy.

I did not care to lie, but neither could I share the entire truth. So I confessed to using Susie's ointment. Mrs. Eton asked me to fetch it. I ran to my room and found the glass jar, and ran down again. When I handed the jar to Mrs. Eton, she removed the lid and sniffed carefully. She rubbed the ointment between her fingers and then scowled.

After suggesting it might be wise to postpone drastic measures for another day or two, my mistress dressed the wound with fresh bandages, deliberately ignored Susanna's ointment, and used a paste she had brought. It had an earthy smell, as if it transported us to a bed of leaves in the darkest forest. It was not unpleasant.

"I shall check again tomorrow. Mrs. Jasper, give her no assignments that would bump her finger or stain the bandage." When she rose, she took my ointment with her.

Once they had left, I smiled to myself, confident in the knowledge that the improvements would continue. My hand—indeed, my life—had been saved.

And there the entry ended. My sister would thrive. I had done my duty.

There were regrets, naturally. Given the harsh words I'd exchanged with Sherri, my relationship with Mark's parents might suffer. I had left my brother in anger, and I had weakened Mark's trust.

Yet Phoebe had good options now. I had made the right choice.

After shutting off the computer I rose, walked to the bay window, and watched the night descend.

CHAPTER THIRTY-TWO

TWO LAYERS OF HEAVEN

Progress on the birth certificate project faltered Friday. I took my phone with me to the third-floor rec room and spent a couple of hours after school surfing the web and making calls.

The people who answered phones at judges' offices were more suspicious than I'd expected. In my case, they had a right to be, but they got there way quicker than I wanted.

However, I did get one cool piece of data in the small number of questions I managed before people hung up on me. A court order didn't have to come from a Wake County judge for the birth certificate to come from Wake County. It could come from anywhere.

My grandparents lived in a different county. Chatham was small, both in area and population. Gran and Granddad had lived there longer than I'd been alive. They went to church and belonged to clubs. Maybe they knew a judge who was dumb or manageable.

It was worth a try. I called the lake house.

Granddad picked up. "What?"

"Do you know any judges?"

There was a pause. "The kind you find in courthouses?"

Not sure what other kinds there were, but no use in pissing him off when I needed something from him. "Yeah, the courthouse kind."

"I do. What have you done?"

I suppressed a laugh. That sounded like something he should be asking Marissa, not me. "I need one for Susanna."

"Why?"

"A judge can issue a court order to file a birth certificate."

There was a long pause. When he spoke, he sounded serious. "Judge Preston Tew. Good guy. Been in office a long time. Gets re-elected because he's conservative and fair. I know him slightly." He grunted. "Are we trying to slip something past him?"

"Yeah, Granddad. Susanna doesn't have any of the documents the government wants, and she has no way to get them. We'll have to fake everything."

"Let me do some research on this and see how complicated it gets. Give me a few days."

"Okay. And Granddad?"

"What?"

"I haven't said anything to Susanna about this. She won't like the idea—"

"If everything works out, it'll be harder for her to refuse."

"Exactly."

"Got it." *Click*.

I blew out a sigh of relief. Now that I had my grandfather helping, this problem might get solved.

"What will I not like?" Susanna spoke from behind me.

Crap. I hadn't heard her walk up to the rec room. I swung around from the computer, mentally sifting through a few convenient lies. "Going to the mall."

Her eyes narrowed. "Indeed, I would not. Your grandfather knows this to be true."

"We thought you might make an exception." Damn, that sounded lame.

"Why?"

What might get Susanna to a mall? Food, maybe. "They have a seriously good burger place."

Her eyes gleamed. "Can you not bring it home to me in bags?"

"Sure." Here I was deceiving her, when just yesterday she'd deceived me. Of course, mine was small in comparison to hers. Crap, I didn't want to think about this too hard. Time to change the topic. "Why'd you come up here?"

Her expression dimmed. "I need your help to locate information on the web."

"Sure." I brought up a browser and my favorite search engine. "What are you looking for?"

"Dorcas Pratt."

I swallowed hard as I tried my first search string. "You want to find out what happened to her?"

"Yes." She drew a chair next to me.

There was nothing. Everything I could think of came back with nothing. She wasn't online, at least not as Dorcas Pratt. "What year was she born?"

"1787."

No good. I searched from 1800 on, looking for a Dorcas Anything in North Carolina. Shaking my head, I turned to her. "Sorry."

Her face was white. "Can you find information on Jethro Pratt?"

I stared at her. Hard. "Why him?"

She sat in her chair, straight and stiff, hands clenched in her lap. "When I saw him yesterday, Mr. Pratt was dressed in the garments of a prosperous man. He rode a magnificent stallion. He could afford neither four years ago."

My fingers flew over the keyboard. It didn't take long to get a hit on Jethro Pratt. "He bought and sold horses."

"Indeed? Mr. Pratt's brother gave him a new brood mare and a slave skilled with horses before I left. He must have learned this business quickly." She stood and turned to go. "Thank you."

"Susanna?" I popped out of the chair and caught up to her. "I'll keep looking for Dorcas."

"I shall too," she said as she descended the stairs. "I must know."

Susanna had been unusually quiet in the two days since she'd returned from the past. It was probably lingering sadness about saying goodbye to her sister. Or worry over Dorcas. Or maybe guilt at what she'd done. I didn't push it.

However, I would've expected *today* to be different. It was October first, her eighteenth birthday, but she hadn't said a thing about it.

No way had she forgotten. Since the age of ten this day had represented the end of her indenture. The day she would gain her freedom. Why had she said nothing?

I headed out after breakfast to pick up her present.

She wasn't in her room when I got home, but it didn't take me long to find her in Mom's garden on the bench, a vivid splash of red against the green of the bushes. I couldn't see her face clearly from the house, yet she seemed so sad, hunched over the way she was.

I joined her. "How has your day gone?"

"I have read about the American War Between the States. I would've preferred not to know that it ever happened." She struggled to smile. "Have you trained this morning?"

"Sure did." I'd gotten it out of the way early, because the rest of the day would be devoted to whatever she wanted. I stood and held out my hand. "I'm going in. Do you want to come?"

She gave a tiny shake of her head. "I shall stay here a while longer."

"It's almost lunchtime. Don't be late."

When I reentered the house, I could hear my parents in the formal dining room, laughing. When I tracked them in there, I saw why.

"Hi," Mom said, smiling from ear to ear. "What do you think?"

It was a little girl's wonderland. Pink and silver crepe paper draped in swags from the four corners of the room to the chandelier. There was a pink tablecloth, pink paper products, and a sequined tiara waiting in front of a chair wreathed in silver balloons.

In the middle of the table rested a Chocolate Dream Cake—two layers of heaven iced with creamy fudge—and four greasy bags from Olde Tyme Grill that smelled strongly of beef and fried potatoes.

I didn't know whether to groan or kiss them. "Wow, Mom, it's perfect. How did you know?"

"Last week, when I asked Susanna what a birthday was like where she came from, she said it was *just another day*. That wasn't all right with me."

I lifted my mom in a bear hug. "Thanks."

She laughed, her dangling feet thumping against my shins. "Okay, son. Love you too. Now put me down."

The security system chirped.

We all turned and looked expectantly toward the hallway.

"Susanna?" I called.

There was a hesitation. "Yes?"

"We're in the dining room."

Footsteps drew closer. "Am I needed?" She stopped in the arched entrance, her gaze flying about the room. First to the cake and the candles—and then to the decorations.

"Happy birthday, Susanna," my mother sang out.

We all applauded.

Her face remained neutral as she stared at the heart-shaped balloons floating from the chandelier. "What are those?"

"We call them balloons. They're painted…bags filled with air, so they'll float." I laughed at her expression of bewildered wonder. "The only reason to have them is because they're pretty."

"They are indeed." Her gaze went next to the fast food bags, eyes shining. "Cheeseburgers?"

"And French fries," Dad said.

The smile she directed at my father was achingly sweet. "Fried food? That is quite a concession."

"My birthday gift to you."

"I am most grateful." She smiled shyly at Mom. "Sherri, it is lovely."

Mom leaned over the table, busily straightening the paper plates. "Every girl needs a princess party at least once in her life."

Dad pulled out the seat of honor for her. "Here you are, miss."

I sat beside her and reached for her hand under the table. She linked our hands tightly, only releasing mine when it became necessary to eat.

The shy smile widened as the meal progressed.

When we were halfway done eating our lunch, my mom patted Susanna's wrist. "I found a job for you. At the hospice center where I work, they're holding a fundraiser. I showed the director a sample of your handwriting. He wants you to address the invitations."

Susanna put down her burger carefully. "How many guests?"

"Two hundred."

"How much time will I have?"

"I get the invitations Monday. You'll need to turn them in by Friday."

"I would be happy to accept this job." Her body seemed to hum with joy.

Mom smiled. "I told him yes already."

Susanna smiled back. "Thank you."

She didn't say much for the rest of the meal, but she did laugh and send me glances that made me wish we didn't have an audience.

Finally, we sang "Happy Birthday" to Susanna, while Mom lit the candles on the cake and pushed it toward Susanna.

She looked at me, confused. "What kind of candles are these? They are tiny."

"We call them birthday candles. There are eighteen of them, one for each year of your life."

"Candles that only decorate a cake?" At our nods, she stared at the dancing flames with awe. "What am I to do?"

"Make a wish and blow them out," Mom said.

"A wish?"

"Yes, ask for anything you want, but don't tell us or it won't come true."

Susanna shook her head. "There is no need to make a wish. I could never imagine anything better than this party you've given me today." She blew out the candles and stared at the cake as if memorizing the sight of it.

After dessert, my mother handed her a box wrapped in pink paper. "Here's your present."

Susanna tore into it like a little kid, lifted the tissue paper, and drew out a T-shirt. It had blue and white stripes and sleeves that would hardly reach her elbows. Beneath it lay a second T-shirt in a solid peachy color with longer sleeves.

I watched her reaction. So far, Susanna had resisted all attempts to expose much skin. Had my mom found a good compromise? Would Susanna ever wear the one that showed her bare forearms, especially when her burn scar would be visible?

Susanna laid the first T-shirt back in the box and caressed it. "It's as soft as silk. It will feel wondrous."

My mother smiled hard. She was totally proud of herself. "Then you like them?"

"Sherri, I shall treasure them always."

Time for my surprise. "I have your gift in the garage. Come on." I led her to the garage door, opened it, and then stepped aside.

Susanna's gaze zeroed in on the present. Of course, how could she have missed it? It was waiting in an empty car stall, tied with a big shiny bow.

"You bought me a bike?"

"Yeah." I felt a sudden nervousness. It had taken more of my savings than I'd planned for. Would she like it? Was it too much? "Take a closer look."

Mom and Dad watched over my shoulder as she approached the bike and wrapped her fingers around a handlebar.

She cleared her throat. "Such a happy color, Mark. Red as cherries."

I hated her ability to hide behind that smooth mask. "What do you think?"

She stared at me, eyes begging for something. Why couldn't I understand? My smile faltered. "What's wrong?"

"Nothing. It's the most beautiful gift I have ever received." Her voice quivered, not at all calm like her expression. "I *adore* it."

My parents backed out of the garage. The door clicked shut.

"Hey." I pulled her into my arms. "Why are you upset?"

"You give me so much. I have nothing to give back."

No point in shrugging that off. I'd probably feel the same way. "This is your birthday. My turn comes in December."

"I cannot give you a bike."

"Already have one." I kissed her. "Mom got you a job. If they like your work, who knows? Maybe you'll get more. Life isn't going to be boring forever."

"I hope you are correct."

"Always." When she laughed, I reached behind her and punched the button to open the garage. "Let's take it out for a ride."

"Now?"

"Sure." I picked up her new helmet. "Here you go."

I made her roll the bike to the street. When we were on a flat surface, I said, "Bike safety, first and foremost."

"Yes." She watched with intensity.

"No gear, no riding."

"I shall always wear my helmet."

"Okay, here are the brakes. They stop the bike. Go ahead and squeeze."

Her hands gripped like she was trying to bend steel.

"Not that hard. Squeeze gently. They'll respond."

She practiced, and with each try she got better.

"Good. It's time to try. I'll hold onto the bike while you ride."

Her breathing sped up, although her face remained calm. I could feel the fear rolling off of her. It made me proud. She wasn't going to give up even though she was scared to death. "Climb on the seat."

"Like a saddle."

"Right, and the pedals are like stirrups."

She did everything I asked, her brow scrunched in concentration. Both feet found their pedals after several tries.

The bike wobbled. One of her feet went down to the pavement. She panted, mouth open.

"Do you trust me, Susanna?"

"Yes." A small, squeaky sound.

"I won't let you fall."

She gave a jerky nod and put her foot back on the pedal.

"Now close your eyes." Her gaze slid sideways to mine. "I have you. I'll move the bike around. Concentrate on the feel."

"Of the seat?" Her voice was tight.

"Yep, and the pumping of your legs."

We stopped after her first loop around the cul-de-sac. "What do you think?"

"Good." She frowned at her feet. "It is a bit difficult to pump my legs."

"It's the skirt. Pants make it easier."

She exhaled noisily. "I shall make do."

"But it would be easier—"

"Hush." She gripped the handlebars, snapped her eyes shut, and nodded at me impatiently.

We completed two more loops of the cul-de-sac. "Better?"

"Yes." A hesitant smile appeared. "This is lovely."

"Okay, let's do it with your eyes open now."

We'd made it halfway around the loop when she said, "It's harder with my eyes open."

"Unfortunately, it's a requirement to ride the bike."

She laughed.

"Let's get bold. Turn the handlebar to your left."

She turned it sharply. The bike jerked, and she went tumbling sideways. I caught her by the waist, holding her free of the bike as it fell. She locked her arms around my neck and banged her helmeted head against my shoulder.

I bit back a curse, eased her into a more comfortable position and said in a calm tone, "You're good. You didn't fall."

"Did I break the bike?"

So that was the real problem. "No. Mountain bikes are designed to take a lot of abuse."

She tensed at the word *abuse*. Damn, I needed to watch what I said.

I lowered her until she supported her own weight, but I didn't let go. I loved the feel of Susanna's body. She still had the strength of her previous life, but weeks in our century had allowed her to fill out a bit, particularly in the places that I appreciated most.

She watched me anxiously. "Is something wrong?"

"Not at all. I like it when you make mistakes."

"And why is that?"

"Then I get to save you. It means I get to touch you anywhere I want, and it's all in the name of safety."

She smiled. "You've never shown a reluctance to touch me."

"Yeah, but now I have an excuse to go public." I dropped a kiss on her mouth, and I liked that one so much I dropped another one, deepening it when her lips moved beneath mine.

She broke it off. "Mark," she said with a laugh, her cheeks turning red. She glanced around the street. "We are in view of your neighbors."

"They've seen people kiss before." I gave her one more, just to prove my point, and bent over to pick up the bike. "Back on. We're trying that again, but this time *barely* turn the handlebars."

It didn't take her long to catch on. She did great, crowing at her own success. As her instructor, I was prepared to take the next big step. "This time around, I'm letting go."

She jammed the brakes and almost went flying off the bike.

"Susanna," I said as patiently as if she were a child. "Watch that, okay? Gently squeeze."

"I'm not ready for you to let go."

"Yes, you are." It wasn't unusual to hear her say that. She was overly cautious about a lot of things. But on this issue, I was the expert, and I knew she was ready. "You can do this."

"Perhaps we should end today's lesson."

"Not until you've ridden by yourself."

"I am weary."

I shook my head and held the bike steady.

She put her feet on the pedals and exhaled with attitude.

"I promise you, Susanna, this will work. You'll go slowly. I'll drop one hand and then the other. You won't even know."

"I'll know," she said through clenched teeth.

We took off, faster than I anticipated but I wasn't going to rock the boat at this point. I dropped my lead hand first and then the other.

She wobbled, corrected, laughed, and pedaled away. Two laps later, she turned to look at me. "I'm doing it."

Shit. She was paying attention to me, not the road. "Susanna," I yelled.

Too late. She ran into the curb and sailed into the yard in a heap of body and machine.

I took off at a flat run to where she lay motionless in the grass and flung myself down. "Susanna, are you okay?"

Her eyes fluttered open and she smiled. "Biking is delightful." She sat up and dusted off her skirt. "I shall enjoy doing this with you."

CHAPTER THIRTY-THREE

BROKE THE CHAINS

My birthday had been wondrous beyond measure. The day that should have meant my release from servitude had become a day of pure joy.

I didn't want it to end.

After my bike lesson and a pizza supper, Mark took me to see a Disney film at an old, nearly-empty theater. He picked this movie, he'd claimed, especially since I was having a princess birthday.

It was a peculiar tale. A common house servant, who wished to be a princess, traveled to a ball inside a pumpkin, which thankfully had been cleaned of its seeds and slime. Inexplicably, she wore glass slippers. Did she not worry they might break and shred her feet? Perhaps so, for she left one of them behind at the ball. Still, she did marry her prince. A charming ending, if not realistic.

We were silent on the ride home. Mark walked me to the apartment and hesitated on the landing outside my door. "It's late. I guess I'll see you tomorrow."

"Please stay."

"Are you sure? It's been a long day."

"Please."

"You're the birthday girl. Whatever you want." He followed me in.

I stood in the middle of the room with my back to him, not sure what should happen next. Would he misinterpret why I had asked him to stay?

Why *had* I?

There was a simple answer, of course. I wanted him to know how happy I was—how much this birthday meant to me. I didn't want our special date to end.

Perhaps we could talk. We could sit on the couch and speak of many things.

We could discuss the film.

No, perhaps not.

I could thank him again for my bike. It was lovely, sturdy, able to withstand...*abuse.*

I hated that word. Truly hated it.

It might be best to sit down and let Mark choose the subject. Yes, that was what we should do.

But first, I must clean. We could not enjoy a pleasant conversation with the apartment in such disarray. It demanded immediate attention.

I plumped up the cushions on the couch and shut the door to the closet. I folded the washcloth on the counter. Then I crossed to the table, closed the open lid of the laptop, and straightened the stack of books.

"Hey. What's going on?" His voice was directly behind me.

When I turned to face him, he was a bare few inches away, reaching for me. My breath quickened painfully. I tried for calm.

I wanted this day to be the beginning of *more*, but I didn't know how. My past had trained me too well.

Mark had once told me that he controlled the possibilities, and I controlled the limits. Yet I had set prudish boundaries, and yearned now to ease them.

Raising my hands, I placed them on his shoulders and gazed anxiously into his face. I wanted more for us. The way I felt about him was not dishonorable. I wanted to be brave.

Mark was tall and strong. His body blocked the light. He seemed to surround me. I edged backward until the table prevented my escape.

There had been another moment like this, not very long ago, when I'd been trapped between a table and a strong man—a man who had been intent on hurting me. He'd locked my wrists behind my back. I had been helpless.

No. I must stop thinking about that. Mark would not hurt me. There was nothing to fear. I had invited him in. I wanted him to touch me.

His hand gripped my waist. Memories of that other day flooded through me.

Panting breaths. Hard hands. The smell of sweat and purpose.

Revulsion crashed in my brain, overwhelming in its power. I strained away from the shame and clawed at those vile groping fingers.

"Susanna, what's wrong?"

The question seemed to come to me from a distance. My chest heaved with the effort to draw in air. "My master…"

I didn't want to remember but the memories wouldn't stop. The rip of my shift. The smirk as he gazed at me. "Please let me go."

"Okay, Susanna." His warmth left along with his hand. "I won't touch you. I promise."

Breathing through my open mouth, I squeezed my eyes shut in a vain attempt to hide from the images of that horrific moment three months ago.

"Whatever you want, Susanna. You're in control…"

I forced my mouth to close. I was in control.

"Tell me what you want me to do…"

I had choices. My fingers uncurled from the fists I couldn't recall jamming against my cheeks.

"Do you want me to stay? Do you want me to leave—?"

"Don't leave me, Mark. Please."

"Fine. I'm right here."

"My master…" I had tried hard to put it from my mind, by sheer strength of will. I reached out, my hand connecting with Mark's chest, the beating of his heart steady and sure.

I could share this tale. Truly, I could. "In July, when I went to old Raleigh, I was away from the Pratts' farm…" I shuddered.

"You were with me and your mother. To take Phoebe."

"Yes."

His calm voice gave me strength. I opened my eyes. He stood before me, arms loose at his sides. He gave me a solemn nod of encouragement.

"My master was very angry." I cleared my throat. "His son had seen us together in an embrace." Our first kiss had been a thing of beauty.

"I remember."

I lifted my hand—it felt shockingly heavy, as if weighted down by chains—and linked my fingers with his. I kept my gaze on our clasped hands. "He accused me of an improper relationship with you. He sought to uncover proof." I couldn't bear to go on and I couldn't bear to stop, as if driven to see this story through to its bitter end. "My master was sure that you had left scratches on my skin. He was determined to see them, wherever they were."

Mark inhaled a sharp breath.

"He undid my bodice and pulled out my stays. He inspected my body."

A sound slipped past Mark's lips, half-moan, half-growl. I collapsed against him, the tears that had not come that day overflowing. The echoes of sheer terror and powerlessness had me trembling. "Hold me."

He enfolded me into a warm and gentle embrace. "I have you, Susanna. You're safe. He can't hurt you. Ever again."

I wept in the secure cocoon of his arms, dreading what must come next. I'd left out part of the story, and I had to say it while I still had the courage. "Mr. Pratt says I have the plump breasts of a cheap whore."

"Bastard," Mark said, deep loathing in the crisp precision of the word. "You are beautiful in every way. Forget him."

He held me for long moments, murmuring in his soothing voice, reassuring me that I was safe and loved. At last I believed, the truth of it seeping into mind and heart. Once the tears stopped, I pressed my wet face to his chest, spent and sad.

"Tell me how to help you, Susanna."

"You're doing it right now."

"You've got me. As long as you need." His hands splayed across my back, bringing a lovely sense of comfort, yet our embrace remained chaste. "Remind me to beat the shit out of him one day."

His words surprised a quick bubble of laughter past my lips. "It's my sincere desire that neither of us see him again."

"I like that plan too."

A faint light teased my eyes, urging them to open. I blinked slowly, disoriented. The door to my apartment stood slightly ajar, the light from the stairwell visible.

I lay at the edge of my bed, tucked snugly under the covers. Yet I had no recollection of how I had gotten here.

From behind me came the rhythmic breathing of another person sleeping.

Carefully, I turned. Mark lay huddled in the middle of the bed. He was still in his jeans and dress shirt, now hopelessly wrinkled. A quilt bunched beneath him.

Memories of last evening returned. Mark had promised to stay until I fell asleep. He had succumbed himself. It warmed my heart to see him.

Slowly, I flipped a spare blanket over him. He stirred and then flopped to his back. I wiggled to my side and drifted away.

I awakened at dawn and watched Mark sleep. Even in profile, he was beautiful.

His eyes fluttered open. Closed. Open again. "Am I in your room?"

"Yes." After the pain of telling my story, the joy of this morning was deliciously sweet. "You slept here all night."

His head turned my way. "What time is it?"

"Six-thirty."

"Good. My mom won't be up yet." He rubbed his face. "I have to get out of here before she figures out we broke the big rule."

"We did nothing wrong."

"No, but I'm sure she wouldn't see it that way." He rolled to his side and dropped his hand over mine.

We lay there, watching each other quietly.

There were, of course, some things that must be said, as much for the person who said them as for the person who heard. "Thank you for being with me. For not being disgusted."

His brow creased in bewilderment. "Disgusted? About what?"

I dropped my gaze to his hand over mine, nestled in the sheets. "Perhaps you might think I didn't fight him hard enough."

"You didn't stand a chance against him. He's huge. I should know; he's taken a swing at me before." Mark tucked a stray lock of hair behind my ear. "Hey, babe, look at me." When I did, he watched me steadily, his eyes wide and clear. "He's a vicious asshole. He is one-hundred percent to blame for everything that happened. *Everything.*"

I wanted desperately to believe Mark. "Mr. Pratt called me a cheap—"

"Stop." Mark pressed his thumb across my lips. "Don't repeat his lies. Don't even think about them. That worthless piece of shit was scared of losing the most amazing person in his life. He wasn't going to let go easily."

What Mark said sounded quite sensible. I needed to take his claims into my mind and allow them to replace the evil things Mr. Pratt had planted.

I nodded at Mark, grateful for his presence. Grateful for *him*.

"Hey." His fingertip caught a tear as it glided down my cheek. "You're the most beautiful girl I've ever known. Really."

It was an outrageous statement, yet the intensity in his voice and eyes proclaimed that he believed it. He'd unshackled me again, as surely as he had two months ago when he broke the chains binding my legs. "You are beautiful too," I said, unable to contain a smile.

"Susanna?" His tone was most earnest.

"What?"

"For the record…I like plump breasts."

I didn't know whether to blush or giggle at the absurdity—yet I could see he meant to please me, however clumsily. "You are sure about this?"

"Completely."

"Then mine will not be a problem for you."

His gaze remained determinedly on my face. "They're a problem all right, just a good kind of problem to have." He yawned, stretched, and sat up. "I'd better be going."

I rose beside him, wishing he could hold me longer, knowing he was right. "Thank you, Mark."

He kissed me and then straightened with a groan. "I can't stand what happened to you, Susanna."

"It is past. We shall talk of it no more."

There was a loud rap at the door. Before either of us could react, the door to the apartment banged completely open.

Sherri stood there, framed in the threshold. "What are you doing?"

Chapter Thirty-Four

Hard and Fast

Ten minutes later, I was perched on the edge of the recliner in our family room, head in hands, breathing in and out through my mouth.

Footsteps approached, the light, fast swoosh of my mother in slippers, the heavier tread of my dad in running shoes.

I was too mad to even look at them. Instead I mentally tracked them across the room. The soft squeak of the couch let me know they were in here, staring at the top of my head. Well, they'd better get used to it, because that was all they were going to see for a while.

"Gran and Granddad are taking Susanna in." Mom's voice was tight.

A long, hard breath hissed through my teeth as I struggled to dam the flood of words that would land me in worse trouble than I already was. "Does she know?"

"Yes, she's packing. Your dad will drive her out to the lake house in a few minutes."

"How long will she be gone?"

"We told you from the beginning, Mark. Sleepovers are deal-breakers."

Holy shit. I catapulted from the chair and forced my fists into the pockets of my jeans, anything to keep them from hitting something. "It wasn't a sleepover—not the way you mean. You saw us, Mom. We had our clothes on. We didn't do anything wrong."

"Except violate a hard and fast rule."

Why the hell couldn't my father have been the one to find us? I shifted my gaze to him. "It was innocent, Dad."

"Sorry, son. Your mother and I are united on this one."

Rage balled in my chest, threatening to explode in a scream. I turned my back on them, anything to get myself under control. "Don't you guys get how stupid that rule is? Telling us 'no sleepovers in the apartment' doesn't stop a thing. It just changes the location." I threw back my head in frustration. "Parental controls are not what keeps us straight. It's her."

Dad's voice rumbled. "Then why did she put this privilege in danger?"

I couldn't tell him the real reason. That was Susanna's secret. "It was an emotional night for her. She was... homesick."

"She's been homesick before."

"It was really bad this time. She told me private things— things that aren't my right to tell you." I faced them, with a feeling in my gut that nothing I could say would make a difference. "She's been abused for years. She's been through stuff that most of us can't even imagine. Whenever she asks me to hold her, I'm not going to check the clock to see if it's convenient for my parents." I watched them. Had I gotten through?

When Mom slipped her fingers around my father's wrist, he gave a slight nod. "It was a rule, Mark. You broke it. You have to live with the consequences."

"Great. Thanks." I stalked into the foyer, wrenched open the front door, and then looked at them over my shoulder. "You guys raised me to do the right thing. Either you trust me. Or you don't."

The door slammed behind me.

I wandered through the neighborhood mindlessly, too pissed off to go home. It was a gorgeous Sunday morning. A lot of people were sitting on their back terraces, drinking coffee and being lazy.

Except the Lewises. We were drenched in drama.

How was Susanna feeling? What had my mother said to her?

Susanna clearly hadn't told my mother any of the story. Not even Mom could've thrown her out after that.

Knowing Susanna, she'd listened to my mom's lecture with a calm face and motionless body. She would've said nothing in her own defense. She would've acknowledged her understanding of the punishment and then looked for a suitcase.

What was wrong with my parents? Susanna was the best person any of us knew. Her previous world had been horrible, but she hadn't given in. She'd sucked it up and kept her sanity and sense of humor. If it hadn't been for Susanna, I would never have known how far I could stretch. I would never have discovered my own strength.

I wanted to be a better person for Susanna. My parents ought to throw us together *more* often, not less.

I cut through a yard to the greenway and followed it away from our house and away from the falls. There was a trickle of bike traffic, normal for this early on a Sunday morning. As I neared the main drag, I could hear the approach of a vehicle as it wound its way through the neighborhood. It braked at the gates to the neighborhood—a half-block away.

Dad was taking her in his Lexus. The bike rack held a shiny new bike. Red as cherries.

I leaned against the wooden fence at the mouth of the greenway and waited. Dad's car pulled onto the road and slowed for the pedestrian crossing directly in front of me.

Susanna sat on the back seat, her head resting against the window. Our gazes locked and held until she was out of sight.

I checked my watch. Eight o'clock. It boggled my mind how quickly life had changed.

What I needed was a long, brutal training ride. I did an about-face and jogged home.

CHAPTER THIRTY-FIVE

AN UNNATURAL STANCE

You'll have to move out.

The words still rang in my head hours later. Clear and angry.

Why had the specter of that rule not haunted me last night? Why had my painful memories—and the comfort I'd found in Mark's arms—been so complete that they banished all other thoughts from my mind?

It didn't seem fair that my master had the power to hurt me even now.

Charlie and Norah had welcomed me into their home once again. I wouldn't be on the streets. I could be happy here at the lake house until I had my identification and could work and live on my own.

But not seeing Mark every day? Having to schedule our time together?

My heart quaked.

I had not liked the look in Sherri's eyes. She believed something of me that was not true. She faulted me for Mark's disobedience. His parents had been good to me. I hated to reflect on their disappointment.

Truly, I had betrayed them. They had surprised me with a wondrous party and made yesterday the best birthday of my life. They had treated me with more kindness and generosity than I had ever known. They fed me, sheltered me, drove me where I needed to go. And my only responsibility had been to follow their rules.

Why had I forgotten?

It had been sweet, so very sweet, to awaken with him next to me, to know that he had kept a vigil until I slept. But had it also been selfish?

Mark didn't deserve their disapproval. I was the one who asked him to stay. Would it make a difference if I shared the reason he'd remained through the night? Did their rules have exceptions? Much in this world did. Yet, even as I pondered this idea, I knew I could not face them and speak the story again. It had been agonizing to tell Mark. I could not imagine telling anyone else.

Sunday became a day lost to time as these questions droned in my mind without ceasing. Thankfully, Charlie and Norah respected my privacy. They informed me of meals, made no comment when I slipped outside often to walk or practice on my bike, and carefully didn't notice when I retired to the loft early.

A book lay on the table beside my bed. *A Whirlwind Tour of Natural History*. Science was an important part of the GED, a subject I had neglected too often to indulge my love of American history. I smiled at Charlie's kindness, for no doubt this was his doing. I plumped up the stack of pillows against my bed and immersed myself in two centuries of wondrous scientific advances. It took no time at all to stifle the disquiet of this day.

I rose as the high round window revealed the gray light of dawn. After a quick shower, I donned a gray skirt with the peach T-shirt Sherri had given me for my birthday. Its sleeves didn't quite reach my wrists, but my burn scar wasn't visible.

When I'd arrived the previous morning and put away my clothes in the closet, I'd found a dress of dark blue, the color of the night sky right before the sun slipped under the horizon. The garment had been made of soft, fluid fabric. Norah had been sewing again.

I held the surprisingly heavy dress against my body. The sleeves would fall to my mid-forearms and the hem to my knees. It was a garment modest by today's standards but more than I could tolerate.

Norah knew better than anyone the state of my legs. She'd seen the scars and understood my determination never to show them. Why was she pushing me so?

Curiosity prickled. I wouldn't wear this dress, beautiful as it was, but I was intrigued that she should have made it for me.

I crept quietly down the stairs to find Norah already in the kitchen, preparing biscuit dough. I paused to watch her in concern. Her movements seemed plodding. I had never seen her act so frail.

"Good morning, Norah. How may I help?"

"I have this under control." She poured me a cup of coffee and picked up her own. "What happened with Mark, Susanna?"

I took a sip before responding, unhappy at the topic but grateful that she'd waited to ask. "We broke a rule."

"That's Sherri's explanation. What's yours?"

"I was assailed by sad memories. I needed Mark's comfort and…" How could I word this correctly?

"And the comfort lasted all night long."

"Yes."

"So my daughter suspects you and Mark have become sexually active."

I blushed at such candor. "It isn't true."

"Doesn't matter whether it is or isn't. It's none of her business."

"Mark and I agreed to follow the rules."

"Maybe they should have picked rules that were more respectful of your maturity." Norah set her mug down hard, sloshing coffee onto the counter. "Sherri'll get over it after Bruce talks some sense into to her."

"He is distressed as well."

"Bruce doesn't like his applecart upset, and he doesn't know what really happened. Once it's righted itself, things'll get better." She coughed into her apron, dabbed a bit of sweat from her lips, and then leaned heavily on the counter. "Listen to what I'm about to say, and think about it hard. You're eighteen now, Susanna. An adult in the eyes of the law. From what I can tell, you've been an adult in reality for more years than are fair. Don't let Sherri bulldoze over you. She's my daughter, and I love her. But right now, she's just a mother scared about losing her baby. Instead of getting worked up and over-protective, she needs to be thanking her lucky stars that she's losing Mark to you."

Norah bent her head over the biscuit dough. I stared at the top of her head, at the thin, precise part in her snow-white hair, and blinked back the moisture in my eyes.

She coughed again and then stepped to the sink to wash her hands. "The Lord knew what he was doing when he created grandparents. We get to have all the fun."

Smiling, I walked around the bar and began to transfer biscuits to a baking sheet. "Thank you."

"For what, hon?"

I nodded in comprehension. The subject of Mark and Sherri was closed. "Thank you for the dress. It is beautiful, but I do not understand why you made it."

"For the winter. It'll give you variety."

"Would not my legs grow cold?"

"Oh, honey, didn't you wear stockings in that crazy place you used to live?"

"Yes, but they were never seen."

She grunted, grabbed a magazine from the bar, and flipped through it to a well-worn page. "This is what I had in mind for you."

The photograph showed a pretty girl in an unnatural stance on a city street. She wore a white dress of similar style to Norah's gift, although the hem stopped closer to her bottom than her knees. Yet it was her legs that had me riveted. They were dark green with tiny white stars sprinkled about. "Are they warm enough for winter?"

"Sure are."

"Do they itch?"

She shook her head. "Mostly, they're silky soft, and we can get them in all sorts of colors and patterns."

I handed the magazine back. "Where do the girl's stockings stop?"

"At her waist."

"Truly?" I tried to imagine how that would work and could not.

"Just a sec." Norah disappeared into the laundry room and emerged immediately. "Here. The stockings are attached to panties."

"Very clever." I studied Norah's stockings thoughtfully, not ready to concede them as a possibility for me but interested nonetheless. "My scars wouldn't show through such a covering."

"Nope. They would not."

"They appear quite snug." I felt the heat of color in my cheeks. "Every muscle and sinew of my legs would be discernible."

"Sure would." She laughed. "As far as Mark is concerned, that's a good thing."

I smiled. "Indeed."

Chapter Thirty-Six

No Trespassing

The separation from Susanna was driving me crazy.

My parents wouldn't let me go over there. Normally, I would ignore something like that, but Susanna wouldn't. She was programmed to obey. Clearly, she already knew the terms of the punishment, 'cause she hadn't tried to call or text or email.

There had to be somebody I could complain to. I got my sister on the phone.

"Hello?" Marissa sounded sleepy.

"Mom and Dad made Susanna leave. She's moved to the lake house."

"Whoa." I could almost feel Marissa sitting up and paying attention now. "That sounds pretty drastic. What happened? Did they catch you in bed?"

Maybe this had been a mistake. "Actually, yes, but it's not what you think."

Marissa laughed. "I've talked with Susanna enough times on the phone to know that it's probably exactly what I think—which is nothing."

"Thank you." I exhaled a noisy, grateful breath. "Too bad our parents don't get it."

"Oh, cut 'em some slack, Mark. They were our age once. They know what it's like to be dying to get into each other's—"

"Stop. That's not an image I need in my head." I sprawled onto my bed and closed my eyes. "I want her back."

Marissa's voice softened. "You will. You're great together. Mom and Dad need to get over themselves."

"Yeah. I hope it's soon."

"It will be." She cleared her throat. "Fletcher might be traveling to Costa Rica next semester."

"Are you paying for that too?"

She grunted. "No, Mark."

"I'm not going to pretend that I like it. He plays while you work. The whole setup sucks."

"Things aren't that bad." Her voice wobbled.

Very interesting. She didn't sound convinced. "Right."

"Really, Mark. It's just that Fletcher thinks…"

I didn't care what Fletcher Mills thought about anything, but my sister had listened to me. It was my turn to listen to her.

Besides, fifteen minutes would go by, and I'd have something new to be mad about.

Keefe Halligan bumped me in the senior hallway, nearly knocking my backpack off my shoulder. I'd managed to avoid him since he won our age division at the Carolina Cross-country Challenge over the summer.

"Hey, Lewis, got any big races coming up?"

I shrugged and kept walking. None of his damn business.

"Going to the Boone Classic?"

I stopped and spun around. We had an audience. The Hungry Mother race and the Boone Classic were the same weekend. I'd already made the choice to spend the weekend in Virginia and race with my dad. Halligan would have to compete in the Boone Classic without me. And, no, I wasn't telling him a thing. Let him sweat out whether I would be upping his competition. "Worried, Halligan?"

He laughed and made a sharp turn into his next classroom.

Gabrielle walked over and linked her arm through mine. "What was that all about?"

I stiffened at her touch and then forced myself to relax. Actors didn't have the same rules the rest of us did. This was casual for her. I had to learn to let it be casual for me. "Halligan and I sometimes compete in the same mountain-bike races. We're trying to psych each other out."

"Sounds stupid to me." She started down the hall, dragging me along with her. "My mom is flying into Raleigh this afternoon with her husband."

In the nearly two months we'd been lab partners, she'd never mentioned them before. "Are they coming for the homecoming game?"

"No. They'll leave by Wednesday."

Okay. A two-day visit wasn't very long. "Did they forget? Maybe if you reminded them…"

She was shaking her head. "They didn't forget. They're just busy people. Mom's husband has a golf tournament in Florida." She pasted on a smile. "I thought I might have a little party so they can meet some of my friends. Can you come?"

We'd reached my classroom. I slipped my arm from hers and moved back a step. "When's the party?"

"Tonight."

"Sure, I can make it." It wasn't like I had any other plans. "Are Jesse and Benita coming?"

She nodded. "You should bring Susanna and your bathing suits. The pool is heated."

Despite the fact that it would never happen, I tried to imagine Susanna in a bathing suit.

A bikini. With tiny triangles for the top. Holy shit.

Of course, a strapless one-piece could be quite nice too, if it were the right one.

A memory surfaced from the day she'd escaped. She'd worn her shift into the bathtub. It had turned into a second skin. Heat flushed through me.

Okay, stop. I was in the hallway. Gabrielle was right here watching me, and she needed an answer.

"Thanks, but Susanna can't make it," I mumbled. I turned toward the classroom as the tardy bell rang.

She caught my elbow, stopping me. "This may not be the time—"

"Uh, Gabrielle, we're late." I glanced at my third-period teacher, who returned the glance with mild curiosity. In fact, everyone in the room could see me, framed by the doorway, with our senior-class movie star.

"This is important. They'll understand." She leaned closer and lowered her voice for my ears only, uncaring that we were the only ones left in the hall or that we were being watched with eager speculation by my entire French class. "The more I hear about your girlfriend, the more concerned I get. She never comes to anything, like she's some princess in a castle and you always have to go to her. Are you sure she isn't taking advantage of you?"

"Gabrielle, in case you can't read faces, mine is saying 'No Trespassing.'" I backed a step away from her and crossed my arms over my chest. "I don't ask about Korry. You don't ask about Susanna."

"You don't have to ask me about Korry. *Teen Trash* can fill you in on all the details you'd ever want."

"Not funny." I stared at her through narrowed eyes. "If you want to stay friends with me, Susanna is off-limits."

"Got it."

"Fine." I headed into the classroom.

"Seven at my aunt's house?" she called after me.

I could almost feel the ripple that went through the class. I glanced at Gabrielle over my shoulder, puzzled at why she was so public about our friendship—if we could even call it that.

She smiled at me, with her perfect face and shining hair and…sad eyes. And it hit me. She spent a lot of her life with people who were paid to be around her. She lived with her aunt, a city councilwoman who was always busy. Her mom flew in for two-day-only visits and missed important stuff in her daughter's life so that her husband could play golf. Korry was on the other side of the world.

All of Gabrielle's relationships sucked.

I nodded. "See you at seven."

CHAPTER THIRTY-SEVEN

A WORRISOME CHANGE

I didn't have the opportunity to relax and read more journal entries until late in the afternoon. I opened Charlie's computer and popped in the DVD. With all of the excitement of researching Dorcas, celebrating my birthday, and then moving to the lake house, I'd put off reading the last journal. Finally, I had the chance to learn what had happened in the months and years after the saving of Phoebe's thumb.

The images in this journal showed grave disrepair. Pages were splotched and torn. Edges had crumbled. I dearly hoped that not too many of the pages in the journal had been destroyed.

April 23rd, 1801

Mrs. Eton gave me this little book. It is a beautiful gift and thoughtfully chosen.

The hour is quite late, almost midnight, and I am too excited to sleep. I burn this precious candle in the need to capture my thoughts.

Tomorrow is the day I leave the Eton household. There will be no chores for me. Letty has retired this evening as junior chambermaid and will shuffle down the stairs in the morning as the senior. A new girl will have my bed before nightfall.

So the final journal was a new one—a gift from Mrs. Eton. Phoebe had received it for her birthday and last day of service. It was a kind remembrance and yet a bit excessive for a departing maid. I should've greatly preferred Mrs. Eton as a mistress to the one I'd had, but that didn't alter how very peculiar it would've been for servants to understand their place in the Eton household.

I shall not be here to observe how the household proceeds without me. I never particularly liked the duties of housemaid, except the needlework. Always the embroidery sustained me.

I look forward with excitement at the adventure I am about to begin. Yet I feel oddly sad to put this place behind me. It is where my sister brought me nearly five years ago to assure my safety. It is where I improved my skills with the needle that secured a job at Mrs. Simpson's. It is where I grew to know and admire Mrs. Eton, Senator Eton, and their children.

I shall be seventeen tomorrow. The years have passed quickly.

May 6th, 1801

Mrs. Simpson is a sour-faced sort, with beady eyes, skin like a dried apple, and long white hairs curling from her chin. Her hands are too gnarled to stitch, but her customers are loyal and her sketches divine.

I do not like this tiny closet where she makes her four girls work. It is hot and dirty, and the light is poor.

I opened the door this morning to let in the sun and the breeze and had my knuckles rapped with a cane for the effort. Why would she do such a thing? I reminded her that I could not do my best work with bruised knuckles.

She made some foolish excuse about keeping doors closed to prevent dust blowing in, claiming that the gowns might become dirty.

I, in turn, suggested it was easier to clean a gown than to sell the shoddy work of workers who could not see what they stitched.

She smacked my shoulder with the head of her cane. The pain stunned me into silence.

After the door leading into the shop slammed behind her, the other girls smirked. I bowed my head over my work and waited for the pain to ease before I added a green vine to a fine linen kerchief.

I, too, understood how it felt to be punished harshly and unjustly for merely speaking the truth. This shopkeeper was the kind of employer I had feared for Phoebe. Perhaps Mrs. Simpson wasn't as bad as the Pratts, but she was deeply unpleasant in her own right.

There was nothing I could do. My sister would have to find her own way.

May 15th, 1801

I do not care for the way Mrs. Simpson speaks to me, as if I were a stupid dog. I am to fetch and obey without question.

Today we had a nasty exchange. She entered the workroom to watch her girls work. She stopped beside me. "I am disappointed in your speed, Phoebe, and yet you come highly recommended. How did you have Mrs. Eton fooled?"

The criticism stung. Perhaps I should have remained silent. But instead, I pointed out the poor quality of the thread she purchased.

It was no wonder it broke and frayed. Boldly, I stated that I could not produce superior designs with inferior thread.

Mrs. Simpson mumbled something about backtalk and then slapped me hard across the mouth.

After two weeks here, I have witnessed the other girls punished as harshly as I. Yet they do not complain. Is this treatment common for a seamstress shop? How can we create beauty when ugliness hovers over us like a hawk?

May 29th, 1801

Mrs. Simpson gave me two weeks' pay after four weeks' work. She claimed that my stitching is poor quality and does not sell well.

I do not believe her claims. I have seen my handiwork on kerchiefs and gowns at the State House on Sundays.

This is intolerable. She is mean and unjust. I cannot bear it much longer.

There are other shops in Raleigh. I may ask about open positions.

"Susanna?" Norah called up the stairs. "Supper."

As I turned away from the computer, I felt a swell of pride at Phoebe's most recent entries. She'd grown into a fine young woman with a strong mind. I had no worries for her future now.

I was eager to resume my reading of Phoebe's last journal later that evening. Indeed, I had curled on the couch in the great room of the lake house, in companionable silence with Norah and Charlie, when there was a knock at the door.

Bruce stepped in, his arms cradling a large box, and nodded gravely at me. "You have a job, Susanna."

He looked so solemn that I feared at first I had misunderstood. Rising slowly, I set the laptop on the coffee table and crossed the room to peek in the box. On top lay a sheet with instructions from Sherri, the date that the work must be completed, and the fee they intended to pay me— which made me blink in happy surprise. The box also held invitations with envelopes of a heavy cream paper, as well as a set of special pens. I lifted one of the pens, noting the shape and weight in my hand. It felt good.

"Thank you for bringing them, Bruce," I said with a shy smile.

"My pleasure." He placed the box on the kitchen table, leaned over to press a quick kiss to my forehead, and then crossed to where Norah and Charlie watched from their chairs.

I treasured that touch. It was the first such caress from him and, coming so soon after the transgressions of Sunday, it did much to ease my distress.

Turning back to the box, I drew out the items, one by one, and arranged them on the table, my hands trembling with anticipation. Phoebe's journals would have to wait. I had a job!

I worked late into the night, finishing much of the work before retiring. Each stroke and flourish of the pen was made with the utmost care. No one would be able to fault the quality of my efforts. I remained confident that I could complete the rest on the next day—pleased yet baffled that I would be rewarded with so much money for so little effort.

Perhaps there would be other such jobs. I allowed myself to indulge in the hope of more.

When I came down Tuesday for breakfast, Norah was not there before me, a worrisome change of behavior. I prepared a simple meal of oatmeal and fruit. Charlie alone appeared for it, confusion etched on his brow.

"My wife is feeling poorly," he said, adding cream and honey to his bowl. "She wants to sleep."

I nodded in acknowledgment and joined him at the table, wondering how much assistance to offer.

The decision was taken from me.

While I collected the dishes, Charlie went to check on her.

"Susanna, please! We need you."

I reached the room to find Norah weeping on soiled sheets. Charlie stood at her bedside, despair in the droop of his head and the wringing of his hands.

"Charlie, we must clean this up now. I shall run a bath. Will you be able to help her with it?"

He cleared his throat. "Yes."

The weeping increased.

"You'll be fine, Norah. We shall take care of you," I said and then departed for their bathroom.

It took no more than a few minutes to have the tub ready, the bed stripped, and the soiled clothes and sheets in the washing machine. When I returned to the master suite, I heard light splashing and Charlie's voice, talking in the most soothing tones he could muster. I continued about the business of airing out the room and changing the bed to fresh linens.

Once Norah was comfortably sleeping again, I fixed Charlie a cup of tea, settled him in his favorite chair, and made a call from the lake house's landline.

Sherri answered instantly. "Hello?"

"Susanna speaking. Are you free?"

There was a cooling from the other end of the call. "I took today off."

"Your mother is ill." Charlie waved at me to stop, but I turned my back to him.

Sherri's voice became brisk. "I'm on my way. Tell me her symptoms."

"Keep her hydrated," Sherri said as she slumped onto a stool across the kitchen bar from me. "And keep my father occupied as much as possible."

With a nod, I continued to scrub the countertops.

"Susanna?"

I looked up.

"Thank you. It was a good thing you were here. Dad is a bit helpless in this kind of situation."

"I am happy to do it." Truly, I was. Tending to the ill was something I knew how to do. My mistress, during her many confinements, had been more feeble than the babies she birthed. If I considered all that Norah had done for me, my actions repaid only a tiny portion of the debt I owed.

"It doesn't change anything about the other situation."

Her words pelted me like ice, freezing me into shock. I glared at her through cold, disbelieving eyes. "You insult me with such a statement." With deliberate movements, I folded the rag, set it by the sink, and walked around the bar to the stairs leading up to the loft. Yet I paused with a foot on the bottom step, needing to say my piece. "Your mother has welcomed me with open arms. I am deeply grateful to her. It is repugnant to suggest that I would use her illness to curry favor with you."

"That's what I hoped this was all about, but I had to check."

"Perhaps you might have checked on Sunday as well." The pain and frustration that had been brewing for days spilled forth. "You interpreted with your eyes and not with your heart. Is that the way justice is meted out in your home? To condemn without full access to the facts?"

Her lips thinned. "Susanna—"

"I do not care what you think of me. I have been planning to leave your home as soon as your world permits it, but I cannot abide what you suspect of Mark. He was only trying to help me. Surely you know your son better than that."

"He broke a rule."

"You believe in your right to punish his transgression. I believe that his reason for breaking the rule deserves a hearing."

Her chin jerked higher. "I don't need your help in disciplining my son."

"Sometimes you treat him like a little boy."

"Sometimes he acts like a little boy." She stared at me, steely-eyed. "Susanna, you're treading on dangerous ground here. I don't answer to you."

I clung to the banister, willing her to absorb what I was about to say in the right spirit. "Mark will turn eighteen soon. You must accept that he's a young man. There are things he's witnessed and things he's done that have forced him to leave childhood behind."

Her face clouded. "What things?"

"Things I cannot repeat." My voice had grown husky. I looked away from her, swamped by memories. There had been Mark's first, failed attempt to rescue me and the panic on his face as he pondered his own near capture and flogging. Undaunted, he'd waited and planned a second attempt, where he'd had to cut through shackles, carry me to safety, fist-fight my master, and elude a pack of dogs. And my wounds? Merciful heavens. He'd cleaned and dressed my raw, bloody wounds even as I fought screams of agony. No, these had not been the actions of a little boy. "I owe my life to Mark."

"He's said that." Her tone was flat.

"Do you think he exaggerates?" I'd failed to reach her. What more must I give to get through? "You saw the infection in my ankles."

"It was pretty grim by the time you got to us, but what exactly am I supposed to think? You've told me that the villagers were good people. If it was so bad, why didn't they put a stop to it?"

"Let me tell you of the townsfolk. They watched my master put shackles on me. They watched me bleed, stumble, and sicken. They looked away from the horror of my *discipline*, because they were hampered by fear and ignorance." I hardly knew what I was doing, for I was suddenly beside her chair, resisting the urge to shake her into understanding. "Mark did not stand by. He risked *all* for me. I am prepared to do the same for him."

She gave a curt nod. "I believe you."

"Then believe me when I say we did nothing wrong." I dropped my head into my hands. "He was just trying to save me again."

"From what?"

"The memory of an evil man."

I could sense her standing now, but her voice, when it came, sounded muffled. "What did your master do to you, Susanna?"

"It is best that you not know. There is nothing you can do about it."

"Mark calls it abuse. Is that the right term?"

"In your world, yes." In my world, it had simply been viewed as my master's right. I fumbled for the couch and sank down.

The cushion beside me shifted under her weight. "I've seen evidence of the physical abuse. What else? Verbal?"

I closed my eyes. My head bobbed in the oddest sort of nod.

Her warm hand covered the iciness of mine. "Was it ever sexual?"

Tears threatened my defenses, but I fought them back. "I cannot speak of this any longer."

She gave my hand a light squeeze. "Susanna, maybe you should talk to someone. A professional. Someone who is trained to listen to your stories and help."

I nodded—but only in acknowledgment. Not in agreement. There was no possibility that I could ever tell of my past. I would have to deal with these things alone. Or with Mark.

CHAPTER THIRTY-EIGHT

MESSY, COMPLICATED, HOT

The Bible arrived in Wednesday's mail.

Excitement rippled through me. I tore it out of its packaging and flipped to the Family Records pages. They were half filled-in. Marriages, deaths, and births—all from the 1940s through 1970s.

I could sprinkle in a few from the eighties and then start filling in the nineties. If Susanna had turned eighteen in 2016, then her birth year had to be 1998. Her family could fit in around that.

Big question, though. Would I sneak the information out of her? Or would I outright ask and run the risk of a fight?

Easy answer. We had been apart too long already. I wouldn't be fighting with her.

If I remembered correctly, her dad was twenty-eight when she was born, and Susanna didn't know his birthdate. Good, I could make it up.

Wait. This Bible was full of names that were not Marsh. It would have to represent her mother's family. Unfortunately, the one time I'd met Susanna's mother, she'd simply been Mrs. Crawford. I didn't know her maiden name.

Damn. I'd figure out how to make ink look old and worry about the names later.

And once Gran felt better, I was heading out to the lake house to talk with Granddad about judges. While I was there, I was getting my hands on Susanna.

Dinner was done. Homework was done. Lawns were caught up.

I had nothing else I wanted to do.

Jesse had sent me a video clip of Benita playing a cello solo with an orchestra somewhere in Virginia. It wasn't the kind of music I liked to listen to, but this was Benita. I might as well watch now.

It was hard to recognize her. She wore a beaded black evening gown. Her blonde hair had been piled on her head in this messy, complicated, hot style. The fingers of one hand flew up and down the strings. It was the first time I'd seen her without gloves. Her hands were slim and gorgeous.

But it was her face I couldn't look away from. With eyes closed and lips pressed together as if in pain, her expression showed how much she suffered along with the music. When the piece was over, I lay on my bed, worn out and wondering if she had been too.

There was a knock on my door.

"Yeah?"

My dad stuck his head in. "Do we have reservations for Hungry Mother?"

"Yes." I snapped the lid down on my laptop.

"Are we both registered for the race?"

I nodded.

He pushed the door wider and wedged his shoulder against the threshold. "Your grandmother's on the mend."

"That's what Mom said."

"We're impressed with how much of a help Susanna was."

I kept my expression neutral. It didn't surprise me.

"When your mother was out there yesterday, she and Susanna had a fight."

"Great," I muttered.

His lips twitched. "Susanna defended you, and she wouldn't back down. I wish I'd been there."

Really? My dad didn't mind? "How mad is Mom?"

"Mad is not the right word. It left her feeling weird in a way she can't describe." He pushed away from the door and reached for the door handle. "We're going to let Susanna move back in." He closed the door.

"Wait!" I jumped off my bed and ran to the door, wrenching it open. He'd almost reached the master suite. "When can she come home?"

"Friday."

This had to be his doing. "Thanks, Dad. That's great."

"Sure thing."

"We won't screw up again."

He waved without turning around. "Save it for your mom."

I took the truck to school on Thursday and drove straight to the lake house from there. It was amazing that I remembered to cut off the engine, considering how fast I jumped out and ran for the house.

"Hey," I called out as I slammed through the door, my eyes scanning for a sign of her.

My grandparents were reading in their favorite chairs. Susanna sat at the kitchen table, in her new T-shirt from my folks, the box of invitations at her side. She'd barely made it to her feet by the time I'd reached her side and hauled her up into my arms, my mouth locking on hers like she was the air I needed to breathe.

"'Scuse me," Granddad shouted.

I laughed and slowly slid her body down mine until her feet touched the floor again. Susanna's face had turned a flaming red, but she smiled just the same.

"I missed you," I whispered.

"I can tell," she whispered back. "I missed you too."

"You can move home," I said at normal volume.

Her eyes widened and then blinked rapidly. "Truly?"

I nodded. "I don't know what you said to my mom, but the punishment ends this weekend."

Granddad muttered, "Friday."

Susanna looked at them. "You knew?"

"Yes," Gran said as she pulled out a chair at the table and sat. "We wanted Mark to tell you."

Susanna slipped her hand into mine and sighed happily. "Tomorrow."

"Yeah, babe." Working around homecoming activities would be tricky. If my grandparents drove her home, that would be a big help. Maybe I could even talk her into coming to the game. "Granddad?"

He stood behind Gran now, his hands gripping the top of her chair. "Yeah, Mark. You want to know what I found out about judges."

That was an important topic too. "Sure."

"Judge Tew is a good man. He plays by the book."

Shit. I'd been counting on a different answer, like it would all be taken care of because my grandfather could solve anything. What next? "Okay, Granddad. Thanks for checking."

Gran raised her hand and waved it like she was back in elementary school. "I know someone better."

Beside me, Susanna stood still, listening intently. Maybe she'd figured out there was more to this conversation than face value, but I couldn't fill her in too much until I understood what I was dealing with. "Someone better than Judge Tew?"

My grandmother gave a sharp nod. "One of his assistants, Peggy Merritt. We're friends at the Heart Association. She prepares all of Judge Tew's paperwork and makes sure it gets clocked in at the courthouse."

"Have you talked to her about our situation?"

"I have. She's willing to hear more."

It was my turn to take a breath—but not too deep, because I wanted to be sure this time. "Does Mrs. Merritt know that we're hoping to get Susanna's birth certificate filed?"

Susanna's fingers clenched around mine, but her face showed no change in emotion.

Gran nodded. "She also knows that the evidence is poor and that there is no lawyer involved at the moment."

I allowed myself a smile. "So what's next?"

"Put together the documents you have and she'll see." Gran's gaze fell on Susanna. "She'll also want to talk to you, hon. As far as I'm concerned, that'll clinch the deal."

Chapter Thirty-Nine

A Wrong Turn

Mark's eyes gleamed with excitement. Clearly, I didn't understand the import of what they were saying. "This is good news?" I asked.

"It's great news." He kissed me lightly. "Hey, I brought my bike. Want to go out? I can explain what we've been talking about."

"Indeed, I would. I've been practicing. Do you have other skills for me to learn?"

"Yep, and the first one is—wear safe clothes." He laid a firm hand on my hip. "Babe, it's hard to ride in a skirt."

"It will test your skill as an instructor."

"Yeah, right." He smiled at his grandparents. "We're going out while the light's still good."

The sun would be out for many hours, but I didn't remind him, for I was eager to be alone with him too.

We rode in parallel up the driveway and onto the main road as he coached me in the use of gears. I tried to understand, but it wasn't easy.

When I'd been by myself, I'd ridden only on trails that were generally flat. But Mark clearly had no paths that he avoided, and I wouldn't ask him to change on my behalf, even though biking uphill had a most unappealing effect on my balance. It required a great deal of effort to keep the bike smooth and steady.

There was no discernible effect on Mark. "Did you get what we are talking about? Gran has someone who can help us figure out your birth certificate."

I nodded, not wishing to waste a precious breath on words.

"It's not a sure thing, but this lady sounds like she could be helpful."

I nodded.

"Do you have any questions?"

There would be time for questions later. Shaking my head, I concentrated on the path and the pumping of my legs. The hem of the skirt kept getting in my way.

He laughed. "It's easier to ride a bike wearing pants."

"It's easier to stay in my good graces if you do not comment on my clothes."

"Point taken."

We finally turned onto a flat dirt trail that paralleled the lake and rode as far as a small park at the water's edge. After securing our bikes, we found a picnic table and sat on its top. I watched the boats speed by. He kissed my cheek and then my jaw.

"Damn." He lifted his head. "I can't wait to get you home."

As lovely and peaceful as the lake house was, I had to agree. "Will you come for me tomorrow after school?"

He drew away from me. "I'm not sure about the arrangements yet. Tomorrow is the homecoming game."

I turned to gaze at him and found him looking out at the water, his face in profile. "Might I infer that you'll escort the movie star?"

He maintained a vigilant watch on the boaters of Jordan Lake. "You told me it was okay to say yes."

"I did indeed. I'm curious why I'm only learning of your decision now."

"You gave me the go-ahead."

"I didn't give you *the go-ahead*. I merely freed you to make the best choice."

"Sounds like we disagree on what that is." He exhaled loudly. "I'd like you to come, Susanna."

"Why should I return on Friday now? You'll be too busy to notice me." We had been apart for five days. During the absence, I'd had no knowledge of what might happen next. Now that the separation was ending, we would remain apart for another day so that he could help a girl in a ball gown walk on a football field.

I felt a strong desire to be away from him. After clipping the helmet in place, I mounted the bike and rode away in the direction of the lake house. It would've been a most effective way to demonstrate the strength of my feelings had I not made a wrong turn—requiring a rescue from Mark.

When we arrived at the lake house, Charlie was seated on the deck, pretending to read a book. I rolled my bike toward the shed while Mark put his in the truck. He called after me, "I could take your bike back with me tonight."

"I'll keep it here until Saturday."

Charlie lowered his book, his gaze locking on his grandson. "Your mother says the exile ends tomorrow. Why would Susanna be here until Saturday?"

Mark's jaw tightened. "I'm busy Friday evening."

"Doing what?"

"I'm on the homecoming court."

"You're going on a date? With a girl who isn't Susanna?"

"It's not a date."

"Sounds like one to me."

"Then you'd be wrong." Mark wrenched open the door to his truck. "Stay out of this, Granddad. I don't cheat on Susanna. Not now. Not ever. She knows it, and so do you."

He slid onto the driver's seat and watched with narrowed eyes as I approached.

I stopped a foot or more away and lowered my voice. "You are leaving now?"

"I don't feel particularly welcome."

Disappointment had me in its grip, yet I couldn't deny that his event on Friday evening made matters between us awkward. "I shall see you Saturday, then."

"Dammit, Susanna. Do you plan stuff like this with Granddad?"

That stung. "You made a decision unlikely to be popular with your grandparents. I can hardly be to blame."

"I've asked you to come to the game with me. I want you to be involved." He snapped on his seatbelt. "This is my senior year. Don't try to make me feel guilty because I want to enjoy it." The door closed with a bang.

I watched as the truck reversed and roared away. Once it had disappeared from view, I sought refuge among the trees, away from my friends and their questions.

Chapter Forty

Fringe of the Crowd

Thursday night ended up being the worst evening since Susanna had left on Sunday. Why? Because we *could* have been together—and we weren't. Should've known the frickin' homecoming game would become a problem.

I was grumpy and pissed and ready to kick something. I'd looked forward to being with her. I'd wanted to stay longer. But with the odds at three against one, I knew better than to hang around.

There would be nothing happening at school tomorrow besides homecoming. No assignments due or exams, which meant no homework, so I actually watched TV. It wasn't too bad, but not a replacement for Susanna.

I showed up Friday morning in a sports jacket and khakis, the unofficial uniform of escorts. The princesses all wore eye-popping dresses. Most looked like they belonged at cocktail parties rather than at school, except Gabrielle. She looked like she was heading to an audience with the Queen. Her white dress covered her completely from shoulder to knee with sleeves that were gauzy and slit down the middle, allowing us a peek-a-boo look at her tanned arms. It should've been prudish but it wasn't. Not at all. It fit perfectly and made guys wonder what it was hiding.

The entire court had a meeting after school, and then I had yet another meeting after that with Gabrielle, Garrett, and her PR person. The rules were surprisingly easy.

1. *Follow any instructions from Garrett without question.*
2. *Stay in Gabrielle's shadow.*
3. *Don't talk to paparazzi.*
4. *Never look directly at the cameras.*

Surreal, if I thought about it, but I could do this.

The only time I put up a fight was when the PR person held out the tuxedo she'd picked for me.

"No, thank you," I said.

"You have to." She gave it a shake. "Come on, Marcus. It's perfectly designed to set off Gabrielle's dress."

"I have my own tux, and the name is Mark. M-A-R-K."

"But this is an Armani—" the woman sputtered.

"Leave him alone, Olivia." She smiled at me. "We'll pick you up around five."

I shook my head—and smiled back. "I'll meet you there."

Olivia's hand-painted eyebrows arched high over her unnaturally green eyes. She checked Gabrielle's reaction, which was still a big smile. With a shrug, Olivia said, "Then you'll need this." She handed over a VIP parking pass.

Finally, something I was willing to take.

After my second shower of the day, I shaved and then worked hard on my hair, since it might make the news.

When I walked into my bedroom, my laptop was pinging. A quick check showed Marissa was checking in.

"Hey," I said as I adjusted the webcam for a clearer shot of my face. "Can you see my hair?"

"Yeah. You need some product."

"You sure?"

"Yeah." She laughed. "Are you psyched?"

"Not yet."

"Liar."

My turn to laugh. "Okay, I'm looking forward to it. A little."

"Granddad is pissed at you because he thinks this is disloyal to Susanna."

"Nice reminder. Like I didn't know that already." I frowned at the camera. "What do you think?"

"I think Susanna needs to learn how to say *no* when she means *no*."

Score. I had someone on my side, which helped a lot. "So why does she do shit like that?"

"All girls do shit like that."

"Okay. Why?"

"We want you to love us enough to read our minds. It's very irritating when you don't."

I laughed. "So there's no way I can win?"

"Not really. The best you can do is manage the fallout."

"Thanks, Marissa. Gotta go."

"Have fun tonight. Later."

I put on every part of the tux except the jacket and the tie, which I left loose about my shirt collar.

"Mom?" I ran down the stairs to find her sitting at the kitchen table, sipping wine and reading something on her phone. She looked up.

"You look nice." She lifted her phone and snapped a quick photo. "Mark, your hair could use some help."

"Marissa said to use product."

"That's not enough." When Mom stood, I saw that she was all decked out for the game—ruffly top, longish skirt, riding boots.

"Looking good."

She wrinkled her nose as she pulled a pair of scissors out of a kitchen drawer. "Sit," she said, and pointed to a chair. In seconds, she swathed me in a huge tablecloth and got to work.

Snip. Smooth. Frown. Repeat.

"Better now. Want me to handle your tie?"

"Sure." I stood patiently while she worked.

When she was done, I slipped on my jacket. She tugged and smoothed. "Perfect."

My dad strolled in from the garage. "Impressive," he said and held out his hand.

We shook. "Thanks, Dad. Are you going to ride with me?"

"No, we don't want to get there so early. We'll see you at the game." He took a swig from my mother's glass of wine. "Is Gabrielle picking you up?"

"I told her I'd meet her there."

"Makes it feel less like a date?"

"Yeah." We exchanged a look. He totally got this. My family had my back. It felt good.

Alexis took her role as the head of the homecoming court seriously. Carlton helped her out of a rented Rolls. She wore a white gown, obligatory for the Queen. It wrapped around her like a mermaid suit, so tight it made me wonder how she was going to walk.

"Hi Mark," she said. Her lips trembled. She was nervous.

I gave her a reassuring nod. "You look great, Alexis."

"Thanks."

I switched my gaze to Carlton. He stared back for a long, tense moment. A year ago, this night would've been impossible. Carlton May and Mark Lewis on the homecoming court? No way.

Of course, it would've also been impossible for Carlton May and Mark Lewis to lose a lifelong friendship over a girl. I hated that it had worked out this way, but there was no turning back.

For tonight, though, we could call a temporary truce. "Good luck," I said and held out my hand.

His eyes widened briefly. "You too."

We shook, and then they were gone, the two of them strolling to where the rest of the court waited.

I waited on the side, taking in the craziness. I'd never seen so many people jamming the parking lot, many with sophisticated cameras. This whole story was bound to generate interest. *Movie star takes time off from her acting career to attend school, ends up on homecoming court.*

Of course people would be curious, and I was Gabrielle's escort.

A limo pulled up in the VIP parking area. Gabrielle's bodyguard got out and opened her door. I stepped forward and offered her my arm.

She smiled as she took it and slid gracefully from the limo, her train slithering out behind her. Cameras flashed from all directions.

Gabrielle looked like she'd been poured into her purple gown. It was high-necked, long-sleeved, and backless down to…damn. In the front, the hem stopped at her ankles, showing off silver stilettos that would have the guys at our school aching forever.

"Hey, you look great."

She smiled at me, her loose curls swishing across the top of that bare back. "Thanks."

The clicking of the cameras was shockingly loud.

We joined the others in a special tent that had been brought in to give Gabrielle some privacy. When we entered, the rest of the homecoming court grew silent. Olivia hustled over with an entourage, introduced us to a reporter, and then arranged some staged candids.

The other princesses watched Gabrielle with undisguised envy. They looked like a bunch of overdressed debutantes who'd finally realized *why bother?*

While the Olivia-appointed photographer organized the princesses for some group shots, Gabrielle handed me her shiny purse. "Watch this, please," she said before joining the others.

Okay, not too happy about holding a purse. I half-sat on a table and set the thing down beside me.

The princesses were on their third grouping when her phone buzzed. And buzzed. Insistently. Until it bounced its way out of the jewel-studded purse. I peeked at the caller ID and figured I'd better answer this call. "Hey, Korry."

There was a pause. "Who is this?"

"Mark Lewis."

He laughed. "The escort?"

"Yeah."

"Take good care of her."

"I will."

"So, put Gabi on."

I looked across the tent. A new lineup had formed, with camera flashes going like fireworks. "She's kind of busy at the moment."

"She'll talk to me."

I didn't doubt it. Holding the phone against my chest, I shouted, "Gabrielle, you have a call."

Everyone turned to stare at me, except the photographer. He was snapping shots like crazy. Actual candids.

Olivia said, "She's tied up."

Gabrielle asked, "Who is it?"

Oh, yeah, this was going to be a moment. "Korry Sim."

There was a loud chorus of "ahhhh" from the homecoming princesses, impatient eye-rolling from Olivia, and an instant expression of delight from Gabrielle. She hurried over and snatched the phone.

"I told you not to call." Her voice made it clear that she didn't mind.

"Couldn't resist, love…" The sound of his voice faded as she walked to an empty corner.

They talked a long time. The game started. The crowd went through the normal cycle of screams and groans—from both sides of the stadium.

Gabrielle didn't hang up on Korry until the cheerleading coach made her move, waving us toward our vehicles. I helped Gabrielle into her spot on the back of a white convertible and then took my place next to the driver. I'd become so used to the photographer now that I barely noticed him.

It seemed stupid to admit it, but I was enjoying the hell out of this night. As I watched Carlton climb into the car behind me, it occurred to me how strange this was. He was escorting the homecoming queen, and I was escorting the girl everyone would remember.

Halftime started. Our band played. The convertibles began their circle around the track.

Everything happened slowly, but time still seemed to blur. One by one, princesses were dropped off at the fifty-yard line. First the freshmen, then the sophomore and junior princesses.

Last came the seniors and the queen.

The crowd definitely saved its biggest roar for Gabrielle, although it was hard to know how much was for her reputation and how much was for the missing back to her dress.

And then it was over. We were back in the convertibles, rolling away from the football field. I scanned the crowd in the stands. Jesse and Benita were up there somewhere, but they weren't the type to scream like idiots.

I caught sight of my parents. My mother *was* screaming like an idiot.

We cleared the stands and slowed to a crawl, waiting our turn to exit through the gate. A bunch of students had gathered on the asphalt, shouting and waving. Gabrielle waved back.

A lone figure stood on the fringe of the crowd, wearing a hoodie in neon green. My gaze zeroed in on it because I had a hoodie in the same color, same style.

Could it be mine?

Nah.

Chapter Forty-One

A New Form of Liberty

Although I didn't wish to think very long about today's homecoming celebration or all of the activities Mark would participate in throughout this day, I could not help but wonder how often he missed fun because of me.

Was our relationship a burden for him? The very thought created an ache inside me.

Should I force myself to go out more? In my mind, I wanted to try, but the rest of me shuddered at the thought.

Perhaps I should plan fun things for us. Perhaps I should try harder to adapt to his world. Indeed, I ought to stop thinking of it as *his* world and start thinking of it as *mine*.

Dodging into the closet of my loft bedchamber, I grabbed a garment I'd been resisting and pulled it on. Standing before a full-length mirror, I studied myself in this pair of pants. The color was a dark blue, the fabric light and supple. The pants had no ties or elastic. They closed with a zipper. Norah had purchased them for me shortly after I arrived. She called them "capris."

Pants might be normal for modern women, but they didn't feel normal to me. Might I like these pants better with a bit of alteration? The width of the pant legs was acceptable, much wider and looser than what most women wore. But I didn't care at all for the hem, which stopped too near my knees. Stockings wouldn't be a reasonable remedy in October when it was still warm.

Perhaps I could lengthen the hem. I would consider this compromise.

After trading my brown skirt for the pants, I headed downstairs. Norah sat in a chair, reading a book. She dropped it immediately when I perched on the couch. "Morning, Susanna."

"Good morning. How are you feeling today?"

"Much better." She inclined her head. "There's coffee waiting for you."

As I smiled my gratitude and walked into the kitchen, the landline rang.

"Would you get that, please?" Norah asked.

I picked up the phone on the counter. "Hello?"

"Hey, Susanna," Mark's sister said.

"You're up early, Marissa." I returned to the living room.

"I have to be at work soon. Is Gran around?"

"Yes. Would you like to speak with her?"

"*No.*" There was a little laugh at the other end of the line. "You're the person I want to talk to. Can you go somewhere so that she can't hear?"

"Just a moment." Surprised and pleased, I lowered the phone and smiled at Norah. "Marissa is calling me."

"How nice." She dropped her gaze back to her book.

I went outside and then spoke into the phone. "I'm on the deck now."

"Okay, I want your opinion about something. I might come home for Thanksgiving. How do you think my family will react?"

"They'll be delighted." Could she have any doubt? Marissa was never far from their minds, particularly Sherri's. "How long will you plan to stay?"

"Permanently?"

"Oh, I see." This news would only heighten their delight, but the questions would be endless.

"Yeah, I'll bet you do." She sighed loudly. "I'm homesick. I miss my family and my friends. I miss North Carolina. I want to be near the ocean again." There was a pause. When she spoke again, her voice had thickened. "Fletcher hasn't said ten words to me in the past two weeks. He's so totally consumed by school that I might as well not be here. I can't continue the way we are."

"I am sorry."

"Don't be. It happens." She sniffed. "Will everyone make me crazy by saying *I told you so?*"

"Mark will."

"Yeah." She laughed. "How is my little brother? Is he excited about tonight?"

I stiffened. "I do not know."

"Have you talked with him about it?"

"Briefly."

She made an impatient sound. "Susanna, homecoming is important to him. You have to let him feel special."

"Thank you for your advice."

"But you're not taking it." She laughed again and then quickly sobered. "Don't tell anyone about Thanksgiving. I haven't made up my mind yet."

"I shall not." And with that, we said our goodbyes. When I reentered the house, Norah looked up expectantly.

"How is my granddaughter?"

"She is well."

Norah's eyes narrowed on me with concern. "You look like you have something on your mind."

"What might I do to help Mark feel special?"

She smiled. "Ask him out on a date."

"That is a lovely idea." I answered her smile with one of my own as my mind raced through the possibilities.

"Perhaps I could prepare a quiet supper for him in the apartment."

"Food is always an excellent option with Mark, but I think the two of you need to avoid time together in that apartment for a while." She gripped the arms of her chair and pushed up, biting back a small groan. "You can fry chicken, can't you?"

"Certainly." I hovered near her, ready to assist if she needed me. "I have not seen this dish served at the Lewis house."

"Not when Bruce is there, much to Mark's regret." She laughed. "I know you can bake an apple pie."

"Indeed."

"Well honey, you have the perfect fixings for a romantic picnic."

"A picnic?" I shook my head. "I do not know what that is."

"It's simple. Pack a basket with food. Find a secluded spot outside, and there you go. The rest is left up to you."

Norah and Charlie took me home Friday night. It must have been unannounced, for when we entered the kitchen, Mark's parents were standing there, dressed to go out.

Charlie shook hands with Bruce and kissed Sherri on the forehead. "Where are you two headed?"

"Homecoming."

They all watched me for my reaction. I had none—at least none I would permit them to see. "I hope you enjoy it."

"Want to come with us, Susanna?" Sherri asked.

We stared at each other intently. It wasn't exactly a battle of wills, more like a testing of the other's mettle.

"An entire football game will be more than I can tolerate," I said.

"We'll leave after halftime."

Bruce blinked at his wife.

Mark had asked me to come, and now his parents were making it easy. It was special to him, and I needed to try. "All right. I accept." I glanced down at my clothes.

"You look fine. It could get cold, though."

"I do not have a wrap." I felt oddly disappointed. For a few seconds, I'd been proud of my decision.

"No problem. We have extras." She disappeared into the laundry room.

"Going now," Norah said, hugging me from behind. "Bravo, honey," she whispered.

Once the door had slammed on Charlie and Norah, Sherri returned, a glowing green jacket in her hand. It was one of Mark's.

"Here you are."

I put it on. It smelled like a freshly-washed version of him. The scent and feel gave me courage. "I am ready."

Huge lights rose like great trees above the stadium, and the noise was daunting.

After five minutes in the stands, I began to fidget. The applause of thousands and the cold hardness of the bench—it all served to shroud me in misery.

Bruce placed his mouth near my ear. "Want me to find you a quieter spot?"

I nodded. We rose and edged out along the aisle and down the stairs.

He stopped near a place to buy food. "Hang out around here. We'll find you after halftime."

"Certainly."

He left, plunging into the crowd fearlessly. There was less noise in my new location, fewer people, and a clear view of the field.

After an hour elapsed, whistles shrieked and then the players ran to their benches and sat down. The people in the stands stood and screamed.

Guards in dark uniforms opened a gate near me. Cars drove onto the odd road that circled the football field. None of the cars had tops. I stood in the shadows as they rolled past.

Mark's car was near the end. He sat in the front seat, but someone else drove. His friend perched high in the back of the vehicle, so high we could see all but her legs and feet.

Gabrielle was more beautiful than I remembered from her photographs and movies. Abundant dark curls cascaded to her shoulders, held away from her face by a jeweled spray of flowers clipped behind an ear.

I walked as closely as I dared to the odd road and watched.

The ritual that followed might have been more fitting in my century than I would've expected here. Girls stepped from white cars on the arms of their suitors. In pairs, they sauntered to the field's center, their gowns dragging in the grass. I blinked with concentration as Mark and Gabrielle stepped away from their car. Her gown was purple except the back, which was the same shade as her skin. Or was it...?

Merciful heavens. The dress left the skin of her back exposed, from her neck to the tops of her buttocks. I blushed at the sight. I didn't wish to know if Mark would touch her there. I looked instead at him.

Once all of the couples had reached the center of the field, a man talked in loud, annoying echoes.

The crowd screamed.

The man echoed more, and then loud music played.

The couples made their way back to the cars.

The entire ceremony had lasted only a few minutes and had displayed a bewildering lack of charm. Why had this been important to Mark?

When his vehicle passed by, he nodded at the crowd, a detached curve to his lips. Then his body stiffened. He leaned forward, staring my way. Had he spotted me?

No, I must've been mistaken.

Mark's parents left early Saturday morning for one of their "turbo errand runs." It felt good to know they trusted us to be alone.

I dressed carefully. First came the blue capris, with the hems lowered as far as the fabric permitted. Then my birthday T-shirt, striped in blue and white. It too had been altered. The sleeve on my left arm had revealed my burn, and that I could not allow. Norah had helped me to add bands of wide, white lace.

As I skipped down the stairs to the kitchen, I ticked off the preparations for the picnic on my fingers. The fried chicken and apple pie that I brought with me from the lake house waited in the fridge. Norah had lent me her best picnic basket, complete with tablecloth and napkins. The basket looked too bulky for transport, but she assured me that Mark would figure it out.

He trudged in after nine o'clock, sweaty and splattered. I watched him from my spot at the table. "Are the trails muddy?" It was a possibility I had not allowed for.

He shook his head. "Not really. I went off-road in an area with a few muddy spots." He stopped at the fridge and drew out a bottle of Propel.

"I would like to ask you out on a date."

He lowered the bottle and swiped his mouth with the back of his hand. "You're asking *me?*"

"I am."

He smiled slowly. "What're we going to do?"

"I shall pack a picnic dinner."

"Cool. Where are we going?"

"Perhaps you could decide. I would like to ride our bikes on paved trails. Is there somewhere close?"

"The Museum of Art. My friends Jesse and Benita say it has a lot of great places to..." He stopped and smiled again.

"Picnic?"

"Right." He laughed. "What time?"

"Shall we leave at eleven?" I felt happy anticipation spiraling all the way to my toes.

"I'll be ready."

We biked on the greenway to the Museum of Art and followed it past the buildings as it wound through their outdoor garden of artwork. We continued up a hill and down into a valley, swallowed by a lovely forest. Once we crested the next hill, we left the pavement and locked our bikes.

Mark carried the basket with one hand and clasped mine with the other. We found the perfect spot high on the ridge, cool and fragrant with pine. Glimpses of the museum's manicured grounds stretched below us.

"I think it's great you're wearing pants."

"Indeed." I smoothed my hands over the fabric against my hips. He had been correct; they were easier to pedal in. I was happy that I had tried them, and happy he'd noticed.

A quartet of cyclists pedaled up the incline, their gears clicking. They passed but didn't glance our way. Perhaps we were hidden from view in this spot.

After spreading out the blanket, we sat down. He immediately grabbed the basket and pulled back the lid.

"Fried chicken?"

"Yes."

"Perfect." He peeled back lids on the other containers.

"Mark." I stared straight ahead, arms wrapped about my knees. "Have you been on picnics before?"

"A lot." He reached up to wrap a stray curl from my ponytail around his finger. "But…this is the first time I've been on a picnic *date*."

That pleased me. "Do you know what happens on a picnic date?"

"Whatever you want."

"I don't know what I want."

"No problem. I have plenty of ideas." His fingers slipped to my cheek, cupped it gently, and turned me toward him. "Kiss me."

I braced a hand on his chest, the muscle hard and smooth beneath the fabric of his shirt. Our mouths clung briefly and then released.

He smiled lazily at me. "That is official picnic behavior."

"Indeed? Picnics involve kissing?"

"The two-person kind of picnic does." He urged me back against the blanket. I shivered with anticipation and uncertainty, but all thought fled at the slide of his lips over mine.

The weight of his hand at my waist held me steady. Our legs entwined. I was surrounded by the warmth of his body. The cool of a pine-scented breeze. And hot, sweet kisses.

He groaned and broke away, his mouth trailing along my jaw to my neck. I drank in air, overwhelmed by the feelings he created.

Voices passed by on the greenway.

I grasped at the excuse. "Mark?"

He pushed up on his arms, gazing at me through half-closed lids. "Hmmm?"

"Can they see us?"

"Uh-uh." He rolled to his back, pulling me along until I lay partially over him. "Babe. If making out is too much for you, we'll stop."

"And that will be acceptable?"

"You're in charge. Always." His lips twitched. "I won't promise not to get grumpy, but better that than scare you off."

"I am in charge?" I must be clear on this magical fact. "Even now?"

"Completely. Totally. Absolutely—"

I hushed him with a kiss.

It had been a glorious afternoon. I had not been so happy since I moved to this century. The time to leave came too quickly.

I packed our trash in the basket while he folded the blanket. We held hands and walked to our bikes in silence, both melancholy that our picnic date had come to an end.

While he secured our things, I stepped to the side of the greenway trail and watched a couple trudging up the incline, absorbed in each other. I felt a sense of communion with them. This was a beautiful place to be in love.

"Susanna, I know this question might sound crazy, but did you come to the game last night wearing my green hoodie?"

"Yes." I looked up the trail, which rose above us before curving sharply around a stand of pines.

"Why?"

I turned to him and squinted. The sun was at his back, outlining him in a golden glow. "It was important to you."

He came closer, his helmet dangling from his hand. "Did you want to see Gabrielle?"

"I most certainly did."

"What did you think?"

I looked away, not entirely sure how to sort through the feelings I'd experienced. Perhaps I should make light of them. "I can understand why she wanted you for her escort. You're quite handsome in a tuxedo."

"You don't need to be jealous of Gabrielle." He hadn't been fooled.

"It isn't envy that I feel." I took a step back and stumbled against the edge of the pavement.

There was a scream and the shriek of brakes even as I found myself jerked into Mark's arms. We twisted and fell. His body took the full blow against the ground.

The bike whirred down the hill even as running feet pounded nearer.

Mark and I stayed in our tangled heap of limbs, breathing hard and in unison.

"Hello there! Are you two okay?"

Mark shifted under me and grunted. "I think so."

"Mark?" a young man asked.

"Hey, Jesse, Benita." There was welcome in Mark's voice. "I guess I shouldn't be surprised to see you here, since you told me about it." His hold on me loosened. "Meet Susanna."

"Hello," I said and turned to look up at them. "I am pleased to meet you."

The couple stood at our feet, staring down, frozen with horror. I craned to see what they saw.

Realization hit me like a punch to the gut, even as Mark whispered in my ear, "Your pants are above your knees."

Unbidden, moisture stung behind my eyes. I mumbled, "My scars." What must they think of the thin lines mottling my calves? Or the shiny pink bands encircling my ankles?

"I'm sorry, babe."

I slid off his body and landed on my bottom, unsure how to proceed.

Mark groaned. "Help her up, Jesse."

His friend pulled me to my feet and then stepped back to his girlfriend's side. I brushed debris from my pants, saddened by the sudden change. It had been a joyous day. The introduction to his friends should have made it even better. For the first time since I moved to this place, I had done normal things. Today, I'd been a girl with her boyfriend out on a date. Except that I had scars that demanded explanation.

"What happened to you?" Benita asked. Her boyfriend jabbed her with his elbow, but she didn't look away.

Mark rose and stood beside me, his arm firmly around my waist, gazing down at me, his silence telling me the decision was all mine.

I'd never had to speak these words. Mark's parents and grandparents had seen with their own eyes as they tended to my wounds. The explanation had come out slowly, piecemeal, in vague bits that his family had woven together on their own.

Today was different. If Jesse and Benita were to be my friends too, there must be truth—however harsh—between us. But how much would be enough? "My master thrashed me."

"Your master?" Jesse asked, his gaze shifting to Mark.

"Susanna was enslaved."

"Oh my god." Benita's eyes widened. "Like, human trafficking?"

Mark nodded. "More like a sweatshop, but close enough."

She gasped. "He must've been a monster. Why did he do that?"

They were horrified—at Mr. Pratt, not me. "It was how he corrected my mistakes."

Jesse and Benita said something in unison—a phrase I had never heard uttered in polite company.

"Yeah, really," Mark said. His hand caressed my neck. "Although they weren't always your mistakes. *Persuasion* was mine."

It had been the first novel I'd ever read, and Mark had given it to me. I had loved reading that book, despite knowing the fury its discovery would unleash in my master. How could any of us have imagined that Mr. Pratt's punishment that time would involve a hot skillet?

I looked into Mark's face, into his beautiful amber eyes. "Mark, please. It was a wondrous gift. Do not *ever* express regret again." Adoration swelled inside me like a living thing.

Benita held out both hands to me, palms up. She wore lace gloves whose fingertips had been snipped off. "Susanna."

I set my hands in hers as we both took one step closer to the other. She was taller than I, with a lovely thin face and expressive eyes of the darkest brown. Right now, her eyes held shock and something else. Something that resonated sweetly and painfully inside me.

Releasing her hands, I turned to Mark almost blindly. When he wrapped me in his arms, I closed my eyes, overcome at the knowledge that I had shared my secret and had been offered sympathy in return. A new form of liberty.

Mark spoke in muffled tones with his friends, but I could not listen to the words. I only knew that, by the time I had recovered my bearings, they were gone.

CHAPTER FORTY-TWO

CHOCOLATE KISS

It poured on Sunday. The gutters became mini-rivers that created mini-fountains at the sewer grates.

Since I couldn't be outside, I finally got to something I'd been putting off for a while—investigating colleges besides Virginia Tech and Brevard.

Mr. Rainey had suggested Duke. I would check it out, even if I remained more skeptical than he did.

NC State had good sports clubs, a ten-minute commute, and a gazillion stops on multiple bus routes. Susanna could get to me if I went to NCSU, but I really didn't want to go there. It would have to be a last resort.

Raleigh had other universities, all private. I'd never been remotely curious about any of them. As far as my parents were concerned, showing a sudden interest in one of them would be too suspicious.

I needed to grow up about this. It was possible to travel home on the weekends from Brevard or Virginia Tech. Or she could come to me, if she ever got her license.

Newman was the *in-between* school. Smaller than Virginia Tech. Closer than Brevard. Good reputation. Great new mountain-biking coach. One thing was for sure. Newman was definitely on the list now. Yeah, perfect in every way, except that two-hundred-thirty mile drive.

I went to their website and clicked on *Admission Requirements*.

Damn. They required an essay and the prompt was painful: *Describe your greatest achievement.*

Why did colleges ask stuff like that? Most high school seniors were seventeen. After twelve years of attending school—a system that only worked well if we did exactly what they told us to do—what kind of achievements did colleges think we had?

Super-brilliant students had achieved interesting things.

Super-bad students had achieved interesting things.

Everybody else had to make stuff up. Actually, I had done something of huge value. My greatest achievement was rescuing an abused girl from the asshole who tortured her. Oh, yeah, and she was living in the eighteenth century at the time.

It was the best thing I'd ever done. It was the best thing I would ever do, and I couldn't tell a soul.

The scent of warm chocolate tickled my nose. I twisted in my seat as Susanna entered the rec room on noiseless feet, a plate cradled in her hands.

She smiled at me, face flushed. Her hair hung down her back in a low ponytail, with wisps escaping to curl against her neck. She looked happy.

"I baked you a treat." She set the plate carefully in my hand.

"It smells great." The brownie was a tiny square, at least by my standards. Susanna still hadn't figured out twenty-first-century portion sizes.

"I tasted one first. It is delicious." She sat cross-legged on a chair beside me. "What has given you this bemused look?"

I wolfed down the entire square in one bite and wanted more. "I'm thinking about applying to another college."

"Which one?"

"Newman College."

"Is it nice?"

"I'm not sure. I've never been there."

Her brow scrunched up, like she was trying hard to take all of this in. "Do you not want to attend Virginia Polytechnic Institute?"

I controlled my smile. Susanna had been surfing the web. "It's one of the places I'm considering."

"Are you likely to be accepted?"

"I am."

"Then why do you apply elsewhere?"

Because everybody did—which was an answer she would think was stupid. I needed a better one. "My guidance counselor recommended it."

She watched me calmly, but her hands were clenched in her lap. "Where is this other college located?"

"Also in the mountains of Virginia."

"How long would it take to drive there?"

"Four hours."

"And the other one is about three?"

I nodded.

Understanding hummed through her body. I wouldn't be here much longer. My first choice was far away, and I'd just told her my second choice was even farther. Unless I found a closer college that had everything I needed, this was how it was going to be. Right?

"When will you leave Raleigh?"

I set the plate down and then linked both of my hands with hers. "Next August. Ten months away. A lot can happen."

She smiled shyly. "A lot can happen in two months."

"I don't want to be separated from you either."

"By then, I shall have my identification. I will have options too."

Susanna with options? I needed to wrap my brain around that. I'd been so focused on getting her an identity—and getting me into a college—that I hadn't planned past either.

My phone buzzed on the desk. "Excuse me a second." I extricated one of my hands, grabbed the phone, and put it on speaker. "Hey, Gabrielle. What's up?"

"Did you take any photos of the last experiment?"

"Yeah. Why?"

"My images are all blurry. Could you forward what you took?"

Susanna stirred restlessly and tugged her hand from mine.

"Can you hold, Gabrielle?"

"Sure."

Susanna had already stood and picked up the brownie plate. "I shall return to the kitchen," she said, her voice low. "I have dishes to clean."

"We're not done, Susanna."

"I know." She leaned over me and kissed me—a hot, brief, chocolate kiss. "There are more downstairs."

"What do you mean?" I didn't know whether to laugh or groan. "Brownies?"

"Indeed." She smiled before skipping down the steps.

CHAPTER FORTY-THREE

A FAR DIFFERENT WORLD

The past week had been a joy. I gave back. I had cleaned, cooked, and cared for Norah and Charlie. I had completed a real, twenty-first-century job.

It was a pleasure to be useful, and I didn't want to return to the days when I hadn't been. Would there be more jobs for pay? Should I ask, even beg, for chores? Would it be proper to remind Sherri of her offer to find me a first-aid course?

This was not, however, the correct week to raise these subjects. Bruce had left today for another trip. There had been an emergency somewhere, but a quick one. Sherri had been angered by the news. Mark had shown a bit of wariness. The family was on edge. I would have to wait.

But I would ask. Soon.

I cleaned my apartment, rechecked my clothes, and visited with Toby. Mark and his mother had already retired for the evening. I would spend an hour before bed with my sister's journal. With all of the activities during my stay at the lake house, I'd been unable to complete my reading.

The next two pages in her journal were filled with the varied crimes of Mrs. Simpson and the dull girls she employed. Why did my sister waste paper and ink on such undeserving people as these?

I was nearly ready to turn off the computer when an entry caught my eye.

June 14th, 1801

Mr. William Eton has returned to Raleigh. He spoke to me outside the State House today following Sunday worship. He checked my thumb and pronounced it as good as new.

Mr. William says he will only be here for a brief visit. He has offers from Edenton and New Bern to serve as a physician. He visits his parents while he ponders a decision.

It is not far from Union Square to the boarding house where I stay. He walked with me the whole way. Mrs. Simpson watched from the window next door.

She told me later not to give myself airs. Mr. William couldn't be interested in a bit of fluff like me.

Why would she say such foolish things? Mr. William was merely being kind. I know this and do not expect more, although it does remind me of what my sister said.

Would it not be lovely to live in a place where there was more familiarity between classes?

I sat back in my chair, mulling over this entry. Had my unthinking words planted a seed in her mind? If so, I had done her a grave disservice. In trying to explain my situation here and reassure her of my contentment, I had given her a thought that had no place in her world.

Another dozen entries passed, with increasing injustice from her employer and, thankfully, no further mention of William Eton.

June 30th, 1801

I received a caning today and declared it to be my last. I packed my things and left Mrs. Simpson's mean employ forever. With the rear door locked, I had to exit through the shop as customers watched in wonder.

Is it wrong to feel pleasure at the scene Mrs. Simpson made? She screamed after me and told me I would come begging back to her. She claimed that no one would want me when they saw what a headstrong girl I was.

But it is she who will be made to look foolish. I shall not go back. I would rather walk to my brother's farm in Worthville and live out my days growing vegetables.

Patty is married now, with a tiny babe. I shall stay with her and her husband until I find a new position. It is fortunate that I do not mind hard labor, for her household has fallen into disrepair. Patty has been too ill to clean, her husband too ignorant, and her mother unable to help due to her own confinement. I fear the scrubbing may ruin my hands, but I shall manage for now. I have no wish to return to Worthville or become a burden on my brother's family.

I stifled a yawn, closed the computer, and crawled into bed, a thankful prayer on my lips that Phoebe had made such a bold and fine decision.

Sherri pulled out of the driveway the next morning, late as usual. It was most fortunate that the building where she worked took hardly more than five minutes to reach.

Mark and I had a quiet breakfast together before he left, although I must say that he seemed a bit distracted. Perhaps there was schoolwork due.

I washed the dishes, fed the cat, and returned to the apartment. My life had fallen into a pattern of sorts, which I liked quite well—especially when my days began and ended with Mark.

The next chore, naturally, was studying for my high school equivalency placement exam. Today my focus would be math. I kept the algebra book from my father open and found myself reflecting on how well this book had stood the test of time.

After lunch, it was time for my sister again. I was nearly done with her journals and I found myself meting out each entry, like a treat that I feared would end too soon.

I brewed my favorite cup of tea, curled in a chair with Toby draped along its back, and read about the next adventure in my sister's life.

July 6th, 1801

I have secured a new position in less than a week. I shall work for Raleigh's new tailor shop. The owner and his wife are eager to make their mark. They wish to sell embroidered gloves and scarves for ladies and will ask me to add whitework to the cuffs of men's shirts.

I feel the burn of excitement at the possibilities.

The wage each month will be low. I have found a small cot at a boarding house a fair distance away. I do not care, for this new position is well worth the peace of mind that comes from working with pleasant employers and not fearing that my hands will be ruined by a cane.

July 15th, 1801

I write my inkwell dry in this journal. Kindly, my new employers have paid me for my first week's wages, and I simply had to buy ink with the pennies remaining after paying rent. I hurried to the stationer's shop and nearly ran into Mr. William as I was leaving.

He told me it was a delight to see me and then tipped his hat.

I curtsied to hide a blush and expected him to move along, but he did not. Instead, he settled in for a brief conversation, asking to see my thumb. He held my hand gently, inspected it carefully, and proclaimed himself to be grateful for my continued health.

I thought surely he would depart but again he surprised me, asking why I had come to the stationer's.

The answer was simple enough. I came to buy ink, and while there, the stationer informed me of a letter that I had received. I knew it to be from Jacob Worth, as his handwriting is bold and distinctive.

Mr. William responded that he remembered his mother teaching me to write.

Truly, I could not allow that erroneous impression to remain. I shared that it was my sister who taught me, since she'd had the finest education a girl could expect, with a father for the village tutor. Then, lest he think that I was not suitably thankful, I added, "I owe your mother the elegance with which I write."

I could see his surprise at the news of my father's profession. It left me oddly ashamed, as if I ought to apologize for my present state. I bobbed my head and whispered a quick goodbye.

July 17th, 1801

Jacob Worth is quite taken with Dorcas Pratt. She is the most beautiful, clever, and elegant creature he has ever met. His latest letter sings her praises without ceasing.

It worries me deeply, for he must surely recognize the obstacles to a relationship between them. It is uncommon enough for close cousins to marry, even if he were to wait until she was of a better age. Nor can he overlook the issue of her health. Truly, a gentleman farmer cannot afford to have a lame wife.

A *lame* wife? Had I read that correctly? My sister's entry seemed to imply that Dorcas was lame, yet she hadn't been when I had last seen her.

I lifted shaking hands to my face. Could Mr. Pratt's ill-timed push have crippled Dorcas permanently? Mark had claimed that her injury was likely to be bad. Whisper Falls had shielded me from what happened after her fall, though I hadn't dreamed that it would change her life.

No longer able to sit still with my guilt, I rose and crossed to the rear window, where I knelt on the padded bench and pressed my palms to the cool glass. Phoebe wouldn't have said Dorcas was lame unless it was true. My dear friend's prospects for marriage had obviously dropped precipitously with a push from her father, yet she'd been educated for nothing else.

Only the wealthiest of men could tolerate the burden of a woman who lacked strength. Yet such a man would have his pick of wives. He would have no need to look past a limp to see her innate grace and rare intellect.

My trip through time had saved one and sacrificed another.

I had to know more. Did Phoebe mention her again? I raced back to the computer and scoured the pages, looking for the name Dorcas. Instead, "William" seemed to leap at me from each image, appearing in nearly every entry.

...Miss Judith and Mrs. Eton paid a visit to the shop. They were quite taken with the adorned gloves. The owners were overjoyed to see them. Mr. William inquired after my hand before waiting outside beside the carriage...

...Mr. William waved at me as he rode past on his horse...

...Mr. William greeted me after worship on Sunday. We spent but a brief time together, yet those minutes were very pleasant...

...William brought me an apple. Perhaps it would seem a silly afterthought, but I had mentioned on Sunday how I longed for a fresh apple and today I have one...

I had not found Dorcas's name, but I had found something more distressing.

Phoebe had dropped the "Mr."

An uneasy feeling settled over me. As beautiful and talented as my sister was, she could never be an acceptable mate for one of the Etons. Oh, my poor Phoebe. If she didn't come to her senses soon, she was bound for heartache.

August 3rd, 1801

Mrs. Nance fetched me from the rear of the shop this day. One of our customers wished to speak a word of praise to the needlewoman who had embroidered his shirt. It was quite an unusual request. Unheard of, even.

How surprised I was when I entered the front of the shop to find William! He was most complimentary of the vines and leaves adorning the cuffs of his newly purchased shirt. "I remain in awe of the dexterity of your hand." He went on to say how delighted he was that a talent such as mine had been preserved.

I am blushing still.

August 10th, 1801

Senator Eton's office is near the State House. I have taken to walking about its grounds on my break, hoping for a glimpse of his son.

William crossed the street today. He said that he had seen me strolling among the trees and had come to offer company. Naturally, I acquiesced.

He stayed with me the whole of my break and escorted me to the shop. He plans to visit Edenton in September, for his decision is imminent and he would like to meet with the townsfolk again.

William is very wise.

It is mad for me to admire him. Utterly hopeless and foolish. Yet his smile is so beautiful and his voice so dear. Can a simple seamstress ever be worthy of a man with his expectations?

I should not dream. No, I must not. It is not done.

Yet I cannot help but cling to the glimmer of hope Susanna gave me. She works as a cook in the household of Mr. Lewis, and she claims they are destined for marriage. My sister would not lie.

There must be places where my years as a laborer could be overlooked.

Phoebe had remembered my words too well. I should never have told her, and could only pray that she wouldn't humiliate herself before him—and that he would be kind to her if she did.

August 31st, 1801

William kissed me. It was the sweetest thing I have ever known and more potent than a fine spirit. I am giddy with joy.

He leaves in the morning for Edenton. I shall miss him desperately.

How easy it has become to yearn for a daily glimpse of the man I love!

I could've written these thoughts myself, but they were wrong for her. So wrong.

My breaths puffed out rapidly, as if I had run a long race. I closed my eyes against her words, fearful of what I would read next. Their feelings could only lead to despair. Yet why should I expect my sister to give up love when I had not?

No, truly, I needed to clear my thinking. I lived in a far different world than she. I lived where it was acceptable for the classes to blend. She did not. An alliance with William Eton could never work. He must know this. Was this a mere dalliance for him?

With a newfound determination, I read on, my eyes skimming over the bits of ordinary life and the foolish musings of a girl who waited.

September 12th, 1801
As I hurried to the shop this morning, a horse stopped abruptly beside me and a young man called my name.

It was a voice I recognized well, though I had not heard it in over a year. Jacob!

He dismounted and kissed my hand, right there on the city street. I could not help a laugh. Had we not had an audience, I do believe that I might have hugged him.

After we exchanged greetings, he informed me of his plans to purchase land near Asheville.

I am most pleased for him, although the import of this news struck me deeply in the heart, surprising the admission from me that I would miss him fiercely.

He laughed and said, "Letters may be posted from Buncombe County, dear friend."

September 20th, 1801
Mrs. Eton separated herself from the crowd after worship and made her way purposefully toward me. "Phoebe, a word, if you please."

I fell into step beside her, trembling at such a visible honor. We strolled some moments before she finally spoke, telling me that her son would return soon from Edenton with the promise of employment.

My heart fluttered with delight at the news and pain at the thought of his departure. How could I bear to never see him again?

She continued, adding that William had received an offer also from the town of New Bern. It was her opinion that New Bern was his preference, given the family and friends he had there.

I nodded, confused as to the point behind these confidences.

She stopped and watched me closely as she stated his plans to practice medicine in Edenton.

Her words surprised a forthright and candid response from me. "Whyever would he choose the lesser option?"

"For your sake."

My face must have reflected my shock, for she went on to declare that William fancies himself in love with me.

I knew a thrill of deep joy to hear this news, but the pleasure was short-lived.

Mrs. Eton opined that his choice was driven by the knowledge that New Bern society would never accept me as his wife—as the Eton family is far too well-known in that city . To them, I would always be a laborer—the housemaid from the home of his youth. In Edenton, he would be able to pass me off as the daughter of a village tutor who married above herself but slightly.

With her little speech concluded, Mrs. Eton turned away from me and resumed her stroll.

I ached from head to toe, as if I had fallen a long way and could barely move, so battered and bruised by emotion was I. When she threw a glance at me over her shoulder, I struggled to catch up, each step dragging as if my legs were weighted down.

She reminded me that I would now be the one with a hard decision to make. She implored me to consider this information with both heart *and mind, remembering that my choice affected the course of two lives, mine and William's.*

My throat felt thick, yet I managed to ask if she had spoken thusly with her son.

Indeed, she had. "It is hard to reason with a young man in love. He believes America is changing, and it is, but not as quickly as he might like."

The rattle of carriage wheels and clip-clop of a horse drew to a stop beside us. Senator Eton jumped down, gave me a nod, and offered a hand to his wife. She placed her gloved hand—one of my creations—in her husband's and bade me farewell. I could hardly hear her parting words.

"Do what you know to be right."

There was a loud rap on the apartment door. I jumped from my seat, startled at the sound. "Come in," I said as I pressed down the computer's top.

It was Sherri, beaming widely, a thick envelope in her hand. "Hey. Got a minute?"

"Certainly." I glanced at the clock. It was barely past noon. "I had not expected you so early."

"It's my lunch break. I'm taking it here today." She crossed to me. "I have your money."

I shook my head, disoriented, craving to know what came next in my sister's story. "What money?"

"From the invitations you addressed." She placed the envelope into my hand. "One hundred dollars—and another job."

CHAPTER FORTY-FOUR

FIERY AND PRIMITIVE

Procrastination paid off.

I checked my web alerts before leaving for school Monday. There were last-minute cancellations Friday and Saturday nights at my second-choice hotel outside Blacksburg. I grabbed one and then canceled my backup.

The day only got better. Susanna fixed me a seriously good breakfast. The commute to school seemed lighter than normal, and the school's morning TV show had a long segment on homecoming. Gabrielle was featured heavily, which meant I was too.

In physics, we had a substitute, the good kind who ignored the lesson plan and told us to do what we wanted.

That was an easy decision. We wanted to talk.

I joined my friends at a free table in the back.

Gabrielle was smiling at the other two. "Did you have fun at homecoming?"

"Sure did," Benita said. "You looked gorgeous in that gown."

"Sure did." Jesse shuddered theatrically.

Gabrielle laid a light hand on my arm. "Mark looked hot in his tux."

"Thanks. You looked great, Gabrielle. From all directions." When I exchanged glances with Jesse, we gave mock-groans in unison. Damn.

"Have to keep up a certain image." Her lips twitched too. "Korry likes that dress."

"I'm sure he does." I shifted to face her. "How late did you stay at the dance?"

"Not much longer than you." She brought up the photo gallery on her phone and showed me a picture of her and Jesse hugging on the floor of our gym. The lights were dim, the other couples were out-of-focus in the background, and his hands were pressed to the bare skin of her upper back. "Jesse was sweet enough to be my partner for the princesses' last dance."

He shuddered. "Sweet is not the word I would use to describe it."

Benita punched him in the arm. "You'd better be careful what word you *do* use."

"It was tame, compared to you." He kissed her cheek.

"Good answer." She kissed his mouth.

"Um, guys, we're in physics," I said with a laugh. How did they get away with stuff like that?

They rolled their eyes at me and then turned the conversation back to the dance. I wasn't careful about tuning in. Lengthy descriptions of dresses were not my thing. I'd rather talk about the football game—which I hadn't been able to see until the second half.

Jesse cleared his throat. "Benita and I met Susanna Saturday."

I refocused. This topic interested me.

"Really?" Gabrielle's eyebrow shot up. "Where?"

"At the Museum of Art." I left it there.

"An exhibit?"

I shook my head. "A date. Out near the sculpture garden." It had been an amazing date. Susanna had been so…brave. I could feel the heat rising in my face.

Gabrielle's eyes widened. She turned to Benita. "What's she like?"

Benita exchanged a long glance with Jesse before answering. "I think Susanna is my hero."

Jesse nodded in agreement.

I sat there silently, soaking up everything they said. It was the first time I'd experienced Susanna through another teen's eyes. Well, besides Alexis, and she didn't count.

Gabrielle frowned. "Why do you say that?"

"She's just..." Benita looked to me. For what? Permission? Encouragement? She wasn't getting either, but I also wouldn't put any controls on what she said. I had to trust them to do the right thing.

Benita looked back on Gabrielle. "I guess you'd have to meet her to understand. She's sweet..."

"Hot," Jesse added.

"Quiet..."

"Hot."

Gabrielle shifted her attention to Jesse. "What makes her hot?"

"The hair? Even better in person than in photos." One corner of his mouth twitched. "And her voice is, like, wow. All low and husky." Then, for once, Jesse lost the teasing smile and looked completely serious. "But it's more than that, you know. She doesn't use many words, but they're the perfect words. And her body language when she's talking with you? It's like you're the most important thing in the world to her at that moment."

He and I fist-bumped. I couldn't have said it better.

"And the way she looks at Mark?" Benita leaned so close to Jesse that their noses practically touched. "I want you to look at me that way."

"What way are you talking about?" My voice sounded oddly raspy.

Benita locked gazes with me. "Like you're heaven itself, come down to earth."

Silence greeted her statement, as if that's what it needed to be savored. I hunched forward on the table, head bowed, wanting to be away from here.

"How do you feel about her?" Gabrielle's question was so soft that it nearly blended with the noise in the room.

"Susanna is everything to me." Something fiery and primitive licked through my veins. "I can't imagine a world without her."

Chapter Forty-Five

Simple Yet Heartbreaking

I joined Sherri in the kitchen for lunch. It took me a few moments to direct the conversation to her announcement about another job. The excitement was hard to contain.

"It's a wedding, which could be a problem. I know the family slightly. You can definitely expect a bridezilla."

I shook my head at the unfamiliar term. "Bride-*zilla*?"

"Oh, sorry." She laughed. "That's what we call a bride who turns into a spoiled, self-centered brat as her wedding approaches."

This didn't sound pleasant, but the payment did. Truly, it would be hard for a "bridezilla" to be worse than the employers I'd had for eight years. "I shall be glad to do the work."

"Five hundred invitations will take a lot of time." She smiled.

Five hundred? I should not like that many people at my wedding. Indeed, the only person I would need at my wedding was… No, I must stop such thoughts. "Please let them know that I accept."

Sherri continued to talk about this new job, her work at the hospice center, and other bits of information that came to her mind. I listened quietly, not always understanding but content to stay where I was. Pleasant visits between us had been rare. I would do nothing to shorten this one.

When at last she went upstairs to her suite, I ran up to the apartment and opened the computer, anxious to finish the pages that remained in my sister's final journal.

September 22nd, 1801

Tonight I shall consider the many reasons a marriage between us can never be.

As my husband, William would be doomed to serve as the doctor of towns distant from his family and friends. Would he not grow weary of this limitation?

I should be the mistress of his home. Could I succeed? I was raised on a farm. I know much about cleaning a large house but little about running the type of household suitable for William. If we entertained, would my humble beginnings be evident to all?

What of my needlework? I love the feel of beautiful fabric in my hands and the bloom of embroidery beneath my fingers. Would I give up adorning linens, gloves, and gowns? Would I be restricted to the useless objects that fine ladies make?

The final reason—the one I fear most—is discovery. What might happen if our deception was ever revealed? How would the townsfolk react? Might they shame us into moving?

Would the constant threat of discovery take the joy from our days?

September 23rd, 1801

William and I love truly and deeply. Is that not a firm foundation upon which to build a marriage? Can there be any stronger?

We shall work hard. Our youth and good health will serve us well.

If we have to move, we shall learn to enjoy our next home together.

And why should the people of Edenton despise us if they uncover my past? It is an old city and a proud one. The ladies of Edenton displayed their mettle ten years before my birth when they refused to drink English tea. They even sent a notice of the Edenton Tea Party to the English newspapers. Such fine and clever women would welcome me, would they not?

September 26th, 1801

A most grievous blow fell today.

Jacob Worth came to the shop at closing time. He has traveled to Raleigh to order the last of his supplies. He plans to leave within a month to arrive in the mountains before snow prevents his journey.

He visited me to say his goodbyes. I wept at his news and told him mine.

Jacob begged me to dry my tears, declaring that I was "a woman meant for laughter. All will be well."

I dearly want him to be correct.

October 1st, 1801

William has returned.

I have walked about Union Square each day, hoping for his return. And suddenly he was there, waiting for me.

We ran into the hiding shade of a willow tree, full of smiles and sighs. Before I had a chance to utter a word, he drew me to him and pressed his lips to mine in long, thrilling kisses.

"I love you, Phoebe." His voice flowed over me like rich honey.

I quickly professed my love to him. Such a slight statement for so much meaning.

"Our time apart seemed an eternity."

Indeed. I laid my head against his chest and closed my eyes against the world around us. It faded from my mind until there was naught left but the safety of his arms.

He spoke of his agreement with the good people of Edenton and that he would have to move there by month's end.

I breathed in his news, the words filling my lungs like sweet air.

"Come with me, Phoebe, as my wife."

Even now, hours later, I can hardly believe it is true.

Did he ask me to marry him or had it all been a dream? It felt real and yet when I strain to recall, it fades away like wisps of fog.

What I have most longed for has come to pass. How shall I answer him? Do I have the courage to claim his offer?

Why had William accepted the position before conversing with Phoebe? If she rejected his offer, he would be honor-bound to move to Edenton nonetheless. Was he that certain of my sister's response?

If she agreed to his offer, did he not realize that their secrets would follow them? His father was a famous war hero and senator. One of William's grandfathers had been a royal governor; the other, one of the state's wealthiest landowners. The whispers would surely reach Edenton. Its fine families would murmur over Phoebe's inability to play an instrument and speak French. They would sniff over how little she knew of planning parties or making aimless conversation. William, who had been raised in the highest of society, would be snubbed because he'd chosen the wrong wife. Would that not chafe over time?

October 3rd, 1801

I received a hand-delivered note today. It is from Jacob Worth. He has asked me to marry him.

He makes no claims of love—not the kind I have with William. It will be a union of friends who wish to prosper in a land of unlimited possibilities.

Jacob returns to Raleigh on October fifteenth, to claim his supplies and, perhaps, me. We could be married in Worthville and begin our journey west the same week.

My head pounds and my heart aches. What is the right thing to do?

Jacob Worth? His offer shocked me. Could he truly wish to marry someone whose heart belonged to another?

I had no objection to Jacob. He was a good man. But he wished to farm orchards, and Phoebe had never lived farther than a ten-minute walk from town. How would she fare in isolation?

October 4th, 1801

William waited for me after worship service today, boldly approaching me, uncaring of those who would see us together. He pressed me for an answer.

I cannot find the words. My indecision is agonizing for us both.

He claims that Edenton delights him, that he has not given a passing thought to New Bern, but I do not believe his protestations. He gives up much for me. Can I ever be enough?

I know what it is to love, and it makes me sadder than any grief I have ever felt.

October 5th, 1801

For a girl who worried that she would never receive an offer of marriage, it is overwhelming that I have received two.

One promises a life of ease with a revered husband. The price is the constant worry that someone will discover I was his housemaid when we met.

The other life will be harder. I shall move far away—to a place where few have gone before. No one will care about my beginnings; there will be no time to wonder about such things. When I do have leisure moments, I shall indulge in my love of sewing instead of the useless pastime of serving tea.

One man I love with the sweetness of a dear friend. The other I adore with all the passions of the soul.

With Jacob, I shall have a life of contentment.

With William, a life balanced between secrets and joy.

Where are you, Susanna? I need your counsel.

It was the final entry. The journal had ended.

What did she decide? It was maddening. I had to learn more, and I would, whatever it took. Thank goodness my skills with the computer had improved.

I searched for Phoebe Marsh, Phoebe Worth, and Phoebe Eton. There was no information on any of those names in the nineteenth century in Raleigh, Edenton, or Buncombe County.

Perhaps I should study the gentlemen instead.

I started with Jacob Worth. I was relieved to find him mentioned on the website at Blue Ridge College. A college student had written a paper about nineteenth-century settlements in the surrounding counties. Eagerly, I opened the document and read.

Jacob Worth had died in a logging accident at the age of 37. His second wife had borne him three sons, each of whom lived to adulthood. And there—at the end of the paragraph on Jacob—was a simple yet heartbreaking statement. His first wife died in childbirth.

The writer of this document failed to name either wife.

I searched next for William Eton. Thankfully, the *Edenton Gazette* had been a weekly publication. The Archives had many of its issues online, although not all years of the newspaper had survived.

There was one mention of him from 1801, expressing excitement that Dr. Eton would be their new physician. The article didn't say whether he was married.

The issues jumped five years to 1806. Two articles surfaced on the computer. One laid profuse praise on Dr. Eton's head for his skill with fevers.

The second article left me numb.

It described the house fire of a prominent citizen and discussed two other fires from recent years. Dr. William Eton's mansion on Albemarle Sound had burned to the ground in 1804. His wife had perished.

Whether she chose Jacob or William, my sister would die young.

CHAPTER FORTY-SIX

THE TEMPTATION TO TAMPER

It was quiet in the apartment when I got home from school. I grabbed a snack and went up there to check on her.

The door stood ajar. I rapped twice and then pushed it open. "Hey."

She sat at the table, staring blankly at the screen. Her eyes tracked to me. "Hello."

"Is something wrong?"

"I seek information on Jacob Worth and William Eton, but there is little to find."

Worth and Eton? I recognized those last names. "Would Jacob Worth be from Worthville?"

She gave a short nod.

"And William Eton is one of *the* Etons?"

"Yes."

I had the sense something was about to change, and that I wouldn't like it. I pulled out one of the kitchen chairs, set my snack on a placemat, and gave her my full attention. "Why are you researching them?"

"They have made Phoebe offers of marriage."

Maybe I had my history screwed up, but I thought girls wanted to be married back then. The earlier, the better. Maybe not, though, because Susanna looked seriously upset. "Are they bad guys?"

"They are both fine young men."

That should be good news, but she looked like she was about to pass out. "Which one did your sister pick?"

"I do not know." She pressed her palms to her eyes.

"Have you learned anything?"

"Jacob's wife died in childbirth. William's wife was lost in a house fire."

The sense of impending doom deepened. Susanna had messed with history when she saved Phoebe's thumb. Had that made a difference in who Phoebe married and how long she lived?

It was too late to know, but it had to be tearing Susanna apart. I needed to reduce the temptation to tamper any more. "Let me see what I can find." I took over the keyboard.

My efforts didn't make a difference. William and Jacob were easy enough to find, but the first names of their wives weren't. "Sorry. I didn't have any luck."

"Where else can we look?"

I wanted her to drop this. I also knew that wasn't likely to happen. "Do you want me to check at the Archives?"

"Yes." Her face remained neutral, except her eyes. They glowed with hope. "Might you do so this week?"

I stood and pushed my chair in. "I'll try."

She stood too. "You'll be gone all weekend."

I wasn't sure whether the manipulation was conscious or not, but it was working. "I'll take the truck tomorrow and go straight from school."

"Truly?" She launched herself into my arms.

Holy shit, I liked the way she said thank you.

I came home from the Archives empty-handed. She read it on my face the minute I walked into the house.

"Sorry, babe. I checked Wake County from 1801 through 1804. There are no surviving marriage records for Jacob, William, or Phoebe."

"I am sorry too." She followed me into the family room.

I flopped onto the couch and held out my hand. She took it and curled up beside me.

The trip downtown and back had been a nasty mess of traffic and non-existent parking. I'd need a moment to recharge. "Deborah Pratt married Aaron Foster in the summer of 1801."

"Truly? Aaron and Deborah? They suit."

I choked off a laugh. "You have snarky down."

She sniffed. "Did you try other counties besides Wake?"

"No, it was closing time. They were pushing people out." I hooked an arm around her waist and pulled her onto my lap. "I don't know how much harder we can try. If she did marry either one of them, the license could've been lost or destroyed in a courthouse fire, which happened a lot. Or so I was told."

She reclined against me. "I must do something."

The steel in her voice sent a shiver down my spine. I shifted her around until I could see her face. She looked very determined. "Why must you?"

"It is my fault that it came to this."

"Why is it your fault?"

"I told her that marriage between classes was possible where I lived now. She has allowed herself to believe it was possible there too."

"Is there really that big a gap between William Eton and Phoebe?"

She frowned at me. "Would the President consider marrying the woman who cleans the toilets?"

"He's already married."

Susanna gave me a look.

I let my head drop onto the couch back, too drained by battling traffic to sit up any longer. "Okay, if he were single, it's unlikely the President would marry the cleaning lady. Not a good career move."

"Indeed. In Phoebe's time, it would be an ordeal to live where their secret was known. They would be foolish to entertain such a notion." She slipped off my lap and walked to the window overlooking the front lawn.

"Maybe she marries Jacob."

"They do not want to marry each other. Perhaps they believe that, since they cannot marry the person they each love, then a friend will be good enough."

"Who does Jacob love?"

"Dorcas." Her voice was flat. "She is too young, and she is lame."

I twisted on the couch until Susanna came into view. Her forehead pressed to the glass as she stared at the front landscaping. Minutes passed—minutes of total silence. It worried me. "What are you thinking?"

"I must get a message to my sister."

That was chilling. "To say what?"

"My advice about what she should do."

"How will that message get there?"

She shrugged.

I rocketed off the couch and stalked to her side. She avoided looking my way.

"Dammit, Susanna. Tell me you won't go back. You'll get caught this time."

Her chin lifted. "I shall not make promises I cannot keep."

"You already promised."

"My loyalty to my sister comes first."

Great. She was considering this. Could I make her realize how completely insane the idea was? "Fine. So you go back and you make it all the way to Raleigh without being caught—even though Pratt knows you're alive and might even have people out looking for you. Let's say you reach your sister. What advice are you planning to give?"

"To marry neither man."

Frustration hissed through my teeth. "I thought girls back then wanted to marry."

"They did."

"More than anything. Like it was practically a necessity."

A nod.

"How does Phoebe feel about these two guys?"

"One she loves as a friend. The other she loves as a…" Susanna sighed.

"As a soulmate?"

"Indeed."

"So the two men she loves most in the world have proposed, and you're going to tell her to wait around in case there happens to be a third."

She tossed her head with attitude. "Her position as a seamstress is a good one. It could sustain her long enough to meet another man and marry."

"Her *third* choice could be a jerk who beats her." I wanted to shake her. "And Phoebe could die in childbirth anyway."

Susanna deflated. "I had not thought of that."

"Which is why you have me." I pulled her into my arms, hoping that what I'd said got through to her. "Leave Phoebe alone to live the best life she can."

"I cannot bear…" Her voice trailed to nothing.

"You can't save her from this one, Susanna. Please put it behind you."

CHAPTER FORTY-SEVEN

A REASONABLE SUGGESTION

I lay in bed later that night, gazing at the ceiling, pondering what I should do.

Mark's words had been wise. Of course, he was right. Phoebe would ignore my advice to marry neither man. In returning to the past, I would risk my freedom to no avail.

Perhaps, instead, I should advise her on which of the two to marry. After all, she did ask my advice.

But whom did I think would be best?

Jacob could give her a simple life, a life that she would understand and enjoy quietly. Certainly his interest in farming and his willingness to move to the wilds of the North Carolina mountains hinted at unknown depths.

I found myself also warming to William, who had been so bewitched by my sister that he was willing to fight his world for her sake.

Both were fine men.

Yet I knew something that they couldn't know. Phoebe wouldn't live long with her husband. Should I allow this knowledge to inform my advice?

Indeed, yes. What value was there in living in the future if I didn't embrace its benefits?

As Sherri and I drove home from a lovely hour of shopping on Wednesday, we passed Mark on his bike not far from the entrance to the neighborhood. Dismay tugged at my gut. I didn't wish to discuss my purchases.

Once the car had stopped in the garage, I hurried upstairs and hid the bag before he could get home.

Below me, I heard the noises of his arrival and opened the door to eavesdrop. In the laundry room, Sherri banged the lid of the washing machine. The tread of Mark's shoes crossed the floor.

"Gross, Mark. Kiss me after you've showered."

"Love you too, Mom."

They both laughed. His footsteps faded toward the kitchen and hers followed. I tiptoed to the stairwell, straining to hear.

"Did you have a good day?" she asked.

"Yeah. Great." The fridge opened and closed. "Where'd you and Susanna go?"

"To the fabric store."

"Why?"

Merciful heavens, she was going to tell him.

"She wanted lace, thread, and buttons."

"Buttons?"

"Yeah, gorgeous buttons made of wood and glass."

I slumped onto the top step of the landing. I had taken a chance in not begging her for silence.

Mark asked, in his most nonchalant voice, "How many?"

Please, Sherri. Don't...

"Forty or so."

A bottle slapped down hard on the countertop. His footsteps sounded on the stone floor, headed this way. I stood and ran back through the door of my apartment.

"Is something wrong, Mark?"

"I'm about to find out." He thundered up the stairs and walked in without knocking.

I stood rooted to the floor in the center of the room. He approached me, jaw taut.

"What are the buttons for?"

"Phoebe. They are currency where she lives."

He crossed his arms over his chest, eyes blazing. "You get points for not lying."

"I do not need 'points.'"

"When were you planning to go?"

"Tomorrow."

"Would you have said anything?"

"No."

He gaped at me in utter disbelief. "You promised not to go back."

"I am breaking that promise." His entire demeanor condemned me, and it was deserved. "I'm sorry, Mark. I meant to honor my promise, but I'm to blame for Phoebe's quandary."

"You were going to disappear again. Just go off and let me wonder."

"Yes."

His eyes closed, as if in pain. "How can I trust you now?"

I stiffened, taken aback at the depth of emotion that crackled about him. "You can trust that I will always to do the right thing for those I love."

There was a long silence, fraught with tension. When his eyes opened again, he looked dazed. "What's the rush?"

"Phoebe must give her answer by the middle of October. Today is the twelfth."

"She gives an answer in 1801, Susanna. You live in 2016."

"The waterfall has always returned us to the same day, different year."

He raked a hand through his sweaty hair, leaving it in disarray. "How about waiting until next spring? Ask the waterfall to take us back to April 1801. Then maybe you can prevent this whole mess from ever happening."

Here was the reason I had hoped to avoid this argument. He'd given a reasonable suggestion which I had no intention of taking. "I cannot bear to wait that long. I need to act now."

He shook his head, over and over again. A dozen times or more. "Okay, Susanna. Let's hear the plan."

"Pardon?"

"How are you going to get there?"

"I shall take my bike."

"You're not good enough."

"Perhaps…" I started to protest but the narrowing of his eyes stopped me.

"You're not good enough yet and you know it. What if you fell and broke something? What if you busted a tire? Would you know what to do?"

I had not considered problems with the bike. "You have given contingencies I had not pondered."

"Great. Give me a moment, and I'll come up with others."

I turned my back on him. I didn't want to be dissuaded. "Phoebe is worth the risk."

"*You* are worth more." He stepped closer, the heat of his breath tickling my neck. "Susanna, your sister is a big girl. She can make her own decisions."

"She might pick Jacob. She will have a hard life and die young." My voice trembled.

"How would marriage to William be better?"

"She loves him." I shook at the intensity of my feelings, unable to imagine the pain of saying goodbye forever to Mark. It would bring grief without end. I could not stand by and let my sister go through the same—not when it was my fault that she'd fallen in love. "If her life is fated to be short, why should it not be at the side of the man she loves?"

He slipped his arms around my waist, his lips brushing my temple. "I'll go."

Had I heard him correctly? "What did you say?"

"I'll go in your place. I'll take the buttons and the message. I'll talk to her."

I spun in his arms. "Mark, it is dangerous for you too."

"Pratt wants you more than me." The corner of his mouth twitched. "I'm faster on the bike. He'd have a hard time catching me. An hour over, an hour there, an hour back. I'll be fine."

"It is too much."

"Oh, you'll pay."

My eyes widened at the edge behind his words. "How?"

"You have to promise to stay here."

Chapter Forty-Eight

Worth a Shot

My phone rang right after supper. "Yeah, Granddad?"

"Got any plans tonight?"

"Some homework. Why?"

"Peggy Merritt wants to take a look at the evidence."

My heart slammed into race-level adrenaline mode. Oh, man, I hadn't expected a response so quickly. "When?"

"Monday."

Why hadn't I anticipated this? "I don't have the stuff put together yet."

He grunted. "That's what I figured. Want to come out here? We could have an evidence-faking party. Gran made cupcakes."

I had to have the coolest grandparents ever born. "Sounds like a plan. Does the typewriter still work?"

"Yep. What else?"

"We need a baptismal certificate."

He sniffed with irritation. "I don't happen to have a spare one at home. I'll have to deal with that later."

Wow. Was it really that easy? "You know where to get one?"

"Sure do, Mark. Unlike you, I attend church every Sunday. I know the process."

"Thanks, Granddad. See you in an hour."

Click.

I ran up to my room, grabbed my backpack, some

I ran up to my room, grabbed my backpack, some printouts, and the Bible. Next, I rummaged in my dad's office for my Social Security card, and my mom's special set of fountain pens.

"What are you doing?"

I looked at Mom over my shoulder. "I'm taking Susanna out to the lake house."

"It's a school night. Why?"

Honesty, in this instance, might be the best policy. "To fake an identity for her."

"Can I come?"

I smiled. "Sure. Meet me at the truck in five minutes."

She took off, running up the stairs at an amazingly fast pace.

I headed up the back stairs to the apartment. It was time to tell Susanna.

Gran and Mom took on the task of converting my Social Security card into Susanna's. I handed them the instructions I'd printed from the web. Gran fed it into the typewriter's roller-thing and soon the metallic tapping began.

Susanna sat beside my grandfather, quietly answering his questions. On the way over, I'd expected her to freak out at the thought of what we were about to do. But she'd surprised me, simply commenting that we would need to speak the truth as much as possible.

Yeah, I could live with that.

"What's your middle name?" Granddad asked her.

"I do not have one." She sat on the edge of her chair, watching him closely, fists clenched in her lap.

"You have to have a middle name." He scowled in thought. "What would you like it to be?"

She squinted at the legal pad he was writing on. "I can choose?"

"Don't see why not. Pick a name from someone you like." He nodded. "We don't want to use your mother's. Susanna *Anne* doesn't sound right. How about your sister?"

"Phoebe?" She shook her head. "It is her own name. I cannot take it."

I pulled out the chair next to her and flopped down. "What about your dad?"

"Josiah?"

"Jo." I smiled. She revered her father. From what I could tell, she'd been a daddy's girl from the moment of birth. He'd taught her more and treated her better than most girls had dreamed about in the eighteenth century, and she'd never entirely gotten over his death. "You can be Susanna Jo Marsh."

She turned to face me and...holy shit. Her expression left me hot and shaky and wishing I could get her alone.

"I shall take Mark's suggestion. Susanna Jo."

"That's a fine name." Granddad pushed the legal pad to the side and opened his laptop. "Now, we need to make a transcript. I copied a homeschool template off the web."

I relaxed in my chair and watched the two of them go. It was kind of fun to be a spectator on this project.

"What is a homeschool?" Susanna asked.

"It's for kids who stay at home every day and have their parents for teachers."

"My father was my teacher."

He laughed. "Hence, the homeschool transcript." He pecked at the laptop's keyboard with his index finger. "We'll put your father down as the school administrator." *Click, click, click...*

Damn, he was slow. "Give it here, Granddad, and let me type. I have homework due this century."

He smiled and slid the computer across the table. I keyed in "Josiah Marsh" and looked at the next field. "Lead teacher?"

"Put me down," Gran said. "And use my phone number." She pulled the modified Social Security card out of the typewriter and handed it to Mom, who carried it into the kitchen. The faucet turned on.

"Okay. The junk at the top is filled in. What about classes?"

I looked at Susanna.

Her cheeks turned pink. "I have taken no classes in eight years," she said in a husky voice.

Granddad scowled at her. "Do you know more about gardens than Mark?"

She smiled. "He knows very little. It isn't fair to compare."

Granddad waved a hand at me. "Give her a botany credit. What about animals?"

"Certainly, I know about farm animals and the creatures of the forest—"

"Another credit for agricultural science. Ever heard about the U.S. Constitution and the Bill of Rights?"

"Indeed. I have studied them closely of late, and my father was rather interested in the document that preceded them, the Articles of Confederation."

"American government credit."

Mom butted in. "Do you know what makes dough rise?"

Susanna nodded.

"Chemistry."

Susanna shifted closer to my chair and watched me type as Granddad and Mom continued calling out ideas. It didn't take long to fill the page. When we were done, I sat back and looked at her. She stared at the transcript, eyes wide with wonder.

"It looks quite impressive," she said, her gaze meeting mine.

"*You* are. Quite impressive, that is."

She jumped to her feet, lips trembling, and ran outside, her shoes echoing briefly across the deck. I stood more slowly to follow her out. When I reached the door, I turned to Mom and my grandparents. "I will never be able to thank you enough for what you did for her tonight."

Thursday had to be the day I traveled back through time. Dad and I were leaving Friday afternoon for Virginia. Even though Susanna had promised to stay put, I wasn't sure I trusted her.

At some level, I almost hoped the waterfall wouldn't let me through. Why did it keep letting us go back in time and tweak things? Did it trust us not to screw up anything big? Did it have a reason for wanting us to stay connected with that time?

Yeah, I needed Whisper Falls to be on top of this, because I didn't want to think about it too hard. My goal now was to keep Susanna safely on this side of history. If that meant traveling two hundred years, I would.

To get ready, I checked out "1801 clothing" online. The shirts were the same, but some of the pants were beginning to look less dorky, like I might be able to get by with a pair of khakis—which I would try because I hated those stupid-ass breeches and stockings. Zippers might be hard to explain, but I didn't intend on anybody getting close enough to have a good look.

Next, I packed all the food, drink, and tools that I could fit in a canvas bag. Then I went to bed early.

At dawn, I dressed in my modified tradesman costume, grabbed the canvas bag and the bag of buttons, and wheeled the bike down to the waterfall.

Susanna stood on the rock in modern clothes. At least that was a good sign.

She turned to face me, dejection written all over her face. "You won't go today."

I stared at the water. It was normal. Not a sparkle in sight. "How long should we wait?"

"It recognizes us, Mark. It knows what we want. It doesn't want us to go through yet." She would sound crazy to anyone except me.

"How does it know what we want?"

"I explained the need to Whisper Falls yesterday."

She didn't leave anything to chance. "Before you went to buy the buttons?"

"Yes."

We returned to the house silently. She waited for me in the kitchen while I stashed my canvas bag in the garage and swapped out shirts.

"Any sign of my folks?" I asked from the relative safety of the laundry room.

"No." She smiled tentatively. "Tomorrow, then?"

"Susanna, I have to go to Virginia."

"You said it would take only three hours to visit Phoebe."

"That's cutting it too close."

"Of course." She gave me a calm nod.

"You promised not to go."

"I promised to stay behind if you went."

My whole body strained with the effort to keep calm. "Does that mean you'll go if I don't?"

"Of course."

"Shit." I stormed upstairs with enough noise to get my parents staring at me out the master suite door.

When I reached the falls Friday morning, the water was sparkling.

My first reaction was to be pissed off. I couldn't imagine a worse day to do this. I texted a message to Mr. Rainey.

heading to newman. an excused absence.

Then I dropped the phone in the canvas bag and lifted the bike. In an instant, I was on the other side. The nineteenth century, this time.

I'd forgotten the feel of being here. Like everything was on hyper-senses. Bright colors. Clear sounds. And the deeply intense smell of earth.

Might as well put that from my mind. I wouldn't be here long and I was never coming back.

I carried the bike until I reached hard-packed dirt. No need to risk the unnecessary noise of riding in the water or on the pebble-strewn bank. Hopping on, I adjusted the helmet and took off.

The main road was deserted. As I pedaled, I thought about what this land would look like in two hundred years. In my century, I'd be biking past all of the small farms that the NCSU Vet School maintained. In 1801, it was rolling hills with no fences, barns, or sidewalks.

I zipped past the future site of the Museum of Art, down a valley that would one day have a multi-lane highway running through it, and headed straight for the heart of Raleigh.

It didn't take long to reach the western edge of the city. Susanna had drilled into me the location of Phoebe's employer; there should be no problem finding it. The pattern of the streets hadn't changed all that much from my century. I hid the bike and made my way into the city, through back streets, ducking this way and that, like I was on some kind of spy mission.

When I reached the right shop, I walked boldly in the door.

"What is it, sir?" A young boy popped up from behind the counter.

"I'm looking for Phoebe Marsh."

"What do you want with her?"

"I have a message."

He disappeared into the back. While he was gone, I looked around. The shop was hardly wider than a closet. Bolts of fabric crowded shelves on one side. Cloth purses and scarves lay in stacks on the other.

A pair of white silk gloves lay on the counter. They'd been embroidered in dark blue with flowers.

Light footsteps approached. Phoebe appeared in the door. "How may I...? Mr. Lewis." She ran forward, offering me both hands. "I am delighted to see you."

"Hello, Phoe..." Maybe that was wrong. "Miss Marsh."

She gave a quick squeeze of the hands and then stepped back. "Tell me, do you have news of my sister?"

"I do."

"Is she well?"

"She is."

Her voice lowered. "Do you bring me happy news?"

"Like what?"

"You have not married." Her smile faded.

"No." Why were these people hung up on that?

"Does she still work in your parents' home?"

That was one way of putting it. "She does."

Her face hardened. "Why do you treat my sister so?"

"What do you mean?"

"She wants to be your wife. She claims to love you."

"I love her too."

"She has followed you to a place I cannot visit. She lost me and I lost her—for you."

Damn. Phoebe had grown up pretty intensely. "Susanna left Worthville because she was in danger."

"I do not see that she is more secure." Phoebe shifted closer to me, a scary glint to her eyes. "Why do you make her wait?"

Getting mad now. "I want to finish college before marriage, but I love her, Phoebe. She is my future."

She studied my face closely and then sniffed. "Very well. I see the truth of it in your eyes. It is not right, but I can do no more." She bobbed her head curtly. "Peter says you have a message to deliver."

Susanna had made me practice what she wanted me to say, carefully worded to hide that she had inside information. "Susanna has advice for you as you decide what life holds in store."

"Shh." She looked over her shoulder and pulled me closer to the door of the shop. "How could she know that I face a solemn decision?"

"I'm not sure." The lie came easily.

A woman appeared from the back, a smile wreathing her face from ear to ear. "Who is our visitor, Phoebe?"

"Mr. Lewis, this is my employer, Mrs. Nance."

Mrs. Nance's gaze sharpened. "Are you family?"

"I am—"

"Mr. Lewis is my sister's husband." Phoebe dared me with a look.

"Oh, indeed." The warmth returned to Mrs. Nance's smile. "What brings you to Raleigh?"

"I am passing through."

"Welcome, welcome." She wobbled back into the darkness of the shop's workroom.

"I am sorry," Phoebe said. "I cannot let her think poorly of my sister."

"Sure." My three hours were ticking down. Better get on with it. "Susanna wrote you a letter." I handed it over.

Phoebe unfolded it slowly and backed up to the light, her lips moving as she read silently.

I hadn't read the letter myself, but it must have been powerful for Phoebe's face changed with each paragraph. Happy, sad, confused, sad again.

Her hand dropped until she clutched the letter to her chest. "This is most peculiar. It is almost as if she knows."

"Knows what?"

"I have indeed reached the age where gentlemen wish to court me." She moved her head slowly from side to side, as if in a daze. "This very month, I have received two offers of marriage, both quite tempting in their own ways."

I would have to pry information out of her—information she might be reluctant to share with me—but it had to be done. "Have you made your choice?"

She nodded slowly. "You may tell my sister that she knows him well. I have accepted an offer from Mr. Jacob Worth. He will return to fetch me in three days." Her smile was slight. "Jacob will be a good husband. He will farm the land and plant an orchard. I shall tend our family and create beautiful needlework. We shall have a good life."

Now came the part I hated to bring up—the part Susanna and I had argued over. "Your sister worries that you might move to a place with no one to help if you become ill."

"It is true, I might." Her forehead creased with concentration. "So here is a message for my sister. Tell her that, when I chose my husband, I did not confer with my fears."

I wouldn't have any trouble remembering Phoebe's message, but I wouldn't want to repeat it. "Does the other man know?"

Her eyes welled with tears. "I shall try to find the words when I see him today."

"Phoebe, your sister—"

Her fingers gripped my wrist, surprisingly strong. "Susanna wrote in her letter that I deserve the best from life. That I should listen to my heart." Tears spilled down her cheeks. "I have listened to my heart, and it tells me that the men I love deserve the best too. Assure my sister I have made the correct choice for *three* people."

If Susanna had been here, she would've argued, but I wouldn't. Phoebe didn't need our help. "All right. I'll tell her."

She nodded briskly, swiped at her tears, and gave me a big smile. "Thank you most kindly for your visit." Her fingers groped along the shop's counter, snagged the gloves I'd been noticing, and held them out to me. "Please. A gift for Susanna."

I nodded as I took them. "She sent you a gift too." I untied the bag of buttons from my belt and handed them over.

Phoebe looked inside and gasped. She scooped up a few and let them slip back with a slow *click-click*. "So many and so beautiful. A true treasure."

Clasping the bag to her chest, she darted forward, kissed my cheek, and disappeared through the rear door.

There were no travelers on the road the entire way back. It was almost too good to be true. When I pedaled past the narrow lane leading to the Marsh family farm, I admired its condition. It looked much better now than when Susanna's mother had owned it.

I thought about Susanna's visit to her brother as I rode the last stretch to the cutoff near Whisper Falls. It had been brave and humiliating for her to visit Caleb, although I still didn't understand why she hadn't set him straight. I wouldn't let Marissa talk to me like that.

Of course, I'd been raised in the twenty-first century. We didn't let our siblings talk trash to us and get away with it. Also, Susanna was a girl. Maybe they had both been raised to believe the girl—the sister—was lesser somehow. Susanna hadn't been in my world long enough to rid herself of all of that old crap yet.

I braked to a complete stop.

Caleb was a lot older than Susanna. Maybe he'd remember the day she was born. I had my phone on me. I could capture a video affidavit.

This could be the final piece of evidence we needed. A witness. And the risk was minimal. I was already here. I had the time.

It was worth a shot.

Chapter Forty-Nine

Simple Repairs

It was noon and still Mark had not returned.

For five hours, he'd been gone. What could be taking him so long? It should only take an hour or so for travel, unless he'd had a broken tire. But surely that would be a problem quickly solved. Mark would've taken what he needed for simple repairs.

Even if I allowed for three hours of travel time, that left the remaining two hours to speak with my sister and, truly, that was not reasonable.

If she were working at her job, she wouldn't be allowed a break of that length.

If she'd left her position, propriety wouldn't permit them to do more than exchange a few words.

And if she were already married, his mission would've ended before it began.

Where could he be?

"Susanna?" Sherri shouted up the stairs.

Mark's mother had stayed around the house for her day off, an unfortunate circumstance. I had expected her to leave, but she had not. Instead, she'd done an unusual number of chores in the kitchen and laundry room. I could not slip out to wait at the falls.

I walked down the stairs from my apartment, displaying a calm that I didn't feel.

Sherri stood in the kitchen, waving a small note at me. "I found a cryptic note from Mark. Do you know where he is?" Her voice was tight enough to snap.

"Yes, ma'am, I do. He visits my sister."

Her brow went from smooth anger to bewildered creases. "Why?"

How much longer could I skirt the truth? "He will deliver a letter for me."

"You can't mail it?"

"She won't receive it if he doesn't hand it to her."

"Why didn't you go?"

My throat ached with guilt. I should not have involved Mark. "I might be recognized."

She tossed the note on the table. "I thought all of those people were gone," she said, her back to me.

"They are. My sister is away from them. She is truly safe."

"If she's safe, why can't you see her?"

"I'm no longer welcome."

She snorted. "So you sent Mark in your place. Have you tried his phone?"

I hesitated. "It wouldn't be wise to call."

"Did you expect him back by now?"

I nodded.

She crossed to the sink and peered out the windows, hands braced against the countertop. "He could be hurt."

"I do not think it likely." My voice was husky with the fear I'd hoped to hide.

"Do you plan to look for him?"

"I shall leave soon."

She brushed past me, heading for the front stairs. "Wait until I've changed. I'm going with you."

"No, ma'am. You may not go with me. You would only slow me down."

Her eyes narrowed. "You can't stop me from following you."

I lifted my chin in challenge. "I shall not leave this house until you promise to stay."

"I won't promise."

I sat down at the kitchen table and folded my hands in my lap, my gaze never wavering from hers.

"Let's go, Susanna. We're wasting time."

"I shall not take you."

A furious hiss seethed through her teeth. "Why don't you turn these people over to law enforcement?"

I shook my head. "Mark's path will not cross that of anyone from the village." I said this with more confidence than I felt.

She stormed from the room, the thudding of her footsteps echoing loudly through the house.

I raced up the stairs and changed into my Federalist costume, yet I chose to keep on the sneakers. They would serve me well if I had to run.

Moving as quickly as I dared, I slipped from the house and hurried along the greenway. People strolled or rode past, glancing curiously at my costume, but I paid them no mind. I had to find Mark and had no idea what that entailed.

CHAPTER FIFTY

THE MOST CRITICAL PARTS

I circled back until I reached the lane to the farm, hid the bike, and jogged the last few hundred yards to the house.

The change in this place was amazing. It looked great, painted and repaired with smoke billowing from the chimney. There was a large vegetable garden to one side of the house. Pumpkins and squash were being harvested by an older woman who had a small girl and baby cradle nearby. A man in dark breeches and a simple linen shirt worked on a fence on the opposite side of the barn, assisted by two middle-school-aged boys.

One of the boys spotted me first. "Papa," he shouted.

The others swung around. The man let the hammer drop to his side as he walked closer, his attitude wary. The woman gestured at the boys to come to her.

"How may I help you?" he asked.

"My name is Mark Lewis."

The man's eyebrows lifted. He exchanged a startled glance with the woman. They recognized my name, which I'd expected.

"How is my sister? The whore?"

Fury jolted through my body with lightning speed. Was that what he'd called her? To her face? No wonder Susanna had been crushed. "If you repeat that, sir, I'll make you regret it."

"Pardon me. How is the runaway who lives with a man who is not her husband?"

What a self-righteous prick. "What makes you think we aren't married?"

"Then you have married Susanna?"

I smiled tightly. Phoebe had warned me, and here it was again. In my century, Susanna was the purest person I knew, and there was nothing I could truthfully say to make these people understand. "Indeed. We're committed for life."

"Well, then." He frowned. "What is your business with me?"

From the corner of my eye, I saw his wife hurry into the house, dragging her children with her. What was that all about? Had she gone to get a gun?

I eased my body to place him between me and their front door. "Susanna grieves your estrangement." I paused, rather pleased with how that phrase came out. She must be rubbing off on me. "I had hoped to explain about her life now—"

"Cease." He chopped the air with his hand dismissively. "I do not care to hear your explanations. Now, go, before I tie you up and turn you over to the authorities." He started to turn away.

I wasn't leaving until I had him on video. "Would you like to see her picture?"

That got his attention. "Pardon me?"

"I have a portrait of Susanna." I pulled out my phone and swiped in the photo gallery to the gorgeous shot where she was dressed in costume at the Avery-Eton House, laughing into the camera with gold ribbons in her hair.

"Let me see," he said.

I held it up to him but drew my hand back when he reached for it. "I don't trust you any more than you trust me."

He leaned forward and squinted for a long moment. "What kind of painting is this?" Despite the gruff voice, his face had softened.

"It is a new type of painting we have in our city. Very expensive." I pointed the phone camera at his face and turned on the VIDEO RECORD function.

"She can afford to have her portrait painted?"

"*I* can." Damn. That sounded so caveman. It probably made perfect sense to him, though. This would be a good way to get him talking. I gestured to his home. "So is this the house where you and Susanna grew up?"

"Indeed, though I moved to Orange County when she was still a young girl."

He was chattier than I expected. "Was she born in that house?"

"We both were." He jerked a thumb over his shoulder. "I moved back to Wake County when my mother died two years go."

I needed Caleb to state when she was born except there was one big problem. I couldn't allow him to say the year. How could we talk around it? "How old was Susanna when she ran away from the village?"

"Did she not tell you?"

Out of range of the camera, I shook my head.

"She ran away just before her eighteenth birthday."

"Her birthday was last week."

"Indeed. October first."

"How much older are you than Susanna?"

"Ten years."

"You probably don't remember her birth."

"Indeed, I do. I remember it clearly. Papa made us work in the barn that day, but Joshua and I kept slipping out, each wanting to be the first to hear the baby scream." He pointed at the front porch which would be out of focus on my camera. "Joshua and I waited right there until the midwife brought Susanna out to us." His brows beetled together. "She had a round pink face. She did not cry, but she seemed most angry to be bothered." The memory left a hint of a smile on his face.

The front door slammed. His wife ran toward us and stopped an arm's length away. When she opened her hand, I saw an oval object with tarnished silver on one side and bristles on the other. "This hairbrush belonged to Susanna's mother. She should have it."

"Frances," her husband growled.

"Caleb Marsh, it is time to put this behind us." She dropped it into my hand. "She is your sister."

He coughed. "So she is." He nodded at the two boys standing on the porch and then made straight for the barn.

Good idea. I was ready to go too. As I turned, I glanced at the phone and flicked off the video capture. The clock time set my pulse racing. I needed to get home before my folks noticed anything.

"Thank you, Mrs. Marsh," I said, stuffing the brush and the phone in the canvas bag.

She nodded tensely as her eyes tracked her husband to the barn.

I had been dismissed.

It didn't take long to retrieve my bike and pedal the last mile to Whisper Falls. A hundred yards out, I hopped off the bike and maneuvered through the forest. Emerging from its shelter at the flattest part of the bank, I wheeled the bike carefully along the creek bed.

"Hello. You, sir."

I stopped and looked around. A young man stood on the bluff above the waterfall. I had no idea who he was, but his stance made me tense. He could easily climb down and block my path.

"Yes?"

The guy cocked his head, listening intently. "I believe you are Mr. Mark Lewis."

Really? I got this close to escaping and somebody recognized me? "I am. Who are you?"

A smug smile spread across his face. "Jedidiah Pratt."

With a ferocious burst of energy, I spun and raced for the forest, dragging my bike beside me, but it slowed me down hideously. Behind me, feet pounded on the trail, gaining with every second.

Just inside the forest, I dropped the bike and dodged at a sharp ninety-degree angle into some bushes, then halted.

His shout of victory quickly changed to a cry of surprise, a metallic twang, a grunt of pain, and a soft thud.

Shit. Shit. Triple shit. He'd stumbled over my bike. How much damage had it sustained?

He roared with outrage. I shifted in the bushes, careful not to rustle anything. My view was only slightly obstructed. He lay prone on the ground, eyes skyward and blinking. With a violent thrust, he went from flat-out prone to standing tall. It took a lot of strength and agility to move like that. I had to adjust my lingering impression that he was a worthless wimp.

A clanging started. Boots connected with metal. The asshole was stomping on my bike.

It was all I could do to stay still. Each bang rattled through me like a hammer's blow to the head. I knew each gear and bolt on that bike. I knew its capabilities, how it responded, its unique balance. A new bike would cost me thousands of dollars to buy and months of training to understand.

I had to lock my jaw against screaming with rage. If I'd had a reasonable chance at winning, I would've stormed out there and beaten him senseless. But even though I'd thrown a few punches at his father before, fist-fights weren't exactly on the list of skills I had confidence in—and Jedidiah looked like he'd grown into the kind of guy who might be able to take me.

So I had to sit here listening to and watching the destruction of my most prized possession, and I had to keep reminding myself that the alternative was an indefinite stint in a nineteenth-century jail.

Finally, footsteps receded back in the direction of the falls. I watched him go as long as I could, forced myself to wait a few more minutes, and then crept from my hiding place, inching ever closer to my bike.

I got as near as I dared and assessed the damage. Equal parts angry and relieved. It was bad. It could've been worse. I wouldn't be racing on this bike over the weekend. I'd have to take it to a bike shop and spend a couple of hundred dollars on repairs, but it was fixable. Good thing that Jedidiah had been too ignorant of the technology to ruin the most critical parts.

I edged forward and peered up the trail. He stood on the bluff, arms crossed, gazing intently into the forest.

Damn. He was smart enough to know that I wanted to exit through those falls, and he was willing to wait.

How long would he stay?

How long could I remain where I was before I took the risk of challenging him?

And how would I get my bike back to the future—where it belonged?

CHAPTER FIFTY-ONE

UNWANTED INTRUDERS

When I reached Mark's rock, I paused to watch the flow. The falls shimmered but barely.

What message did the falls send? Would I be able to pass?

Tentatively, I stepped through, two hundred years tingling against my skin. Yet the sensations lacked intensity. Was the waterfall losing strength, or had I been given a warning?

I stood on my favorite rock and listened, reconciling myself to my old world. It was warm in Worthville—warmer than modern Raleigh on the same day, and less overcast.

The rhythms of the forest sounds were not correct. The creatures had been disturbed. There must be people nearby.

I hoped that Mark was near. Yet if he was, he was waiting for the opportunity to leave, and there could be no good reason for that. Who else was here?

With careful movements, I slipped into the cave behind the falls. The insects kept their wary chirps. The birds chattered indignantly at the unwanted intruders.

Horses' hooves thundered down the path, drawing sharply to a stop overhead.

"Jedidiah, we need help with the horses. Why have you taken so long with your errands? Why are you simply standing here?" The enraged voice belonged to Mr. Pratt.

Tension coiled in the pit of my stomach. His voice sickened me.

"You were right, Papa. Mr. Lewis has finally come."

I wavered on my feet. Was Mark close by? Was he all right?

"He has come? Oh, indeed." The saddle creaked. "Where did you see him?"

"In the forest behind us. He has not emerged since I posted myself here."

"At last, I shall extract justice." Mr. Pratt's merciless laughter chilled me. "Remain here. I shall round up the slaves and the hounds. We'll run him to the ground like the animal he is." Hooves pounded down the trail toward the Pratt property.

Mark was out there, no doubt listening, as I was. Being hunted by dogs would terrify him, even as it frightened me in my position of relative safety. Once captured, he would be punished fiercely—flogged and imprisoned—for rescuing me from Mr. Pratt.

I must save Mark *now*.

What could I do to create a diversion? Offer myself in trade?

Merciful heavens, I trembled to think about what would become of me if the next few minutes went wrong.

Before I had time to decide how to proceed, Mark burst from the depths of the forest and raced down the creek's bank.

"You cannot escape me," Jedidiah shouted. There came the gritty crunch of boots against granite and a deep grunt. Not five feet away from where I stood, he crouched on a flat rock, facing away from me, fists clenched in a boxer's stance.

In the five years that had elapsed in my old century, Jedidiah had grown tall and muscular from hard work. Mark would never slip past this strong and intimidating young man. I had to distract him. Since I didn't have the strength of body to stop him, I would have to use the strength of my mind.

Stepping from the cave, I emerged onto the ledge behind him. Mark skidded to a stop, eyes wide with horror.

"Jedidiah, I am the one you want, not Mark. Let him pass."

The young man whipped around, surprise striking him mute.

"You and I were well-acquainted once, Jedidiah." I inched closer. "We should talk."

He blinked. "Why?"

"I have much I wish to know. How is Deborah?"

Remarkably, the tension eased in his body. It was as if our relationship of old had returned. Wary and respectful. "She is well."

"Mark," I said, my eyes remaining fixed on Jedidiah's face, "fetch your machine and leave."

"Susanna, are you insane?" Mark bit out through clenched teeth.

I shot him a quick glance, begging him to obey me for once, and then looked back again at Jedidiah, whose eyes were scouring me from toe to head.

"You look well, Susanna, and prosperous. Are you Mrs. Lewis now?"

"She is," Mark said before I could respond.

Jedidiah flinched at the response. "Why have you returned here?"

"My sister is to marry soon. Had you heard?" I looked at Mark, whose eyes flickered with sympathy. Phoebe had not chosen as I'd hoped. The knowledge stabbed through me with a pain that shook me to the core. I dragged my gaze back to Jedidiah. "She will wed Jacob Worth."

His brow creased. "I had not heard, but surely you do not expect to attend their wedding."

"Of course not." I didn't have to feign sorrow, for it clawed at my heart. I had to resist its pull until we were safe.

Mark must have discerned my ploy, for he'd begun to back away toward the forest. I smiled at Jedidiah calmly, praying that he hadn't noticed. "I should like to know about Dorcas. I have missed her."

"Of course you have missed her. She was always your favorite."

There was no use denying it, but the faint petulance in his tone surprised me. "How does she fare?" I awaited his response anxiously.

"Dorcas is lame now. She will never be right."

I winced in genuine distress. "I am most grieved to hear it."

"She does not need *your* pity." The muscles bunched beneath his jacket. He raised fists to his chest, yet he moved no closer. "It was your fault."

"It was not." I shook my head slowly. "Who made that outlandish claim? You did not hear it from Dorcas."

"Papa told me."

"I thought so." I sighed with exaggerated heaviness. "Did he also tell you that I had already eluded his capture that day? Did he tell you that he pushed Dorcas *after* I was safe?"

"I do not believe you."

"You do not have to believe me. Ask Dorcas. Share my story with her, and see what she says." Mark had appeared in the creek again, carrying his bike. He moved quickly and not silently.

When Jedidiah looked over his shoulder and saw the source of the noise, his attention shifted to Mark.

"Let him go, Jedidiah. I am the better prey." I took another step forward, dislodging a rock to draw his gaze. "Do you worry about your sister's prospects?"

Jedidiah swung back to me. "Of course I do. Who will want her now?"

"She is a beautiful girl." I nodded with confidence. "She will make someone a witty and charming wife."

"Who?" His voice throbbed with anguish. "Who will want her?"

Mark had passed me now, his boots thumping on my favorite flat rock. He grunted, and the bike clattered against a boulder on the other side of the falls.

"I promise you, Jedidiah. Someone will want Dorcas. Truly. She is too lovely and vibrant to spend her life alone." I strained to hear behind me. What was Mark doing? What was he planning?

Jedidiah's expression was grim. "You have not seen her, have you? You cannot know the extent of her injury's effects. She limps badly and tires easily. No man wants a wife who cannot keep his home or who brings ridicule and pity with her."

A shiver of dismay passed through me. Perhaps I had not realized the depth of the damage, or perhaps Mark's century had altered my perceptions of those with disabilities. But Jedidiah was right. A visible flaw could not be forgiven in the upper classes—not even for someone as wondrous as Dorcas.

I frowned at him. "I did not know how bad—"

Hounds bayed in the distance.

In an instant, Jedidiah transformed from pained brother to snarling man. Before I could think what to do next, he'd lunged across the distance separating us, locked his fingers around my wrists, and yanked me to him. "Enough of this talk. I've got her now, Mr. Lewis," he sneered. "Better leave and save your own hide while you can."

The taunt didn't go unanswered. Mark hurled himself forward but missed us, for Jedidiah, moving with remarkable speed, had slammed me into the granite cliff, knocking the breath from my lungs. While I gasped for air, he gripped both of my wrists with one hand while he reached for his neckcloth with the other.

Mark rose with a roar and kicked back with his leg, his heel connecting with Jedidiah's knee.

There was a loud popping sound, and then I was free.

A screaming Jedidiah fell to the rocky ledge, his face contorted in agony.

Mark caught my elbow. "Go. Now." Swiftly, we leapt through the waterfall and landed on the other side, fumbling to avoid his battered bike that lay half in the creek, half on the land.

When Mark would have turned to look back, I stopped him. "There is nothing you can do for Jedidiah. Let us go."

"But I hurt him." The knowledge didn't sit easy with Mark.

"I know." I touched his cheek lightly. "That injury will save him from the wrath of his father."

He gave an understanding nod and lifted his bike. Together we walked silently up the greenway to the gate at their house, detouring to the small barn to hide his damaged bike.

When I would've turned to go, he yanked me into his arms. "That was frickin' stupid. What were you thinking?" he growled into my hair.

"I had to save you."

"Good idea in theory, but you put yourself in danger and then *I* had to save *you*."

"Without my appearance, you would be there still." I smiled that we were arguing over who had saved whom. Perhaps it was easier to think of that than what might have happened.

"The way you stood there, talking Jedidiah down, giving me time to escape? That was awesome." He gave me a hard kiss and then muttered against my lips, "I saw the curtains twitch in the master bedroom. My mom must be home."

"Yes."

"Then my dad must know too."

"Indeed."

"She's probably watching out the window, wondering what we're doing behind the barn." He straightened. "So here's the plan. We'll race for the house. You head straight to the apartment and get out of those clothes. Mine are normal enough that they might not think too hard about them. I'll distract them until you can get back downstairs."

"It is a good plan."

"Right." He smiled. "See you soon."

When I entered the kitchen a few minutes later, it was quiet on the first floor of the house. I looked into the family room and saw Mark's parents sitting beside each other on the couch.

"Mark will be right back," Sherri said.

They watched me take a seat and said no more. I was glad of that. I would be glad if Mark did all of the talking.

It was my fault, of course. I should never have placed Mark and myself in harm's way. I should never have tampered with Phoebe's life. Had I not given her medicine for her thumb, perhaps she would've married Silas the stable boy and had a long, pleasant marriage.

No, I must stop such thoughts. I didn't regret my actions. They had been made with the finest of intentions. A pleasant existence wasn't good enough, and Silas might have been, as Mark suggested, a jerk who beat my sister. I could never know what type of future I had interrupted, but I did know that a crippled hand would've been lifelong torture for her. Better to be happy and useful a short while.

Mark had changed history for my sake, and I had changed history for my sister's. We had to forgive ourselves for the parts that went awry.

He came clattering down the stairs and strode past an empty chair to drop on the floor at my feet. He reached for my hand, gave it a light squeeze, and didn't let go. "Okay, Mom, Dad. What do you want to know?"

"Where are these people?" Bruce asked.

"I didn't go to the village, Dad. They live too far away now."

"Tell us where you went then." Sherri's eyes narrowed on me.

Mark gave my hand another squeeze. "Susanna's sister is getting married soon. I took her a wedding present."

"Wait." Sherri frowned. "Isn't she a little young?"

"There are extenuating circumstances."

Sherri exchanged a glance with her husband before looking our way again. "Why the secrecy then?"

"I had to go today. We were running out of time."

I gasped and averted my face. To have Mark allude so unexpectedly about my sister's fate stole my breath away.

"Hey, babe." Mark kissed my hand. "It'll be okay. Phoebe looked really happy."

"What's wrong, Susanna?" Sherri asked.

Mark's voice was low and muffled. "Phoebe is…terminal, Mom."

The tears started, and they would not stop. He hauled me from the chair and onto his lap.

Footsteps crossed the family room floor and faded. Mark and I were alone, and still I cried.

He held me close until my weeping eased. Even as I quieted, he didn't move except to hold me more comfortably. Perhaps ten minutes passed before I heard Bruce's voice in the hallway.

"Soon, son."

"Okay, Dad."

I looked up into his face. "What does he want?"

"We have to leave for Virginia."

I struggled to sit up, but his arms remained firmly around my waist. "Of course, you must leave."

"We'll get there." He settled me on his lap again and kissed my brow. "Not sure about the race. My bike is in bad shape."

In the excitement, I had not thought about the impact of his damaged bike. His mechanical beast. On the day we met, I had seen it before I saw him, and now it was useless. His frustration rolled from his body like the oppressiveness preceding a storm. I didn't know what to do. There could be no comfort at such a moment. "What will you do?"

"Guess I won't be able to race."

I placed a light hand on his cheek. "You can take my bike."

He looked at me. His quick smile faded into a more solemn expression, one that I could not read. "Thanks. That's a good idea." He turned his head until he could kiss my palm.

"You can still compete?"

He grunted as he fumbled in the canvas bag. "Phoebe sent you a gift."

I unfolded a pair of white silk gloves and drew one on. A spray of dogwood blossoms flowed from the back of my hand and spread around my wrist. They were exquisite.

"There's more." He handed me a small, silver-backed brush.

I gasped. "This was my mother's." I lifted wondering eyes to him. "Where did you get it?"

He held up his phone. "Your sister-in-law gave it to me."

"Frances?" Shivers cascaded down my limbs like icy showers. "Did you speak with Caleb?"

"Yeah. He told me the story of the day you were born. I caught it on video." Mark brushed the surface of his phone and then tapped.

My brother's face filled the screen. He spoke in a low and precise tone. He had the air of a man reminiscing about a beloved sister. The video was a balm to my heart.

After a few seconds, Mark tapped it off again.

"Will it be enough for identification?" I choked out.

"Damn straight."

CHAPTER FIFTY-TWO

HER TRUTH

I went to find Susanna first thing after we got home Sunday night. She was waiting for me on the landing outside her door.

"Hello," she said, eyes bright with welcome. "You had a good time."

"Sure did." I pulled her back into the apartment. No point in giving my parents an eyeful, but I did leave the door open. "Missed you."

She nodded, her smile widening. "I'm glad you have returned."

Enough talk. Time to make out. I indulged in dozens of short, sweet kisses while my restless hands reacquainted themselves with the feel of her.

"Mark." She laughed and drew back. "Tell me about your weekend."

Keeping our hands firmly linked, I crossed to the couch and sat down, cradling Susanna in my arms. One long, hard kiss later, I felt restored enough to speak. "Yesterday was the Hungry Mother race. It was fun."

"As you said on the phone last night. What did you do afterwards?"

"We hit a sports pub and hung out with some guys we'd met from Virginia Tech."

"And today?" She watched me calmly. "What was Newman College like?"

I wanted to stay non-committal, but it was impossible. "The campus is gorgeous, and the people are really nice." Even though we'd arrived on a Sunday—on a weekend with nothing specific scheduled for prospective students—a guide had met us and shown us around. She'd arranged for a meeting with a faculty member of the Conservation Biology program and then the new coach of the mountain-biking team.

My dad had once said that, when the college was the perfect fit, it would feel like home. Now I knew exactly what he meant. Newman *did* feel like home.

"You would like to go there, I think."

I shifted my arms around her more snugly, pressed her head to my chest, and rested my cheek against the rose-scented silk of her hair. With my every sense filled by Susanna, it was hard to think clearly. Would I like to go there—with its eight-hour commute most weekends? "I'm not sure, babe. I guess we'll have to see."

After a school assembly on Monday, my friends and I found an empty table in the cafeteria to wait for the bell schedule to sync up again.

Benita pounced on Gabrielle the minute we slid onto our seats. "Okay, let me see it."

Gabrielle extended her right hand. A large brown gemstone, surrounded by a swirly, twisty gold setting, weighed down her index finger. "It's a gift from Korry. He knows me so well. Gorgeous, isn't it?"

"Yes," Benita said, studying the stone like it was the object of an experiment that required careful observation.

Gabrielle looked at Jesse and me. We nodded dutifully—although Jesse obviously didn't see the big deal any more than I did.

"What's the occasion?" he asked.

"No occasion. What's it to you?"

"Um, okay," he said into the uneasy silence that followed. Jesse shifted on his seat and looked out across the dining room.

"Damn, Gabrielle," I muttered.

"What?" She rounded on me, lips thinned angrily. "Don't you ever give Susanna presents?"

I tried to imagine how Susanna would react if I gave her a piece of jewelry. It boggled the mind. "The only thing she wants from me is my time."

Gabrielle jammed her hands into her pockets. "What are you trying to say, Mark? That Susanna is perfect and Korry isn't?" There was a sharp edge to her voice, like she was spoiling for a fight.

"Susanna *is* perfect for me, and Korry doesn't spend enough time with you."

"He's busy with things that matter."

I exchanged glances with the other two, and they were just as surprised as me. Without speaking a word, Jesse and Benita slid off their bench and headed for the door.

"Who told you that bullshit, Gabrielle?" I wanted to get through the next few moments like I wanted a whole series of rabies shots, but it had to be said. "Getting your diploma matters. Being normal for once matters."

"Having a career matters."

"Yeah, and when you're done with your education, your career will still be there, because you're a good actor." I turned sideways on the seat to watch her, but she wouldn't meet my gaze. "Jesse didn't deserve your harassment, and why go all weird about Susanna? You don't even know her."

"How about explaining why we haven't met?"

"You will one day."

"When?"

"I don't know. When Susanna's ready." I looked at the tabletop, my eyes tracing the graffiti gouged into the top as I wondered what to do next.

"Why are you such a wuss about her?"

I'd had enough. "Why are you such a wuss about Korry?" I rocketed to my feet, outrage and pity warring inside me. "I don't know what's going on between the two of you, but if you're not happy with the way he's treating you—"

"I *am* happy."

"No, you're not. Take it up with him, and leave off judging Susanna until you know her."

Gabrielle sat on the seat, still as a statue with her dark hair partially hiding her face. She was the total picture of dejection. Was it an act?

Probably not. Korry might be one of America's favorite movie stars at the moment, but he treated Gabrielle like a jerk. That ring didn't strike me as a "no occasion" gift. She had to be miserable.

Pity won. "Look, Gabrielle. You hang out with Benita and Jesse. They're amazing together. You hang out with me, and I'm drunk in love with Susanna. If the comparison hurts, do something about it with Korry. Don't lash out at the three of us."

As I stalked away, I heard something that sounded like a sob.

I called Granddad as soon as I reached home. "Are we still on for tonight?"

"Wouldn't miss it for the world."

"Do you have the baptismal certificate worked out?"

"Sure do, and it's a beauty." He chuckled. "I signed as the lay leader. The pastor whose signature appears at the bottom passed away last year. Susanna's name has been added to the church's registry for 1998. She was the last baby baptized that year."

I shook my head in amazement. "Granddad, don't you feel guilty about faking something at your church?"

"Mark, there is truth, and there are facts. They're not always the same thing. Susanna was baptized as a baby. I don't feel even the slightest twinge of guilt for my participation in her truth."

"Thanks, Granddad. We'll be out there soon."

"You bet." *Click.*

CHAPTER FIFTY-THREE

THE SHROUD AROUND MY PAST

I dressed carefully for this meeting. I wanted to look as modern and normal as possible.

Sherri had helped me shop for winter-season apparel. I purchased a new pair of clogs with the money I earned from my handwriting. Sherri said the shoes were a bargain. I was overcome at the thought of owning three pairs of shoes at the same time.

The clogs looked nice with my blue capri pants, although my shins were visible. But that couldn't be helped. I slipped on the buttonless, striped T-shirt that Mark's parents had given me for my birthday, and I left my hair loose.

Mark and I didn't speak the entire drive to the lake house, but he did hold my hand.

Peggy Merritt waited at the kitchen table with Norah and Charlie, sipping tea and eating cake. She was tiny and thin, with hair red enough to be nearly purple. She had to be as old as Norah was.

After the introductions were over, Mrs. Merritt gestured at the others. "Go. I'll talk to Susanna privately. There's no point in looking at the evidence or pushing further if I don't believe her story."

Mark kissed my cheek and followed his grandparents out the door.

Mrs. Merritt leveled a bright blue gaze at me. "Where were you born?"

"North Carolina."

"Where else have you lived?"

"Only here."

"Where were your parents born?"

"Both in North Carolina."

Her fists dropped to the table, still joined. "Why don't you have original birth records?"

"The village didn't care about such things. Papers were never created."

"Will you ever go back to this village?"

"I cannot, nor would I wish to." My actions had placed Dorcas and Phoebe on new paths. The two people I loved most after Mark had been forever changed, and I could only pray that it would eventually be for the better. I'd made a promise to Mark and to myself that I would leave the past behind me. I had to keep it, although the *not knowing* would be agonizing.

Mrs. Merritt watched me, hesitation in her manner. When next she spoke, her voice was soft and low. "I know this will be difficult, but you need to tell me about the abuse."

Mark had suggested several questions to me. Yet neither of us had anticipated this one. Could I get through it?

Of course I could, because I had to. I focused out the window at the trees rimming the garden, their reds and golds muted in the fading light. "Mark calls it abuse, and I must agree that my treatment fits the definition. Yet I didn't think of it as abuse. At the time, it was merely the way the world had to be. There were families in need of servants, and there were families with excess children. Some learned to be satisfied with their situations. I was one of the unfortunate children who did not.

"Mistakes required correction, and I made many. Indeed, I was a most difficult girl to discipline, but my master gloried in the effort."

A shadow crossed the window and then back again. Mark was pacing. His unrest strengthened my resolve. My hands clawed into fists, as if rending the shroud around my past. "I didn't like my treatment, but I survived. What else could I do?"

The chair squeaked beside me. When Mrs. Merritt spoke, her tone was soothing. "Why have you not turned these people in, Susanna? There are ways to deal with them."

"Truly, are there?" I met her gaze frankly. "How well does the government manage abuse cases? Are all children protected from the people who hurt them?" I shook my head. "My master didn't abuse his children. He didn't abuse his wife. He abused *me*. The government would be better occupied with saving children who need its help. I am safe now."

Silence greeted my speech. Sympathy softened her expression, and there was something more. Something hopeful.

She rose to her feet, stretched for the window, and rapped sharply. Seconds later, Mark and his grandparents came in.

Mrs. Merritt made a casual gesture at the other chairs. "Let me see the evidence."

Mark yanked me from my chair and wrapped me in a tight hug. I lay in his arms, drained from telling my story. It wasn't over, but perhaps it was close.

It took five minutes to spread the documents before Peggy. She scrutinized each item and then opened a small case at her side. "I'll take the baptismal certificate, the school transcript, and a photo of the Social Security card."

"Not the Bible?" Charlie asked.

She shook her head. "The easiest to fake. It would be suspicious."

Mark nudged the DVD with Caleb's speech. "What about the video affidavit?"

The corner of her mouth tilted upward. "It may be the most compelling for you, but I can't use it unless it's written, signed, and notarized." She smoothed the documents together and placed them carefully inside her case. She looked at each of us in turn, her gaze landing last on me. "There are three places where this whole gamble could fail. Judge Tew might notice what he's signing and refuse. When I go to clock the court order in, someone might notice it doesn't have a case file. Once it arrives at Vital Records, they might try to check up on the evidence. But after it gets that far, you're home free."

Charlie cleared his throat. "How long before we know anything?"

She pursed her lips. "The timing has to be perfect. I'll have to catch the judge on a busy day, and I'll have to hit the courthouse on a Friday at four-forty-five. Could be as early as Thanksgiving. Could be as late as the New Year."

Gran leaned against the bar, a cup of tea cradled between her palms. "What happens if this doesn't work?"

"Susanna will have to hire an expensive lawyer and spend a lot of years in legal limbo."

It was time to ask the questions that had gnawed at me since I learned of her involvement. "What happens to you if you're caught?"

She tilted her head, considering me. "Worst case? I'll retire, which I'm about to do anyway." She closed her case and stood, preparing to leave.

"Why are you doing this, Mrs. Merritt?"

She reached out and clasped my hand briefly. "I've spent enough time working in the judicial system to know that justice isn't always what we get. Every now and then, it's nice to see the law bent to fit the circumstances."

CHAPTER FIFTY-FOUR

THREE LITTLE WORDS

I pulled into the parking lot of Olde Tyme Grill. It was full and I was late. My study group was already here.

As I jogged through the maze of cars, I tried to think about the not-so-secret pop quiz we'd be having tomorrow in physics, but it was hard to keep my thoughts there. Too many other topics had me interested.

Thanksgiving was a week away, and already the wait for Susanna's birth certificate was making me crazy. For the past five weeks, she'd had nothing to say about it. She'd found plenty of things to do instead. Susanna's handwriting business was taking off. At the moment, she was swamped with orders for invitations to holiday parties. She'd also taken a set of first-aid classes that my mom found for her.

Most important, though, was her "study program," as we'd begun to call it. Granddad had offered to turn her fake high-school transcript into a legal homeschool diploma, but she declined. Susanna wanted a "real" education, and to her, that meant getting ready for a GED. She was cramming hard even though it would be months before she could even take the placement exam required by the community college. Math scared Susanna the most. Dad, the engineer, had become her tutor whenever he had time.

I'd finally made a major decision about college—to *delay* my decision. November first came and went without me applying early to Virginia Tech. Dad was disappointed. He kept hoping I would make the commitment, but I just couldn't. Not yet. January would be soon enough to send out applications, and May first would give me plenty of time to choose. Much as I hated to admit it, I didn't have my head straight about Susanna—what to do about me and what to do about us. I needed the extra time.

The study group was already seated in "our" booth. Jesse was slumped into a corner, his glazed eyes staring into space. The girls were talking rapidly and laughing a lot. I slid onto the bench beside Gabrielle and grabbed a fry. "What's the topic?"

Jesse moaned.

Benita sighed dreamily.

Gabrielle squirmed happily. "I went to London this weekend."

I turned to look at her. "Why?"

"To see Korry. He's still filming on a soundstage there." Her lips curved into a tiny smile that hinted at stuff that wouldn't be shared. "It was fun."

"London, Mark. Did you hear that?" Benita poked my hand with an incredibly strong index finger. "She went to England for a *weekend*."

"She's sitting right next to me. Of course I heard." I ate another fry, surprisingly curious to know more details. "So what did you do?"

"We talked and did touristy things and…" Gabrielle grew serious suddenly. "Okay, guys. I have to apologize. I've been a pain in the ass lately, and I'm sorry."

"It's a cute ass," Jesse offered helpfully.

Benita's strong index finger jabbed him in the head. "Girlfriend present."

"Yes, my love, my goddess." He leaned close and whispered something in her ear.

She blushed and said, "Officially forgiven now."

"I thought so." He kissed her neck.

"Really, guys?" I looked at Gabrielle. "Proceed."

She shrugged. "There's not much else to say except…" She straightened, eyes bright. "He'll be here during Thanksgiving break for a day. Do you want to come over and meet him? There'll be a few other people over."

Benita and Jesse nodded in unison.

"Maybe," I said. Never could be too sure about my plans. I had no intention of missing a single moment of Susanna's first Thanksgiving.

"Mark," Jesse said, his voice sharp.

"What?"

He jerked his head toward the entrance to the dining room.

I turned to see what was so important, and had to grip the table to keep from falling off the bench.

Susanna stood in the doorway, scanning the dining room.

My heart seemed to swell until it filled my chest, my throat, my whole being.

Other than the four of us, nobody else paid her any attention, because she looked completely normal. She wore a navy dress I'd never seen before. It left her throat and forearms bare and stopped at her knees. But most amazing, she also had on leggings and riding boots.

I catapulted from the booth and tore across the room. Her gaze met mine almost instantly and there it was. One of those rare, gorgeous, heart-stopping smiles that I lived for.

"What's going on? You look beautiful." My hands went straight for her waist and I hauled her up against me. "How did you get here?"

"Bruce dropped me off."

"Why?"

"Mrs. Merritt called."

Three little words that crackled down my spine like lightning. "What did she say?"

"It is over." Her joy radiated like a blazing fire. "I exist."

"Really?"

She nodded.

Locking my arms around her, I gave her a hard, brief kiss. A kiss of relief. Happiness. Wonder.

"Mark," she said, blushing and trying to wiggle away. "We have an audience."

"Let 'em watch." I buried my head against her shoulder. It took all of the most manly thoughts inside me to keep the tears at bay.

The noise dipped in the room before returning, even louder than before. If Susanna hadn't made an impression when she walked in, my display of affection guaranteed she'd be noticed now.

"I cannot breathe," she said with a laugh.

I released her slowly, hardly able to take in the news. It was over. The past was behind us now. She could get a real job, get her education, whatever she wanted. And my world—*our* world—would let her.

"Hey," I said, sliding my hand into hers, "come with me."

When we reached the booth, Benita jumped up and scooped Susanna into her arms. For a fraction of a second, Susanna froze, and then she relaxed and even made a clumsy attempt to hug back.

I reclaimed her hand and said, "Susanna, meet Gabrielle."

"Hello," Susanna said with a nod, her smile still glowing. "It is nice to finally meet you."

"Yes, it is." Gabrielle's answering smile was cautious. "I was just telling the others that I'm having a party at my house on Thanksgiving. You should come."

"Perhaps we shall." Susanna looked up at me, her eyes searching my face for something. She looked happy and serene and…

I wasn't sure what exactly that look was trying to tell me, but I knew that I wanted to find out alone. To focus on her. To celebrate her victory.

"Guys," I said, my gaze never leaving hers, "we'll see you later." I turned around and practically ran from the room, dragging her along with me.

When we reached the relative privacy of the parking lot, I cupped her face in my hands and kissed her until we were both dizzy, not stopping until I felt her cool fingers clutch at my wrists, holding on for dear life.

"Mark?"

"Yeah?" I could not get enough of this Susanna. This beautiful, *ready* Susanna.

"Where are we going?"

I took off again, heading for the truck. "I don't care—as long as you're with me."

ACKNOWLEDGMENTS

There are so many people to thank that it's hard to know where to start. First, I offer grateful praise to the writing community (especially Rubies and Retreaters) for their generosity to me and all authors. Please don't stop. To my family and friends, thank you for your interest and loyalty—and keeping me honest. To the fabulous people who contributed personally to this story, I am so grateful for your roles in making it the best book it could be: Angela, for her insights into the justice system; Jeff Thigpen and the Guildford County Register of Deeds, for their insights into birth certificates; Alec and Andrew, for helping me understand Mark; Mike Mazzella and Jan DiSantostefano, for answering questions about ruining knees and thumbs; Trish Halley, for knowing beautiful places in the mountains; Llewellyn, for lending her writing skills; Tom, for his patient advice on bodyguards, athletes, and life; Laura Ownbey, who is a true gift to literature; the transformative Jessica Porteous and Richard Storrs and the rest of the team at Spencer Hill Press; and Kevan Lyon, my extraordinary agent. Finally, to my amazing daughters and husband, thank you for being the kind of family that allows dreams to be possible.

Also by Elizabeth Langston

I Wish

ELIZABETH LANGSTON

November 2014

February 2014

HEATHER McCOLLUM

SIREN'S
SONG

Jule Welsh can sing. She enthralls people with her bel canto voice. But it takes more than practice to reach her level of exquisite song; it takes siren's blood running through her veins.

THE LOST IMPERIALS

The Tesla Institute is a premier academy that trains young time travelers called Rifters. Created by Nicola Tesla, the Institute seeks special individuals who can help preserve the time stream against those who try to alter it.

The Hollows are a rogue band of Rifters who tear through time with little care for the consequences. Armed with their own group of lost teens—their only desire to find Tesla and put an end to his corruption of the time stream.

WELCOME TO THE WAR

Book A Trip To The Bermuda Triangle

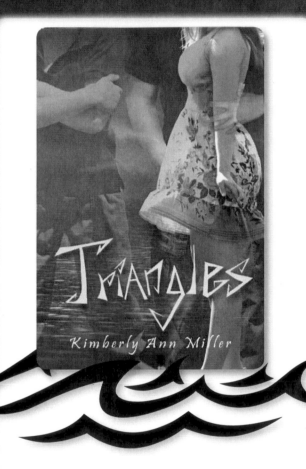

A cruise ship. A beautiful island. Two sexy guys. What could possibly go wrong?

In the Bermuda Triangle—a lot.

THE DOLLHOUSE ASYLUM

MARY GRAY

A virus that had once been contained has returned, and soon no place will be left untouched by its destruction. But when Cheyenne wakes up in Elysian Fields--a subdivision cut off from the world and its monster-creating virus--she is thrilled to have a chance at survival.

"Having a crush on another demi-angel is one thing, but now a demon is after my soul? This is so not how I pictured my senior year."

In the battle for her soul... which side will she choose?

Milayna

Bestselling Author
MICHELLE K. PICKETT

It is hard being good all the time. Everyone needs to be bad once in a while. But for seventeen-year-old Milayna, being good isn't a choice. It's a job requirement. Born a demi-angel, Milayna steps in when danger and demons threaten the people around her, but being half angel is not all halos and happiness.

ABOUT THE AUTHOR

Photo by Liza Lucas

Elizabeth lives in North Carolina (mid-way between the beaches and the mountains) with two daughters, one husband, and too many computers. When she's not writing software or stories, Elizabeth loves to travel, watch dance reality shows, and argue with her family over which restaurant to visit next. *A Whisper In Time* is the second book of the Whisper Falls trilogy.